Turn to the back for an excerpt from Suzanne Arruda's new
Jade del Cameron hardcover, *The Leopard's Prey.*

Praise for the
Jade del Cameron Mysteries

The Serpent's Daughter

"[A] rollicking tale of adventure and suspense . . . stellar."
—*Library Journal*

"Captivating . . . Jade's escapades should appeal to fans of Elizabeth Peters's Amelia Peabody series or the Indiana Jones movies."
—*Publishers Weekly*

"Jade del Cameron . . . is closer to Indiana Jones than Miss Marple in a book that is part adventure story, part mystery, part travelogue—and overall a rattling good read."
—Rhys Bowen, author of *Her Royal Spyness*

Stalking Ivory

"Suzanne Arruda is fast creating her own unique and popular niche in mystery fiction. With deep research and rich imagination, she gives us Africa, in the 1920s, and a bold new heroine in Jade del Cameron. This is a series that deserves a long life."
—Nancy Pickard, author of *The Virgin of Small Plains*

"In Arruda's spunky second throwback adventure . . . the resilient Jade will charm readers as she asserts her independence in rugged Africa."
—*Publishers Weekly*

"British East Africa is the seductive setting of this sequel to the author's exuberant debut, *Mark of the Lion*. . . . Like its predecessor, this book is deliberately over-the-top, and great fun to read."
—*The Denver Post*

"Another top-notch mystery. . . . Fans of Ernest Hemingway and Agatha Christie alike will find this second tale of Jade's exploits a ripping good yarn."
—*Richmond Times-Dispatch*

"Arruda's second Jade del Cameron novel sizzles with mystery. The protagonist is a gutsy, affable heroine whose tenacity is evenly matched with her intellect."
—*Romantic Times* (Top Pick)

continued . . .

Mark of the Lion

"From the extraordinary opening sentence in the shell-torn trenches of France in the Great War to the green hills of British colonial East Africa, *Mark of the Lion* sweeps the reader along with an irresistible narrative and literary drive. If you're looking for a fresh new mystery series, a vivid historical setting, and an especially appealing heroine, look no further. One of the most memorable mystery adventure stories I've read in a long time."
— *New York Times* bestselling author Douglas Preston

"Jade del Cameron... brings new meaning to the word *gutsy*. Vividly portraying the long-ago age of shooting safaris and British stiff-upper-lip attitudes, this novel is filled with appealing characters." — *The Dallas Morning News*

"This debut novel delivers on its unabashedly romantic premise and for good measure throws in a genuine mystery.... It's storytelling in the grand manner, old-fashioned entertainment with a larger-than-life heroine far ahead of her time." — *The Denver Post*

"Set in 1919, Arruda's promising debut introduces a heroine who's no ordinary Gibson girl.... Most readers will close this charming book eagerly anticipating the next installment of Jade's adventures." — *Publishers Weekly*

"Jade del Cameron is smart, capable, and insightful... and although *Mark of the Lion* would be a good read just for Arruda's encyclopedic knowledge of Africa, it is Jade herself... that readers will remember best. Arruda has given us a literary hero in the tradition of Sir Richard Burton and H. Rider Haggard, but without the burden of nineteenth-century sensibilities."
— Max McCoy, author of the Indiana Jones Series
and *Hellfire Canyon*

OTHER BOOKS IN THE
JADE DEL CAMERON SERIES

THE
SERPENT'S
DAUGHTER

A JADE DEL CAMERON MYSTERY

SUZANNE ARRUDA

AN OBSIDIAN MYSTERY

OBSIDIAN
Published by New American Library, a division of
Penguin Group (USA) Inc., 375 Hudson Street,
New York, New York 10014, USA
Penguin Group (Canada), 90 Eglinton Avenue East, Suite 700, Toronto,
Ontario M4P 2Y3, Canada (a division of Pearson Penguin Canada Inc.)
Penguin Books Ltd., 80 Strand, London WC2R 0RL, England
Penguin Ireland, 25 St. Stephen's Green, Dublin 2,
Ireland (a division of Penguin Books Ltd.)
Penguin Group (Australia), 250 Camberwell Road, Camberwell, Victoria 3124,
Australia (a division of Pearson Australia Group Pty. Ltd.)
Penguin Books India Pvt. Ltd., 11 Community Centre, Panchsheel Park,
New Delhi - 110 017, India
Penguin Group (NZ), 67 Apollo Drive, Rosedale, North Shore 0632,
New Zealand (a division of Pearson New Zealand Ltd.)
Penguin Books (South Africa) (Pty.) Ltd., 24 Sturdee Avenue,
Rosebank, Johannesburg 2196, South Africa

Penguin Books Ltd., Registered Offices:
80 Strand, London WC2R 0RL, England

Published by Obsidian, an imprint of New American Library, a division of Penguin Group
(USA) Inc. Previously published in an Obsidian hardcover edition.

First Obsidian Trade Paperback Printing, October 2008
10 9 8 7 6 5 4 3 2 1

OBSIDIAN and logo are trademarks of Penguin Group (USA) Inc.

Obsidian Trade Paperback ISBN: 978-0-451-22465-1

The Library of Congress has catalogued the hardcover edition of this title as follows:

Arruda, Suzanne Middendorf, 1954–
The serpent's daughter: a Jade Del Cameron mystery / Suzanne Arruda.
p. cm.
ISBN: 978-0-451-22294-7
1. Women private investigators—Kenya—Fiction. 2. Americans—Kenya—Fiction. I. Title.
PS3601.R74S47 2007
813'.6—dc22   2007014972

Set in Granjon   •   Designed by Elke Sigal

Printed in the United States of America

This book is dedicated to the real "Bert boys,"

James and Michael, who soar as eagles.

I love you guys.

ACKNOWLEDGMENTS

My THANKS TO the Pittsburg State University Axe Library Interlibrary Loan staff for all the books; National Wild Turkey Federation's Women in the Outdoors program for continuing opportunities to experience aspects of Jade's adventuresome life; Terry (Tessa) McDermid for her help as my writing buddy; Dr. John Daley and Neil Bryan for information on rifles and sidearms; Sgt. First Class David Brock for advice on handling a knife; Dr. Dan Zurek and Dr. Judy Berry-Bravo for help with the Spanish; Mssr. Arnaud Blanc-Nikolaïtchouk of Les Doyennes de Panhard et Levassor for his help with Jade's Panhard; my brilliant sons for applying their aerospace engineering knowledge to my understanding of rigging Curtis JN-4 airplanes (Jennies); Mike and Nancy Brewer for original and inspired musical accompaniment to my Web and publicity CDs; my NAL publicists, Tina Anderson and Catherine Milne, for all their hard work; my agent, Susan Gleason, and my editor, Ellen Edwards, for their continued belief in the series; all my family: Cynthia, Dave, Nancy, The Dad, James, and Michael for helping me shamelessly promote the books. I especially wish to thank Joe, the greatest husband and webmaster a writer could ever want, for all his help and support.

Any mistakes are my own, despite the best efforts of my excellent instructors.

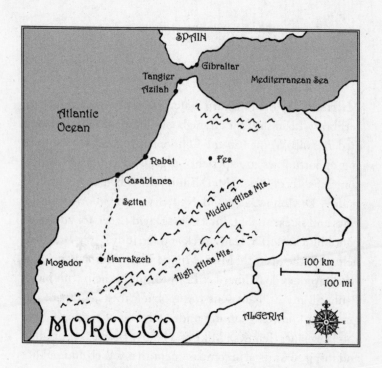

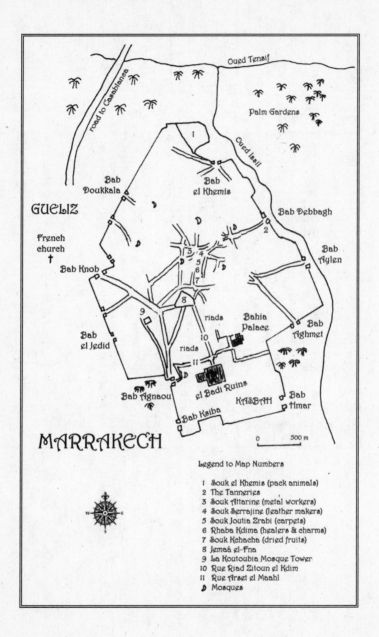

Oued Tensif

road to Casablanca

Palm Gardens

Oued Issil

GUELIZ

1

Bab
Doukkala

Bab
el Khemis

Bab Debbagh

French
church †

2

3 4
5
6
7

Bab Aylen

Bab Knob

8

9

riads

Bahia
Palace

Bab
Aghmet

Bab
el Jedid

10

riads

11

el Badi Ruins

Bab Agnaou

KASBAH

Bab
Hmar

Bab Ksiba

MARRAKECH

0   500 m

W   E
S

Legend to Map Numbers

1 Souk el Khemis (pack animals)
2 The Tanneries
3 Souk Attarine (metal workers)
4 Souk Serrajine (leather makers)
5 Souk Joutia Zrabi (carpets)
6 Rhaba Kdima (healers & charms)
7 Souk Kehacha (dried fruits)
8 Jemaâ el-Fna
9 La Koutoubia Mosque Tower
10 Rue Riad Zitoun el Kdim
11 Rue Arset el Maahl
♪ Mosques

CHAPTER 1

Morocco is a land of contradictions. Desert and oasis,
palaces and clay huts. It is Africa, yet distinct from Africa. The Moroccans call it
the Maghreb, *the 'land of the western sun.'*

—The Traveler

"One should never trust the shopkeepers," declared a young man seated across from Jade. "They will cheat you."

Jade stifled a yawn and switched her attention from the busy Tangier streets below to the speaker. Woodard Kennicot's creamy white linen suit and broad-brimmed boater-style straw hat blended visually with the scenery, but his yammering mouth clashed; his voice nasal, his tone condescending. *And that hair. It's like staring at an inferno.* The blaze, she noted, continued in a small brush fire above his lips.

Why does Mother always have to hold court? Jade fidgeted in her chair. Mother had arrived just yesterday from America via London with the intention of wrangling an Andalusian stallion from her cousin to take back for stud on the family's New Mexico ranch. This time she wanted Jade to join her, a prospect that didn't thrill Jade. But when her mother had suggested they first meet in Tangier, rather than in Spain on her family's estate, Jade had jumped at the opportunity. The

I

social atmosphere in Andalusia was stifling at best, and visits home to their New Mexico ranch weren't much better. Jade and her mother always ended up arguing about Jade's life, her unladylike style of dress, and her short hair. But Tangier, Morocco, was a "neutral" spot, and Jade had hoped the two of them could come to an understanding. She prayed that her mother had become more accepting of, or at least resigned to, Jade's chosen profession as photographer and writer for a magazine, *The Traveler,* and the life that entailed.

Their meeting last evening when her mother's boat docked had been cordial enough. They had even managed to share a room last night without killing each other, thanks in part to her mother's exhaustion. But instead of a quiet mother-and-daughter breakfast, Mrs. del Cameron seemed positively determined to introduce Jade to this hodgepodge of people who'd shared boat passage with her mother from America and England. Jade took a final sip of coffee from her delicate china cup and fidgeted with her crystal water glass.

To Jade's right, Doña Inez Maria Isabella de Vincente del Cameron reigned over the assembly. In her blue and white, straight-skirted, crepe de chine dress, she was the picture of decorum and style, without a trace of pretension. The band of her mother's straw hat echoed the dress' blue satin waistband. Its down-turned brim shaded but didn't hide her regal face and, at forty-nine, Mrs. del Cameron's flashing blue eyes and creamy olive complexion took second place to no one. Even her jet-black hair, which she wore pulled back into a tight bun at the base of her neck, bore no trace of gray. *Correction: one strand.*

Jade sighed, and her mother noticed. "What is the matter, Jade?" she asked in a hushed aside.

"Nothing, Mother."

Jade lied. She'd been thinking of her sixteenth birthday party. Jade had hoped for a barbecue and a hoedown. She even went so far as to invite their foreman and the ranch hands. But her mother had other plans: a sit-down banquet and ball. She invited the territorial governor and other, more local, dignitaries along with their stuffy sons, the youngest ten years older than Jade. Jade had pleaded with her father, but he just patted her hands and told her it was probably for the best, as if he were resigned to a boring evening himself.

Her mother had paraded Jade before the assembly until Jade felt like a filly on exhibit at a fair; she expected someone to place a bid on her at any moment. In the end, she told one young man, who spoke of nothing but his money and prospects, that he could bore a grizzly to death, and walked out of the room. After that, her mother forbade her to leave the house for a month. *Why did I think this tour of Tangier would be any different?*

"I was merely admiring the view, Mother. Perhaps I should take some photographs down by the beach while you visit? I know my magazine would appreciate it."

"There will be time for that later, Jade," pronounced Inez. "We have guests. How many times must I tell you that a hostess must make her guests feel welcome?" Inez nodded to Jade's plate. "You haven't finished your breakfast."

"Yes, Mother." Jade didn't want to argue. There was no point to it. The only thing left to do was endure this brief stay in Morocco and the subsequent visit to Andalusia. Once her mother procured her desired Andalusian stud, Jade could go her own way with a clear conscience, knowing she'd done her best to make peace between them. She picked at the fruit basket and chose a small mandarin orange, the type many tourists called tangerines after this port city, which first shipped them to Europe. As she peeled it, she kept half her attention on the others at the table and the rest on that mesmerizing view below.

White-robed men scurried through Tangier's narrow streets, while white-shrouded women haunted the screened, flat rooftops. Trace minerals in the stucco tinted the city's older buildings a delicate pink, painting a youthful blush on the aged. Every dwelling butted against the next like plants, sending a new shoot to grow. Early morning shadows stretched from house to house, caressing them with cool blue fingers, often bending where one house rose or fell compared to its conjoined neighbor, but never breaking.

Liquid and light. Jade inhaled the invigorating scents of ocean air and fish and let her gaze drift from the jumble of cracker box buildings below her high terrace to the turquoise Straits of Gibraltar, speckled with sunlight and white sails. The only jarring note in this symphony of pure light and water was the steamship anchored offshore; that and Woodard Kennicot's nasally voice.

"You're so right about the Tangier shopkeepers, Mr. Kennicot," said Libby Tremaine, a tiny but pretty young American woman on her honeymoon with her husband, Walter. "One horrid-smelling man tried to overcharge me for a pair of leather slippers yesterday. I refused to buy them and walked away." Her head bobbed emphatically, sending into motion the numerous assorted flowers on her hat. "He'll think twice the next time he tries that." She patted down the few strands of fine hair, the color of pale strawberries and golden dawn, that had broken free.

"I believe you are expected to bargain with the sellers," said Jade. She sectioned her orange and popped one slice into her mouth.

"Applesauce! Whoever heard of such a thing?" remarked Mrs. Tremaine as she took a second croissant. "May I have the marmalade, please?" She flashed a brilliant smile at Patrido Blanco de Portillo, the Spanish merchant to Jade's left, even though the jam pot sat closer to Jade's right.

Inez picked up the bowl of marmalade, but when she reached across to hand it to Libby, her hand bumped both the salt cellar and the pepper pot, spilling a spray of black and white specks across the tablecloth. "Pardon me." Inez scooped up a portion of the salt and tossed it behind her.

"Allow me to assist you," said de Portillo. He swept up the remainder of the spilled seasonings, then exploded in a sneeze as he inadvertently flung stray pepper grains into his nostrils.

"God bless you," said Chloe Kennicot primly. It was the first thing the woman had said during breakfast, deferring always to her husband.

"It is nothing. Only the pepper," replied de Portillo with a sniff as he brushed the remaining errant grains from his silk cravat and sumptuous gray waistcoat. "But Miss del Cameron is correct. Bargaining is tantamount to a sport for the commoner."

"Well, that's a system that's all balled up," said Mr. Tremaine. "Sounds like a lot of bushwa to me. How am I to know when I am getting a bargain or am being cheated?" He glanced from one to another, as though seeking agreement, and stroked his baby-smooth chin.

"Being cheated is, unfortunately, the price one must pay, so to speak, when you leave the civilized familiarity of Europe and come to a barbaric city," said Mr. Kennicot, arching one brow, the other lid drifting down to shade a gray-green eye against the morning sun. He sat stiffly upright with his hands tented, fingertips touching as though he were trying to look like an experienced man of the world about to issue an edict. His flaming red hair did nothing to assist that illusion. Jade thought he resembled a circus clown more than a serious world traveler.

"Barbaric?" exclaimed Jade. "Tangier's about as barbaric as an egg timer." She waved her hand to encompass the surrounding area. "We are sitting in a French café, dining on croissants, using the finest bone china and linens. Most of us are staying in either the Spanish or the French hotel, and across the street is another one owned by a Scotsman. The main newspaper is in Spanish, and every other person on the street is a European or an American. It's no wonder the Moroccans call Tangier the infidel city. One might as well be in your civilized Europe."

As she finished her speech, she noted her mother's furrowed brow and tightly pursed lips, as clear a sign of exasperation as a cat's twitching tail. "Of course, that's just my opinion," she added to try to soothe her mother's irritation. "I understand Fez is very unique." She finished her orange and prayed for breakfast to end.

"Do not be deceived by these familiar surroundings, Miss del Cameron," said Mr. de Portillo. "A great deal of barbarism lies directly under the veneer." He pointed to a small procession in the street below. "Do you see that man in the embroidered *djellaba* and the large turban, the fat one followed by the five young girls and the old woman?" Jade nodded. "And what do you make of them?" Patrido asked.

"Normally I would guess that the older woman is his wife and the girls are his daughters," said Jade, "but here in Morocco I suppose those are all his wives."

"And you would be wrong on both counts," said the

Spaniard. "I have seen that man many times in my trips here to purchase leathers. He is a slaver of sorts. Oh, rest assured he will have papers for the authorities that proclaim every one of those beauties as his daughters, but they are not. They are probably from Circassia or the Caucases, possibly Armenia. Their parents are likely poor and sold them off. He will take them into the interior with the old woman, who may in fact be his wife, to watch over them. Then they will be sold at market. Some will be house servants; others might become wives or concubines if they are pretty enough."

"How horrid," said Chloe Kennicot.

"See here," declared Woodard Kennicot. "I happen to know for a fact that the French stopped that practice several years ago."

Patrido de Portillo bowed once, slowly. "Indeed they did, Mr. Kennicot. But the sales happen nonetheless. They are only less open, less regular than before." He turned back to Jade. "So you see, Miss del Cameron, the *Maghreb,* the land of the western sun, is still barbaric."

Libby half closed her eyes and sighed. "I suppose that's what makes it seem so romantic. Like something out of Arabian Nights."

"Are you touring some of the local sites in Morocco for your honeymoon, Mrs. Tremaine?" Inez asked.

"Walter is taking me to see the Caves of Hercules later today," Libby replied.

"And we'll take a gander at Volubilis, tomorrow," added Mr. Tremaine, "before we travel to Marrakech. Both the caves and Volubilis are laced with Greek and Roman history. I studied both subjects at Yale, you know."

Marrakech? Jade examined the bride with more interest. The young woman's white gloves, long sleeves, and huge straw hat were designed to protect her alabaster skin and strawberry blond hair from the sun, but they wouldn't help much in the desert or the mountains. *She'll cook like an egg on a hot rock.*

"I understand that there are some interesting inscriptions on the cave walls," said Mr. Kennicot. "They are in Greek, a language I read as a lowly student of scripture." He nodded his head in a gesture meant to show humility. "Legend suggests they were written by Hercules himself."

Jade chuckled. "Mark Twain has a humorous notation about that very fact in his book *Innocents Abroad*. He wrote that Hercules must not have traveled much or else he wouldn't have kept a journal." No one else laughed. In fact, Jade noted, most of them—all except her mother—stared at her with blank expressions. Jade cleared her throat. "Of course if you aren't familiar with Twain's writings, I don't suppose it would mean much." She picked up her fork and poked the orange rinds on her plate, wondering why she felt like a naughty child waiting for permission to leave the table.

Her mother glared at her until she put her fork down.

"So, you are a biblical scholar, Mr. Kennicot?" asked de Portillo.

Mr. Kennicot bowed. "Yes. My wife, Chloe, and I hope to do good work bringing enlightenment to this country."

"Ah, you are missionaries," concluded de Portillo. "Most interesting. I think you might find your task very difficult outside of Tangier. The Arabs are ardent Muslims."

Missionaries! thought Jade. That explained the severely tailored lines of Chloe's tan linen suit and the lack of lace or other frippery. Her interest renewed, she studied Chloe more closely. Jade approved the simple roll with which she'd bound her walnut brown hair. Like her mother's style, it looked elegant, not austere. Chloe's sapphire blue eyes took in everything with an interest that bespoke intelligence.

"Woodard and I wish to preach to the Berbers," said Chloe. "We don't believe they are ardent, as you put it, in anything."

"If anything," added her husband, "they still hold to their ancient pagan ways."

"How interesting," said Libby as she clasped her hands together and leaned forward. "And just what sort of pagan rites do they practice?"

Jade took a deep breath and gritted her teeth. The girl acted as though she expected and reveled in hearing about human sacrifices. Something brushed her legs, one of Tangier's innumerable cats. Jade smeared butter on a roll and dropped it for the cat to lick clean. It landed on de Portillo's leather boots before plopping to the side. Jade noticed most of the butter stayed on the boot.

"I was under the impression that the Berbers are Muslims," said Mr. Tremaine.

"They are whatever they need to be," said de Portillo. "Some, like St. Augustine, were Christian. I believe some were Jewish, as well. Most have followed Islam, at least superficially, since the Arabs brought it here. Their last holdout was one of their vision-gifted queens. *Kahinas,* I believe these women were called." The cat settled in for a meal, licking de Portillo's boot.

"So you agree that they can be converted?" asked Kennicot.

Mr. de Portillo shrugged. "Why should they? It is true that they are not fastidious about praying five times a day, nor do their women veil themselves, but they have at least gained token acceptance among the Arabs. They would lose that if they turned Christian, and possibly gain nothing in the process."

Chloe Kennicot put a gloved hand to her face and gasped. "Such shocking commentary!" she said. "To think they would gain nothing. Why, they would gain their souls, Mr. de Portillo."

Woodard Kennicot patted his wife's other hand to soothe her. "Do not agitate yourself, my dear. I am certain that Mr. de Portillo only meant they would not gain any political or social standing, and meant no offense." He looked at de Portillo when he said this. Patrido waved his hand and nodded, as if to agree without having to actually say so, and Mr. Kennicot took this as a chance to continue explaining their mission.

"I subscribe to the idea that the Berber people are the descendents of the Canaanites," he said, "and they still hold fast to ancient beliefs in spirits and fetishes, making food offerings at springs or to certain trees."

"There is evidence that they practice traces of an old worship of a heathen goddess, Astarte," added his wife. "One can see it in the dreadful henna symbols they tattoo on themselves."

"Evidence," said Mr. Kennicot, "that they may actually have intermarried with Phoenicians."

"More likely they only traded with them," said de Portillo. "When different people trade in goods, they sometimes trade beliefs, as well."

"Imagine, Canaanites in the mountains," said Libby. "How thrilling."

"They were not always in the mountains," added de Portillo. "These tribes once extended from Libya all across northern Africa—the *Maghreb,* as they term it. They only retreated there to escape domination by Romans and later the Arabs."

"Yes," agreed Inez. She nodded to de Portillo. "We Spaniards know the extent of Arab domination from when the Moors invaded our country."

De Portillo shook his head and leaned forward. "Ah, forgive me for contradicting you, Doña del Cameron. The Moors that entered our beloved Andalusia were Berbers who had risen to power, not Arabs. And I do not think, Mr. Kennicot," he said, as he turned his black eyes on the missionary, "that you will find them any more trusting of a Nazarene, as they term a Christian. You will not easily shake them of their belief in spirits."

Walter Tremaine's brown eyes brightened with renewed interest. "Spirits! Now, that is great fun. Don't they call them genies? Like the genie in the lamp in Arabian Nights?"

"I believe the proper plural is *jnūn* or *jinni,*" said de Portillo. "*Jinn* is one spirit, unless it's female. Then it is a *jenniya.*" He crossed his right leg over his left, tossing the still-feeding cat aside. The resulting bump against the table, hiss, and scrabbling of claws startled everyone but Jade, who'd been watching from the corner of her eye.

"Sounds like one of them now," Jade said. Inez closed her eyes and raised her chin, a sure sign to Jade of her mother's displeasure. Jade resigned herself to the inevitable scolding and lecture on decorum once breakfast was over and they were alone. Not that her mother would go so far as to yell at her, but only because raising one's voice was as improper as poking fun at the conversation.

Mr. Tremaine acknowledged Jade's humor with a weak smile and plowed ahead. "Well, from what I understand, they blame spirits for everything. Run of bad luck—it was an evil *jinn*. Commit adultery—blame it on a seductive lady *jenniya*." He waggled his eyebrows. "Apparently the worst of the lot is some spirit that actually seduced Adam before Eve was created. What was her name?"

"I believe she was known as Lilith," replied Mr. Kennicot. He took a deep breath and placed his hand on his chest. "A demon, a veritable daughter of that serpent Satan." Beside him, his wife gasped in horror.

Jade felt a shiver run up her spine, though not from any biblical bedtime story. During the war she had been courted by a young British pilot, David Worthy. He died in a plane crash after entrusting her with the task of finding his missing half brother. The search in East Africa revealed that David's own mother, Olivia Lilith Worthy, was capable of monstrous crimes to prevent even her own husband from finding this lost youth. No, thought Jade, one didn't need to look to folklore to find something evil. *Does Lilith know about this mythical she-demon?* Perhaps Mrs. Worthy fancied herself to be a modern version. Jade shook her head as though to clear out the image. Her mother arched one brow and seemed about to ask her if she were all right when Walter Tremaine jumped back into his tales.

"Well, according to those Berbers," he said, a big grin on his boyish face, "she still wanders the area looking for new victims." He licked his lips, caught his bride's wide-eyed, shocked look at such a risqué topic, and quickly added, "Not that *I'd* ever fall prey to her, darling." He rapped on the table three times.

Chloe Kennicot pounced on the topic. "You have no idea how pervasive this dreadful belief in *jinni* is, Mr. Tremaine. It governs their lives. One must not whistle, because that's how these spirits speak. You must fold your clothes at night or they will wear them."

"Sounds like a good way to get children to do their chores, right, Mother?" said Jade. Inez did not reply.

"One must avoid blood at all costs," added Mr. Kennicot. "It is terribly haunted. Salting meat keeps the *jinni* away."

"But meat in the markets is never salted because some of the butcher's best customers are *jinni* and it would not pay to offend them."

Everyone turned to see this new speaker. A slender young man of moderate height stood behind Mr. Kennicot and next to Inez. A wayward strand of blond hair peeked out from under his straw hat. It was echoed by a well-groomed brushy mustache that just covered the top of his lips. Jade couldn't see his eyes behind the darkened glasses, but his face looked pale.

"Pardon me for interrupting your charming breakfast," he said. His voice was hushed and mellow, like a person used to speaking quietly. It reminded Jade of a librarian's voice. "I could not help but overhear the end of your conversation and had to intrude. It's a topic I find fascinating." He nodded to everyone at the table. Libby Tremaine flashed him a broad smile, and Jade could have sworn the girl batted her eyelashes at him.

"Not at all, Mr. Bennington," said Inez as she raised her hand to him. He took it and bowed over it, displaying very old school manners that Jade knew would impress her mother. "I was hoping you would join us. But where is your aunt? Is she not leaving her room again today?"

"Alas, Aunt Viola is not feeling particularly well this morning. She is unused to these warmer temperatures and refuses to go out until evening. Even then I doubt I'll get her to stir much, since she'll likely fret over the night air." As if to comment further on the rising temperature, he pulled a kerchief from his trouser pocket and mopped his brow. A small English coin tumbled out and onto the café floor. Chloe leaned over to retrieve it for him, but Mr. Kennicot stopped her with a solemn shake of his head.

"I am forgetting my manners," said Inez. "You know everyone else here, but you have not met my daughter, Jade. Please allow me to introduce you to her. Jade," she said, turning to her left, "this is Mr. Jeremy Bennington. He is traveling with his great aunt from England to the Continent."

"How do you do?" said Jade. She didn't hold out her hand, as she detested having it kissed or bowed over.

"Charmed," replied Mr. Bennington in his breathy whisper. "Your mother spoke of you on board ship, but I see she did not do you justice."

"You will join us?" asked Inez.

"Alas, no. I only came out for a breath of air and a newspaper. I do not get out much. Aunt Viola will be expecting me to read to her over her breakfast."

"Sorry you have to stay so shut away, Bennington," said Mr. Tremaine. "Must be quite a drag."

"Yes," agreed his wife. "We'd just *love* to have you join our little party." To Jade's disgust, the young bride actually pouted at Mr. Bennington.

He made a delicate shrug. "If the truth be known, I am engaging a hired nurse to escort my dear aunt back to London. It is painfully obvious that her condition is beyond my care. If I do secure this nurse, then I shall only be in the way."

"Then perhaps you can come along after all," said Walter. "We're thinking of forming a touring party today to the caves or someplace equally haunted by those *jinni*. Sounds like good sport. I know Libby is very rah-rah about it."

"Then you should also go to see Azilah," Mr. Bennington

said. "From what I read, it was built on the ruins of an ancient Phoenician city. I'm told it has delightful old passages running underneath that are, of course, the abode of your *jinni*, since they are underground. But I fear you must make your plans without me today." With that parting bit of advice, he bowed to the ladies and walked back toward his hotel.

"Such a fine young man," declared Inez. "So devoted to his great-aunt. She is a charming lady herself, although I only saw her at table once. I believe she gave her nephew the evening off to write his own letters. But he has stayed so shut away inside that I imagine such bright light disagrees with him."

That would explain the dark glasses and the pale skin, thought Jade.

Mr. Tremaine signaled the waiter, then took out his wallet from his jacket's inner breast pocket and extracted a few bills. "Well, I for one intend to see these Caves of Hercules and anything else associated with these so-called *jinni,* if I can manage to get a guide." The waiter, a gaunt-looking Moroccan in a white robe, approached. Mr. Tremaine paid for the breakfast and dismissed both the waiter and Inez's protests with a flap of his hand. "In fact, I might just have some fun and see how many Moroccans I can scare by making them think I'm a *jinn* myself. Threaten someone with an old evil eye, eh?" He glanced around the table. "Anyone else game?"

Jade scowled. "That sounds like a childish prank, Mr. Tremaine. We are guests in this country." She heard her mother gasp.

Libby edged closer to her husband, as if rallying to his defense. "I hardly see how razzing them hurts anyone. These are ignorant people. They should be shown how foolish their silly belief in genies is."

Jade made one huffing snort of disbelief. "Now, there is a perfect example of the unwashed calling another person dirty."

"Jade!" scolded her mother.

"It's true, Mother," Jade said, raising her hand to token no more interruptions. "All of you are equally guilty of superstitious belief."

A round of disclaimers and affronted gasps went round the table, excepting Mr. de Portillo, who leaned his chin on his folded hands and watched Jade.

"I am an ordained reverend," declared Mr. Kennicot. "How dare you accuse me of being superstitious."

"Then why did you stop your wife from picking up that coin? I'll tell you why. It's because it fell tail side up, and that's bad luck. And your wife invoked a very old superstition when Mr. de Portillo sneezed earlier. I believe people say 'God bless you' because it was thought the soul flew out of the body when you sneezed and a devil could enter in."

Walter Tremaine chuckled. "She's got you there, Kennicot. But," he added as he turned his eyes on Jade, "just how am I guilty of any hokum?"

Jade smiled. "You keep a four-leaf clover in your wallet. I saw it when you paid for the breakfast. By the way, thank you very much. You also knocked on wood earlier when you told your wife you wouldn't be led astray by a temptress. And I saw your wife cross her fingers when you spoke about getting a guide for the caves."

"And myself and your esteemed mother?" asked de Portillo. "Are we also guilty?"

"Well, Mother threw spilled salt over her left shoulder, but to be honest, Mr. de Portillo, I cannot recall any such superstitious expression on your part. So I correct myself."

De Portillo's lips twitched in what may have been amusement or perhaps scorn. Jade couldn't tell, so well did he mask his emotions. Like her mother, he wore a studied expression of polite indulgence to those around him, an expression worthy of royalty granting an audience to lesser nobles.

"You are indeed charming, Miss del Cameron," he said with a bow. "Your mother's praise did not do you justice."

Walter Tremaine rose and held his wife's chair. "I'm sorry to break up this swell morning, but if we want to see the Caves of Hercules, we must be off to hire a guide." He tipped his hat to the others, exposing a mop of straight brown hair, long on top and short on the sides as was currently in vogue among young men. "If anyone should care to join us, you will find us in front of the hotel in an hour."

"I shall not be in your party, pleasant as it sounds," said de Portillo, rising from his own chair in deference to Libby Tremaine's standing. "I must make my own arrangements if I am to carry out my business. I am again in Morocco to see about exporting more of the wonderful leather that they make here. In particular I must make ready to journey to Marrakech." As the Tremaines left, he walked around Jade with head high and shoulders back and bowed to Inez, taking up her right hand and kissing it. "Doña del Cameron, I trust we will see each other again. I understand you are going on to Andalusia in a day or so. If you remain there for longer than a week, I should be able to join you. I believe you have my card."

Inez inclined her head in a graceful bow. "I do, Don de Portillo. And you have mine. It would be a pleasure for us to receive you at my cousin's estate."

De Portillo bowed again to Mrs. del Cameron, to Jade, and lastly to the Kennicots. "Good luck to you both. If nothing else, I'm sure you will have a very interesting experience among the Berbers."

The Kennicots inclined their heads in token bows, then rose as one from the table. "Breakfast with you has been most interesting," said Mr. Kennicot with a sideways glance at Jade. "We won't be leaving Tangier for another day at least. I'm sure we will both see you again. Good day." He tipped his hat, took his wife's arm, and they left.

Jade waited until they were out of earshot for the scolding she knew would follow. She wasn't disappointed.

"Jade! How could you be so rude to my guests?"

"Mother, I was not rude. You wanted me to stay and engage in conversation. I did!"

"By insulting them."

"I didn't insult them, Mother. I spoke the truth. After hearing Tremaine babble on about fooling the natives, I'm almost ashamed to be an American. Yale graduate," she said with a snort. "That boy probably majored in dad's money. And did you see his wife flirt with your Mr. Bennington? Is this your idea of polished society?"

Inez gasped. "A *lady* is gracious to *any* guest. Jade, I sent you away to England to gain some manners, and I am despairing of it ever happening." She waved her hands in a sweep that encompassed Jade from head to toe. "Look at you in that old brown skirt. It's hardly suitable for a breakfast engagement. You dress as if you were on safari. You don't even have a hat or gloves."

Jade took a deep breath to contain her mounting exasperation. "I don't need any polish, Mother. I'm not a floor. And I'm not dressed for a safari. On safari I'd have on trousers and I would wear my big old felt hat."

"You embarrassed me in front of these people."

"Mother!" Jade took a step towards Inez, her hands outstretched. Inez took a step back and Jade let her hands fall. Right. No public displays of affection. "Mother, these people are a perfect example of our problem. *You* say a lady would know how to be gracious to them, but *I* say anyone with sense wouldn't bother with them to begin with." She shrugged her shoulders and shook her head, her black waves jiggling around her face. "You are a smart woman, Mother. Why do you insist on inflicting these boors on yourself and," she added, "on me?"

"I had hoped that becoming friends with Lady Beverly Dunbury would have taught you proper society manners," said Inez, referring to Jade's friend, whom she'd first met during the Great War. "Instead, you seem to be corrupting her into joining your wild escapades."

"Wild escapades?" Jade took a deep breath and calmed herself. "Mother, have you forgotten your own youth? Dad said you used to outride him all over the countryside. You knew how to shoot and fence, and once raced a stallion half-way across Andalusia to win a bet."

"I don't recall doing any such nonsense. But even when I did practice fencing and shooting, I always dressed and be-haved as a lady. Why haven't you let your hair regrow? Only women of poor morals wear hair cropped like that."

"It's more practical, Mother."

"And that horrid mark on your wrist," she added, point-ing to Jade's crescent lion's tooth tattoo, which she'd received from a Kikuyu shaman during her naming ceremony. "How could you do such a thing? I cannot imagine what Mr. Ben-nington or Don de Portillo would think if they ever saw it. No decent man will want to marry a woman with such a marking."

Jade flung her hands up in front of her. "So that's it. You want me to marry one of those two. Mother, I love you dearly, but no. I thought you invited me here to spend time together before we went to cousin Ramone's estate. I'd hoped you were finally ready to accept me and my life, but you're still trying to mold me into some . . . some parody of yourself." As soon as the words erupted from her mouth, Jade regretted them. They might be true, but saying them was only going to make the situation worse.

"I am thinking of your best interests, Jade."

"I'm sure you think so." Jade collected her bag, an old cloth satchel containing her new Kodak camera and her notebook. *Good Lord, I've made a hash of this now.* "I'm sorry, Mother. I didn't intend to have words with you." She pointed down from the terrace to the busy streets below. "I want to see the shopkeepers. Will you come with me to the souks?"

Inez turned aside, arms folded across her chest, chin out, a hurtful look on her proud face. "I have another appointment," she said. "I should call on Mr. Bennington's aunt. I would invite you, but you would probably consider it too dull for your adventuresome tastes."

Jade rolled her eyes heavenward. *Why didn't Dad come?* "Very well, Mother." She kissed Inez on the cheek before her mother could pull away. "See you for lunch?"

Inez shook her head. "I will still be out of sorts with you then. I'll join you for afternoon coffee. Be at the hotel lobby at four, and don't be late. You know I cannot tolerate people coming late for appointments."

Jade watched her mother walk away, her back stiff with pride. She sighed. How many times had she tried to impress Inez, only to receive this same response? Yet Jade knew if she pretended to be a proper, sedate lady, her mother would still be disappointed. *All these years and we don't know each other, Mother.*

Where in the name of St. Peter's fishing pole is she? Jade paced in the lobby, occasionally dodging another guest. She looked at her pocket watch for the seventh time. *4:40.* Mother was never late. To her, punctuality was a mark of good breeding. Jade remembered when her mother hosted the Lady's Art Society dinner for the establishment of a traveling library. Women who arrived "fashionably late" were greeted graciously and sat down to whatever courses of the dinner were left. Even her father joked that he wished his wife was in charge of the seasons so spring would never be tardy.

"Pardon me," Jade asked the clerk, "but are you certain there are no messages for me?"

"No, miss. Did you look in your room? Perhaps Mrs. del Cameron left a note there."

"She didn't."

"Perhaps it fell to the floor?"

Jade tried a different tack. "Did you see my mother leave with anyone today? I know she planned to meet with a Mrs. Bennington, but I don't know if she had any appointments afterward."

"I'm sorry, Miss del Cameron. I can't say that I did."

"Then can you be so good as to tell me if the Benningtons are registered here? Perhaps they know where my mother went."

The clerk consulted his books. "They were here, but Mr. Bennington checked out for himself and his aunt around midmorning. I believe they were taking the steamship back to Spain."

Jade returned to the room she and her mother shared to

look once more for any message. *If this is Mother's idea of disciplining me for being ten minutes late . . .* Jade hadn't intended to get lost in the souk. *Blasted convoluted streets.* Of course, the two hours she had spent watching the snake charmers, jugglers, and other entertainers hadn't helped.

Jade looked on and under the bed, beneath the desk, in the waste can, in the powder room, anywhere a note might have conceivably been left or dropped. Nothing. The room appeared as immaculately as before; no sign of haste. Even her old notebook, the one she'd used in East Africa on her first trip to western Tsavo, the wild territory east of Mt. Kilimanjaro, was aligned precisely with the edge of the end table instead of on her bed where she'd tossed it.

Mother must have put it back, but where is she? That's when Jade noticed her mother's blue and white dress hanging neatly behind the door. *Of course. She went touring.* With the Benningtons gone, her mother would have had time to see some of the sights and she'd never wear a morning dress to someplace dusty.

Jade opened the chifforobe to see what was missing, in hopes it would give her some clue as to where Inez went. Unfortunately, Jade hadn't paid much attention last evening when her mother hung her dresses. Maybe her shoes would give some insight. She knew her mother had a pair of practical, ankle-high walking boots. She stooped to look at the remaining shoes more closely and saw the crumpled note on the floor.

Please join us at the Europa Hotel at eleven, and we can tour Azilah. The note was in a woman's hand and signed with a first name in a close scrawl. Jade moved to a window and held the paper to the light to read it better. The ink on the signature was smudged but looked like "Libby." *So she went to*

Azilah with the Tremaines. Jade chuckled as she imagined her mother's consternation. She must have expected to be back by now or she'd have left a message for Jade. *I'm not going to let her hear the end of this for a while. Mother, you're late. Do you know how rude that is?* Well, maybe she wouldn't go *that* far, but it did promise to be fun.

Jade pocketed the note and headed for the terrace where they'd breakfasted. She chose a seat near the front walk where she'd have a clear view of her mother when she returned. In the meantime, she'd enjoy a cup of coffee. That was a pleasure she didn't care to postpone any longer.

She was into her second cup when she spotted the Tremaines strolling up to the door. Jade called to them. "Mrs. Tremaine. How did you enjoy Azilah? Where is my mother?"

Libby Tremaine looked as though she'd bitten into a lemon when she saw Jade. "Miss del Cameron. I have *no* idea what you're talking about. Walter and I went to the Caves of Hercules."

"My mother didn't go with you? She received a note from you asking her to join you in a tour of Azilah."

"You're mistaken, Miss del Cameron," said Mr. Tremaine. "My wife just told you that we went to the Caves of Hercules. We went alone. Wherever your mother went, it wasn't with us."

CHAPTER 2

Morocco boasts one unique political distinction; it was the first
world power to recognize the United States as an independent country, a
distinction bestowed on the new nation in 1777. Ironically, the American Legation
to Morocco is in Tangier, which is not one of the Imperial capitals.
If anything, Moroccans tend to disown it as an infidel city.

—The Traveler

JADE, RENDERED MOMENTARILY SPEECHLESS, sat blinking stupidly like an owl dazed by one of her photographic night flashes.

"Why did you think she came with us?" asked Mr. Tremaine.

The question jarred Jade back to rational speech. "Um, your wife's note."

"*I* didn't leave any note for your mother."

"Isn't this your signature?" Jade held out the paper.

Libby snatched it from Jade's hand and scrutinized it. "That's not my handwriting. More like a lot of hokum." She flung the note back to Jade. "Maybe your mother is playing a trick on you, teaching you a lesson for being so rude this morning."

Jade didn't answer, her mind too busy turning over the fact that her highly disciplined, notoriously prompt mother was missing. The question was, Where? Had she gone to

Azilah, anyway, or was she lost in the twisted streets of Tangier?

"I don't understand about the note, but I'm sure she's all right," said Mr. Tremaine. "She didn't strike me as being gaga."

"I beg your pardon. My mother isn't *what*?"

"Gaga. You know, someone crazy or silly. Gee, I thought you were an American. No offense meant to your mother."

Libby appeared to wilt of a sudden and fanned herself. "Walter, I'm all in. Take me inside."

"Of course, darling. Poor bunny." Mr. Tremaine hastened to clasp his wife's arm. "Good luck, Miss del Cameron."

Jade watched them go inside and wondered about Libby's sudden case of fatigue. Was she avoiding any more questions? The girl didn't seem very outraged to find someone had forged her name, even as a prank. If this was Libby's idea of a joke, then Jade would kick her across the Straits of Gibralter once she'd located her mother.

Maybe her mother thought she'd missed the Tremaines and decided to go on to Azilah herself. How would she get there? *A donkey?* Definitely not. Mother was an expert rider, but she wouldn't ride unless someone hired out good horses. A motorcar? Jade had seen a few, mainly near the ambassadors' residences, but she wondered how her mother would hire one since she didn't speak any Arabic and her French was horrid at best. No, she probably went with someone. But who?

Jade studied the note's signature again. The letter *L* was relatively clear, but her assumption that it was Mrs. Tremaine's first name appeared to be false. She shoved the note into her skirt's side pocket. Heaven knew how many of the other passengers her mother had made alliances with on the voyage.

Her best hope lay with tracking down her mother's transportation. Jade jumped up and ran inside to ask the clerk. "Pardon me, where can I hire an automobile?" The clerk gave her two names as well as directions to their homes. Jade wrote these in her newest notebook and thanked the man. "If my mother returns before I do, please tell her to wait in our room for me." Then she hurried out the door and spotted the Kennicots, walking with Patrido de Portillo.

"Hello," Jade called, and noticed Chloe Kennicot stiffen. Maybe her mother was right. Maybe she did have a tendency to open her mouth first and think about consequences later.

"Good afternoon, Miss del Cameron," said Woodard Kennicot. Mr. de Portillo bowed formally.

"Good afternoon," said Jade. "I'm looking for my mother. Would you happen to know where she is?"

"I saw your mother sometime after breakfast," said Mr. Kennicot. "I'm not certain exactly, but it was not noontime yet. She appeared to be waiting for someone."

"Did you speak with her?" asked Jade. The minister shook his head.

"I'm certain she's perfectly all right, Miss del Cameron," said Mr. de Portillo. "I saw her with a native guide. I heard him say something in French." He paused for a moment. "*La ferry* or something to that effect."

"Laferriere," said Jade. "Madame Laferriere is one of the names the hotel clerk gave to me. She has a motorcar for hire."

"Well, then," said Mr. Kennicot, "it appears your charming mother went touring with one of our other passengers. Nothing to be alarmed about."

"No, probably not." Jade took a deep breath and tried to convince her heart to stop racing. "Thank you all very much.

You've been most kind." She consulted the directions given to her by the clerk and headed toward the *medina*, the old walled part of Tangier cornered by the great Kasbah.

The narrow streets never went straight for very long, a pattern aimed at confusing enemies. Jade didn't doubt it. It certainly confused her. Even with the directions she got lost twice. It was after the second retracing of her steps that she had the feeling she was being followed. She turned several times to sneak a look back, but couldn't pick out anyone in particular either time. The Westerners, in their straw boater hats and ivory linen suits and dresses, all looked alike, and the native Moroccans blended into a sea of white. She decided it was her imagination and continued on.

Finally she turned onto the Rue de la Petite Maison and found Madame Laferriere's address. Like most of the buildings, the pale pink mud-brick walls were crumbling with no obvious attempts at recent repair. A heavy wooden door, its paint blistered and peeling, guarded the entryway, a small latticework at the top allowing the inner occupants to look out with relative anonymity. Unlike the other buildings in the vicinity, a narrow alley bordered one side. Jade glanced within and saw a battered motorcar. Confident that she'd found the correct house, she knocked at the door and waited. The sensation of being watched returned and made her skin prickle, but when she looked around, she saw no one. She knocked again.

"Hallo?" The voice from the other side of the grating was a woman's. Jade could only make out her eyes behind the latticework at the top.

"Madame Laferriere?" inquired Jade.

"*Oui.*"

"I am looking to find my mother," Jade said, continuing

in French. "A Spanish-looking lady. I believe she and her friends came here to hire a car from you."

The door opened a few inches and Madame poked her head into the crevice. Jade caught a glimpse of brown eyes and a long, thin nose with a mole on one side. Although she was possibly a woman of middle age, her skin didn't look as if she had spent years baking in the sun.

"Yes, my car was rented by a man today. He said he was taking two ladies to view Azilah. But they have come back. The car is here." She pointed towards the alleyway. Three Arab men passed by, having what sounded like a heated discussion. Several more followed behind. None of them paid any attention to Jade, an unveiled Nazarene woman.

Maybe they just returned, she thought. She knew if her mother was now waiting at the hotel, no amount of explaining was going to be adequate, but Jade could face that. *As long as she's all right.* "How long ago did they return with your car?"

"Two hours ago, at least."

"Two hours!" *Then where the tarnation is Mother?* "Did both ladies come back?"

Madame shrugged.

"Do you know the man's name? The one who hired your car?"

"What do I care for his name? He had money."

"What did he look like? Did you see the ladies?"

"He looked like any man. He said he was going to Azilah. The car, it comes back. The ladies did not? *Voilà,*" she pronounced, as though Jade were a simpleton to not figure it out. "Perchance the ladies stayed there. Now, do not disturb me unless you have more to offer to me than air." Madame Laferriere waved Jade off and shut the door.

"Wait. I'll pay you." The door opened a crack. Jade rummaged through her canvas bag for her wallet. The door opened wider and Madame Laferriere stuck out a hand, palm up. Jade peeled off several francs and handed them over. Madame Laferriere did not look terribly impressed. Jade added two more. All the while her mind struggled with her dilemma. Should she go back and seek help from the authorities or go on searching on her own? Tangier was such an international city that no one seemed to be in charge. Besides, it might take hours to get an audience with the American consulate, and Jade didn't want to wait hours.

"The man may have been English, perhaps American. I cannot tell. He spoke French but not as well as you do."

"Young? Old? Tall? Short?" Jade added another franc.

"Not old. About your height. I did not pay much attention. If you want, then hire my car and go there yourself."

Jade's exasperation rose. She wanted to push her way inside, throttle the woman, and demand answers. That's when she made her decision. With no other information to hand over to either the French or the Spanish authorities, there was little they could or would do. She could see it now. The American diplomat would say she needed to see the French since a French woman owned the car and Azilah was French territory. The French would say she should see the Spanish since her mother was traveling next to Spain, and both would pass Jade back over to the Americans again.

"I want to hire your car."

The twenty-eight-mile road to Azilah was in surprisingly good condition, the French doing their level best to bring order into Morocco, beginning with its coastal cities. Madame Laferriere's Panhard Sport was another matter. The machine had once been a thing of beauty, with gleaming black hood and cedar side panels. Now rips ran the length of the convertible top, the split leather seats belched out stuffing, and the cedar was cracked. The infernal thing rode low in the rear, probably, Jade thought, due to a worn-out suspension. She may have been the best mechanic in her ambulence unit during the war, but she'd be blasted if she'd stop and work on this woman's car now. Instead, she gave it the gas and sped on to Azilah.

Other than a nearly constant view of the Atlantic to her right and an occasional Moroccan on a donkey in front of her, the trip had little to recommend itself. It didn't matter. Jade's single focus was her mother. Inez was proper to a fault, often domineering, always aggravating, yet Jade loved her and, despite their clash of personalities, respected her.

Mother would have assembled the entire valley if I were missing. In fact, Jade recalled, she did once. Jade had been only six then, and her father was away selling livestock. Before he left, he took his family to the high pasture where they'd camped under the stars. Jade's mother, suitably attired in a full, overlapping wrap skirt of her own design, rode astride without exposing any improper limbs. Even up in the mountains her mother reigned over the campfire with as much dignity and grace as she did the household. Two weeks later, Jade, bored with life at the house, decided to have her own camping adventure. She just didn't bother to tell anyone else. Two days later she woke to thirty-seven assorted ranchers and hired hands approaching on horseback. Her mother sat at the head of the column like some warrior queen. Once they got home, her mother thanked everyone for their help, offered them refreshments, said good-bye to each personally, then proceeded to "explain" to Jade in the woodshed what she'd done wrong. Jade couldn't sit a horse again for a week.

When I find her, I'm going to yell at her till I'm blue in the face.

Jade spied the ancient stone walls of Azilah and headed for them, wondering where to look for the tunnels. She had had only two months of intensive study with an Arabic-speaking shopkeeper before leaving Nairobi, only to discover that the Arabic spoken here had strong Berber influences. Still she decided to attempt her rudimentary Arabic and ask directions of a ragged-looking man and a boy leading a donkey ahead of her. Judging by their knee-length white tunics, partially shaven heads and lock of hair behind an ear, they were Berbers. She hoped they also spoke Arabic. As she drove closer, her car suddenly lurched, the back end rebounding and slamming down again. *Blasted hole. Didn't see that one.*

"*S-salamū alekum,* peace be upon you," she greeted as they turned to see what had caused such a commotion. "I'm looking for . . ." *Oh, tarnation. What's the word for "tunnels"?* She tried the word for "holes," then, getting no response, said "*Jinn,*" hoping they'd point the way to the nearest haunted location. Hopefully, it would be the tunnels.

The boy's black eyes widened and the man scowled. He covered his son's eyes with one hand and held up a small silver charm shaped like an eye around his neck with the other. Then after muttering something, he turned and headed for the nearest gate, driving the donkey and the boy in front of him.

Well, that didn't go well. Had the man covered the boy's eyes because she was an unveiled woman? Then she remembered that Berber women didn't wear a veil. Was he afraid she would give his son the evil eye? Perhaps he held up that charm for protection. She turned at the sound of approaching footsteps behind her. The man's lone lock of hair, knitted white skullcap and his shortened *djellaba* labeled him as another Berber. He wore a black-and-white striped robe over his dirty white *djellaba*. Judging by his black beard, he was relatively young, perhaps in his thirties. *"S-salamū alekum,"* Jade said.

The man returned the greeting. *"Wa alaykum s-salam."*

This time Jade decided to avoid the dreaded invocation of *jinn,* flipped through an Arabic phrase book she'd pulled from her bag, and tried for a combination of "ground" and "holes" instead. The man smiled. *Probably just asked him where the toilet is.* "Parlez-vous Français?" she tried.

He held out a hand, index finger and thumb close together and said, *"Petit."*

A little French, thought Jade. *Now we're making progress.* She kept her French very simple and asked him how to find the tunnels.

"You look for where the night people live?" asked the Berber man in moderately good French.

Jade assumed that "night people" was a euphemism for *jinni* and nodded.

The man motioned for her to follow him. She parked the car against the stone wall in an angled recess where the wall jutted out near a set of stone steps, grabbed her canvas bag and followed. Jade noticed the diamond-shaped symbol woven in red and brown on the back of his hooded robe. He led her along the towering wall towards a city gate protected by a round, crenelated tower left from the Portuguese occupation nearly four hundred years ago.

"Through here," he said, then passed inside. Jade followed. Azilah did not wear its age as gracefully as did Tangier. Inside the fortress walls stood tightly clustered houses made primarily of *pisé*, a dried mud similar to adobe. Most were crumbling. All wore a peeling coat of whitewashed plaster. The high walls blocked the early evening sun and painted the interior in darkness, relieved only by the occasional glow from a second-floor window. As in Tangier, the narrow alleyways zigzagged without any discernable pattern until Jade could tell direction only by the muted sounds of the ocean surf to her back.

Jade stopped, her eyes darting back and forth in the gloom, watchful for any sudden shifting of muted shadows. She listened for the telltale sounds of an ambush: the soft brush of a body against the wall, and the deep intake of breath. A rat braved the town's feline population and scuttled past her boot. Above her, a stork settled in on the adjoining rooftop. *Nothing*. Most importantly, Jade's left knee didn't ache, and while she didn't want to admit that it was able to predict imminent danger, she had to admit the connection went beyond coincidence. Somewhere close by, one of the Moroccan owls known as the Little Owl sounded its questioning *kee-uhk*. Her guide turned back to her and motioned her on. She followed.

At the backside of the city, the houses abutted the wall, or perhaps considering the age of some of the dwellings, formed the wall. The Berber paused to collect his bearings, then led Jade to an ancient wooden doorway, partially broken, tucked into a narrow recess. A stylized black hand, fingers touching and pointing down, marked the door. Inside the hand was a red diamond shape. Remnants of stonework indicated that this had once been an interior doorway, the surrounding structure long gone. None of the nearby dwellings showed signs of habitation or other use. Clearly people shunned this area. Even the local cats avoided it. Her guide nodded towards the door.

"Inside?" asked Jade in French. The man nodded again. She pointed to the man's chest. "Will you come, too?" This time he shook his head and stepped back a pace.

"The people who shun salt and iron live inside," he said.

The man feared the spirits he believed dwelled within. Well, spirits or no, Jade needed to find her mother, and if she was still inside, Jade meant to go in after her. She removed her portable flashlight from the bag and switched it on.

The dirt by the door showed signs from where the door had been dragged open over it. Footprints overrode some of the drag marks. The question was, How recently were they made? In this alcove the air smelled stale, as though it didn't circulate often. There probably wasn't enough wind then to blow the sandy dirt, which meant the door could have been opened today or last month. She squatted down and tried to sort through the number of footprints but couldn't make out anything clearly. Rising, she tugged on the door and forced it open.

Her guide tapped her shoulder. When she turned, he pressed a chunk of iron into her hands, the remains of a worn knife. "It has *baraka*," he said.

Jade had read about *baraka*, a term for the holiness attached to certain objects, people, or deeds. It seemed to be fragile, easily lost by doing something harmful. Jade acknowledged his gift with a nod, then stepped into a wall of stale air, redolent of decay and earth. A hint of ammonia wafted past her, an indication of stale urine. Startled by the door's noise and the sound of her footsteps, a family of mice scurried past. Jade caught a brief flashing of some object in one mouse's mouth. Packrats of some sort, she thought, and paid no more attention. She scented dampness in the air, perhaps moist sea air collected and held in the stone and earthen walls. Once more she turned her head to silently question her guide. He stood pressed against the opposite wall of abandoned dwellings, as far from the doorway as possible, his right hand raised in front of his face, fingers splayed in some sign to ward off evil. His left hand held a piece of iron.

"Wait there," she said in French, then added, "please."

Her flashlight played across the floor and the stucco walls, but did little to penetrate the gloom beyond. She walked slowly, pausing every ten steps to listen and to sweep the floor with her flashlight beam. Someone had walked in here, but how long ago was still unclear. She stooped and examined the prints, hoping to find something indicating her mother. Then it hit her. She had no idea what type of shoe or boot her mother had on. There was certainly a print here that looked small enough to belong to her.

"Mother," she called into the black recesses. Her voice echoed off the walls and disturbed a few bats hanging near the entrance. They fluttered past, their wings brushing against her hair. *Probably just woke up some jinni.* She wondered if they'd frighten her guide into vacating his post. Jade decided she'd follow these footprints as far as she could before heading back. If she didn't find her mother soon, she'd return to Tangier and demand help from the American Consulate.

The tunnel led straight back for fifty yards before it turned left and angled down. Stone walls replaced the stucco as she descended beneath the floor of the present city. The air smelled dank with mold, the walls moist and green. It turned cooler as she continued, like entering into a cave. The tunnel took a sharp right down a flight of worn stone steps, their surface polished by countless feet. Another right, and Jade knew she was heading back under the city.

A new odor tickled her nostrils, a human smell. She sniffed, testing the air. She detected stale perspiration and something else; something cloying, reminiscent of a meat market. *Blood.* She hastened forward and saw that the tunnel forked ahead. In her haste, she nearly tripped over the body.

There, at her feet, lay a Moroccan on his right side, a knife in his back. His length spanned the width of the tunnel, his left arm pointing to the right fork.

CHAPTER 3

The Atlantic coastline bears witness to the multitudes of cultures that have laid claim to Morocco at one time or another. Portuguese fortresses sit on top of Roman foundations, which sit on top of Phoenician storage cellars. Most of the underground levels have been filled in or forgotten by everyone except the jinni. *The ones who shun iron and salt seem to favor caves, ruins, and dirt, rather like children.*

—The Traveler

A STRONG SENSE OF SELF-PRESERVATION, honed by Jade's service driving an ambulance at the front lines during the Great War, quickly replaced her initial shock and disbelief. She instantly crouched against the wall and switched off her light. If the murderer lurked nearby, she didn't need to present herself as the next target. After several uneventful minutes, she risked turning her light back on and scrambled over to the body.

Jade put her fingers to the man's neck below the jawline. *No pulse.* His gray, waxy face verified what she already knew. *Definitely dead.* The right side of his face had turned a purplish red where the blood pooled after death. The blood from the knife wound spread down, a macabre blossoming in his otherwise white robe. She turned her attention to the knife, or at least the hilt, since most of the blade was deep in the man's back. The intricate filigree design on the hilt looked Arabic and continued up into the fan-shaped end. The empty scabbard tucked into the man's waistband hinted that this was his own weapon.

She tried to move his left arm, the one pointing into the tunnel. It moved, but reluctantly. *So he's been dead for only a few hours, maybe three or four.* Surely, she thought, he didn't land in this position. Someone must have placed his arm that way to leave a message, and they did it not long after killing him. These tunnels weren't the most popular tourist spot, but someone counted on the body being found and wanted the discoverer to go farther into the right tunnels. *Is Mother in there? Is it a trap?*

She tiptoed eight paces to the fork, stood with her back to the left branch, and played her light along the floor of the right one. A slight breeze wafted over her face as another bat fluttered past her on its nocturnal flight. Jade opened her mouth to call once more for her mother when she heard voices murmuring from deep within. She cocked her head to hear better. They came from the left tunnel, and one voice belonged to a woman. Jade pivoted and entered the left branch.

Jade tugged her handkerchief from her skirt pocket and covered the flashlight to dull the beam. She could still see, but with less risk of being seen. Then she tiptoed along the narrowing passageway. Again the echo of a woman's commanding voice, followed by whispered murmurs. *Not Mother's voice.* This one was higher in pitch, although maybe the tunnel's acoustics played with it.

Now the voice turned pleading, and an argumentative male answered it. *Where's it coming from?* It seemed to be everywhere at once: behind her, before her, and beyond the walls. Jade took a deep breath, her head foggy from the stale air. Again the voice drifted away to her left. She followed it, drawn along as sailors were drawn to the siren's song, no longer watching the walls for other branches.

The constructed stone walls gave way to natural earth and stone. Jade saw lines along the walls and floor where ancient tools had picked and hammered out the passages. *Phoenicians? Romans?* Once, she accidentally kicked aside a fragment of an urn. Jade picked it up and turned it over in her hands. She recognized the shape as that of an amphora, golden leaves painted on a black glaze. Perhaps these had been storage warrens when the city was a trading port. Jade carefully set it aside and continued along the passageway, pausing only to let her light expose an occasional shallow alcove carved out of the wall.

Finally, the voices became clearer, as though the speakers stood just around the next corner. Jade pressed herself against the wall in one of the alcoves and switched off her flashlight. She couldn't make out what language these people spoke, but oddly enough, she understood them.

"Take this amulet, Igider, but do not wear it," commanded a woman.

"Elishat's amulet," said a man's voice, breathy with awe.

"The very same."

"Dahia, I have obeyed you in all else, but I cannot do this. It will mean your death."

"I am already dead, Igider. What is important is that the rule of the *kahina* lives on. My sons will do as I say to save my people. They will join the invaders to stop the warfare and our extermination. *You* must do as I say to save my daughter's legacy."

"Your daughter?" Igider's voice was incredulous. "Dahia, no one . . ."

"You are correct. No one knows of my daughter. I have

kept her hidden in the high mountains for her twelve years to keep her safe."

"Then you knew of this day?"

"Yes, I foresaw it," the woman replied, her voice riddled with sorrow.

"But still you fought?" the man asked, his voice softened with respect.

"To foresee is not to surrender. But it is to make preparation."

There was a brief pause, as though both parties searched for something to say, something to bring hope to a desperate situation.

"Now go," said the woman. "Slip out the tunnels into the night and make your way to my sister. Give the amulet to her for my daughter."

"And you, my *kahina*?"

"I will wait a while longer before I, too, slip away. Have no fear for me, Igider. They will not capture or kill me tonight."

The voices ceased. Jade remained still lest one or the other go past her and see her, but no one passed her way. Whoever these people were, they didn't seem to be involved with her mother.

Mother. Perhaps she was back at the hotel. Maybe she'd been there all this time, waiting for Jade, worrying. Jade shook her head to clear the foggy feeling enveloping her. That's when she noticed that even her left palm hurt.

As she switched her light back on, she realized that she was gripping the old iron blade her guide had given her. *What in the name of Pete?* Jade couldn't recall taking it out of her pocket. *I've got to get back. Report this body. Find Mother.* She started to turn back when her light reflected off a thin band of white at her feet. Something white and grainy made a neat semicircle around the nook where she'd hidden. Jade bent down and picked up a few coarse grains, then touched one to her tongue. *Salt.* Where did it come from? She flashed the light into the alcove and saw another half-filled urn. She reached inside and pulled out a handful of sea salt. *What's going on here?* Salt in an old urn was one matter, but the circle of salt? She didn't remember seeing that when she'd hidden herself. Her skin prickled with goose bumps.

That did it. She ran back down the tunnels, trying to remember every turn she'd taken. Just keep turning right, she thought. Finally she stumbled out the doorway and into the city alleyway, collapsing against the opposite wall. The stork nesting above her clacked its thick beak in alarm and flapped away. Jade gulped in the fresher air, not minding the smell of rat urine and stork droppings. *I'm out. Away from that body and those voices.* That's when she remembered the body. She hadn't seen or tripped over it on her way out. It was gone. So was her guide. Only the Little Owl remained, ruffling his rufus-red feathers. He opened his beak wide and, after a few convulsive twitches, regurgitated the pellet from last night's meal; then hunkered down for the day.

Jade stepped back as the owl pellet plopped at her feet and cracked apart against a stone. From inside, something golden winked in the light. Jade's first thought was that a little pack mouse had met his end when he ran out into the night. She reached down and picked up the trinket, a charm shaped like a moon eclipsing the sun. Jade turned it over in her hand and blinked as it flashed sunlight into her still dilated pupils. *Sunlight! It was sunset when I went in. Sweet Millard Filmore on a bicycle. How the hell long was I in there?*

CHAPTER 4

*Tangier is an international city governed in part by a committee of nations.
Basically, this translates into too many officers and not enough soldiers.
Everyone and yet no one is in charge. Consequently, it's the perfect place to
conduct illegal activities. One would suspect that every third person
and his cat is a smuggler, and there are a lot of cats in Tangier.*

—The Traveler

"I TELL YOU, LIEUTENANT GERVAIS, there was a dead man in the tunnels. I saw him."

"Of course, Mademoiselle. And what did this supposed dead man look like?"

"Like he was dead. Monsieur Lieutenant, I have already described this man to you twice." She stood in the small reception room of the French military post in Azilah, facing the lieutenant who sat at his desk, twirling his pencil. Why, she wondered, did he insist on treating her like some hysterical female? She caught his bemused glance at her clothing and knew why. Her clothes were covered in dirt, old whitewash and a few smudges of what smelled like bat guano. She could only imagine what her face and hair looked like. She could almost hear her mother's admonishments in her ear. One in particular stood out. *You must never show your emotions when dealing with others. It gives the appearance of a lack of control and awards them the upper hand.* All right.

Time to curb her rising temper if she wanted him to take her seriously.

"He was dressed like a Moroccan Arab in a long white *djellaba* with a black sash around his waist and a white turban on his head."

"And you say he had a scimitar?" He made a notation in his little book.

"No. I did not say that. I said he had the scabbard for a small knife tucked in his sash. He wore the knife in his back."

Monsieur Gervais ignored her sarcasm. "I see. And how long was this knife?"

"I don't know. I didn't pull it out of his back. But the scabbard was about twenty centimeters long." She held out her hands like a fisherman does to depict the size of the catch.

"And this man spoke to you?" He held his pencil poised, ready to write.

Jade scowled. *He's mocking me.* "How could he speak to me? I told you he was dead."

"But you said he told you to go down one of the tunnel passages?"

"His arm lay stretched out, pointing down the right-hand passage. But I went down the other branch. I heard voices and thought it might be my mother."

"And these voices, Mademoiselle, they were not attached to any people?"

That's it! "Monsieur. I'm sure they were, but I didn't see them. I was hiding. Now, if you don't care about the dead man, will you at least help me find my mother?"

The Frenchman closed his little book and pocketed it in his shirt. "Mademoiselle del Cameron," he said, his voice patronizing, "I'm sure you can now see the bad judgment in an impressionable girl such as yourself wandering alone in such dangerous passages. Of course the experience would over-stimulate any untrained mind of a romantic turn. I would suggest you go back to Tangier and you will most likely find your mother waiting for you at your hotel."

Jade wouldn't hold back her temper any longer. It was one thing to suggest she had made up her story to feel impor-tant, but to accuse her of being a silly twit of a girl fresh out of finishing school? She stiffened into a military posture, star-ing over the man's head. "*I* am a decorated ambulance driver of the Great War, where I served the French Third Army. I pulled simpering, babbling soldiers from the trenches and drove them under shell fire to the hospital and earned the Croix de Guerre. *You* are an idiot, Monsieur, and I shall re-port you to your superior officer."

She drove back to Tangier in a furor; angry at the French representative in Azilah for treating her like a child, and at her mother for wandering off without letting her know where she was going. When her conscience prickled and suggested she should be angry with herself for causing their argument the other morning, she pushed the thought aside and focused on her mother's antiquated notions of propriety as the root.

She drove past the *Bab el Kasbah*, or "Gate of the Fortress," and followed the Rue de la Kasbah southeast to a smaller gate into the *Medina*. Eventually, after wending her way through the tangled, narrow streets cluttered with people, stray dogs, and a few donkeys, she turned the car into the side alley by Madame Laferriere's residence. No one answered her knock, so Jade ripped a page from her notebook, scribbled a brief thank-you in French and shoved it under the door. Then she hurried as quickly as she could back to her hotel.

Jade was taking the front steps two at a time when a slender man in a French military uniform stopped her at the door.

"Mademoiselle del Cameron?" he asked.

"Oui." She supposed that the officer at Azilah, thinking better of her, had sent a wire to his colleague in Tangier. "Have you found my mother?"

"You must come with me," he said, gripping her left arm.

Her stomach lurched as she envisioned identifying her mother's dead body at some barracks headquarters. "Answer me, please. Have you found my mother?"

"We are hoping you will tell us where your mother is, Mademoiselle. She is under suspicion for murder."

Jade jerked her arm free. "What?"

"And," the officer continued as he grabbed her arm again, "there has been a complaint filed against you for stealing an automobile."

"That is ludicrous," she retorted, her voice sharp with anger.

"Which charge would that be?" asked the officer as he led her to a waiting car and gently pushed her into the backseat. He slid in beside her and tapped the driver, a private, on the shoulder.

"Both charges," replied Jade, as the car raced through the crowded streets. The driver honked the horn continuously as pedestrians scrambled out of the way. Jade saw a few tourists point at her and recognized the Tremaines. Libby, in particular, watched with a smirk pasted on her pretty, insipid face. *Wonderful. That should fuel the gossip.*

"If you go to Madame Laferriere's home, I can prove I did not steal her Panhard."

"Ah, then you do know her car."

"Of course I know her car. I drove it. Only I did not steal

it; I hired it out for the day. She probably became concerned when I didn't return it yesterday evening."

"And why is that?"

"Because I was in the underground tunnels of Azilah all night. I was looking for my mother."

"And you hid her away in these tunnels after she murdered a man?"

Jade's emerald eyes opened wider. "Mother didn't murder anyone."

"That remains to be seen, Mademoiselle."

"Please, Monsieur . . ."

"I am *Captain* Réné Deschamp."

"Captain Deschamp. If you will allow me to explain. I am not trying to hide anything. On the contrary, I need your help. My mother is missing."

"I am aware of that, Mademoiselle del Cameron." They stopped in front of a clump of crumbling houses that Jade recognized from this morning. "We will first pay a call on Madame Laferriere."

Captain Deschamp led Jade to the door, keeping a firm grip on her right arm with his left. He rapped on the door several times, but received no reply.

"If you look in that alleyway," said Jade, "you will see her Panhard. And there," she pointed to the slip of paper peeking from under the door, "is the note I left for her."

Captain Deschamp ordered his driver to inspect the alley and then the automobile itself once the man verified that the vehicle was parked there.

"It appears to be in order, Captain Deschamp," said the private.

"Hand me that note," ordered Deschamp. The private

did, and Deschamp read it. He handed it back to the under-ling and motioned for him to replace it.

"It seems that you are guilty of nothing more than tar-diness in returning Madame's car. At least," he added, "in this matter. There still remains the issue of your role in your mother's crime."

"My mother didn't commit a crime," Jade said.

Captain Deschamp escorted her gently but firmly back to the car and ordered his driver to proceed to headquarters. "Perhaps," he said as they sped along the narrow streets of the *Medina*, horn honking, "you should tell me everything."

Jade flinched as one white-robed Moroccan dodged their Peugot, dropping his basket against her window as he stumbled. Cucumbers sprayed into the air, several bouncing against the glass. "I've been trying to ever since you arrested me." She explained yesterday's events quickly and concisely, omitting nothing but the owl pellet, and that only because she hadn't given it any more thought after pocketing the charm. By the time she'd finished, they'd arrived at a tidy, two-story building outside the *Medina* walls.

"A most interesting tale, Mademoiselle. But you will par-don me if I do not believe all of it. This overheard conversa-tion, for instance, is most fanciful." He looked sidewise at her and pursed his lips as though amused. "Please come inside. I have something to show you." As he led her past the front desk, several privates and one sergeant saluted. All stared at Jade as though they'd never seen a woman before. "In here," he said, indicating a back room.

Jade stepped inside, her attention immediately arrested by a shrouded figure lying on a long mess table. Captain Des-champ pulled back the sheet.

"That's the man I saw dead in the tunnel," said Jade. "Who the hell is he and how in thunder did he get here?"

"Both are interesting questions," said Deschamp. "We believe he is Achmed ben Sayid, a local guide for hire. A maid found him in your rooms this morning. He had this in his hand."

He held out a blue leather pocketbook, engraved in gold with the letter *I*.

"My mother's pocketbook! But it wasn't in his hand before, and he wasn't murdered in my room."

"And you are certain of that?"

"Dead certain. I saw him in the Azilah tunnels. His knife was in his back. He had no pulse. His arm was just starting to stiffen, but not his lower body."

"As you can see, Mademoiselle, this man's arms are by his side, which makes me question the veracity of your statement."

Jade thought for a moment, her mind replaying the events in the tunnel. "How was he lying when you found him?"

Deschamp made a point of consulting a report. "Lying facedown."

"Then he was moved," Jade said, triumph in her tone. "Look to see where the blood pooled in his body. I think you'll find it wasn't where you'd expect if he died facedown in our room. You might also discover that his left shoulder is dislocated where someone forced it back down after rigor set in."

The captain inspected the corpse briefly, then snapped his head around to Jade. "You are right. It is pooled on his right side, and his arm has been forced. Such a thing does not change when a body is moved. But how is it a young lady such as yourself knows of these things?"

"I drove an ambulance during the war, Captain, so I am on intimate terms with blood and death. Even before that, I hunted and I know what happens to the blood in game animals if they are not bled out."

Deschamp studied Jade's face as if seeing her for the first time, taking her measure. "It would seem that you are a remarkable young woman," he said. "One would assume that your mother is equally remarkable."

Jade caught the tenor of his statement. "She is not a murderer, Captain, if that is what you're suggesting. She would consider it unladylike."

"Perhaps. But would she kill in self-defense? What if this man attacked her? I have made inquiries. Your mother hired this man to be a guide and translator for her."

Jade studied her words carefully before speaking. "Have you considered all the inconsistencies here? You suggest this man was brash enough to assault my mother *in her hotel room*? Then my mother stabbed him in the *back* to escape, but the man fell to his right side, where he lay long enough for his blood to pool before he rolled over onto his face? That my mother would then not have the presence of mind to retrieve her pocketbook from him before running away?" She shook her head. "No, I am convinced someone abducted my mother, possibly in the Azilah tunnels. I beg you to help me find her."

"We will find her, Mademoiselle, but I must ask you to remain in Tangier until we do."

"You still think I have something to do with this man's murder? Do you think *I* killed him?"

"I do not know what your role was, but I would prefer not to have two fugitives to search for. There is more at stake here than just the murder of this man." He stopped and studied

Jade again, locking his brown eyes on her green ones. "Why were you meeting your mother in Tangier?"

"Mother planned to spend time at her old home in Andalusia. She wanted to acquire a horse stud for our ranch in the States. She asked me to join her."

"That does not answer my question. Why did you meet in Tangier? Why not in Spain?"

Why indeed? "I was in British East Africa. North Africa seemed a good place to meet. Someplace neutral."

Deschamp made a notation in his notebook. "So you spend quite a bit of time in East Africa? Do you travel to Mombasa often?"

Jade's senses again went on alert. What was this man fishing for? "No."

"I have been given a dossier on you, Mademoiselle del Cameron. It is a most interesting read."

"The devil, you say," retorted Jade, outraged at the idea. "Who in tarnation sent you that?"

Deschamp ignored her question. "Am I correct that drugs were once found in one of your safari vehicles?"

"It wasn't my vehicle."

He looked up and arched a brow. "No?" He turned a few pages back in his notebook and read. "You hired a Harry Hascombe to run your safari, did you not?"

"Yes, and he hired Roger Forster and Roger hired the cars."

"And you shot Forster?"

"Yes."

"I see." He made another notation. "Apparently *you* do not consider such an act unladylike."

Jade took a deep breath and struggled inwardly for a grip on her temper. Losing it would not help her position. "I presume, Captain, that you are making some sort of connection, but I'll be deuced if I can see what it is."

Deschamp closed his book. "We searched your rooms, of course, and found a packet of hashish in your mother's luggage. There has been quite a lot of hashish entering my native country of late."

"What?" Jade felt as if the bottom had fallen out of her world and she'd been sent plummeting into hell. Her mother was missing, possibly injured or dead, and now they were accused not only of murder, but also of smuggling drugs. Her head ached and a sudden pain gripped her stomach. Finally she felt enough in control of her voice to speak. "Captain, I told you I found a note for my mother, which I thought came from the Tremaines. Perhaps you should question them. If nothing else, surely someone noticed a person or persons entering the hotel with a dead man."

Deschamp didn't answer immediately. He just watched Jade as if evaluating the truth behind her reaction. "I shall contact you at your hotel as soon as we know anything more." He bowed stiffly, dismissing her for the moment.

Jade didn't budge. "I'm not convinced, Captain, that you have the authority in Tangier to confine me to the city, much less my hotel. The American Consulate will likely have something to say about this."

"As you wish, but I assure you, the consul would prefer not to be involved in a murder investigation in a French city."

"Tangier is not a French city. It doesn't appear to be *any* government's city."

"No, but Azilah is, and you have been most insistent that the murder took place there. I thank you. You have given me all the authority that I need." He smiled, his head bobbing slightly in smugness. "Should you try to do anything rash, you should know that we hold all your travel papers. You cannot leave."

Jade stormed back toward the hotel, stopping once when a sound or a shadow or some unidentified sense alerted her to another presence. She pivoted, hoping to catch sight of whomever dogged her steps, but saw only the usual assortment of white-robed men. *Deschamp probably has someone watching me.* Once in the hotel, Jade ignored the desk clerk and gave a cursory glance to the lobby. Empty. She took the steps two at a time up to her room, feeling the need to think and sort everything out before deciding her next move. She didn't have the chance. There on the desk was a typed note.

Missed you in Azilah. Come into Marrakech to the Jemaâ el-Fna and come alone.

The note was signed with a picture of a full moon eclipsing the sun. The picture troubled Jade, but not nearly as much as knowing that *Jemaâ el-Fna* translated into "the Square of the Dead."

CHAPTER 5

One would expect the Moroccan peoples to be upset about handing over a major port city to foreign interests. But it may be the Sultan's way of herding the scum into one location and keeping the majority of the infidels out of the rest of the country. All things considered, it is not a bad plan.

—The Traveler

A MOON ECLIPSING THE SUN. Jade's right hand went to her skirt pocket and retrieved the charm she'd pulled from the owl pellet. They matched. She'd taken the trinket out of the owl pellet as a curiosity, the mouse's attraction for something shiny perhaps having drawn the owl's attention. At the time it merely struck her as an ironic lesson, applicable to human greed and demise. And now? Now it took on a far more sinister meaning. Whoever had hidden in the tunnel had waited for her. *I took the left fork. That's why they missed me.* Jade hadn't followed the dead man's signal. She'd followed the voices instead.

Then who were the people she had heard talking in the left tunnel? Were they connected in any way to her mother's abduction or to the Moroccan's murder? Did the charm belong to one of them? It could have fallen from a man's watch fob, a woman's bracelet, or it may have even been a protective talisman worn by the dead guide. If the latter, Jade thought, it ended up being as useless as a lucky rabbit's foot was to the rabbit.

One thing seemed certain. Someone in the right tunnel had something to do with her mother's disappearance. This note in her room proved that. Someone had wanted her to take the right-hand fork. She hadn't; they had waited, then left. *Probably hauled the dead man back with them.* She imagined them toting the corpse back to the hotel, perhaps pretending the man was drunk rather than dead. That alone told her they were not waiting to warn her. Was she supposed to be kidnapped, too, or were they going to demand ransom? Whatever the question, the answer waited in Marrakech.

Jade ransacked her and her mother's belongings for anything of value that she could use to barter for her mother's freedom. It didn't amount to much, just her mother's opal necklace and earrings. She rolled the results in some dark hosiery and shoved it in a carpetbag along with a clean dress for her fastidious mother. Then she exchanged her filthy skirt for a pair of trousers, decided that might be too scandalous for the Moroccans, and pulled her old ambulance corps skirt out of her trunk to wear over them.

The calf-length garment, designed to be worn over her corps trousers and boots, felt like an old ally, and aroused a rush of sensations. She closed her eyes and heard her comrade Beverly's melodic laugh, tasted Bovril's strong beefy flavor, smelled the pungent aroma of carbolic acid soaps, and felt the rumble of not-too-distant artillery fire. She exchanged her walking shoes for her stout pair of high boots, equipped with a knife sheath. She tucked her trouser legs inside the boots to hide them, and slipped her hunting knife into the sheath. Most of the francs went into her pocket; a few into the carpetbag along with a packet of coffee, a tin of matches, and a compass. The flashlight went into her camera bag.

I'm ready for you, you sons of hyenas. To perdition with Deschamp. The man would only claim she had typed the note herself. No, she'd head to Marrakech alone. She snatched up her carpetbag as well as her canvas camera bag and headed out only to stop abruptly at the door. *Think,* she told herself. If she left in broad daylight, Deschamp would stop her. She'd better wait for dark.

Jade dropped her bag by the door and paced the room, feeling very much alone when, on the third pass, she realized she didn't need to be. She'd wire Beverly and her husband, Lord Avery Dunbury, in London, where they awaited the birth of their first child. Avery had connections everywhere. Surely he'd be able to enlist someone here to come to her aid. Jade wrestled for a moment about also sending a wire to her father on their ranch in New Mexico and decided against it for the time being. There was nothing he could do besides worry, and she wasn't sure she could reach him, anyway, since he'd be up in the high pastures, making the rounds of the flocks.

She sat down at the desk to compose her message to Bev and Avery. Would Deschamp find out? Probably, if he was having her tailed. Might as well make it difficult for him. *Wonder if he reads Swahili? How in the world do you say "kidnapped" in Swahili?*

After a moment's reflection, she settled on the following message: *Mother stolen. We are suspects in murder. Going to Marrakech. Reply as received here. Later messages to mission there.* She signed it with her Swahili name, *Simba Jike.*

Jade frowned. If Deschamp did see this, he'd know she'd gone to Marrakech, but she couldn't conceive of a way to disguise the city's name and still get the information to Bev and Avery. Then she remembered that the imperial city stood just north of the Atlas Mountains. Jade burned the first paper, took another blank sheet, and rewrote the message, disguising Marrakech as "the red city holding up the world." She hoped they'd look at a map and make the connection. Of course what they could do, Deschamp could, too. Well, she had to try something. She just wished her Arabic was better to help her enlist the aid of one of the area children.

She took a seat on the hotel's lower terrace and ordered coffee, sipping as she watched the assorted Moroccans parading in front of her. Of particular interest was a boy about eight or nine years old selling oranges. She watched him accost several tourists like a natural-born salesman. He spoke French!

"Here," she called to him in French. The boy trotted over with his basket of fruit.

"Fresh oranges, Mademoiselle," he said, and named an outrageously high price.

Jade offered a fourth that amount, and the boy countered with something closer to half the original cost. Jade picked up an orange, turning it over in her hand as though scrutinizing it. In the meantime, she motioned the boy to lean closer, pointing to the orange. When he did, she spoke slowly and softly in French.

"Can you keep a secret?" The boy nodded once, his brows furrowed as he contemplated her with obvious skepticism. "Good," she continued. "I want you to take a message to the telegraph office, but you must make it look like you are just selling your oranges somewhere else." She held up several francs, enough to have purchased several baskets of oranges.

The boy, suddenly enthusiastic, grabbed for the money. Jade pulled it back. She could barter, too.

"Only this much now," she said as she held out a third of the money. "You must go back this evening for a reply. Bring it to me and I will pay you the rest. But you must tell no one. Will you do this?"

The boy didn't hesitate. "Yes."

Jade slipped the money and her message into his hand as the boy gave her a second orange. To an onlooker, it seemed like any other transaction between a foreigner who couldn't barter and a shrewd Moroccan who knew how to overprice his goods. "Come back here this evening," she whispered as he left.

The boy didn't reply. Instead he strolled off, occasionally hoisting an orange and calling out its virtues. But Jade noticed that he didn't directly approach anyone else to press them into buying his fruit. Instead, he made his way down the narrow street until she lost sight of him where the street made one of its many twists.

Now for the hard part, she thought, waiting. She wanted to call on Madame Laferriere again and convince her to hire out her car for several days, but knew if she went now, Deschamp would find out and put an end to any hope of leaving Tangier. Jade finished her coffee and left the terrace, strolling at a leisurely pace towards the souks. To her right she saw a uniformed man study her. When she stared directly at him, he put his hands behind his back and looked away as though he was merely keeping the peace on this corner. Jade took advantage of his pretense, reached into her pocket, and tossed several coins into the street behind her while he wasn't looking.

Immediately, a host of beggars and children scrambled after the coins. The ensuing melee drew the officer's attention from Jade. She slipped into a side street and escaped. Forty minutes later she strolled back to the hotel with a woven bag stuffed full of sundry purchases hanging from one arm. She smiled at the panic-stricken officer and waved, watching him breathe a sigh of relief that she hadn't escaped during his watch. *Later. When you're less vigilant.*

The trick to this waiting game was not to let down her own guard. Jade detested playing the role of prey. Lie still, don't move, wait it out, then run like hell. Too passive, and often too futile. Her father had taught her to observe all animals and study their behavior, to always think like a predator in dangerous situations. She searched her mind and settled on a smaller predator, the weasel. In this role, she again had to avoid detection by a guard animal, but for a more aggressive reason. Avoiding capture wasn't the only goal. She had her own prey to pursue. Metaphorically speaking, she intended to slip past the guard dog and across the fence to raid the chicken house. Only the chicken she wanted was in Marrakech. Stealth and camouflage became her key weapons, night her ally.

Jade went back to her room and away from watching eyes. She rummaged in her bag, took out a whetstone, and honed her knife before slipping it back in her boot sheath. Then she studied her hand-drawn map of Morocco, memorizing the new roads, the villages and the French outposts on the way to Marrakech. She would have to be watchful. With an incomplete rail system and limited vehicles, very few tourists pushed as far as Marrakech. That meant she would be more noticeable. It also meant that any non-Moroccans she met might be the kidnappers.

She tried to rest but sleep eluded her, her mother's face imposing itself every time she began to doze. Once she dreamt of her mother hosting a banker for dinner, convincing him to loan her husband a large sum with very low interest. A second dream showed Inez organizing a school for the pueblo children. In most of the dreams, her mother appeared impatient at Jade for taking so long to show up. Jade got up again and took out the dark blue woven robe and the dozen blue and black scarves she'd purchased from a street peddler.

Eventually her stomach announced it was 5:30. She tossed the robe on the bed, took a seat back on the terrace and made a pretense of watching the people while she devoured stewed chicken with apricots and drank cup after cup of coffee. Patience, she counseled herself, but inwardly she felt like an unexploded shell, ready to blow apart at the slightest provocation. Deschamp's watchdog still stood on patrol, looking more relaxed slouched against a wall. Jade pretended not to see him while her eyes searched the milling throngs for a smaller form.

Presently the boy appeared, wending his way from person to person, his high voice proclaiming the virtues of his wares in French and Arabic. "Sweet oranges. Golden as the sultan's throne."

"Here. I will buy an orange." Jade saw the young officer watch her for a moment, then relax again when she did nothing more unusual than sniff a couple of the small globes before selecting one. What the man didn't observe was the paper slipped to Jade with the fruit and the extraordinarily high price Jade paid for that orange.

Jade shoved the telegram into her skirt pocket and calmly peeled her fruit, feeling the paper practically burn a hole in her pocket, taunting her to read it. She resisted. No one should suspect her of doing anything other than obeying Deschamp's order to remain in Tangier. She finished her orange, then as the muezzin called the faithful to evening prayers, Jade rose and went to her room and ripped open the return telegram. The Dunburys had followed her example and written in Swahili.

Roughly translated it read: "Received. Gathering help. Be careful." At least she assumed the Dunburys said to be careful. They used *hatari,* a word that literally meant "danger" but was also used to express the need for caution. Jade had no idea what help they were gathering, but hoped Avery could persuade one of his many contacts to pressure either the American Consulate or the French to help her.

She looked at her watch. Seven o'clock. Ten minutes after sunset. Another hour for the deeper darkness to descend. The earlier hours had been difficult enough to endure. This last hour seemed next to impossible. Jade forced herself to remain calm and busied herself knotting the scarves together into one long rope. She had wanted a room with a view of the Kasbah, but her frugal mother had insisted on the less expensive room whose windows looked over the narrow back alley.

"Why pay more to see something from your room when we don't plan on spending much time there?" she'd said.

"Thanks, Mother," muttered Jade as she tied one end of her silken rope to a bed post. "You've just made sneaking out of the hotel much easier."

Finally she decided the time was right. Deschamp's watchdog would assume she'd gone to bed and would relax his vigilance. She slipped on the dark robe, tossed the rope and her carpetbag out the window, and shinnied down the outer wall.

CHAPTER 6

There are two distinct cultures that call Morocco home. In the cities are
the Arabs, who resent the French intrusion into their home despite the new roads,
schools, and developing railroad. They forget they themselves have only resided here
since A.D. 682 and ousted another peoples up into the mountains. Long before their
arrival, the entire Maghreb was peopled by tribes now known as the Berbers.
The history of these people is as mysterious as they are.

—The Traveler

KEEP TO THE WALL, HUG THE SHADOWS. Jade grimaced when she imagined her mother's reaction. She could almost hear her snap, "You pretended to be a weasel? Will I never see you behave like a proper lady?" *Sorry, Mother. I'm a lost cause.*

The narrow, dark alley afforded some cover, but it didn't extend beyond the building adjacent to her hotel. Eventually, Jade would have to risk being seen. She just hoped Deschamp's watchdog was napping now, preferably in the hotel's lobby. With her carpetbag tucked under her left arm and with her right hand clutching the robe's hood in front of her face, Jade paused at the alley's end. *It's now or never.* She stepped into the slightly wider side street and matched her pace with the natives around her.

No one paid any attention to her. To the few Moroccans still about, she was just another body. To the more numerous Europeans enjoying the Tangier nightlife, she represented something to be avoided, a possible beggar or a thief. No one saw her as female since she wasn't swaddled in white veils.

Jade passed one of the popular tourist watering holes, a French café of sorts that served wine and spirits late into the night. This one attracted a larger number of tourists by purporting to present Moroccan entertainment. She heard the wailing of some wind instrument and the hypnotic, hollow *thum dum* of a clay drum. Over this background rose and fell a man's tremulous voice, singing what had the earmarks of a tragic love song. Jade caught the words "lost," "beloved," and what might be "soft hair." *Probably singing about his favorite goat.*

Through the window Jade glimpsed a swaying form, a woman in baggy red trousers and a gaudy red-and-blue striped coat that hung to her knees. Silver bangles adorned her wrists, ankles, and forehead; those on her wrists jingled as she twisted her hennaed hands about in time to the music. The woman was fully clothed, but managed to hold nearly every man's attention with her softly undulating hips. *Little Egypt all over again.*

Jade started to walk away when she noticed Walter Tremaine at one of the tables. He didn't appear to be particularly interested in the dancer. Instead, he sat staring into his tiny cup of thick, black coffee, lost to daydreams. Jade pulled her hood down lower and moved on.

Once she was past the more popular European sector, she relaxed a little and turned into the *Medina* and toward Madame Laferriere's house. The souks, teeming earlier with shopkeepers and customers, sat silent. Only a stray cat trotted by. It must have spotted some prey, as Jade heard it make a sudden dash, its claws scrabbling for purchase up a wooden crate.

Suddenly Jade stopped and hugged the wall. The cat wasn't chasing a rodent. Something had frightened it. She listened, ears filtering through the silence for anything unusual. Nothing. She waited a moment longer and heard the soft *oof* of a stifled cough.

Jade sprinted down the narrow street, dodging garbage and the occasional sleeping dog. Each time the opportunity presented itself, she turned left, hoping to eventually double back behind her pursuer. It would have been easier if the streets were straight and built on an orderly plan. In the end, she had only a general idea of where she was, except she had run uphill more often than not.

She forced herself to breathe slowly as she took note of the buildings. Nothing looked familiar. She sniffed and sorted through the myriad smells. Among the scent of dog refuse and lingering sweat, Jade caught the faint scent of spices creeping out from the tightly shuttered shops. *Ah! The street of the doctors and herbalists*. She listened again for the sound of pursuit, heard none, and slipped back into the street and to Rue de la Petite Maison.

Several lights burned inside Madame Laferriere's residence. Jade pushed back her hood to expose her full face lest Madame think robbers were afoot, and knocked at the door. From inside came the shuffling of slippered feet.

"Who is there?" the woman asked in French. The voice sounded much older now than it had yesterday.

"Jade del Cameron. I'm an American. We spoke yesterday about your automobile."

"My automobile? Go away."

"Wait. I'm sorry you had to report it stolen to the French. I was delayed." When the woman did not respond, Jade added, "I will be happy to pay you more in recompense."

The door opened a few inches, but where Jade expected to see a woman an inch or two shorter than herself, she saw a tiny, old, hunched crone. "Madame Laferriere?" Jade asked. The woman nodded. "I must have spoken with your daughter yesterday. Is she here?"

"I have no daughter. And I do not know what you are speaking of. I have not been to see any police. I have been ill. At least I think so." She rubbed a clawlike hand across her forehead. "Someone left me a gift of new wine at lunch yesterday. I drank it and fell asleep. I did not wake until this morning. Ooh," she said as she passed her hand across her eyes. "My head still hurts."

"Madame, may I please come in and talk?"

"No!" She started to shove the door closed, but Jade stuck her boot in the crack and blocked it.

"Then at least let me hire your motorcar again for several days." Jade had no doubt that someone, the same person who later reported the robbery, had drugged the old woman and taken her place yesterday.

At the mention of possible revenue, the old woman pulled the door back a few inches and peered up at Jade. "How much will you pay?"

Jade opened her canvas bag that hung from her shoulder and extracted several francs. "Will this be enough?"

The crone began to reach for the money, then hesitated. "No one has used it for many months. It may not even run anymore."

Jade smiled, gratified to see that the little creature had a conscience despite her need. "That is no problem, Madame. I am a mechanic. I served France during the Great War, driving an ambulance for the army."

At the mention of a beloved homeland, now so distant,

the old woman's eyes misted over. "Ah, I would love to go home again and see my country and my nieces."

Jade pulled out all but a couple dozen francs from her pocket and held out the roll of money. If the amount in the carpetbag was not enough to pay a ransom, and she knew it wouldn't be even without spending this, she would wire for money from home. Right now she had a better use for it. The Panhard, new, might have cost over ten thousand francs. Now the woman would be lucky to get five hundred, but to Jade it was invaluable. It was worth her mother's life.

"Take this, Madame. Let me buy the car. If you sell your house, together it should be more than enough to get home again."

"It is yours, and bless you," said the woman without counting the bills. She picked up a jerry can from beside the door and handed it to Jade. "There are a few liters of extra fuel in here."

Jade went into the alley and fastened the can to a sideboard. She'd just finished when a calloused hand touched her shoulders. She jumped and spun around, landing in a crouch, her right hand slipping the knife from its boot sheath. The man in front of her raised his right hand directly in front of his face, palm out, fingers spread. It might have been an expression of peace, but something about the action seemed familiar.

"Who are you?" Jade asked in French. "What do you want?"

"I can help you get to Marrakech." The man stepped forward one pace into the dim light. Both hands were empty.

"You! You're the man who showed me the tunnels in Azilah." She sprang forward, gripped the man by the neck with her left hand and pushed him against the wall, her knife at his throat. "What have you done with my mother?"

The man closed his eyes and held one hand in front of his face, muttering something in a language Jade didn't recognize. "By all that is holy, *Alalla,*" he said in French, but using the Arabic equivalent of "Madame," "I have done nothing with your mother."

"Then why are you following me?"

The man opened his eyes but kept his head turned so he never met Jade's piercing stare. "I have been told to bring you back with me. I heard you talk with this woman. You want to go to Marrakech. I can help you."

Jade relaxed her grip on the man's neck and stepped away, her knife still poised for defense. "Why should I trust you? And what did you mean when you said you were told to bring me back? Back to where?"

"To . . . to Marrakech."

Jade scowled. "How convenient," she mumbled to herself in English. "Look me in the eyes!" she commanded. "Did you leave a note for me in my room?" She pushed the knife tip closer to the man's throat.

The Berber forced himself to meet her intense gaze. "No. I swear by all that is holy, I left no note for you."

Jade studied his eyes. He didn't look aside when he answered. If anything, he seemed terrified to look at her at all. Either he was telling the truth or was *very* experienced in lying. She wasn't convinced she could trust him. Still, she reasoned, it might not be such a bad idea to go with this man. If he was an enemy, it was better to have him in her sight than dogging her steps. If he was a friend, well, she needed all the help she could get right now.

She released him and motioned with the knife for him to precede her. "I will take you with me, but do not try to trick me." She picked up her carpetbag from the cobbled pavement and tossed it to him. "Go crank the car." She tucked her knife into her belt where she could retrieve it instantly and climbed in on the right on the driver's side.

The Panhard started up easily enough and, after her companion climbed into the passenger's side, Jade drove out of the alley. She maneuvered the silent streets uphill to the Kasbah, paid the gatekeeper to let her out, then exited from the *Bab el Kasbah*. Once outside the gate, she headed downhill, the great souk with sleeping camels and donkeys to her left and the Atlantic to her right. "What is your name?" Jade asked in French. She noticed he kept his eyes averted again.

"Bachir."

"Well, Bachir," she continued in French, "I am not taking you to Marrakech or anywhere else until you answer some questions." Jade stopped the car and turned to him. "Who sent you to find me and why? How do you know who I am, how did you find me in Azilah, and why did you leave before I came out of the tunnel?"

Bachir turned partway towards her, still avoiding her eyes. "I will answer all, *Alalla,* but not here. We must move on. You will be discovered if you stay here."

As much as Jade hated to admit it, he was right. By morning, Deschamp would expect word from his watchdog. After he reported that she hadn't come down to breakfast, someone would go up to her room. Then they'd know she'd slipped away. She searched her memory for anything she'd told him. Nowhere did she remember mentioning Marrakech. She'd received that message later.

"I agree, for now. But once we are safely away, I expect answers." Bachir didn't bother to reply.

Jade put the car in gear again and followed the track to Azilah. The acetylene headlamps didn't work and they drove in the dark with little more than the sound of the surf to their right until the moon rose half an hour later. Three days past full, the still-swollen orb spilled its creamy light across the road from behind her left shoulder, illuminating every hole and bump. When she reached the far side of Azilah without meeting or overtaking another living soul, Jade decided it was time for some answers.

"Now, who sent you?" she asked, still driving west.

Bachir kept his eyes ahead. "The *kahina*."

CHAPTER 7

The stories of the Berbers' origins are as fanciful as a tale from Arabian Nights.
Some people claim they were chased from Israel when David overthrew
Goliath. Others align them with ancient Egyptians or the Phoenicians. No one
asks the Berbers. They call themselves Imazighen, or in its adjectival form,
the Amazigh people. It means the "free people."

—The Traveler

THE PANHARD SLID SIDEWAYS as Jade hit the brakes. In her head she again heard the voices in the tunnel and the word *kahina*. Her hand gripped her knife hilt and her voice dropped to a low rumble. "Who, in the name of all that is holy, is this *kahina*?"

"She is our leader, *Alalla*."

"My name is Jade. So, this *kahina* of yours leads the Berbers?"

The man's chin went up, an expression of pride. "That is what others call us. It is an insult. We are not barbarians. We are the Imazighen." To Jade's ear, it sounded like *Im*-ah-*Zirr-en*, the *r* sound being made as a deep, throaty rasp. "My own tribe traces itself back long before even the Roman people came. Our leaders were mighty people."

"I see. And what was your *kahina* doing in the Azilah tunnels?"

The man's ruddy face paled and he gripped a silver talisman around his neck. "She was not in the tunnels, *Alalla*

Jade." He brought his left hand up as an open-handed shield between himself and Jade as he muttered something in his own language.

"Why do you do that?" asked Jade, as she raised her hand in imitation of his. "There was another Amazigh man and a boy outside Azilah. The man did that and he also hid the boy's eyes and mumbled something like an incantation. Why?"

"This sign is the hand of the *kahina*. It has much *baraka* because the hand has five fingers. Five is a holy number," replied Bachir. "It is protection against the evil eye and he would say, 'five in your eye' to stop you. He feared that you would look at his son's eyes and make him ill with the evil eye. Tell me, *Alalla* Jade, about your walk in the tunnels."

Jade hesitated, not sure whether or not she could trust this man. Raised in relative isolation on a New Mexico ranch, Jade always approached strangers with caution, viewing them as possible threats until proven otherwise. Her opinion of people in general hadn't changed during the war, but she had learned to read character more readily. That, and that blasted, odd shrapnel wound in her knee didn't ache. It always seemed to hurt when something was trying to kill her. She decided in Bachir's favor, mainly because she needed an ally right now. *But if he tries anything, the evil eye is the least of his worries.* "I went inside and found an Arab man dead, stabbed in the back."

"Is that all?" Bachir seemed to suggest that the dead man was of no consequence to him.

"Is that *all*?" echoed Jade. "Isn't that enough?"

"You were inside a long time," he explained. "Did you not go in deeper?"

"Yes, I did. I heard voices and I followed them. I thought my mother was with them."

"These voices, what did they say?"

"Nothing to do with my mother."

Bachir persisted. "What did they say?"

Jade felt her irritation rising. When this man told her he'd been sent to take her to Marrakech, she naturally assumed it was to lead her to, or help her find, her mother. But he didn't express interest in any details pertaining to her mother's kidnapping.

"They said foolish things," she snapped. "There was a man and a woman. The woman wanted the man to take something from her, a . . ." She searched for the correct word in Arabic or French to convey a talisman and decided on "charm" in Arabic. As she said it, she heard Bachir's sudden gasp. "The man did not want it. He said something about the woman's death. He called it Elishat's charm."

Bachir muttered soft phrases under his breath, and Jade saw him grip something under his robe. Clearly the man was spooked. "What else did you hear, *Alalla* Jade?"

"The woman said it was not her time to die. She talked about a daughter. I think the man was surprised about her daughter. I don't think he knew she existed. Now, what," Jade demanded, "does this have to do with my mother?"

"I do not know," Bachir replied. "Did the woman give her name?"

"I don't think so. But," Jade added after a moment's reflection, "I think the man did. He called her Dahia, but he also called her *kahina*. That means this Dahia sent you to find me?"

Bachir's face paled to an ashy gray, as though the blood had drained from his head. For an instant he reminded Jade of the corpse in the tunnel, enough so that she forgot her irritation in concern for the man's health. "Are you ill?" she asked.

Bachir shook his head. "Have you told me all?"

"Yes. But I was in longer than I thought. When that man and woman quit talking, I found I was standing in a circle of salt, and it was morning. The dead man's body was gone, too." She stared at the man, hoping to intimidate him as she often did others with her deep green eyes. Apparently she didn't need to stare here. People were afraid enough about the evil eye, Bachir among them. He would not look at her. "You were gone when I came out. Did you take the body, Bachir? Did this *kahina* woman take my mother?"

"No." He shook his head again. "I followed you inside once I made my protection. I carried iron and salt and burned white benzoin to frighten away the *jinni*. I saw the body and I saw by your light that you did not go the way the man pointed. When I found you, you were standing still as a rock, barely breathing, your eyes open and fixed on nothing. I put the circle of salt around you to guard you from the *jinni*. When I left, the body was already gone."

"You put the salt around me?"

"Yes, *Alalla*. As I told you, the *jinni* prefer to live in the old ruins and tunnels. But they do not like salt or iron. I knew I had to protect you, but I feared I was too late."

"If you were in the tunnels, Bachir, then you must have heard those people talking, too."

"No, *Alalla*. I heard no one."

"Then why did you leave?"

"I did not have enough benzoin to last very long. I went and hid in the back of the automobile."

"Wait a minute," Jade exclaimed, remembering the low-riding rear end on the first trip to Azilah. It occurred to her that the car didn't ride that way this time. "You hid in the back and rode from Tangier, didn't you? Then you jumped out when I came to Azilah. You were the person following me in Tangier."

"Yes, but I did not ride inside. I hung on to the back, my feet on the metal crosspiece."

"This woman in the tunnels, the one I heard, do you know where she went? Maybe she knows who took my mother."

Bachir's hands trembled as he again gripped whatever protection he wore under his striped cloak. "You heard the voice beyond the dead, *Alalla* Jade. The Dahia *kahina* led our people in rebellion against the Arabs six hundred and eighty years after your Nazarene prophet was born."

CHAPTER 8

*Morocco, while now a French protectorate, is still ruled by a Sultan,
who has opulent palaces in many cities including Marrakech, the red city.
The city's rust-red, earthen ramparts carry a grandeur amplified by the cooling
beauty of palm groves in the middle of desert and the looming magnificence
of the nearby Atlas Mountains. It's a splendid setting worthy of any ruler.*

—The Traveler

NOTHING MADE SENSE ANYMORE, and as Jade grew more and
more tired, she entertained the idea that she had actually died
during the war and gone to hell. Why else would she be driving an old French car without lights through the Moroccan
night with a lunatic Berber at her left? Any hope she had of
getting assistance from him vanished as soon as he explained
she'd heard a 1,240-year-old disembodied queen talk. Then
he clammed up, turning his face to the blackness around
them, the scalp-lock dangling behind his right ear. Eventually she saw his head droop, and heard a gentle snore. She'd
debated shoving Bachir out the door at one point, then decided he might still prove useful as an interpreter, and left
him to doze on.

The Panhard had half a tank of fuel when she left Tangier
and a full spare can strapped to the sideboard. It wouldn't be
enough to get to Marrakech, though. The problem would be
getting more. Most likely only the French authorities had any

gasoline, and once Deschamp spread the word that she was on the run, she couldn't very well afford anyone knowing where she'd gone.

For that matter, she needed to sleep. That's why, when she finally made it to Rabat, she drove around and parked a half kilometer away from the city. Once again she enveloped herself in her black cloak and stole into the European sector, a siphon hose from the toolbox and the now empty fuel can in tow.

Jade found a likely government vehicle parked away from any others and promptly siphoned off enough gasoline to fill the can. She started to leave when the truck's own spare can caught her eye. She nabbed it, as well. Then, feeling guilty, she pulled three francs from her pocket and placed them on the seat, anchored with a rock.

From Rabat, Jade drove another hour southwest along the coast and pulled off the track to sleep. She awoke at dawn to something nibbling on her shirt collar.

"What the . . ." she exclaimed as she bolted upright in the seat. A brown nanny goat with its forehooves on the chassis stared back at her with its unreal-looking horizontal pupils. The goat *maa*ed and stretched its neck for her collar. Jade pushed it aside, and it dropped down to the ground as she got out of the car. She found herself in a small herd of the inquisitive beasts. "Shoo. Back off," she scolded as a white nanny made a grab for her overskirt. She looked around for Bachir and found him bartering for fresh goat's milk and one flatbread with a small, woven bag. He appeared to be unsuccessful.

Jade offered them francs, only to find they had no inter- est in the French money, either. *Fine, we'll find something else to barter with.* She opened her carpetbag, found the wrapped parcel of ground coffee she'd thrown in lest she be caught without her precious brew, and tossed it to Bachir.

"Maybe they will take that," she said.

· The goat herder, a nomadic Berber judging by his short, black-and-red striped robe, sniffed the packet. He grinned, exposing more open gums than teeth. In a moment Bachir was back, followed by a boy leading one of the nannies and a little girl carrying two clay pots and the bread. The girl handed the bread to Jade, taking care never to look her in the eyes. Then she milked the goat while her brother held its head. She poured half the milk into the second jar and handed both to Jade. Jade passed one on to Bachir along with half the bread.

"*Shukran,*" said Jade, thanking the girl. "*Besmellāh,* in the name of God," she added, giving the proper invocation used before just about any activity. She guzzled the warm milk, her hunger taking over all sense of decorum. "Bachir," she said between mouthfuls of bread, "ask them if they have seen another car, one with a woman in it."

Bachir translated her question into Tashelhit, the language of the Atlas Berbers. Judging by the goatherd's confusion, he spoke a different dialect, but with the insertion of the few Arabic words that the herder recognized and a lot of gestures, the man finally comprehended. The same process repeated itself in reverse until Bachir had the answer.

"He says he saw a car yesterday morning with two men."

Jade's shoulders slumped until it occurred to her that her mother might have been bound and gagged, lying down and out of view. "Can he describe the men or the car?"

After another painstaking exchange, Bachir gave the exhaustive report: "Black."

Jade cranked the car and climbed back in. As she reached

over the side to release the brake, the boy approached her. He pointed first to his upper lip then made several strokes across it with his finger.

"A mustache?" Jade murmured in English before saying "nose hair" in Arabic. It seemed the boy understood some Arabic, for he nodded. Jade recited possible colors beginning with black, followed by brown and yellow. The boy shook his head at each, looked around, and picked up a kid whose creamy tan fur was coated in the red dust of the *bled,* or wasteland desert, turning parts of it a pale rusty-butter mix.

"This color?" asked Jade. The boy nodded. She rewarded him with a franc.

They drove on to Casablanca, where Jade hid while Bachir purchased two cans of fuel from one merchant and food from another, then headed due south across the expansive wasteland towards Marrakech.

Except for one lone well where Jade tinkered with the car's engine, refilled the radiator, and emptied her own in a much-needed personal stop, there was little to interest her. There were no villages, no trees, nothing but a flat land of rock and brick-colored dirt. Under the track itself the earth had submitted to so much pressure from countless hooves and feet that it had been pressed into a polished red rock, as hard as any stone floor. Bachir's reticence increased each time Jade asked any more questions or attempted to engage him in conversation. Instead, he watched the never-changing landscape and sang in an atonal tenor voice a mournful-sounding tune. Perhaps he missed his distant home somewhere up in the Atlas Mountains.

Around noon, she skirted the military post at Zettát, careful to avoid detection. She sent Bachir into the post with the empty gas can and some of her few remaining francs to purchase much-needed fuel. She only hoped they wouldn't ask too many questions of him, such as, Why do you need gasoline? But the soldiers at the post seemed too bored with inactivity to be concerned about Bachir's request. Perhaps, Jade thought, they were in the habit of acting as a refueling station for the few people crossing the rocky desert.

From the outpost there, the road stretched out for miles across the wasteland to the gorge of the Oued Ouem. Beyond the river the road climbed gradually for fifty kilometers, striving to reach an elusive, hazy vision of the Djebilets Mountains. Jade began to think she'd taken the wrong road out of Casablanca, except there hadn't been any other option. Then as the Panhard struggled and wheezed up to the top of the pass, she glimpsed an island of emerald green in the distance, a palm oasis. Somewhere tucked inside that jewel lay Marrakech. As if to prove the city's existence, a lone tower shot up above the trees.

Just as seagulls are an indication that land is near, the presence of more people bore witness to the presence of water and a nearby city. They appeared walking beside donkeys, or sitting astride camels that moved in a languid motion, rocking the rider gently into oblivion throughout their long treks.

By the time they sputtered over the ancient stone bridge over the Oued Tensif's broad but shallow course, Jade wanted only to throw herself in the little river and let it wash away the dirt and exhaustion covering her. She skirted around the north side to the west through the palm grove and its welcoming shade, waiting for Marrakech to reveal itself beyond the towering minaret standing sentinel above the trees. Beyond the palms grew olive trees and past them sat the newer, whitewashed buildings of Gueliz, where the French resided. Jade barely noticed them, her gaze riveted by the immense red wall rising up out of the soil as if the Earth itself had risen and hardened. *Marrakech*.

The ramparts of the red city loomed above her, the wall interrupted periodically by a gate. But what Jade found most curious were the evenly placed indentations that punctuated the wall. Some had chunks of timber sticking out, and she realized that the wall had been built up in sections by packing the earth in and around the scaffolding.

She glanced across at Bachir, remembering that he was told to bring her here. *Well, we're here.* If there was a time to watch for tricks, it would be now. She waited for him to make a suggestion, give an order, do anything. Instead he stared ahead at the first gate into the city, his face a stoic mask. "We're here, Bachir," she said after a lengthy silence. "Where do I go now?"

"To find your mother," he answered, without turning.

"Yes, but where?"

He shrugged.

Jade began thinking aloud, hoping to catch Bachir's reaction for any evidence of his involvement. "Mother was not taken by a Moroccan. They would not brave the *jinni* in the Azilah tunnels." *But you did, didn't you, Bachir?* "Now, where would a European hide Mother in Marrakech?" She remembered the note telling her to come to the Square of the Dead. Would Bachir suggest she go there, as well?

Instead, he pointed to the French settlement of Gueliz. "There," he suggested.

Okay, that was a point in Bachir's favor. She had no intention of blindly walking into any place called a Square of the Dead. Maybe it would be useful to make some inquiries as to new arrivals. She turned the Panhard down the closest avenue, looking for what might be a hotel. The eucalyptus-lined street boasted three cafés and a few pitiful shops displaying European shoes and other Western items before it ended abruptly at a deep ditch. She put the car in reverse, spun around, and stopped at the nearest café, where she inquired where new visitors might find lodging.

"We have a room above the café," said a poorly shaven, portly little Frenchman.

"Oh? I thought it was taken already. I understood two men traveling from Tangier arrived yesterday. I'm sure you've seen them. One has a reddish-blond mustache."

"No, Mademoiselle. Very few visitors venture this far into Morocco."

Jade persisted. "They were traveling with a woman. She may have been ill. They might have carried her inside."

"I have seen no one new besides yourself. Did you wish the room for yourself?"

"*Merci,* no. I must try to find my friends. I will try the consulate's office to see if they have gone there."

Seeing that he couldn't pawn off his room, the Frenchman grumbled under his breath for a moment. "You might try the Hotel de France. It is in the next avenue south."

"*Merci.*"

Jade tried the hotel, only to hear again that no one new had taken rooms for several months.

"When they come, do you wish me to tell them you are here?" asked the desk clerk.

"No. That won't be necessary. Perhaps you can tell me something about Marrakech. What is this Square of the Dead I have heard about?"

The man chuckled. "Ah, that is a name for the great open plaza in the heart of the city. It took its name from the quaint old practice of once displaying the salted heads of executed prisoners there. Now it is a great gathering place," he said, waving his hands in large circles. "Many shops, many story-tellers. The Berbers, the Tuareg of the South, and others who do not reside in the city and so do not keep shops in the souk, gather there and sell their wares. Most entertaining," he added, "especially in the morning and evening hours when it is cooler. You might find a few people beginning to meet there now. But you must enter the gates before sunset. They are closed soon after that."

Jade thanked him again and returned to the city gate only to find that Bachir was not waiting for her at the Panhard. *Where did he go?* She spied him standing outside a great gate, speaking with a cluster of Berbers.

"*Alalla,*" he said as he left the men, "they have seen the men you seek. They came yesterday with rugs to sell, and a black machine came like a wild camel through the *Bab Agnaou*. They say one was a Nazarene. The other was an Arab."

"Where did they go?"

"They went to the street of the *riads,*" he said, using the term for palatial town houses. "There are many princely houses there. And, *Alalla,* they said there was a woman with them. She was wrapped entirely in white robes."

One of the Berber men edged forward, avoiding Jade with the caution one showed when approaching a potentially dangerous reptile. He held his arms in front of him, elbows bent and wrists crossed above his chest while he spoke. Bachir listened, nodded, and turned back to Jade.

"*Alalla*, he says the woman's hands were bound."

Inez, still groggy, felt herself being lifted and carried. A slight nausea rose in her throat, and she struggled to fight it back. She heard the sound of a heavy bolt sliding against metal and felt herself drop. Whoever had carried her had deposited her, without ceremony but not roughly, onto a hard surface. She fell to her side and felt the bonds on her wrists being loosened. Then a heavy door shut and she again heard the bolt slide in its traces. *I've been locked in, but where?* She couldn't see anything.

She wriggled her hands and discovered she had limited range of movement in her arms. Suddenly the nausea increased, as well as a sense that she was suffocating. Her hands clawed at the fabric that enveloped her head and upper torso. Her nails worked a small rent in the fabric, and Inez forced her fingers inside and pulled, rending the thin cloth. She sat up, forced her arms and shoulders through the gap, and yanked the cloth back from her head and face before she collapsed to the floor, gasping and retching. Her stomach didn't deliver anything up, a fact that registered with her brain. *I haven't eaten in a long time.*

With the swaddling cloth gone from her face, she was again able to breathe freely. She inhaled deeply several times to clear her head. *What is that smell? It smells like . . . ?* Suddenly she stood up and let the rest of the cloth drop from her onto the floor. *Ether!* The fabric had been soaked in ether to drug her. She kicked it away.

Myriad sensations welled up inside her: hunger, fear, loneliness, dread. She longed for her husband's strong arms to encircle her and hold her. "Richard," she whispered. Would she see him again? Or Jade?

Jade! What had happened to her? Inez remembered finding a note in her room from her daughter, entreating her to meet her, telling her she was sorry. Inez had gone to the rendezvous willingly. She'd wanted so much for them to reconcile. That, more than getting any stud horse, had been the ultimate point of this trip. She wanted to bring Jade home with her so that her daughter could take her proper place in Taos society by Inez's side. The task of hosting endless committees and dinners wouldn't be so lonely then. So when the English-speaking Arab man outside the hotel offered to be her guide, she went with him.

But Jade hadn't been at the rendezvous. Now a fresh terror welled in her gut. Her heart raced, pounding hard against her chest. What had they done to her daughter?

The bolt slid back in its slot and the door opened. Inez blinked against the sudden glow of a candle. An Arab with a wicked-looking knife tucked inside a broad sash quickly set the candle on a low table. Next to it he put a plate holding a small mug of water, a flat circle of bread, and something that smelled like a spicy stew.

"Eat and drink," he ordered. Before Inez could react to his unexpected entry, he slammed the door shut.

Inez threw herself on the door just as the bolt slid back into place. She pounded her fists on the thick wood and shouted with all the breath she could muster.

"What have you done with my daughter?"

CHAPTER 9

The Arab population resides in very interesting homes. Their houses are built without windows to the outside, at least on the ground floor, and those on upper floors are heavily screened. Instead, all the windows open to the interior courtyard. This provides beauty, light, and privacy for the ladies of the harem, thereby allowing a man to describe his wife or daughter as a pearl of inestimable beauty without risking contradiction.

—The Traveler

JADE WAS NEVER A STRONG BELIEVER IN COINCIDENCE, so she quickly dismissed the possibility that another woman had been abducted. *It has to be Mother*.

"Bachir, do you know the way to this street they spoke of?"

"Yes, but there are many houses there. How will we know which one holds your lady mother?"

How, indeed. As Jade considered this dilemma, she noticed an Arab made a wider detour around Bachir and herself. Jade remembered Mr. de Portillo's observation that the Berbers were not always fastidious in their prayer, and Mrs. Kennicot's comment that the mountain dwellers weren't particularly ardent Muslims. *Treating us as infidels*. It gave her an idea.

"Bachir, if there were Christians living in the city, Naza-renes as you call us, how could we find out? Would the out-side of the house look different? Would the Arabs put a mark on the door to warn others?"

"I know of no such mark, *Alalla*. You think these people who took your mother are Nazarenes?"

"They would claim to be, Bachir, if they were asked. But know that a *good* Nazarene would not abduct or murder anyone."

"If they are Nazarenes, they would drink wine?" Bachir asked.

Jade smiled, understanding where his questions led. "Yes, they probably would. And they would eat pork. So if someone delivered a basket of such forbidden foods to a door looking for the people who bought it, perhaps someone would point out the house of the Nazarenes."

"If they do not slay us first, *Alalla*."

"That is a danger *I* will face," said Jade. "Will you help me?"

"I will help you find your mother, *Alalla,* if you will then help the one who sent me to bring you."

"I will do what I can, Bachir," she said, remembering that it was Bachir who found out the section of the *Medina* where her mother was taken.

Jade decided she'd draw less attention to herself in the square if she were on foot. She drove the car into a small gully at the edge of the olive grove. Considering the Panhard was completely covered in the desert dust, it should be well camouflaged. Then, leaving the idling car, she took her knife and carved out a niche in the ravine's mud sides, large enough to hold the bulky carpetbag. She shoved it inside and covered it with the dirt. If Moroccans truly feared the *jinni* that haunted buried treasure, then the bag with the opal jewelry and spare clothing should be safe in the dirt. To be certain, however, she parked the car against the wall, blocking the bag with a wheel. Then she walked back to Gueliz district, carrying only the dwindling money reserves, her flashlight, the matches, a spare dry cell, and her small Kodak in the canvas shoulder bag. She doubted the utility of her camera, but if an opportunity to photograph the culprit presented itself, she wanted to be ready. Her knife went back into her boot sheath.

This activity only served to keep her anxiety from rising to the point of hysteria. Still, the dread for her mother's safety became a bitter taste in her mouth. *Blast it! Why would someone do this?* If it was a kidnapping for ransom, surely they would have demanded some sum of money in the note.

Besides, her mother never gave the appearance of looking wealthy. As long as Jade could remember, her mother declined any offer of diamonds or other showy gems from Jade's father. Instead, she preferred the simple opal jewelry that Richard del Cameron had presented to her when they were first married. Inez had always said the ranch and her family was all the wealth she needed or wanted. *Dad!* The thought of his grief if anything happened to his wife overwhelmed Jade and she stumbled. *Don't think those thoughts. Mother is alive. She's too proud to let anyone do her in without her consent.*

Jade returned from the French district just before sunset, armed with two bottles of wine and a hind leg from a wild boar. There was little meat worth eating attached to the shank, but that didn't matter. All Jade wanted was for a cloven hoof to stick out in view. Bachir met her with a small woven basket, and Jade tucked the offending pig's foot in with the wine bottles and draped her pocket handkerchief over enough of the contents to cover the gaps and make it look full.

"Allāhu Akbar. Hayya 'alas-salāt," came the quavering call of the muezzin from the towering minaret. "God is the great-

est. Make haste towards prayer." Immediately all the activity ceased as the faithful hastened towards the closest mosque. A few of the Berber people followed, but most did not, electing to either pray where they were or not at all.

"Show me the way to these houses, Bachir, but stay clear of the square. These bad men told me in a letter to meet them there. They will be looking for me." She pulled the hood of her dark robe over her head. "I will knock on the doors and find the correct one."

Bachir ran his gaze over her weak disguise and shook his head. "It will not do, *Alalla*. You wear a man's cloak, but it is not striped like that of an Amazigh man." He stuck out one leg, exposing a bare calf and a foot shod in a plain leather slipper. "Your boots are not that of my people, either." He pointed to her head. "You have no cap and your head is unshaven. No one will believe you as an Amazigh peddler." He reached for the basket, taking care not to touch the hoof. "I will go to the doors. You keep watch."

Bachir led the way into the city through the massive stone arch of the *Bab Agnaou* into the Kasbah. In the gathering dusk, Jade couldn't make out much of the gate's ornamentation, but then her attention was held prisoner by thoughts of her poor mother lying captive somewhere inside the city. She paid more attention to the mosque in front of her, trying to memorize the exit path. They jogged left in front of the mosque and turned east onto the broader Rue Arset el Maahl. Past the mosque rose another wall to their right. Bachir shied away to the opposite side of the avenue, his right hand held palm out against evil.

"What is it, Bachir?" Jade asked.

Bachir pointed to the wall. "El Badi," he said. "Many *jinni* live there now."

Jade wasn't sure what El Badi was, but if it didn't involve her mother, she didn't care.

Once again, the streets began filling up with people as they emerged from the mosques, and several street vendors and water sellers in their distinctive wide-brimmed, fringed red hats took advantage of the evening traffic to gather some late-day business. A few feminine voices drifted down from the sheltered rooftops as the ladies enjoyed the evening coolness. She heard a child cry and a woman speak in soothing tones. Her own mother used to speak that way to her long ago, back in the hazy memory of toddlerhood. Then it ended. The love was always there, but the songs were replaced by instructions in proper etiquette. Jade wiped away a tear of longing and followed Bachir farther into the city.

Jade expected each house to bear some token of individual tastes, but from the exterior, there were few clues to indicate that these houses sequestered the wealthy and powerful. Perhaps fewer feral dogs lounged in the streets, but the plain wooden doors and the red-plastered exterior walls held no boasts of hidden opulence. A canopy of reeds covered the narrow passageway providing welcome coolness and privacy during the day's heat but now effectively blocking out much of the lingering twilight.

Jade found a dark recess and snugged herself against a wall to watch Bachir as he knocked on a door and shouted to the occupants within. So far the results had been discouraging. No one came to the first door, the next two occupants cursed Bachir for carrying food of the infidel, and at the fourth, an aging slave merely slammed the door in Bachir's face. Now, after yet another twist in the narrow road, Bachir tried again, this time stopping at a house with a door knocker shaped like a large insect. This was the first piece of ornamentation Jade had seen so far.

"I have delivered your food and drink."

The door opened inward, exposing a short entryway and an ornately tiled wall. Jade knew that the entries to these houses were convoluted with a set of *chicanes,* halls that twisted and turned, designed not only to block the view from the street but also to impede the progress of anyone entering with unfriendly intent. It made the defense of the home much easier. Barring any entry to this one stood a veritable black giant. The formidable doorkeeper wore a resplendent robe of snowy white trimmed with a broad green sash. A curved dagger with a shiny silver hilt lay tucked in the sash within easy reach. Jade did her best to catch the rapid exchange.

"Who are you?" demanded the doorkeeper.

"I have brought the food and drink the master of the house ordered."

"My master has ordered nothing. What do you have there?"

Bachir held up the basket. The doorkeeper immediately drew his knife and grabbed Bachir's cloak. "Dog. Would you pollute my master's house? I should kill you."

"Have pity," wailed Bachir. "I mean no disrespect. This is for a Nazarene. Only I do not know what house to go to, and I will not be paid unless I deliver it to him."

The doorman released Bachir with a slight shove. "You look for the house of an infidel dog of a Nazarene?" The man spat at Bachir's feet. "I have seen one enter the last door." He pointed to the end of the street where the houses formed a cul-de-sac. "Now go, and do not pollute this area again."

After the door slammed shut, Jade called softly from the shadows. "You did well, Bachir. Thank you."

"What will you do now, *Alalla?*"

"Get my mother."

"You cannot go inside through the front, *Alalla*. The passages twist and turn. Someone will see or hear you."

Jade smiled. "I'll go in the way the women do, by way of the roof."

Inez, her hunger abated by the stewed lamb and apricots, picked up the candle and looked around the room for a means of escape. Her prison measured about fifteen feet square, but contained nothing more than a worn rug and pillow in one corner and the wobbly little table beside the door. Something that looked like it might be a chamber pot sat in the corner opposite the rug. Apparently she was supposed to sleep on the rug. Inez brought the candle over and sniffed the pillow, her nose wrinkling in disgust. It smelled of old sweat and mold. She was sure the carpet was loaded with fleas.

Well, that settles that. I have no intention of staying in here. But how to escape? The room had no window, and the door was bolted from without. *The hinges.* Inez set the candle on the floor and picked up the little table. With a twist, she pulled off one of the three legs, revealing a rusty, hand-hammered nail. She pushed the nail against the floor while holding the leg, forcing the nail to push up until she could pull it free.

Somehow, she sensed it's what her daughter would have done in this situation. At least it matched the sort of antics Jade always tried at home. Like the time Inez took away Jade's knife when the girl had carved her initials underneath the dining room table. The next thing Inez knew, Jade had flint-napped a knife blade and strapped it to a piece of elk antler with some rawhide.

Inez dug the nail into the wood around the middle hinge.

As she slowly whittled away at the door to free the hinge, she sighed. What had she done wrong in raising that little wildcat of a girl? She did everything her own mother had done. She hired a tutor, she gave her lessons in proper decorum, but nothing worked. Of course Richard was partly to blame, as much as she hated thinking ill of her beloved spouse. He indulged the girl by taking her along on hunts. And those ranch hands. They were nice men in their own way, but they'd made a pet out of Jade and taught her horrid games like mumbly-peg, where they threw knives at targets on the ground. Perhaps if she'd been able to have a son it might have been different.

You don't have a son. You have one daughter and you love her no matter how aggravating she's been. She attacked the wood with greater vigor and scratched her knuckles against the door. *She's a lot like you,* taunted a voice in the back of Inez's brain. *Remember when you slipped away in the night to see the Gypsies?*

"But I always behaved myself in front of others," Inez muttered to herself. If Jade had left that note as a ploy to force her to visit the souks with her . . . she let the thought dangle and worked the door with fresh resolve. *I'll get out of here, find the authorities, and have them take me back to Tangier, and then that girl is going to get the scolding of her life.*

Jade and Bachir padded softly down the deserted side street, keeping close to the walls to avoid detection in case someone kept watch from within. Not so much as a glimmer of lamplight shone from the latticed windows on the second floors. Jade peered up at the flattened roof two stories above her. The domain of the women, rooftops had access to the interior courtyards. But how to get to the roof from out here? From the roof of another house?

She studied the adjacent house. Two loosely nailed boards barred the entrance, and a white handprint marked the door. It reminded Jade of the handprint at the entrance to the Azilah tunnels. *Must be haunted.* Further proof of its uninhabited state came from the small pile of debris that had blown against the door. A tug on the barricades loosened them. One good jerk would free each one.

"What does that hand mean, Bachir? Is this house the abode of *jinni?*"

"This house bears a curse, *Alalla.* Perhaps someone killed himself. It is now the abode of *jinni.* The hand warns us. The Arabs call it the hand of Fatima, but the sign is older than that. Our *kahina* carried that sign before the Arab invaders came."

"Well, I'm not afraid of any *jinni.* I'm more afraid of what my mother will do to me if I don't get her out now. So listen carefully, please. I am going to pull off the boards from that door and go inside. Then I'm going to go across the rooftop to the other house. When I throw some plaster down to the street, you knock on the door and keep their attention on you."

She reached into the basket, pulled out the pig's foot, and tossed it aside. "That will probably only create more trouble," she muttered to herself. A stray dog lounging in the corner grabbed the bony tidbit and ran off with it. "Just give them the wine, Bachir, and argue over payment while I find my mother. I only wish there was time to discover who these people are."

"Send your mother out to the rooftop. I will help her down while you search the house."

Jade stopped to think over the proposition. She wanted to just get her mother and run, but without some proof of their innocence, Deschamp would never let them leave Tangier. This might be her only opportunity to get that proof. "She might not trust you, Bachir." Jade studied the sturdy little man, with his lone lock of hair dangling from his knitted cap and his homespun clothes fluttering on his short frame, and wondered if *she* trusted him. So far, at least, he'd proven honest.

"She will if you tell her to, *Alalla* Jade."

"Very well." She reached around her neck and pulled a gold chain over her head. On it hung the ring that her sweetheart, David Worthy, had pressed into her hands just before he died. "Mother will recognize this. I will tell her to follow the man holding it." She added two of her last francs. "Pay the gatekeeper to let you and her out. Take my mother to the French church in Gueliz and wait for me there. Do you understand? This is my *mother,* Bachir. If something happens to her, you will wish *jinni* were chasing you rather than me."

Bachir replied with perfect serenity. "Your mother will be safe with me, *Alalla* Jade."

Jade pulled out the two boards from one end and let them hang to the side. Then, drawing her knife from her boot, she opened the door onto the inky blackness within. "I need a light." She took out her flashlight, thought a moment, then removed a tin of matches from the camera bag. She handed the bag to Bachir, deciding that she wouldn't be able to take a photograph inside the house, anyway, without adequate light.

"Here. Take this. It will only be in my way right now." She put the tin of matches in her front trouser pocket, turned on her flashlight, and entered the abandoned house.

After the usual set of right-angle turns from the entryway, Jade found herself in the expansive central courtyard. The dry fountains stood as dead sentinels, and the once-gorgeous tile work lay under a thick coating of dust, dried leaves, and animal droppings. Most of the smaller plants had long since withered into dry stalks, but one citron tree flourished, watered by early spring rains. Left unattended and unpruned, it had pushed up to the broken skylight in a riot of sprawling limbs. At its base grew a clump of jasmine, the white flowers opening in the night and filling the courtyard with a wash of perfume that nearly masked the stench of droppings.

If *jinni* took the form of mice, insects, and spiders, this house had its fill of them. Owl pellets crunched under her boots and one Little Owl fluttered off at her approach. It settled on an exposed ceiling beam and watched her with golden eyes.

"*S-salamū alekum,*" she whispered in greeting. "I think I met your cousin in Azilah." The owl trilled its quavering *kee-uhk* in response.

She walked the courtyard's perimeter, looking for a means of gaining the roof. Nothing. *How the blazes did the women get up there?* There had to be stairs or a ladder somewhere. She repeated the circuit and tried all of the doors off the courtyard. Several opened up into what had once been sumptuous rooms lined with intricate ceramic tile mosaics in green, turquoise, and blue. The tiles formed five-pointed stars and other complex geometric shapes. Binding them all was a running network of white tiles, representing the interlocking network of life.

Now these beautiful rooms housed rotting silken hangings and shredded cushions. Rustlings and squeaks showed the new occupants lived inside the aging pillows. A narrow door in the corner was locked. If the stairs were behind it, someone had made sure it wasn't usable.

Finally, one door at the back of the court opened into

another, less ornamental suite of rooms. Discarded clay jars and charcoal braziers lay in one corner and a broken loom reclined against the opposite wall. *A women's work area.* A set of broken stairs, built into the back wall, led up to additional living quarters. Jade tested the first one before putting her full weight on it. Her light dimmed, and she opted for haste instead of caution.

The upper floor was divided into several large rooms, which again circled the main courtyard. Another set of stairs at the back led up to the rooftop, the place where women could hide behind screens and safely take the air and watch the street below without being seen. Jade also knew from her stroll in Tangier that the rooftop was the way women paid visits to each other. Sure enough, a wooden ladder was long enough to allow a woman to climb safely up and over to the other side. Presumably, it could also span the narrower alleyways between one row of houses and the next.

Jade's flashlight dimmed again, then died. She shoved it into a hip pocket, hoisted her leg over the screen, and scrambled across. Now to alert Bachir that she was ready. She grabbed a handful of broken plaster and tossed the rubble down to the street. Immediately after, she heard Bachir's insistent knock. She listened for the door opening, then scurried across the roof to the stairs inside.

Despite this house's current habitation, the stairs were in worse shape than that of the boarded-up building. Apparently no one used the roof here; further proof that the occupants either didn't hold with the traditional code for the harem or didn't have any resident females. The steps were bad enough going down to the upper rooms; they became nonexistent shortly after that. Once again the formal stairs to the lower floor were barricaded, this time from the top. Jade found the set used by the slave women coming from the kitchen. Two steps down from the top floor, Jade's foot searched in vain for a purchase.

Blast the bad luck. She could easily drop down to the first floor as the ceilings were low, but getting back out would be another matter. She heard voices in the distance, arguing— Bachir and the guard. His distraction wouldn't hold out for much longer. She needed to move now. Jade knelt down, took hold of the last step, and slid over the side.

She landed with a soft plop. By now her eyes had adjusted to the darkness and she made out the remains of a brazier, a few pots, and a cracked *tajine*, once used for cooking savory stews. Whoever lived here didn't use the kitchen area, either. At best, this was a temporary residence, a place to hide out. *Now, where's Mother?*

So far the floor plan of this house matched that of the abandoned one next door. That meant a large central court-yard to the front and an array of rooms radiating from it. The ground floor had no windows for prying eyes to peer in, which made any of those rooms perfect for a prison. Jade padded down the dark corridor, hugging the walls, her knife hilt snug in her right hand.

Bachir's voice drifted towards her. She caught snatches including "gift" and "Nazarene." Apparently he was trying to convince someone that the wine bottles were a gift they should accept. At least he hadn't alerted them to her. That was a point in his favor. The courtyard opened in front of her, bathed in the house's lamplights. This one had been bet-ter cared for in more recent times, as at least one stout orange tree thrived among a wealth of jasmine. The central fountain trickled weakly into a tiled basin at the floor, and the wet co-balt and emerald tiles shimmered in the flickering light.

That same light, now a blessing to help her find her way around, would easily become a curse if anyone came back. She hugged her dark robe more closely about her and stuck to the shadows behind the thick pillars as she made her circuit and listened at each door. After the third door, she decided to try the other side of the courtyard rather than risk getting any closer to the entryway and the guard. That's when she noticed the recessed hallway in the back corner.

Tucked away inside was a narrow wooden door, painted in faded bronze and deep greens to resemble potted trees in bloom. The white plastered wall forming the top of the doorframe was cut into three slender minaret tops, the central one higher than the others. The door itself was made of two wide panels opening down the center. What most intrigued Jade was the stout iron bar bolting the door shut. There were fresh gashes along its side, as though it had been recently slid into place. She put her ear to the wood and listened. A persistent scratching from the other side rewarded her.

"Escupe fuego y ahorra las cerillas!" A slight lisp accompanied the *s* sounds, the remnants of Castilian Spanish laced with years of New World Spanish.

Mother. Who else would say "Spit fire and save the matches"? "Mother, it's Jade," she whispered. Immediately the scratching and the muttered imprecations ceased.

"Jade? Is it really you?"

"Shhh," Jade admonished. From the front she heard Bachir invoking charity and pity in Allah's name on a poor servant. Other than that one guard at the front door, the house appeared to be empty. The others were presumably lying in wait at the Square of the Dead. Still there was no sense in making any extra noise.

The solid door had no bars or latticework to admit any light into the room beyond. Jade slid the bolt back and eased the door open. It wobbled on one lower hinge. Inez emerged carrying a lit candle in one hand and a thick, rusty nail in the other. A quick visual inspection told Jade that her mother, while disheveled and dirty, was not injured.

A surge of relief and inexpressible joy rushed through Jade. *Thank you, God!* She wanted to grab her mother in a tight bear hug, but resisted and put her finger to her lips for silence instead. They were too exposed here. She motioned for Inez to come out, then eased the door shut and pushed the bolt back into place. If no one opened the door to check on the prisoner, they would assume she was simply asleep inside. Jade pointed to the back of the house and led the way.

Once they were safely in the unused kitchen area, Jade embraced her mother, but only for the briefest moment before Inez gently pushed her back. *Mother never did approve of public hugs, not even in private.* Jade let her arms drop and risked a few words. "What the hell happened, Mother?" Inez stood with her proud chin covered in grime, her green linen walking dress tattered and soiled. Her knuckles bore fresh scrapes and scratches. She softened her tone. "Are you hurt, Mother? You look like something the dog dragged in."

"I'm not hurt, and I do not know what happened. I went to our room to prepare for my visit and found that message from you apologizing and begging me to meet you. So as soon as I changed into something suitable for walking in those souks, I hurried back out to find you. Where *were* you?"

Jade heard the hurt in the voice and knew her mother felt betrayed and blamed all this on Jade's supposed negligence. "I didn't send any message to you, Mother."

"What? But it looked like your hand. You, er, the note

said to meet you at the cloth sellers' on the Place de la Kasbah."

Jade sighed. "Mother, there are no cloth sellers there. I
tried to teach you about . . . oh, never mind. What happened
then?"

"I left the hotel and one of those innumerable guides
came up and asked me where I wanted to go. He spoke English well enough, so I told him. He said he knew the shop
and led me down all sorts of dirty streets to one of those little
plaster buildings. Someone came from behind and put a rag
over my face. That's all I remember until I woke up in an automobile. By then I was bundled head to foot in ether-soaked
cloth, my hands tied in front of me. They put me in there
with one candle." She held up her nail, an evil-looking, hand-
crafted spike more than two inches long. "I pulled this out
of that weak excuse for a table and was taking the hinges off
the door. I had one off already," she said, her voice proud, her
chin thrust out.

Jade grinned, pride for her mother's courage replacing
relief. "Well done. Maybe I've been a good influence on you
after all." Inez gasped, and Jade immediately regretted the
attempt at levity. "I can get you out, but it will not be easy.
Do you see those stairs?" She pointed up at the top two steps,
dangling into space. "I'm going to put my hands out like a
stirrup. You step up and I'll boost you as far as I can. Do you
think you can pull yourself up the rest of the way?"

"Jade! In this dress? And what about you? How am—"

"Mother, we do *not* have time to debate this. You are
wanted for murder back in Tangier, and I need to clear up
this mess." Jade took a deep breath as her mother gasped
again. "When you get to the upper floor, continue up those
stairs to the roof. Climb over the latticework to the house next

door. Go down those stairs and work your way to the front of the house. There will be a man waiting for you nearby, a Berber man named Bachir. He has David's ring. Go with him."

"Where?" Inez began, but Jade cut her short again as she heard the heavy front door slam shut. Footsteps echoed from the courtyard: a man walking slowly. She heard him call to her mother, taunting her, then, receiving no answer, walk away. A moment later she heard another inner door close.

"Just go," Jade hissed. She locked her fingers together and when her mother stepped into them, hoisted the smaller woman as far as possible. Inez grabbed the lower step and tried to pull herself up. Part of the worn plaster broke away in her hands and clattered to the floor.

"I can't do it, Jade."

Jade took hold of her mother's legs and lowered her to the ground. She rubbed her shoulders to ease the pain from her exertion. Inez did the same. *Think*, Jade told herself. *There must be another way*. Her mind raced through everything she'd seen so far. *The orange tree in the courtyard. It should reach the second-floor court*. "This way, and hurry."

Jade peered around the doorway into the courtyard, looking for the guard. *Empty*. Grabbing her mother's wrist, she towed her along to the large tree growing near the fountain. "Climb," she ordered as she shoved her mother from behind and up into the lowest branches.

Her mother glanced down at her, her blue eyes questioning. Jade gave an encouraging nod and flashed a confident smile. "I'll catch up to you after I have a look around," she mouthed, not daring to speak. She handed up the flashlight, then made a shooing motion, flapping her hands forward. Inez turned and clambered up the tree as quickly as her straight skirts would allow. Once she was safely in the upper floor, Jade decided it was time to finish her reconnaissance, find some way to identify these people, and leave.

A quick scan of the unswept floor around the court revealed the three rooms most frequently visited. One was her mother's former prison. Of the other two, Jade decided to try the one farthest back. She listened at the door and heard the guard snoring within. So far so good. She opened the next door a few inches, ready to bolt for the tree at a moment's notice. No one challenged her from the black space within, and Jade opened the door wider, wishing she still had her flashlight. Then she remembered that the battery had drained itself. *Mother won't be happy about that.*

She wished she'd picked up her mother's candle. It was like peering into a pitch-black cave. *My matches.* Jade patted her pockets and located the match tin. She removed one, shoved the tin back into the pocket, and felt the lid slip off, spilling the rest. *I'll deal with it later.* Jade struck the match on the rough plaster. It flared instantly and Jade caught the flash of something shiny within the room, glinting like autumn sunlight, just before someone struck her from behind.

CHAPTER 10

The more palatial of these homes are called riads. *They are adorned inside*
with rich geometric mosaics, stained glass clerestories, rippling fountains, and, in some,
interior gardens. The more extravagant might even boast its own bathing room
so that the occupants have no need of the public bath, or hammam.

—The Traveler

INEZ STUMBLED IN THE DARK, always working towards the
front door and freedom. Jade's flashlight did not work. *So*
why give it to me? She'd left her candle back in the first house
by the broken stairs. Now she wished she had it with her.
That and some matches. And maybe some water. Her right
foot collided with a chunk of plaster the size of a mountain
beaver, and she grabbed for her toes, rubbing them through
her thin leather shoes.

"*Millard Fillmore dulce en una bicicleta,*" she swore, unconsciously using her daughter's favorite oath.

There was a time, she thought, when she would have been
prepared for an adventure like this. A time back in Andalusia when she rode her horse across the land when and where
she willed. After all, she recalled, her nanny-turned–lady's
maid doted on her and the tutor was so easy to elude. And
her mother? Inez frowned. She didn't remember what her
mother was doing then. Probably supervising maids or enter-

taining the other landowners. Was that how it had been between her and Jade? she wondered. No. She had kept a closer
eye on Jade, which is why she got caught when Inez hadn't.
Her thoughts returned to her own girlhood excursions. She
always traveled ready for anything back then, her saddlebags
holding an assortment of dried meats and fruit, flint and
steel, a pistol, and something to trade with at the Gypsy camp.
She couldn't think of anything in her possession now worth
trading for food or water. But surely her daughter had come
prepared. Jade was good at that, she had to admit, and was
surprised at her own feeling of maternal pride. Another toe
stubbing brought back her annoyance with her daughter.

Patience, she counseled herself. But patience was never one
of her virtues, and she was fast losing what little she had.

Starlight over the courtyard helped her a little now as her
eyes adjusted to the darkness, and she found her way to the
first turn of the entryway. Feeling along the walls, she maneuvered the *chicanes* and located the door. She put her ear to
the panel and listened for sounds of pursuit outside. Hearing
none, she opened the door into the street.

A small man of her height met her, dressed in a calf-
length white robe and the striped outer garb of the mountain
people. He held up Jade's ring and motioned for her to follow
him. She did, at least until they'd turned a corner and were
out of sight of her house of imprisonment.

"Stop," she said. The man turned around.

"We wait for Jade," she said. The man shook his head
and again motioned for her to follow. "Where are you taking
me?" she demanded, not moving an inch from her spot.

The man first cocked his head to the side and then shook it
to indicate he didn't understand her. She tried again in Spanish. This time he added a shrug to the gesture. Finally, when

she seemed adamant, he handed the ring to her, repeated "Jade," and motioned forward. He added something in Arabic, then what sounded like French. Inez didn't know what he said, but judging by the tone of his voice, it wasn't "So happy to see you alive and well." More likely he said something akin to "Follow me, woman, and quit asking questions."

Frustrated that she couldn't communicate, Inez decided she needed to trust her daughter's choice of protectors and followed the man through the maze of lamplit streets.

"Oooh." Jade woke to a throbbing headache. She tried to rub her head and discovered that her hands were tied behind her back. *What the hell happened?* When she attempted to shift her legs she realized her booted ankles were also bound. She took a deep breath and tried to sort through the pain and accompanying nausea to remember something. *Mother.* She'd found her and gotten her out of the house, she hoped, and to Bachir and safety. But how much time had gone by? Did they know she was captured? Were they still waiting at the French Church of the Holy Martyrs, or had they come back to find her?

Jade squirmed into a sitting position and nearly passed out from the stabbing pain in her head. She put her head between her knees until her nausea and light-headedness faded, then slowly rose and looked around. The bare room was dimly lit with one smoking lamp set on a stone shelf built into the wall. No furniture, no windows, no grillwork in the heavy wooden door. Judging by the dankness of the floor, she had been thrown into a lower level of the building, a dungeon. A pair of glittering eyes flashed in the lamplight before a fat rat waddled off to join several of its companions.

Think. Someone hit me from behind. Why? Because I freed

Mother? Because I saw something? The last thought triggered a mental image, something shining in the last room, something that glinted yellow. *Gold?* Maybe. Was it stolen? What if it was? Why, she wondered, would *any* smugglers in Marrakech kidnap her mother and frame her for a murder in Tangier?

It hurt to think. It hurt to hold her head up, but Jade didn't want to give in to the overwhelming desire to lie down. For one, the stone floor was disgusting, and she hated to think what had already crawled onto her. She tried to sort through the recent events as an exercise in clearing her mind. *Mother got a note to meet me. Mother is kidnapped. I find the note. I go to Azilah.*

She stopped in midthought. Her mother didn't get a note asking her to go to Azilah. Instead she got a message purporting to be from Jade that took her to the Tangier souks. That crumpled note in their room was left there as bait for Jade, not for her mother. Then whoever left the note also left a man dead in those tombs. What would have happened if she'd gone into the right-hand tunnel as the dead man directed? Would she have been kidnapped, too? Killed? What was the point of all this?

If someone wanted ransom, they were going about it all wrong. True, her mother had inherited a sizable fortune, but Jade had no access to it. Her income amounted to a salary from *The Traveler,* provided she turned in copy to them four times a year, and her share of the sale of foals from her five mares on their family's ranch.

On the other hand, if someone was looking for a scapegoat to take the blame for their illegal activities, two lone women might not be a bad choice. Especially if the thieves smuggled contraband into Spain and knew of her mother's plans in Andalusia. But who, in the name of St. Peter's tailor, would know that?

Someone on the ship with Mother? Right now Jade's bets were on Tremaine. Who else in Tangier had a red mustache? Well, maybe a lot of people, but not many who knew her mother. The silly Yale graduate act was probably just a ploy to win over Inez. *Mother!* Jade could just imagine what she was thinking now as she waited impatiently for her delinquent daughter to join her. *She'll probably try to pack me off to a convent this time.*

Jade tugged at her bindings. The leather wasn't very thick, but she didn't have the muscle to snap it. Next she tried reaching for the knot, but someone had been careful to tuck in the loose ends. Maybe if she scooted back against a wall and rubbed them over a rough rock? She peered at the visible walls in the little room and sadly saw that they were all plastered.

The sound of heavy feet stomped down a flight of steps outside the door, a key rattled in the lock, and the door groaned open. Several rats scurried off to their respective holes. A man of medium height and build, made larger by a thick turban and robes, loomed in the doorway. His most notable facial feature was a crooked nose, hooked to his right where it had been broken once. He put his fists on his waist, just above his broad red sash, and planted his booted feet far apart.

"Good, you are alive," said the guard in Arabic. "Allah be praised." He opened one fist and tossed a handful of dates onto the floor. "There," he said with a laugh, "root for your food in the dirt like an infidel pig." He slammed the door behind him, his laughter mingling with the jingling of keys.

Jade eyed the half-dozen dates with a mixture of disgust and extreme need. She wasn't the only creature coveting sustenance. One of the bolder rats trundled out of hiding towards them. "Oh, no, you don't," she yelled, and pivoted around on her rear to face it. The rat squeaked and ran, but not far. Jade scooted around the floor, herding the dates into a pile using her feet, and was about to actually try to reach one with her mouth when an idea came to her.

Using her bottom as a pivot point, she raised her legs and spun halfway around so that her back was to the dates. Then she slowly scooched back until she could easily reach the pile. Two of the rats watched her from a few feet away. "You'll get your supper. Just wait."

Jade's slender fingers selected a date and wriggled it about, shoving the soft fruit into the tiny space between the overlapping leather strips. She did this to the next four dates until her fingers began to cramp. The last one she simply smashed into the knot by leaning into it. "Okay, guys, come and get it."

It didn't take long for the rodents to overcome what little fear they had of her. Within minutes, first one, then another started eating the mashed dates. Once they finished with the exposed fruit, they started chewing on the date-encrusted leather. Jade felt their bristling whiskers brush her wrists, heard the rapid gnawing of sharp yellow incisors scraping against leather and lower teeth.

She steeled herself to remain motionless as a twitching nose sniffed her bare skin. The touch both tickled and revolted her. Jade closed her eyes and tried to concentrate on her next move. Tying someone to a rat seemed like a promising start, but hardly practical.

One of the rats grazed her fingers with its teeth, and Jade jerked. "There's plenty on the blasted leather," she scolded. "You don't need to chew my fingers." But the movement gave her a fresh stirring of hope. The bindings were weakening.

She was able to move her wrists more. When the same rodent tried for her fingers again, Jade decided enough was enough. They must be running out of smashed dates on her bonds and trying for the bits on her hand.

She strained her wrists and heard the leather rip. Another twist and pull and the bindings snapped. *Free!* Jade quickly set to work on the knot around her ankles, swatting one of the more persistent rats away with her right hand. "Go find something dead to gnaw on."

Once her feet were free, Jade stood up slowly, careful to avoid another bout of dizziness. First she walked across the cell a few times till she felt steady on her feet. Then she rolled her shoulders and flexed her arms to regain circulation. When she felt competent to take on her guard, she gathered up the leather strips, tossed them into the darkest corner, and resumed her original position on the floor, hands behind her. Her captors had taken her hunting knife from her boot sheath, but with any luck, she'd soon have a replacement.

"Help me," she called out in English in what she hoped was a piteous voice. "Water." She called for water again in Arabic. *"Lma."* She repeated her plea for water in both languages until the guard stationed somewhere outside opened the door.

"I need water, please," Jade said. She let her head droop. *"Afak,* please, water." Through the limp black hair hanging across her eyes, she studied the man, evaluating his center of gravity. He didn't appear to be too broad shouldered. A good shot to the gut ought to do the trick.

"Hmph," he grunted and moved towards a bucket just outside the door. Jade watched as he dipped a pottery goblet into the bucket and carried it, dripping, back to her.

She prayed he wouldn't notice that her feet were no longer bound. A quick flutter of her chest distracted him. She licked her lips as though anticipating the water and drew her knees closer to her as if to make room for him to get closer.

The man squatted down in front of her, grinning. Gaps showed among his brown teeth. Jade could see bits of bread and other foodstuffs still stuck in his chin-length beard. Just as he held the cup to her lips, she shot her feet out and hit him square in the chest. The cup flew from his hands and shattered against the wall as he toppled backward. He started to right himself, but Jade kicked again, this time in his gut. The man doubled over in pain, his hands gripping his midsection. That's when Jade landed a hard right to his chin.

The guard fell to his side, his head hitting the floor as Jade pounced on him. She pulled his curved dagger from his sash and held it to his throat, but the man was stunned, if not already unconscious. Jade knew he wouldn't be out for long so she changed her grip on his knife and thwacked him hard on the back of the head with its hilt.

That's one, she thought, as she massaged her sore knuckles, already feeling them swell. She knew she'd have a hard time slipping out unobserved. They'd taken her dark robe, so she needed a new disguise. Quickly she divested the man of his outer robe and slipped it on, tying it at the waist with his sash. Next she took his turban, hoping he didn't suffer from head lice, and his keys. The robe hung a few inches longer on her slender frame, so she sliced off part of the bottom and used it as a gag on the guard. Finally she retrieved the leather used to bind her feet and tied his hands behind his back, not an easy task with a sore right hand.

"Enjoy the company here," she muttered to the man as she locked him in her cell.

. . .

Inez bounced along on the little donkey, feeling like a sack of potatoes. The shady palm gardens were far behind, and all around her lay rock-festooned flatlands. A few spring flowers bloomed along the route, at least until the donkey stopped and ate them. Inez suffered another jolt as the donkey stumbled. She didn't know whether to be grateful, vexed, or outright angry and so she oscillated among the three emotions; mostly the first two.

True, she was glad to be out of captivity and knew she owed her freedom to Jade. But where was her daughter now? How exasperating! That girl never thought out the long-range consequences of her words or actions. She just had to stay behind and snoop. And for what? Inez didn't care about who had captured her. If they'd been after ransom money, they didn't get it. She just wanted to get away, leave this country, and find refuge in Spain. She couldn't do that until Jade rejoined her. Instead, she was sitting sideways on some miserable little donkey, her once-good dress in ruins.

Anger flooded through her once again. Couldn't Jade have found someone who spoke English or Spanish? This Bachir didn't speak either, so Inez had no way to get answers to her questions, and she had a lot of questions. For one, what was all that nonsense about a murder and someone blaming her? She hadn't murdered anyone. The ridiculous claim was what kept Jade back at that horrid house. Just where did Jade expect to meet her?

Where was she going, and why wasn't Bachir going with her? After he had led her on foot to some gate, two other men dressed much like Bachir met him with three donkeys. Bachir had lifted her up onto one of them, thrown a heavy woolen robe about her, and gone back into the city. She'd expected to be taken to some French official's house or a mission church.

Instead she'd found herself riding on in the night across a flat wasteland, and now they were heading up into the snow-capped mountains, using the moonlight to find their path.

Suddenly worry replaced her anger. Maybe this was actually another kidnapping. That Bachir person might have done something to her Jade. That girl seemed to have a knack for associating with the most unsavory people, despite all Inez's attempts to train her otherwise.

I'm not going a step farther. Inez tugged on her donkey's short mane and attempted to turn him around. The man behind her blocked her way and pointed up the trail. Inez kicked the little donkey in the flanks, hoping to spur him on past her captor, but the poor beast just brayed and sat down. Inez tumbled over, rolling to her left and off the donkey's rump. By now, the lead man had dismounted and run back to assist her. Gently but firmly he raised her, then put her back on the donkey.

The other man said something she didn't understand and pointed up the mountain trail again. Inez had no intention of complying, but the lead man took care of that problem. He attached a rope of braided grass around her donkey's neck and took hold of the other end. For a brief moment, Inez considered jumping off and making a run for Marrakech, but decided she wouldn't get twenty yards before they caught her again. Then they might tie her to the animal. She decided to trust that this was all part of Jade's plan.

But wait till I see that girl again!

Jade's exploration had revealed no other person in the house, but she had no idea how long she'd been unconscious. It could be morning, evening, or several days later as far as she knew.

I need to get out of here and get to Mother. She wasn't sure she should risk the front door in case someone else was keeping watch. If she could just make it to the central courtyard, she reasoned, she could climb that orange tree and get out onto the roof from the second floor.

She listened for sounds outside the guard's room, heard none, and opened the door a crack. She was in luck. This was the same room she'd heard the snoring sounds come from just before she was captured. She wasn't far from the orange tree and freedom.

Because she couldn't see through the garden foliage to the other side of the courtyard, Jade didn't venture out immediately. Someone might be sitting out of view on one of the stone benches, and she knew her disguise wouldn't withstand close scrutiny. *Forget the tree. Just head for the rear.* No one seemed to use the back part of the house and she could always hide there until the coast was clear. She might even be able to stand on something and pull herself up onto the lower of the steps, something her mother hadn't been able to do.

Mother's going to have a conniption fit. She took three steps out of the room, then froze.

"What news?" The words were in unaccented English, and the voice came from near the fountain.

Jade couldn't return to the guard's room. If these people decided to check on her, they'd come this way and spot her immediately. She slipped into the next room and eased the door nearly closed, keeping an ear to the crack in an attempt to eavesdrop. Unfortunately the voices, low to begin with, were now almost completely muffled. She thought she caught the word "escaped."

Good. Mother did get away. She risked opening the door an inch to hear better.

"... still have ... daughter." It was the first voice again.

Something about it sounded familiar. Jade tried unsuccessfully to match it with voices she'd heard at breakfast in Tangier.

The second person spoke English with a strong Arabic accent. "He has arrived."

"Show him in."

Jade heard footsteps approaching, stopping. "Is all in readiness?" asked the newest arrival.

Jade's interest perked up even more. That voice and the Spanish accent definitely sounded familiar, but the thick door made it difficult to hear clearly.

"Not quite."

Whoever they were, they were coming closer. Jade looked around for a place to hide and was amazed at what she saw. The room was an old bath complete with a large sunken pool, now dry and cracked. Daylight filtered down in an array of colors from a multicolored glass skylight two floors above. Tiles of emerald green, gold, and sapphire graced the walls, while colored light danced on the once white floor. But it was the bright flash of bronze leaf from the red leather pouches stacked high in the corner that caught Jade's eye. This was the room she'd glimpsed just before being hit. *Was it the bronze I saw before, and not gold?*

She had just enough time to snatch one of the pouches before jumping over the side of the dry pool. She slipped the pouch over her head and a shoulder, ran for the water conduit, and backed into it. No sooner had she pulled her head in like a turtle retreating into its shell than she heard the footsteps enter the room.

"As you can see, many of the bags are here, but the rest of them will not be ready for another week." The voice, English, had the pitch of an Irish tenor, but softer, as though the speaker were hoarse. Jade had to strain to hear from inside the conduit.

"Only a small part has arrived," continued the nonaccented voice. "These people are intolerably slow. I shall have to have my men encourage the pouch maker to work faster." There was a brief pause.

"And the other shipment? Has it arrived?"

"No, but then the passes through the Atlas have only recently opened."

"You should have sent around to the west and up to Essaouira."

"Too dangerous now. The damned French watch those old Portuguese ports."

Jade heard the sound of leather being manhandled, then tossed back onto the pile. "I can wait if the quality of the rest will match this," said the familiar-sounding man. He had shifted position and his voice came into the pipe more clearly. "It must be perfect. It is becoming dangerous even to do business out of a city as ungoverned as Tangier."

Sweet Millard Fillmore on a camel, that is Patrido de Portillo. But who is he talking to? Jade tried to peer out the conduit but all she could see were trousers. There was no way to glimpse the other man's face unless she stuck her head out of the pipe. She pulled back farther instead. Knowing one of the kidnappers was enough for her. *Wait till I tell Mother. He said he was here to buy leather, but apparently that's not all he's taking out of the country. What are they waiting for to come down through the mountains?*

"You need not worry. I have taken steps to ensure you will not be harassed," said the Englishman.

Patrido de Portillo blew out his breath in a cynical, laughing snort. "A bribe, I suppose. The business becomes too expensive with so many officials wanting their cut."

"Not a bribe," said the other man. "Something more effective, I think. I do not wish to appear rude, but I'm afraid you have interrupted me in the middle of some important business. I will be in contact with you."

"Of course," said de Portillo. "You know where to find me."

The men left the bathing chamber, shutting the door behind them. Jade squirmed out of the pipe and headed for the door. It would be only a matter of moments before they discovered her escape. She needed to get up that orange tree now. She grabbed the door handle and pulled, but it didn't budge. *Locked! The bastards have bolted the blasted door.*

CHAPTER 11

Women in well-to-do Arabic households are kept in seclusion. Intricate window and
roof screens allow them to see out but not be seen. Except to visit a saint's shrine, a
hammam, *or to cross the roof to see a neighboring woman, they spend their lives in their*
indoor household gardens and harem. Gossiping with the women from a neighboring
house is their only excitement, but it's hard to imagine what they have to gossip about.

—The Traveler

JADE TOOK A DEEP BREATH AND FOUGHT FOR CALM. *Okay, this room has a glass skylight.* Maybe she could climb up, break the glass, and get onto the roof. She looked for anything to help scale the walls and saw nothing but slick mosaic tiles. There was no way she could reach that ceiling. Could she break down the door? Was there anything to use as a battering ram? *Not without being discovered.*

Then her gaze rested on the dry pool and the water conduit. If she couldn't go up, maybe she could go out through it. After all, it had once carried water into the building from some outside source. It was wide enough here to fit her, and pipes usually narrowed near the outlet, not closer to their origin. The big question was, just how far did it still go?

Jade removed the turban and pulled off the robe, keeping only the guard's knife and the leather pouch. She squirmed back into the pipe, this time going headfirst, keeping the knife in front of her. *Better not be any blasted rats, bugs, snakes, or any of Bachir's* jinni *in here.* According to him, this was just the type of place those denizens of the underground preferred. Handy creatures, though. It seemed if anything went wrong, just blame it on a *jinn*. Jade wondered if her mother would believe such an excuse. *Sorry, Mother. I was right behind you when this* jinn *grabbed me.* What was she supposed to say if she met one and it tried to give her the old evil eye? *Five in your eye? I'll give 'em five in the eye.* Only she'd put a fist in their face instead of a flat palm.

The baked clay duct climbed slowly for about fifty feet before it divided at a T-shaped juncture. Jade reached out and felt with both arms. One went up, or at least so it felt to her touch; the other sloped down, presumably to another building also with dry baths. This portion of the city's princely houses had fallen into disuse and Jade wondered why they'd been abandoned.

She took the upward path, still squirming on her belly through the accumulated debris. It was pitch-black inside, but happily a little bit wider. She still couldn't rise onto her knees, but at least there was enough room that she didn't brush the top with her back. Another juncture, another slight rise before the pipe took a turn to her right and leveled off. The debris on the bottom now included substantial chunks of the upper pipe, some still sharp. Jade slowed down before she accidentally sliced her hand on anything.

Time stood still in the tunnel, with only the pounding of Jade's heart to mark its progress. By now her captors would have discovered her escape from their dungeon, but did they know where she'd gone? Had they opened the bathing room and seen the guard's clothing? Each time she paused, she listened, dreading to hear an echo of pursuit. Her hands hurt, her shoulders ached, her head throbbed, and ever since that last turn, she'd been getting wet. She pressed on. The blasted tunnel had to end somewhere.

It did, in a pile of collapsed clay and dirt. Jade lay in the pipe, struggling to register the brutal fact that she couldn't go any farther. As long as she'd been making progress, she could ignore her throbbing knuckles and tired arms. Now they seemed to scream at her for attention. *Idiot! That's why the pool was dry.* She started to shiver and recognized the signs of muscle fatigue.

Well, she couldn't very well go back to that room and wait for them to find her. She needed another plan. For a moment, she thought about digging through with her knife. She patted the obstruction, trying to get a feel for how packed it was, until she reached to the far right and felt water. It seeped through in a steady trickle that flowed at perhaps a cup a minute, but who knew how much lay pent up behind the barrier? She might release a torrent and drown.

No, thank you.

There seemed to be no option but to wriggle backward and try one of the other pipes. True, they'd empty into another house's pool, but from there she might make it to the roof. She decided to follow the water and started to shinny back down until she found the most recent T branch. She discovered it at the point she'd first started getting wet.

Not wanting to back down this pipe, Jade retreated a little bit into her old route, then, feeling with her hands, found the juncture that took the tiny stream and headed into it. It sloped down, which meant she'd end up in someone else's plumbing. She just prayed this pipe didn't get any narrower and that the end wasn't covered. At least she hadn't run across any vermin. *I feel like a blasted cave salamander.*

By the time Jade found the end of the pipe, she was ready

to crawl through a den of *jinni*, she was that desperate to get out, and for a moment, she entertained the notion that she might have to. It was the sound of high-pitched conversation that set off the idea. She listened carefully and picked out three distinct female voices and at least one giggling child. *A harem?* She inched closer, careful not to make a sound. If someone thought anyone was creeping up on them, they might call for help or even close the pipe and leave her trapped inside. She didn't relish either option.

Finally she could see the end. *What do you know. There is a light at the end of the tunnel.* It seemed since the water flowed so slowly, they didn't bother to ever close the water conduit. Instead, they simply let it trickle into the bathing pool. From her vantage point a few feet back, Jade could see two of the three women. One, a girl of about fourteen years, stood in the pool with water to her ankles, holding on to a toddler's hand. The naked baby marched in place, giggling and cooing as he splashed the young woman. The other, a middle-aged woman in green, sat on the edge and watched. The third was out of view, but Jade could tell from her voice that she was much older.

Jade gathered her wits about her, preparing to make her dash to freedom. Then with a sudden flurry of movement, she literally oozed out of the pipe and into the shallow pool. All three women screamed, their high-pitched voices reverberating off the enclosed walls. The young mother snatched up her son and pulled the folds of her scarlet and gold vestlike robe around him.

"*Jenniya,*" said the oldest, followed by something that might have been a plea for their lives.

Jade stood up and put her finger to her lips. "*Ana mra,*" she said repeatedly. "I am a woman." *What the tarnation was the word for "friend"?* "*Sāheb.*" She knew she must look a fright so she quickly stooped and splashed some water on her face to clean off the worst of the mud.

The oldest woman, a wrinkled thing swathed in a black robe, calmed down first and dared to address Jade. "Who are you?"

Jade wasn't sure that these three women, possibly secluded since birth, would understand if she told them she was an American. Instead she decided to repeat the word for "friend," then pointed to herself and told them her name. "*Ana* Jade." Then, taking her time to get the words right, she explained her predicament. "Bad men held me in a house. Will you help me, please?"

The thought of adventure and the novelty of a strange female emerging from their bathing-room pipe pushed aside the women's residual fear. The three descended on her as one, touching her short black hair, matted with wet clay. They fingered her shirt and the brown overskirt, lifting it to observe the trousers underneath. Their own pants ballooned out from under their tight-bodiced robes, the younger girl's in scarlet with designs embroidered in gold threads, the middle woman's in green and blue. Even the old woman's wrists and ankles jingled with gold and silver bangles from which hung many coins. The bracelets glittered as the women pawed and patted Jade. Clearly, they considered her homely brown clothes and lack of jewelry to be as much a subject of pity as her recent capture.

"Have you no brothers? Is your father poor?" were some of the questions they pressed on her. Jade said she had no brothers and her father lived very far away.

The eldest remarked that Jade clearly came from a distant land, as she spoke Arabic in an odd way. The woman's pale blue eyes watered as her thoughts drifted to a different place and time. Perhaps Jade's presence triggered some long-dormant memory in her mind, a time in her youth when she was sent from Circassia on the Baltic Sea to become the property of some man she'd never seen before. The moment passed, and the old woman patted Jade's arm. A few words to the younger women and the three were galvanized into action.

The youngest held her baby and acted as a watchman, listening at the door for voices or unusual activity outside. Under the elder woman's direction, the middle-aged woman slipped out and returned with the all-encompassing white veil worn by women when they ventured onto the roof or, more rarely, into the streets. She wrapped it around Jade and showed her how to hold it so that only her eyes showed. Satisfied that Jade looked like a proper woman on a simple visit, they escorted her from the bathing chamber towards the stairs to the roof. Jade need not have worried about being seen. No man other than the head of the house would have dared intrude upon the women's quarters.

At the foot of the stairs, the old woman tugged at Jade's arms to stop her. Then she pulled three of her own silver bangles from her arm and gave them to Jade. "To buy food," she said.

Jade turned to the little woman, now stooped with age, and wondered if she were the mother of the house or the first wife. She looked seventy, but might only be fifty if her life had been a hard one. Jade smiled and took the lady's wrinkled hands in hers. "*Shukran,* thanks," Jade said, and repeated her thanks to the other two women.

"Where will you go?" asked the youngest. Her soft black eyes expressed the horror of being alone in the streets, something unimaginable to one who had always known protective walls.

"To my mother," said Jade.

"Ah," said the others, nodding. That was well, then. She would be with family.

Yes, thought Jade, there was safety in the family, even one as odd as her own. After wishing them peace with many *besmellāh,* she bounded up the stairs and made the roof just as the muezzin called for noon prayer.

From the rooftop, Jade could see the high tower of the great Koutoubia mosque and reoriented herself. She was two streets over from the house where she and her mother had been held prisoner. After seeking out the best route to the French district, she looked for a way down. The roof was about fifteen feet off the ground, and Jade wasn't sure she wanted to drop that far. That's when she heard a woman's voice call to her.

The second oldest of the three women popped her head up through the hole like a groundhog from its burrow. She pointed to the far edge of the roof. Jade followed her hand and saw a flimsy pole ladder lying next to several thin boards. The ladder, meant to carry a woman up and over the rooftop latticework to the neighboring house, barely reached the roof when Jade lowered it to the ground. She eased her weight onto it and scrambled down as quickly as she could, with the veil swaddling her. Once on the ground, she hurried through the maze of streets, using the position of the red Koutoubia tower as a bearing. Finally she exited the old city near the tower, discarded the white veil, and hurried west towards the Franciscan church.

The few European people walking about in the afternoon sun eyed Jade as they might an escaped lunatic, uncertain whether they should ignore her, offer aid, or call for an official. Jade ran her dirty fingers through her hair in an effort to make it less wild, and headed for the rectory. Just outside the church she ran into a priest wearing the brown robes of a Franciscan.

"Father, can you take me to my mother? Her name is Inez del Cameron. I believe she came here last night. She was held prisoner in a house in the *Medina*."

"You are mistaken, my child. No one has come here under any such circumstances. It has been very quiet."

"But she must be here," Jade insisted. Just then she saw Bachir and ran to him. She grabbed him by the front of his woolen robe and glared at him. "What have you done with my mother?"

CHAPTER 12

The Atlas Mountains are the guardians of Marrakech. They hold back aggressors from the Sus, or south, cause rain to fall on the Marrakech side, and send life-giving water down the slopes from the frozen reservoir of snow. Marrakech would probably not exist except for the Atlas, and it is into these sanctuaries that the Berbers sought refuge.

—The Traveler

"Your mother is very well and safe, *Alalla* Jade. Just as I promised she would be." His mouth was set in a determined line, as though his honor had been impuned.

"She's not *here*. I told you to take her to the French church." Jade hissed the words, her face inches from Bachir's.

"*Mademoiselle,*" called the Franciscan as he pulled Jade away from Bachir. "What is the problem? Why do you attack this poor man?"

Jade kept her green eyes riveted on Bachir's. She watched him raise his right hand in front of his face, fingers spread upward in the sign against the evil eye. *You have no idea just how evil it's going to be.*

"*Mademoiselle,*" repeated the priest. "What has happened?"

Without taking her eyes off Bachir, she answered, "My mother was a prisoner in one of the old *riads*. Someone kidnapped her in Tangier and brought her here. This man," she said as she pointed in Bachir's face, "was there in Tangier. He said he could help me. I went into the house to free her and I trusted him to bring my mother here, but she is *not* here. He has abducted her *again*."

"I see," said the priest. Turning his attention to Bachir, he addressed him in Arabic. "Where is her mother? Did you take her?"

Bachir, perhaps to show he was no uneducated fool, answered the priest in French. "I did not steal her mother. I told the *Alalla* that I would keep her mother safe. And I have. She is with my people. It is the only way I could be sure the *Alalla* would keep her promise and help us."

The Franciscan, acting now as a negotiator, turned back to Jade. "Is this true? You promised to help this man in return?"

Jade nodded. "I did. And if Mother is indeed safe, I will. I keep my promises."

"Very well," said the priest. "It seems you both must learn to trust the other." He let his hands drop from both of their shoulders and folded them inside his sleeves as he appraised Jade. "You have seen some trouble, that much is clear. It is my counsel that you go to the authorities at once. The Resident General is away at present, but surely his aid would help you."

Jade shook her head. "No, Father. Not yet. They would only arrest my mother and myself for a murder we did not commit."

He arched his brows in surprise at this new revelation, then furrowed them just as quickly as another thought occurred to him. "Wait. What is your name again?"

"Jade. Jade del Cameron."

"Come with me. I have a message for you."

They followed him to the rectory door as he explained that a telegram had come yesterday for her and that they'd spent much of the day debating what to do about it. "We decided it was a mistake, but it appears now it was not. Wait here." He went inside for a moment, then reappeared with the telegram and a loaf of bread and two chunks of cheese. Jade took the telegram.

Jade. Help on the way. Be careful. Lilith disappeared. B and A.

Bev and Avery had sent help. Jade wondered what kind. Probably pulled in some favor with the British Consulate in Tangier, who, hopefully, carried weight with either the French or the American consulates. But what was this about Lilith Worthy having disappeared from London? Her deceased beau's mother always ran her schemes of murder and drugs safely from her London town house. Did they think she was also on her way to Morocco or perhaps Spain? Jade folded the telegram and shoved it into her trouser pocket.

"Thank you, Father," she said. "You have helped me more than you can know."

He handed each of them a chunk of cheese, followed by the bread. Jade, suddenly ravenous, bit into the bread. "Where do you go now?" the priest asked.

Jade, her mouth full, looked to Bachir. He pointed out the window across the flatlands to the white-capped mountains in the south. "There. We go to my village." Jade coughed as she suddenly inhaled a bit of bread.

"I think you will need more food," said the priest.

A half hour later, Jade stood at the Bab el Khemis, the gate on the northernmost point of Marrakech. Its small, plainly carved scallops rose over the brick-worked archway and made a tolerable attempt at being ornate without any scroll-work or other pretensions. More interesting to Jade's eye was the oddly crenellated top, made of zigzagging tiers narrowing at their tops. This *bab,* or gate, did not cater to the rich, but to ordinary travelers in need of mounts.

It was Thursday, and the great market had been going on all day. No aroma of attar of roses here, just the earthy smell of camels, donkeys, mules, and an occasional swaybacked horse. While most business had been conducted in the cooler morning hours, a few men lingered with the remains of their stock. About a dozen other men loitered about, looking at the animals, and their chatter mingled with invitations to buy. Jade frowned. She certainly wouldn't get the pick of the litter at this time of day. Perhaps she should have hurried over here, but she'd accepted the priest's offer of water to clean her hair and face. No one would have sold anything to her looking like a wild woman.

"Come see this fine mule," beckoned one man. "She is a pearl beyond measure, a rare gem. Only three years old."

Jade opened the animal's mouth and examined the teeth, at least what remained of them. "She was three years old when Allah sent the great flood," she said. Someone laughed behind her. Jade turned.

"Ah, the lady knows a nag when she sees one," said the man who laughed. "Here I have fine animals, strong as the mountains but gentle as kittens. Only one hundred fifty dinar each."

Jade ran her hands over one animal's legs, examined the hooves and teeth. All the while she wondered how she was going to pay for any beast, much less provisions. Her mother had her camera bag with the last of their money. The priest had pressed four loaves of bread on them, along with two water skins and a cooked chicken, but that would hardly take them to Bachir's village. She'd sent Bachir into the souks with one of the silver bracelets given to her by the old woman to buy food and a few cook pots.

The bracelets turned out to be great gifts, each finely crafted with coins dangling from them, part of the old lady's dowry. Jade hoped one of the other two bracelets, equally beautiful, would be accepted here. The problem was, she had no idea how many dinar they were worth. She hoped by flaunting them, the merchant would give her some idea.

"It is not too bad an animal," Jade said with little enthusiasm as she began the bargaining game. "But I am a poor woman and I need three mules." She raised her hand to her forehead to flaunt the bracelet, and sighed as though many troubles beset her. It wasn't a far stretch, either. The afternoon sun glinted on the silver links and danced off the coins. "I am not sure I could find even thirty dinar."

The merchant took the bait, his eyes riveted on the glittering bangle. "You are Nazarene," he said, "and so must be very rich."

Jade shook her head. "Ah, if you only knew my troubles. Evil men stole my mother. It took all my money to get here. Now she has been taken away again. All I have left is what I wear. Would you leave me bereft of everything?"

"Charity is a virtue, *Alalla*. I will let you have three mules for one of the bracelets."

Noting how quickly the man suggested the new price, Jade gained some insight to the bracelet's value. "I can do without a saddle if I must," she said, as though speaking her thoughts aloud to herself, "but how can I make my aged mother ride without one when I find her again?"

"I will take the loss, *Alalla,* waiting patiently for my reward in heaven. I will let you have three mules and two saddles for the bracelet."

As willing as the man was, she knew she still had bargaining room, but the deal was fair. She wouldn't have the man think the worst of a Nazarene. "I accept your offer *if* you let *me* choose the three mules and the two saddles."

Now it was the merchant's turn to appear distressed, as though such a bargain would break him, but he agreed. Jade selected her animals, choosing the best but settling for the more worn but still serviceable saddles, leaving the newer and more ornate ones behind. Her own kindness in that matter did not go unnoticed by the merchant.

"Allah go with you on your journey to find your mother," he said, after the nearby scribe had recorded the sale. Any guilt Jade might have harbored for taking advantage of the man disappeared when she saw the delight with which he took possession of the bracelet. *Probably worth an entire herd of camels.*

Jade thanked him and, after many wishes for blessings were exchanged, led her animals to the gate to wait for Bachir. He found her shortly after, his success evident by the sacks of provisions: onions, sugar, salt, meal for couscous, grain for the mules, a cook pot, a teapot, two cups, a bag of mint, and another of green tea. Jade grimaced when she saw the latter. What she really wanted was a good cup of coffee, but if a person had to endure tea, at least the mint tea was heavily sweetened. He obviously was a better haggler than she was, since he returned the bracelet chain to her with one coin left on it.

Bachir approved of the mules. "We can leave in the morning, *Alalla.*"

"We will leave now. We have at least five good hours of

daylight left." Jade fastened the saddle girth on her mount, a jenny with soft brown eyes and velvety ears. "We will put the supplies on this one," she said, pointing to a large-boned jack mule.

By the time they left Marrakech, it was just after three o'clock by Jade's pocket watch. The sun, while hot, didn't scorch like it would later in the summer. Water for the mounts wouldn't be a problem since the spring melts brought plenty of water down from the snowcapped Atlas, and the mules could find forage close to the streams. If anything, the spring runoff would make fording some of the rivers interesting.

The route south took them past several deep wells, which Bachir said tapped into the underground clay conduit pipes carrying water from the mountains to Marrakech. Jade thought about the conduit she'd wallowed through. It must have been part of this vast system, but a part that had collapsed on itself, much to her good fortune. Water left to run wild, still cold, raced by in sharp ravines, and a few children splashed along the edge with a herd of black goats, while the children's parents dug at the wet clay along the edge, making bricks to sell. Jade and Bachir stopped only to water their mules and themselves, pressing on until the increasing dark made it too difficult to see.

Bachir started a fire by an oasis of scraggly olive trees and heated water for tea while Jade tended to the mules. When she sat down by the fire, she broke out the food and handed the chicken to Bachir to take first pick. He tore off a leg quarter, and Jade did the same. She studied her guide out of the corner of her eye, wondering what motivated him to travel all the way to Tangier to hunt for her. After all, he'd never even seen her before. Who was behind this?

"Tell me, Bachir, do you have a family?"

"My father and mother live," he said, without looking up from his meal.

"Then you are not married? You have no children?"

"No."

Jade finished the leg quarter, sliced a hunk of breast meat from the chicken, plopped it on a thick slab of bread, and passed it to Bachir. She did the same for herself, letting silence fall naturally into the conversation. Her companion's reticence seemed almost palpable. Jade could tell he would not appreciate being interrogated, nor did she wish to. She needed his goodwill, but she also needed information. She had no clue what she was walking into up in the mountains.

"May I ask you about your village?"

"What do you want to know?" he asked as he poured hot mint tea into two mugs. He took one for himself and offered Jade the other. She took it. It wouldn't pay to offend him by doing otherwise.

"How do you grow crops up there? Do you have village festivals?" She purposely chose nonpersonal questions first, to put him at ease. While she waited for his answer, she sipped the sweet tea and felt it scald her throat.

"We make flat steps into the mountain," he said, using his left hand to illustrate the wide terraces. "Every family has their land and their use of the water. We celebrate when someone marries." He sighed, his shoulders sagging. "Then there is a big feast and dancing."

Jade heard the sorrow in his voice and knew with a flash of feminine insight that he mourned a wife. She decided to take a chance and address it as a certainty. "I am sorry, Bachir. I'm sure she was a good wife." She saw him startle and clutch the talisman he wore under his robe.

"It should not surprise me that you know, *Alalla*. You have the gift."

"I don't have any gift, Bachir, except experience. I have known many people who mourned someone. I am one of them myself." Bachir nodded. "What was she like?"

He stared at his mug of tea without answering for half a minute. "Young. A quiet woman, but you are right. She was a good wife. Allah took her and my infant son when she was in labor last harvest."

"I'm sorry, Bachir."

He shrugged as though resigned to his lot in life. "My mother picked my wife."

Jade didn't know if her next question would seem impertinent or not, but she asked anyway. "Will you marry again?"

"Yes. It is unholy for a man not to have a wife. But we paid a very high bride price, and I have not yet enough goats and silver to marry again. I do not hurry," he added. "There is no unmarried girl I want." He stared into the fire and began singing his tuneless lament.

Jade sensed he did not wish to pursue the discussion, so she let it drop. She understood how he felt, in a way. Everyone she knew was always trying to play matchmaker for her, including her mother. After a while, it made the entire prospect a trifle annoying. It seemed apparent that Bachir would marry again out of spiritual necessity. It also sounded as if he had not been very much in love with his first wife. *Then what was he mourning?* She replayed his words, *There is no unmarried girl I want.* Was that it? Was he in love with another man's wife and dreaded facing the family again? She wondered what he really saw in the fire. Was he imagining a face or perhaps a home full of children?

"Is that why you were chosen to find me?" Jade asked. "Because you do not have children to care for?"

"I volunteered to go for the good of my village." He filled his mouth with a large bite of bread, a clear signal that he did not wish to talk anymore.

They devoured the entire chicken and a loaf of bread each before curling up in their saddle blankets to sleep. Jade couldn't sleep right away. She thought about her own parents. They were devoted to each other; that much was evident. But she wondered if their love had diminished over the years. They still rode together, but less frequently and never very far afield. The days when her mother had joined them on camping trips had ended when Jade was still a young girl. *Why?* Her father had told her stories about her mother, how they met at a Gypsy camp in Spain. *Not that Mother would ever admit it now.*

At least her parents loved each other, she thought as she stared up at the stars. Now, David's parents were another story altogether. She shivered again, thinking of her former beau's mother, Olivia Lilith Worthy, remembering when she first met her. Jade had gone to London to express her sympathy for the loss of Mrs. Worthy's son as a pilot in the war. She was in need of sympathy herself. But she received a very cold reception. Mrs. Worthy, a widow, had appeared dressed in proper black, but with a sense of style and wealth that didn't bespeak of much sincere mourning for either her son or her recently deceased husband.

Then later, Jade learned that the woman had actually orchestrated her husband's death in Nairobi when Gil Worthy had returned to seek out his illegitimate son. If that weren't enough, evidence hinted strongly that much of Lilith's wealth did not stem from her husband's successes. Instead, she ran several smuggling operations, bringing heroin into Nairobi and rifles into Abyssinia. She'd planned on becoming empress of that country, ruling with the man who ran her guns. Had David known any of this? He'd rarely spoken of his mother. Was that why? What would have happened if Jade had married David?

Thoughts of marriage led Jade to think of the newest man in her life, Sam Featherstone. She'd met him in January while photographing elephant herds on a remote mountain in British East Africa. He'd proven himself to be a trusty ally when slave raiders and gunrunners kidnapped a Kikuyu boy in her care. An American pilot who lost his lower right leg in the war, Sam was smart, funny, good-looking, and clearly interested in her. In their adventures together he'd proven his trustworthiness many times over, and whenever he was near, Jade's senses became acutely alive. Still, his pursuit of her scared her, and she wasn't sure why.

Jade wrapped her blanket more tightly around her and remembered Sam's warmth when they shared a hammock on Marsabit one night. That led to thoughts of a burning kiss, when they were chained together in a lava waste desert. Jade felt warmth spread across her face and down her limbs. She missed him and wished she could talk about this situation with him, or just share the campfire and the sky. What was he doing now? Was he back on Mount Marsabit in East Africa, filming the elephants? Or had he gone home to Indiana to start life anew and try to fly again? It wouldn't be easy to operate rudder pedals with only one leg. A gaping yawn intruded on her thoughts, and Jade submitted to sleep.

She slept fitfully, dreaming of *jinni,* dank tunnels, and Little Owls popping out of red leather bags with silver charms in their talons. Every time she tried to catch one of the owls, the moon eclipsed the sun and everything went dark. Then she'd find herself back in one of those tunnels again.

By four o'clock, two hours before sunrise, she'd had enough and got up to rekindle the fire. Bachir again made tea flavored with mint and sweetened with chunks from their sugar loaf. Jade felt the morning chill in her back and left knee, and so drank some for the sake of the heat. She wondered if she could leave out the tea and just drink hot, sugared mint water instead. That might not be too bad. They ate more of their bread, put out the fire, and packed up.

"How far is it to your village from here, Bachir?"

He peered south towards the mountains. "Another day's journey, maybe more if the waters are too high. We came as far yesterday, but the climb is harder." He picked at the woven panniers, making certain the teapot was securely inside.

"You must be anxious to get home to your parents," said Jade.

Bachir shrugged, but Jade noticed that he packed more rapidly this morning, as though he was anxious to get home.

They broke camp and began the long climb up into the Atlas Mountains. At first they passed through fragrant cedar forests, once startling a male red deer, his antler nubs pushing up the velvet. White and pink flowers worked their way up through the needles along with leafy ferns. As they climbed higher, they gradually left the great cedars behind, picking up stumpier vegetation confined near riverbeds filled with spring melt. Here the underlying nature of the mountains revealed itself in layer upon layer of faulted rock the color of old rust that had darkened the way blood does on drying. At times the color gave way to the brighter brick orange where erosion had clawed fresh wounds into the mountainsides. In the distance, the Atlas took on a cool hazy blue color, always topped by snow. And above it all was a sky so perfect, so intense, that it might have been poured from a bottle of cerulean blue.

Several times the mountains seemed to begrudge them any room for a path. More than a few times, Jade's overskirt brushed the rock wall to her left as she made the effort to avoid going over the precipice on her right. Below her the accumulated spring runoff roared by in deep chasms. It was not a place for someone with vertigo. Bachir never cast so much as a glance to the plunging valley, which spoke volumes on his familiarity with the trail. If anything, Jade noted, he sat up straighter and searched the heights eagerly. Once again his flat voice drifted back, singing softly in quavering notes.

They rode past a bank of shrubs whose slender, finger-length greenery gave way to a cluster of five-petaled pink blossoms at the tip. Jade picked one and examined it more closely. *Oleander?* She asked Bachir its name.

"The French call it rose laurel. Very deadly," he added. Jade dropped the flower by the trail.

The path reminded Jade of the mule ride down into the Grand Canyon. Besides following the curves of the mountain, the trail continually switched back and forth in an effort to climb as well as make forward progress. As they rounded a turn, Jade glanced down and saw that they'd advanced only a few hundred yards south from the last matching switch. The hawk flying to her right made better time than they did.

Once near a tributary, they broke to rest the animals and let them graze while Jade and Bachir finished the last of the bread and cheese. Bachir started a fire with flint and steel and heated the teapot for the inevitable hot mint tea. Jade felt too impatient to sit for long and soon wandered up the tributary a few hundred feet. She amused herself by scanning the fresh red mud for animal tracks and found several from smaller animals, including one that looked like a fox. As she turned, she noted the shadows in the mud. Something had left a very large print, and she bent for a closer look. She expected to see a human shape from some sandal. She did not expect to see the distinct pug mark of a large lion. Luckily it led up the valley and away from them.

"Bachir," she called. "Come and look at this."

He put down his tea and hurried to her side.

"Do you see it?" Jade asked, her voice ripe with excitement.

He nodded, his knitted cap bobbing. "It is *Izem*. That is what we call the lions of these great mountains. It is a good sign. We are close to my home now."

"A Barbary lion," whispered Jade. "I didn't think there were any more left."

"Very few, *Alalla*. Very few. Soon they will be gone, like the bear that once walked these mountains." He sighed. "We are safer, but we are poorer now, I think."

Jade looked at the track again, wishing she hadn't left her camera with her mother. "We'd better get back to the mules before this one returns for dinner."

By late afternoon, Bachir had led Jade onto a branch of the trail that headed more easterly, rather than the main path that continued to climb up to the pass. The sun started to dip below the peaks just as they reached a broad, swiftly flowing stream.

"We will cross tomorrow," said Bachir.

"But you said we were close," Jade argued.

Bachir jerked his chin to the fast-moving stream. "It is not safe to cross it now. Too cold, and they"—he nodded to the animals—"are too tired."

Jade nodded, curbing her impatience to see her mother

safe and sound. He was probably right, although she suspected him of stalling more than once, almost as if he wanted to make sure they didn't overtake her mother before they got to the village. Still, crossing these ice-cold waters would be bad enough in the daytime when the sun's rays could dry them out afterward. At dusk? They'd risk taking shock from the cold for themselves and the mules. She also knew the animals had a better chance of crossing without slipping when they were well rested.

Jade hobbled the mules, put some grain in their feed bags and slipped the bags over the animals' heads. Bachir started his fire and soon had a pot of couscous simmering, seasoned with cumin and onion. They ate in silence, completed their private ablutions and needs, then settled on their separate saddle blankets.

She soon heard Bachir's soft snore, but sleep eluded her long after the gibbous moon climbed over the peaks. She kept reviewing everything she'd learned so far and kept coming back to the fact that she'd heard Patrido Blanco de Portillo's voice in that *riad*. Clearly he was smuggling something for someone, but wasn't in charge of operations in Marrakech. That job belonged to the other man, the one who said he had "taken steps," done something "more effective than a bribe." The fact that de Portillo thought he'd meant a bribe indicated he was not the author of her mother's kidnapping.

But right now he's all I've got to clear our name. She stoked the fire with the remaining pieces of brush. And this other man in Morocco, was he the brains? The warning from Avery made her wonder if Lilith wasn't behind it all. Jade could have easily stumbled onto another branch of her illegal operations. But Lilith always ran them from London. *You don't know that for certain.* So where did Bachir fit into all this?

So far he'd proven useful, but not entirely trustworthy. He'd sent her mother out of Marrakech and up into the mountains against her orders. Just what did he and his people want from her? She would have to be extra wary tomorrow.

Jade closed her eyes and slept, her brief night haunted by the distant *harrumph*ing roar of a male lion.

The next morning, Jade and Bachir crossed the stream, then dismounted and walked, leading their mules along the narrow path, the sheer mountain wall rising to their right, a precipitous drop to the swollen river on their left. It was a good thing she hadn't pressed to continue last evening. This was not a route one took in the twilight hours. Treacherous as it was, it had the grace to be short. After a few hundred yards the trail turned south, away from the river and towards a small valley. There, along the stream, lay Bachir's village, or at least the fields and orchards.

Jade looked in vain for any houses until she let her gaze stray up from the fertile floodplain. Nestled directly against the mountain wall, the village itself rose, the red plastered buildings nearly invisible, so well did they blend with the mountain. The houses climbed the Atlas in terraces, leaving the more hospitable ground open for farming and grazing. Dominating the higher terrace stood a one-family *kasbah*, its four-turreted corners marking it as a building of importance. The span between the towers had the same odd crenellation as the gate where she'd purchased the mules. Each crenellation looked like a set of stacked *z*'s, narrower at the base and coming together in a wide, flat top. Even the fortress itself was constructed in a reverse of this plan, with a wide base gently sloping inward to the parapets. More zigzags were carved into the outer wall. The lines rose and fell like mountains with valleys between. No one stood at the top or below.

In fact, aside from a few goats and chickens, the village appeared abandoned. It wasn't.

Bachir called out in his own language, and immediately the village erupted into life. Men poured out of every building, each one armed with either a flintlock rifle, a hoe, or a knife. They held up their weapons. Clearly they had known someone was approaching, and had kept vigil until they knew whether it was friend or foe. Behind the men came nearly a dozen children, and to Jade's amazement, several women. None of them wore veils and many stood in bare feet, their legs exposed halfway up their calves. The Berber people truly were different.

Bachir and another, older man clasped each other in a bear hug and began a lively conversation. Judging by the glances in her direction, she was the topic of discussion. Finally Bachir turned to her. "Come, I must take you to the *kahina*."

He led Jade to a multistory building at the far edge of the village. The first floor served as a combination barn for the livestock and storage area. Terraced about it were the living quarters, all made of *pisé*, the lower story as bricks, the upper as a solid mass of earth mixed with straw. They climbed up to the second floor.

"I have brought her," said Bachir from outside the door. He pushed Jade inside.

As her eyes adjusted to the dim light, she saw an elderly woman sitting in one corner next to a ceiling-to-floor loom, a pile of wool at her feet. She wore a brown-and-red-striped woolen cloak, or *handira,* like a dress over some lighter-weight, knee-length tunic. Two ornate silver pins pierced the *handira* and locked into large silver rings in front of each shoulder. A thick silver chain dangled between the pins, suspending a large silver amulet shaped like a diamond, which rested on her chest. The pins reminded Jade of the *fibula* worn by Romans for the same purpose. The woman's hair was hidden under a turbanlike wrap of red and gold fabric. A shuttle rested against her leg.

A younger woman of about eighteen to twenty years and dressed in similar garb sat beside her, weaving on a loom attached to the ceiling beams. A little girl of two, wearing a light cotton garment, played with a drop shuttle at her feet, spinning it like a top.

"I knew you would come today," said the old woman in Arabic as she looked up from her spinning. "I heard *Izem* call last night, something he would not do unless another lion came into his territory. Welcome to our village, Jade de Cameron."

CHAPTER 13

*Berber villages appear plain on the exterior, but inside, they are a riot of color
and artistry. Culture is often inherited through the maternal line, and the women
decorate pots, walls, and their weaving with symbols handed down for ages,
symbols that give blessing and protection to the family.*

—The Traveler

"You know my name." A split second after she said it, the
reason seemed obvious to her. It also filled her with an incredible sense of relief. Her mother really was here. "Mother told
you."

The old woman smiled, the creases of her face folding
into a broad grin. "Ah, your lady mother." She chuckled.
"For one who does not speak our language, she was very able
to express her demands."

I can imagine. But this time Jade didn't blame Inez, not
after all her mother had endured. Jade wanted to issue a few
orders of her own, but tempered her requests. "I would like
to see my mother, please."

The old woman nodded to the younger woman, who rose,
scooped up her daughter, and left the house. As soon as she'd
departed, the old woman dismissed Bachir with thanks and
gave her full attention to Jade, inspecting her from bare head
to booted toe. Her blue eyes were remarkably clear for one so

old, and Jade knew that this woman could stare down one of the famed Barbary lions. *A woman after my own heart.*

"I knew your name before your mother came," the old woman said. "Just as the last lion in this valley knew you as a lioness."

Simba Jike, my nickname, lioness.

Before Jade had a chance to question the old woman about her sources, the younger one returned, and with her a third Berber woman. At least that was what Jade thought until she noticed the soiled green linen dress peaking out from under the woven wrap and saw the woman's face. "Mother!" She reached for Inez to embrace her. Inez countered by taking hold of Jade's hands and pressing them between her own. "Thank God you're all right, Mother."

Inez patted her daughter's hands. "Of course I'm all right. Why didn't you follow me out of that house? You've had me worried to death, and no one here can understand me or tell me anything." She looked at Jade's clay-encrusted clothes and let out an exasperated breath. "What happened to you? You look as if . . ."

"As if I've been wallowing. I know, Mother." She drew back her hands, again remembering that Inez deemed such public displays of emotion and concern improper, and let her face go blank, wiping away any hidden hurt she felt. "Please sit down, Mother, so we can discuss what is happening."

Inez caught the sudden change in tone and topic. "I didn't get a chance to ask if you are all right, Jade. Did you have some difficulties?"

Jade couldn't help but laugh at her mother's understatement. *Difficulties.* "A few, but I'm fine."

Inez persisted. "What happened? I want you to tell me. I have a right to know why you made me come all the way up here, bouncing like so much baggage on that little donkey."

Jade sighed, hurt that her mother's expression of concern still smacked of disappointment in her daughter. "I'm sorry I kept you waiting, Mother, but I was captured, locked in a dank dungeon, had rats chew on me, thwacked a guard on the head after I kicked him in the gut, and crawled through a maze of filthy conduits to get out. I'm afraid I've behaved in a most unladylike manner. Now if you would *please* sit down," she added, while directing her mother to a woven rug, "I think we are keeping our hostess waiting." Jade knew that her mother would hasten to sit once she realized she was committing some breach of etiquette. Jade wasn't disappointed.

"Oh," murmured Inez softly, as though taken aback by all that Jade had endured.

As soon as they were seated, the younger of the two Berber women brought out a beautifully crafted pottery teapot glazed with a warm ochre color and decorated in red and black with an assortment of designs, including zig-zags, some of which resembled a tree, and diamonds within diamonds. The woman put a handful of dried green tea leaves into the pot and poured hot water over it. Then she added mint leaves and a thick dollop of wild honey in the comb. The older woman maintained her silence during the younger woman's preparations, as though this were a serious ritual.

Jade took advantage of the lull to inspect the home's interior. The walls of the single whitewashed room were lavishly decorated with stripes, triangles, and diamonds in vivid red, blue, yellow, and green. The floor-to-ceiling loom dominated one corner, and a shelf, three feet high, ran around the other two walls and part of the third, ending at the doorway. A low shelf that looked like a seat was built into one corner, and several cubbyholes painted in blue and red dotted the vertical space under the main shelf. The result was a room with considerable storage space for pots and platters, while the floor area was kept clean.

Jade noticed another doorway partially hidden at the back of one shelf, tucked behind a curious square vessel. This pot, painted a vivid red, had two large wooden stoppers in the top and four small stoppers in the front, two above and two below. Carvings of leaves, zigzags, and diamonds covered the container. She recognized one pattern as imitating the *kasbah* crenellations. Even the ceiling was ornate. Beams of silver birch and palm trunk supported an interlocking latticework of dyed bamboo, interlaced to form chevrons and diamonds in red, yellow, and black. The effect was an ornamental and strong ceiling that supported more *pisé* above it.

Finally deeming the concoction ready, the younger woman served the tea, stretching up her arm and pouring it from a great height into colorful pottery mugs. She handed them first to the older Berber woman, then to Inez, and finally to Jade before taking a cup for herself.

"Hold it with your right hand, Mother," whispered Jade. "Never use your left hand. It's rude.

"Besmellāh," said Jade as she raised her cup.

Her mother repeated the word, took a sip, and smiled. "What did we just say, Jade?" she whispered.

"You literally said, 'In the name of God.' It's a blessing. Just say it before you do *anything* and you'll be all right." Jade also sipped the tea. "Thank you," she said in Arabic to the two women. "And thank you for taking in my mother."

"It is my honor," said the older woman. "I know you have many questions. It is good you speak Arabic. It is not my tongue, but Bachir learned it and he teaches me as he teaches my daughter and her husband, Mohan, French. So we will talk without him. You will explain," she added with a nod to Inez, "to your lady mother." The old lady adjusted her *handira,* woven from soft goat hair. "I am Zoulikha and this is my daughter, Yamna. I am the *kahina*."

She waited a moment while Jade translated the introductions to her mother and introduced herself and Inez. Zoulikha poured more tea for her guests and nodded to Yamna, who rose and began preparations for a later meal. She went to the curious red pot, tugged open one of the uppermost stoppers, stuck her hand inside, and pulled out a handful of semolina grain.

Zoulikha saw Jade's fascination with the pot. "It is called an *akoufi*. It is where we store the household's grain for making couscous. It will hold a week's worth of grain."

"It's beautiful," said Jade.

"Red is the color of blood, so it means life to us. The grain also gives us life. It is proper for the two to go together."

Jade wanted to ask about the designs, but the old woman took up another topic.

"I will tell a story," said Zoulikha. "We are the Imazighen, the free people. This village is the village of the Ait Izem, the children of one who bested a lion and so took Izem's name as his own. Once the Amazigh people lived all over the *Maghreb,* the land where the sun sets. Our tribes each had a *kahina,* a woman versed in healing and lore. Many also knew how to control the *jinni*. Some could see the future. The strongest in learning were those . . . ." She paused to ask Yamna something.

"Descended," said Yamna in French to Jade and Inez.

"Yes," said Zoulikha. "They came from the family of the great queen, Elishat. The Romans called her Dido, which meant 'wanderer.' "

Jade felt an involuntary shudder twitch across her back and shoulders as she recalled the name of Elishat spoken in the Azilah tunnels. Even her mother seemed to take notice when the old woman spoke Dido's name.

"Don't you remember reading Virgil's *Aeneid*, Jade? He describes Dido as the founder and first queen of Carthage."

"That's right," said Jade. "In Tunisia, which is also part of the *Maghreb*."

Zoulikha continued her story with occasional assistance from her daughter. "Elishat passed on her knowledge and a powerful amulet to her sister, Annah, before her death. This amulet was also a sign of our lineage. From Annah it went on to her eldest daughter and so down the line to the *kahina* called Dahia. Dahia led her people when the Arabs first came to the *Maghreb,* bringing Islam. Many of the Imazighen had left the ancient ways to become Nazarene or to follow the Israelite people, but always a *kahina* led them, though many had lost some of their knowledge."

The old woman paused a moment to sip more tea and quench her throat, giving Jade a chance to relay the tale so far to Inez. "Dahia knew that the ways of the *kahina* would be lost completely, for the Arabs keep their women locked away. So she united the Amazigh people to do battle. The Romans had already built and rebuilt many ancient fortresses, most with deep tunnels. The Imazighen would not go in them, knowing the people of the night dwelt there. But Dahia could command them to do no harm to her. She had protection, for she carried Elishat's amulet. It was more than just a symbol of her authority. It was a talisman of great power and holiness."

Once again the conversation in the tunnels came back to Jade. "The *kahina* gave up the amulet to some man named Igider to give to her daughter," she whispered.

Zoulikha heard her and smiled, as though she guessed what Jade had said in English. "You know of this already, Jade," she said. "You know how she gave up the amulet so that her hidden daughter would bear the power and become *kahina*. Igider was her general. But in doing so, Dahia lost its protection and hastened her death. She sacrificed herself to save her people from destruction."

Jade nodded, feeling slightly dumbfounded and more than a little bit unnerved. Inez noticed, as well.

"Jade, you're pale. You look as if you've seen a ghost."

"Close, Mother. I believe I heard one." She translated Zoulikha's tale to her mother, then explained first in English, then in Arabic, her experience in the Azilah tunnels. Zoulikha and Yamna exchanged knowing looks and smiled as though all this was perfectly normal. Jade caught the look. "Wait. Was it Yamna in the tunnels? Did Bachir take her there so I would hear this story?"

Zoulikha shook her head. "Yamna has not left the village."

"What is the rest of the story?" asked Jade. "There must be a reason you are telling me this. The man I heard in the tunnel, her general, seemed surprised that this *kahina* had a daughter."

"He was," said Zoulikha. "The girl was kept secret, for Dahia herself had foreseen this trouble. She knew the girl would be hunted down and killed, so Dahia instructed her sons to adopt Islam to save her people from more war. But she had secretly trained her daughter in the ways of the *ka-hina* and hid her in the mountains to the southwest. Over the years, the tribe made its way here, where we have lived for many generations. I am now the *kahina*, and carry the wisdom passed on from Elishat. Yamna is my daughter and my pupil, as her daughter, Lallah, will be hers."

"So you rule this village?" asked Jade.

Zoulikha shook her head. "No. The men choose a sheik, a chief, to oversee the village. He lives in the *kasbah*. But the heart of the tribe is carried by the women. And even the sheik seeks my advice."

Jade saw Yamna smile and wink at her. "What?" she asked.

"The sheik is my father," said Yamna. "The man with the favor of the *kahina* is most likely to oversee the village."

"I still do not understand what *my* role is in your story," said Jade. "Bachir said you wanted my help."

"Elishat's amulet has been taken from us. We need you to get this talisman back."

"Are you certain it has been stolen? Possibly it is misplaced?"

"No. The amulet usually remains in a hidden place of which I will not speak at this time. I wear it when I must assume duties of the *kahina*: at healings, births, settling disputes. It has not been lost. Someone took it from its hiding place."

"Then it must be someone in your own village."

Zoulikha sighed deeply, as though such a thought were a terrible burden to bear. "Perhaps."

"Have you searched the houses?" Jade asked.

Zoulikha nodded. "Two women claim some of their bracelets were gone, as well. Silver bracelets belonging to their mothers and handed down through the generations to wear at weddings and harvest festivals."

"So someone is a thief. Why do you need *me* to find this amulet?"

"Because," said Zoulikha as she reached across and caressed Jade's cheek with her wrinkled fingers, "it should not be handled by just anyone, and you are also a daughter of the great Dahia."

CHAPTER 14

Jinni are feared, all the more so because they are so difficult to spot. They may come in the disguise of an animal. Others appear human. Men report having been married to a jenniya, which is a very handy explanation for not getting along with one's spouse. The easiest way to get rid of such a wife is to let a jackal eat her. Jackals have a taste for jinni.

—The Traveler

INEZ LOOKED AS IF SHE MIGHT EXPLODE when Jade translated that last tidbit. Then, remembering her manners, she managed to control both the volume and tone of her next statement. She could not, however, disguise the quiver in her voice, which alerted Jade to just how upset her mother was.

"This is . . . not possible, Jade. Neither your father nor I am . . . Imazighen."

"But you *are* Andalusian, Mother. I believe a goodly number of people have left their, er, mark there, including the Gypsies and the Moors."

"The family of de Vincente traces its line back countless generations," said Inez. She held her head high and proud. "Some of your ancestors served in the court of King Ferdinand and Queen Isabella."

"What is bothering you, Mother? What if this story *is* true? Are these people too barbaric for you? Are you afraid some snob in Taos will take offense?"

"Jade! How dare you accuse me of such thoughts!"

"This news angers your lady mother," observed Zoulikha. "Does it also distress you?"

Jade shrugged. "I am not sure I believe it. It is one thing to say I am Dahia's daughter. It is another to prove it."

Zoulikha adjusted her position on the floor rug, exposing her right leg high above the knee. She took up a drop spindle and a pile of combed wool and deftly began to spin yarn by rolling the spindle shaft down her thigh with her right hand. With the left, she played out the combed fibers, her fingers moving out of memory. The rhythmic motion of rolling, catching the spindle at the knee, and scooping it back up to begin again made a hypnotic background for weaving her story.

"Perhaps you know of the Almoravids, Amazigh tribes from the desert south. They became mighty rulers and spread across the waters to Andalucía," she said, shifting the accent to another syllable. "They took with them many others, both Arabs and Imazighen, to make their nation and to fight the Nazarene living there. At that time, the *kahina* holding El-ishat's talisman bore twin girls. The midwife told her which one was born first, but the *kahina* taught them both. The eldest became *kahina*, and the second girl married a *kaid*, a regional chieftain, who went to Andalucía to serve the ruler." The old woman looked up from her spindle without stopping her motions and peered deeply into Jade's eyes. "This girl's blood runs in your veins and in the veins of your mother."

"It is a pretty story," said Jade after she translated for her mother, who responded by folding her arms across her chest. "But hardly proof."

Without breaking either her gaze or rhythmic motions, Zoulikha continued. "Why else do you dream warnings and feel them in your bones? And why else can you speak to *jinni*?"

"I have never spoken to *jinni*," countered Jade. She didn't bother to contradict the first question. The dreams of danger in the grass or elephants trumpeting to her could easily be explained as her mind sorting through likely scenarios in Africa, but there was that blasted knee ache. Ever since she had received the shrapnel wound during the war, it seemed to throb just before something tried to attack her or her closest friends. Now that she thought on it, it had also ached just before she was taken prisoner recently.

"I saw you in the desert and on a mountain. You spoke to an old man, Boguli."

Jade started as the old woman named the mysterious and aged native tracker that had helped her elude and eventually apprehend the poachers on Mount Marsabit. "Yes, but he wasn't a *jinn*. He was a . . ." She hesitated, not knowing the Arabic or French word for "elephant." Instead she extended her right arm next to her nose and waved it, making trumpeting sounds. From the corner of her eye she could see her mother's eyes widen, wondering what in the world her daughter was doing now. Then it occurred to Jade, this woman called Zoulikha actually knew about her recent adventure on Mount Marsabit and the northern desert. Either she had very good informants or she really did have some unusual abilities.

"Yes, *Al-Fil*," said Zoulikha, giving the Arabic word for "elephant." "*Giwa* in our language." She smiled, her wrinkled face creasing as she watched Jade's mouth open in astonishment. "This surprises you."

"What is going on?" demanded Inez. "What are you talking about?" After Jade explained, her mother said, "We'll talk about this business of you chasing poachers later, Jade, but with all due respect to our hostess, this is silly. If you are descended from this Dahia, then I am, as well. But *I* don't talk to spirits or have premonitions."

Zoulikha anticipated Inez's argument and answered before Jade could translate her mother's statement into Arabic. "Your lady mother does not walk with death." She nodded to Jade's left leg. "You do. It entered during the war and stayed there. When it did, it awoke that which was hidden inside you."

"Let us say for the moment that what you say is true, lady *kahina*," said Jade. "What can I do that you or your daughter cannot do? If you could see me with Boguli, you can surely see who has your talisman."

Zoulikha's right hand stopped working the shuttle and her left hand drifted down, still holding the tufts of carded wool. Distress and dismay played in her eyes. "I cannot," she said softly, "and neither can Yamna. A very powerful *jinn* must hold the knowledge underground. I thought once it was in the old *kaid*'s *kasbah* farther up the valley. I thought that he held it to take away our authority to rule ourselves. He is a stern overlord and often demands many goats from my husband as tribute."

She resumed her spinning. "Then I saw a great and mighty stone gate made of many arches nesting one over the other. Storks sat upon the top. But now all I see when I look into the spring is dirt and old walls or heaps of goatskins. Something in my heart tells me the amulet is in the red city below the mountain. Sometimes I almost see the charm. It tries to call to me, but it is dim, as if something shadows it as when the moon passes over the sun."

Jade snapped to attention. "I know that symbol, a moon

eclipsing the sun." She reached into her trouser pocket and pulled out the charm she'd found. "I found this outside the tunnels in Azilah. It was in an owl pellet." She turned to Inez. "This symbol was also on a note left for me in our rooms after I came back from Azilah."

As she turned back and forth, her sleeve brushed the leather satchel that still hung around her neck. "I nearly forgot about this. I took this pouch from one of the rooms in the *riad*." The front was coated in dried clay from where it had been dragged through the culverts, but now a bit of dirt fell away, revealing a golden-colored glint. Jade put the charm back into her pocket, grabbed the end of her skirt, and used it as a rag to wipe away the grime. As she did, she exposed the tooled image of a full moon nearly covering the sun. The sun had been embossed with a bronze leaf, while the moon was stained black. "See? It's here, as well."

The old *kahina* reached across for the bag, so she could inspect it more closely. "Yes," she croaked. "That is the symbol of the most powerful of the *jenniya*. The one that Adam first took to wife before our Lord God made Eve. To pronounce the name of any of the people of the night is to invoke them. King Sulaiman, son of David, could do so because of his magic ring. But to pronounce *her* name could mean death." She handed the bag back to Jade. "Cover it up. Do not let her see her symbol lest she come for it."

Jade turned the bag upside down, not out of fear of mythical *jinni,* but to respect the old woman's beliefs and wishes. As she did so, she shuddered. *Lilith.* That was who Zoulikha meant. Again that woman's name came up. Jade always suspected that someone had steamed open her mother's letter to her last January in Nairobi. Someone spying on her, trying to find information. The only person with a motive to do that was Olivia Lilith Worthy. That meant the woman had known of Jade's plans to meet Inez in Tangier. *It would be like her to assume the symbol of a legendary demon whose name she bore.* And Avery had said she'd left London.

"I don't see how you can help them, Jade," said Inez after Jade explained the situation. "She should send some of her own people to find this talisman. Marrakech is a big city. You don't even know where to begin looking."

"I think I understand why they need me, Mother. The *kahina* Zoulikha is, of course, too old to make the trip. Her daughter is too valuable to risk. She's the next in line. Besides, she has a baby to care for."

"And you, on the other hand, are expendable? I don't think so. Let her send some of her men. That Bachir can go."

"You don't understand, Mother. You and I may not believe in them, but these people fear these spirits. They won't, they *can't* try to fight one."

"Well, that still doesn't mean you have to," argued Inez. "Let them get one of the French officers in Marrakech to help if they cannot."

"Do you honestly think they would listen? Or care?" Jade placed a hand on her mother's shoulder and held it there. "Besides, Mother, I made a promise to help. I do not go back on my word."

"You were probably tricked into making that promise," muttered Inez. "Always doing foolish things, rushing in to save someone. Risking yourself in that horrid war."

Jade sighed. "That's what Beverly tells me, too. But, Mother, that promise was the price for your freedom. I wouldn't have found you without Bachir's help."

Zoulikha tended to her spindle during this conversation;

her daughter made the final preparations for the meal. Inez spoke to them first.

"How is my daughter supposed to find this talisman? And if this *jenniya* is so strong, how can I be sure my daughter will be safe?" She turned to Jade. "Translate for me, please." Jade did.

"The talisman has much *baraka,* holiness, to it," answered Zoulikha. "It will try to hide lest someone unholy wear it and it loses its holiness. It will recognize a daughter of Dahia and call to Jade. Your daughter has already proven that she can control some of the night people. That is how she was able to command the ones in her prison to chew her bonds. It is how she went through the underground pipes without harm."

"And will my Jade be able to command this dark *jenniya* you speak of?"

Zoulikha shook her head. "This one is too powerful. Her symbol is very evil. But if Jade can get Elishat's amulet, she will be safe."

Inez grumbled a bit under her breath about obstinate, headstrong daughters and reached for the leather pouch. "I'm not afraid of this symbol. I want to see what it looks like." When she hefted the bag, she paused. "Feels a bit heavier than what I would expect for something this small."

Jade reached for the bag. "I hadn't noticed, but then I had it around my neck and across my chest the entire trip." She also held it in the air, testing its weight. "I see what you mean. It does feel heavy."

She drew the guard's knife from her boot sheath, ignoring her mother's startled outburst that she'd even have a place in her footwear to hide a knife. After squeezing the bag along the sides and bottom, she inserted the knife point along a seam and slit upward. "It's not one layer thick, but two. There's a secret pocket sewn in each side and, I think, another on the bottom."

Jade put down the knife and slipped her slender fingers into the bottom pouch. "I can feel at least five coins in here." She withdrew a solid gold Roman coin. *"Septimus Severus,"* she said as she read the inscription. She tipped the bag and let the other four coins spill out.

"What's in the side pockets?" asked Inez. "More gold?" She reached for the coins and inspected them.

Jade felt inside the narrow pouch. "Not gold, but something else that might be worth killing for." She pulled out a small paper bundle and sliced it open, exposing a dark reddish-brown brick. "Monsieur Deschamp claims you've been smuggling hashish, Mother. I think I found it."

CHAPTER 15

*Amazigh life has a rhythm and structure to it. There is order in irrigating
the field, a job regulated by the village sheik who knows the landholdings
of each family. There is similar harmony and order within the house,
women generally ruling the domestic arena. This structure is mirrored
by the loom and the rhythm is echoed by the act of weaving.*

—The Traveler

IF JADE HAD ANY HESITATION about assisting the Berbers before, it vanished when she saw the hashish. Their fates were
somehow bound together. She didn't know who Patrido
de Portillo worked for, but he was involved. It was a start.
Talking about it wouldn't make her mother happy, but Jade
couldn't let that stop her.

"I'll leave tomorrow morning," Jade said first in Arabic,
then in English for her mother's benefit. Immediately both
Zoulikha and Inez protested her decision, the old *kahina* for
practical reasons.

"You are not ready, Jade," Zoulikha said. "Your mules
must rest. Bachir must rest. *You* must rest. You have *baraka,*
but it is not enough. There is much I must teach you." She
motioned to her daughter to serve some food. Yamna, who
had just resumed her weaving at the great loom, rose and
filled two bowls with steamed couscous topped with chunks
of onions and cucumbers and something that looked like

159

eggplant seasoned with cumin. She handed the first bowl to Inez.

"How do I tell her thank you?" asked Inez.

"In Arabic, you say *shukran*." Jade repeated the word to Yamna as she took the second bowl.

"Shukran," said Inez. She looked at the bowl in confusion, uncertain how she should eat this. "There's no fork," she whispered to Jade.

"Use your right hand, Mother. Never use your left. It's considered unclean. And remember to say *besmellāh* before you begin." Jade had only had a little practice herself with this style of eating, but she managed to roll a bit of vegetable into a ball of couscous and pop it into her mouth after first saying the blessing word. Her mother, to Jade's surprise, deftly rolled up a tidy ball of the steamed grains as if she'd done so all her life.

"It's very good," said Inez. Jade agreed and passed on their praises to Yamna. "Are you not eating?"

Yamna explained that they would all share in a large meal that evening, but knew their guests would be hungry now. Then, satisfied that everyone was well served with more hot mint tea, she returned to her loom, her daughter now asleep at her feet.

Jade watched the younger woman pass the wool by hand through the warp strands. Then she raised the heddle, a rod balanced on stones on either side of the loom, to raise the alternate warp threads, and passed the wool through in the opposite direction. Her dexterity spoke of long practice from an early age, the rhythm second nature. Most of the strands were brown and white, but now Yamna began to run a red stripe through them. Jade recalled the stripes she'd seen on Bachir's cloak and the eyelike design in the center back.

Zoulikha looked up from her spinning and studied Jade's interest. "Weaving is our life," she said. "We have a saying: Life is a loom, and God holds the threads. And when a woman has a baby, we tell her that her weaving has been granted happiness."

"What is the symbol on the back of your cloaks?" asked Jade.

Yamna nodded to the bird sitting in the cage nearby. "It is the eye of the partridge. It keeps watch against evil." She pointed towards some designs on the grain bin. "The sheaves of grain represent fertility. The design from the *kasbah* roof means 'fortress,' or 'strength.' " She looked across to her mother and smiled.

Jade caught the glance exchanged between them as she ate another ball of couscous and onion. *Looks like my education has already begun.*

"Finish eating," Zoulikha said, "and we will walk."

Jade quickly downed her food, licked her fingers clean, and rose. Her mother, not knowing what had been said since Jade hadn't translated, did the same. From the look on her face, Jade could see she had no intention of letting her daughter out of her sight.

"What are we doing?" asked Inez.

"Taking a walk, Mother. Care to join us?" It was a rhetorical question at best, and Jade didn't wait for the obvious answer. Instead she gave a hand to Inez before she crossed over to Zoulikha and assisted the old woman to her feet.

Outside, Jade was once again struck by the efficiency with which the village scaled the rocky mountainside, making use of unfarmable land. Now from this height, she also noted the breathtaking beauty of their valley. A stream wended its way a hundred feet below, carrying snowmelt from the higher peaks. As it meandered in the more level plain, it watered their flocks and crops. As far as there was a water channel, there grew a verdant belt like a living green ribbon.

An orchard of date palms and olive trees flourished on the near bank next to the rocky slope. Silver birch shimmered in between, forming a barrier against icy blasts. Across the water grew more crops, barley and corn among them, right up to the twisted and faulted layers of rock. Narrow irrigation channels cut across the fields at each level, ready to service even the higher terraces. She couldn't imagine what life was like here in the harshness of winter, but right now, it seemed to be a garden spot.

"Come," said Zoulikha. She led the way along a dirt path to the village center. They stopped first in a small, sheltered courtyard where a woman sat on the ground next to a long coil of clay. The new pot grew as she added coil upon coil, like a snake winding around on itself. Next to one bare foot sat a fired length of clay, painted to resemble a snake. Jade noticed the snake's tail was broken. "This lady is Fatma," said Zoulikha.

Zoulikha greeted Fatma in their native language. The woman immediately got up and hurried inside her house, emerging with a teapot and the ingredients for mint-flavored tea. "The snake," explained Zoulikha while the potter fetched cups, "keeps watch against evil. It protects her pots so they do not break when they are fired." She motioned to the ground. "Let us sit."

Fatma returned and poured hot water into a beautifully crafted pot and added the usual handful of tea leaves, a huge dollop of honey, and several sprigs of mint. She did not look up at any of her guests, even when Zoulikha introduced them and inquired about her pottery making, translating everything for Jade's benefit. Jade, in turn, translated into English for her mother, and so the conversation progressed slowly.

"I am worried about these pots," said Fatma. "I think they might break when I fire them. Already the people who fear salt are making mischief. My snake lost his tail last week."

"It is not his tail that strikes at evil," replied Zoulikha. "Do not fear."

They sipped tea for a while, and Jade twice caught the potter's sidewise looks at her and her mother; curious but afraid to make eye contact. *Afraid I might have the evil eye, I suppose.* Towards the end of the visit, the old *kahina* spoke softly to Fatma and the potter relaxed, then nodded emphatically.

"I have told her you are here to help us," Zoulikha explained. "I said we will hold a *haïdous* for you tomorrow. It is a creation dance."

They made their good-byes and walked farther down to another house. Zoulikha announced herself at the door and ushered Jade and Inez inside. Once again, a pot of mint tea, the mark of good manners in any household, came out. This time the conversation dwelt on the spinning and the innumerable knots that showed up in the wool.

They went from house to house, each place with its own concerns. The flat loaves of bread burnt too quickly, or a nanny goat gave less milk than before. Jade drank so much tea, she didn't think she could face another cup no matter how much honey or loaf sugar was put in it.

"I think I'm going to be sick," she whispered to her mother after her eleventh cup, "if I don't explode first."

"You don't need to drink all of it to be polite," replied Inez. "Our hostess, Zoulikha, only takes a sip, but I've noticed it's polite to slurp it and make noise. You should have done that."

Jade groaned and excused herself to find a secluded rock pile outside of the village. Leave it to her mother to catch all the nuances of polite society even in the mountains.

"You will sleep tonight, Jade," said Zoulikha when Jade returned. "Tomorrow we will show you the springs."

They returned to Yamna's home, where she was getting ready to serve a *tajine,* a traditional stew named for the pot it was cooked in. Her husband, Mohan, had returned from the fields and sat outside the door. Jade noticed that most of the village men left much of the village, especially the hearth and the town's well, as the women's domain, preferring instead to sit together in a sort of central plaza when their work in the fields was done. She wondered why Mohan didn't join the men, but assumed he preferred his own threshold and knew his meal would soon be ready.

Zoulikha led Jade and Inez to the well where she drew a bucket of water from its depth, and ladled some over their hands before doing the same to her own. "Come," she said as she gazed at the setting sun slipping behind the western wall of their valley. "We will eat and talk of unimportant things so as not to disturb our digestion."

They returned to find another, much older man talking to Mohan. The newcomer wore a white turban that matched his short, snowy beard.

"This is my husband, Izemrasen," said Zoulikha. "We often join Yamna for our meals. My husband wants to see his granddaughter, Lallah."

They sat on woven rugs around a central platter of flatbread and a large but shallow clay dish with a tall conical lid. Yamna removed the lid to reveal a delicious-smelling concoction of lamb, onion, apricots, and dates. Once again, the scent of cumin tickled Jade's nose. Everyone took chunks of flatbread in their right hand and used it to scoop out portions of the stew to eat. Izemrasen offered choice bits to little Lallah, who sat in her grandfather's lap. The little girl ate very daintily while her large blue eyes took in everything Jade did.

"Your daughter is beautiful," said Jade to Yamna and Mohan.

Mohan called to the child, who toddled quickly around to her papa, arms outstretched. He sat her on his lap with her back to Jade and fed her. His affection for the little girl was evident, and Jade smiled. For some reason, she'd assumed a girl child would not be as welcome as a boy. This was one time she was glad to be wrong.

As Zoulikha promised, they spoke only of insignificant things: the food, Jade and Inez's clothing, the weather. No mention was made of Inez's or Jade's recent imprisonments, the mysterious leather pouch with gold and drugs, or the *kahina*'s missing amulet. After they finished the *tajine* and several cups of mint tea, Yamna served a platter of sugared almonds and dates. As soon as she set it out, a familiar voice called from without. *Bachir*.

"God's blessings on this house," he said in Tashelhit as Yamna translated into Arabic for Jade's benefit. Izemrasen welcomed Bachir and bade him enter and sit down. "We will speak French again?" Bachir said, this time in French. Jade saw that he wore a fresh, clean *djellaba* under his striped robe, and he smelled of fresh spices and cedarwood. He smiled briefly, almost shyly, at everyone in the room except for Yamna and Mohan. He avoided looking directly at the former and nodded only perfunctorily to the latter.

Lallah giggled and squirmed in her father's lap. Zoulikha also welcomed Bachir inside and made room for him between herself and her husband, but the old sheik excused himself to return to his own home, motioning to Zoulikha to stay longer. Yamna handed Bachir a cup of mint tea while Mohan scowled.

"Do you speak French every night?" Jade asked in French after Izemrasen had gone.

Yamna took over as spokesperson for the household and answered in Arabic, giving a nod to her mother. "Mother does not often have time to learn. But my husband and I try to learn as often as we can, with Bachir's help."

Bachir explained. "I fought in the war with a Moroccan regiment. We fought in the Sus," he added, using the term for the area south of the Atlas Mountains. He pulled aside his outer robe and revealed a Croix de Guerre pinned underneath on his knee-length, homespun *djellaba*.

"It looks like your medal, Jade," remarked Inez. While no one understood her English, both Zoulikha and Bachir caught the implications in Inez's gestures as she pointed first to the medal, then to Jade.

"I, too, served with the French in the War," said Jade. "I drove an ambulance for the wounded in France."

Bachir translated for everyone, and Zoulikha smiled. "Ah, this is where death visited you," she said.

"Bonjour," piped Lallah during the ensuing silence. Mohan kissed his daughter and fed her another sugared date as a reward for her cleverness.

"Blessings on this house," called a woman from outside. "Zoulikha *kahina,* I need your help. My son is sick. There is a *jinn* in his stomach and it has entered my head."

Zoulikha struggled to her feet, Jade and Yamna assisting her. "Yamna, you stay here and learn," said her mother. "You already know the cures for this trouble. Jade will come with me."

The old woman gathered up a bag woven in myriad designs from finely spun wool. Jade recognized the partridge eye, the zigzagging snake, and the handprint, but the central print grabbed her attention. It resembled a stick woman made of a triangle for the body with her arms upraised and a horn or crescent moon on her circular head. Jade had seen it before in a study of ancient history in college. It was a symbol for Astarte, a key goddess of the Phoenicians. Suddenly several similar lessons flashed into her mind. Dido supposedly became a goddess after her death, one closely associated with Astarte. It made sense. A culture that honored this ancient queen would honor even the symbols tied to her. Just who were these Imazighen? Was the speculation that they were the remains of ancient Phoenicians true? Or had they simply lived in close enough contact with the Phoenicians, trading together, that they exchanged cultural ideas as well as goods?

The woman with the sick child glanced sideways at Jade. She remembered not to make direct eye contact until Zoulikha explained her presence. This was not a woman that Jade had met during her afternoon tour. A few "ahs" and nods from the woman told Jade that she'd be tolerated at least, if not openly accepted. She followed the two Berber women through the quiet streets to a home at the far end and down one terrace. The boy lay on a sleeping mat in a corner, moaning and gripping his stomach.

As Zoulikha questioned the mother and then translated both the questions and the responses into Arabic for Jade, Jade managed to pick up a few snippets of Tashelhit, words like "husband," "son," and "dates." Jade surmised that the boy suffered primarily from stuffing himself with too many dates. Zoulikha made a brew of mostly mint leaves and gave it to the boy to drink. Then she turned her attention to the mother's headache.

From her pouch she took out a small square of cloth and poured a handful of eucalyptus seeds into it. She brought the four corners together and twisted the cloth until she made a tight ball. Next she rubbed the ball of seeds into the woman's hand, releasing the seeds' essential oils. Finally, after pouring the seeds back into a jar and returning them to her pouch, she handed the cloth to the woman and instructed her to inhale the fragrance on the cloth and in her hands.

By the time Jade returned with Zoulikha, Bachir had gone. Yamna offered more tea, but Jade declined, feeling she'd float away if she drank more. Zoulikha came to her rescue. "Our guests must sleep now. Tomorrow will be full of many preparations."

Zoulikha kissed her daughter and granddaughter goodbye and led Jade and Inez through the village to the *kasbah*. While this four-turreted building lacked the size and majesty of a great city's *kasbah*, which might house an entire village, its stark severity carried its own dignity. They passed through a smaller portal in the closed wooden gate and made the usual set of turns, which made the fortress more defensible.

"The village stores its grain here," explained Zoulikha.

Once past the twists, they crossed through a narrow alley and another gateway into an open courtyard the size of a moderately large dance hall. An upraised platform ran the length of one inner wall. At the far end of the courtyard, Zoulikha turned right to lead them up a flight of stairs, but Inez stopped her with a respectful touch on the old woman's arm.

"Jade, please tell our hostess that I can find my way now. I'd hate for her to stay away from her husband any longer on our account."

Zoulikha smiled, her wrinkles creasing up as Jade translated. *"Shukran,"* she said.

"Do you and your husband live here all alone?" asked Jade. "Why don't Yamna and Mohan join you? Then your husband could see Lallah more often."

Zoulikha shook her head. "But then he'd also see Mohan more often." With that, she wished God's blessing on them for the night, turned, and went to her own quarters to the left of the courtyard.

Now Inez took over as guide and led Jade up a narrow flight of steps. The stairs went straight, turned a sharp left, and went up three more steps to a short landing and a T junction. From there one could either go down three steps and proceed ahead to a suite of rooms, or turn left again and continue up. Inez went down the steps and ahead into a receiving room off which was a corner closet-sized room and three larger chambers.

"That is the latrine," Inez said, pointing to the closet.

Jade peeked inside and saw a low shelf around the outer walls with a hole in the middle. "It's like the ones we saw in some of the old castles in Europe," remarked Jade. "Very clever."

Two of the other rooms were bare. The third contained brightly colored floor rugs and two sleeping mats woven in black and brown stripes. In the center of the room, a large coal-filled brazier sent out heat and light.

"Cozy," said Jade. Her eyes brightened when she saw her camera bag. "Oh, good. It wasn't lost. I can take pictures in the village tomorrow." She settled herself on the mat nearest the bag and took off her boots, while her mother stretched out on the other mat.

If this room lacked the hominess that came from regular

inhabitants, it did offer privacy and the warm fire, which someone had thoughtfully kept going during the day to warm the room against the night cold. Jade took out her notebook and pencil. She needed a moment to gather her thoughts before discussing their situation with her mother, and her notebook seemed to provide the best distraction. She jotted down a few impressions and sketches, then closed her book and set it on her lap. Finally, alone with her mother and ready to talk, Jade could bring her up to date on all the events in Tangier and Marrakech.

"I certainly find it hard to believe that Patrido Blanco de Portillo is involved in any way," Inez finally said. "He is a man of impeccable manners and breeding."

"So was the kaiser," countered Jade. "That didn't stop him from waging war on half the world." Her mother didn't reply. "All I'm asking, Mother, is that you think for a moment with an open mind. Is there anything that you can recall seeing or hearing that might help us figure out not only who else is behind this outrage, but also why they have targeted you? Perhaps if you tell me what you know about your fellow passengers, it might help."

"Surely you don't suspect any of them?"

"Mother, we didn't suspect de Portillo either, but *he* is a smuggler. Someone left a note for you with my name on it. Who else but one of the other passengers would know my name? And didn't you say I apologized in the note? Who else but someone at breakfast would know you were perturbed with me?"

Inez sighed and ticked off a list of people on her fingers. "You met several of them already. Don de Portillo, the Kennicots, and the Tremaines. The Tremaines came over from America. The others embarked in London along with

Mr. Bennington and his elderly aunt. I met the captain, of course."

"Is that all?" Jade started to write their names in her book, then stopped when her mother didn't present anyone new in the list.

"Well, those are all that *I* spent time with from when the boat left England. I met others coming from America, but several passengers got off in England. I shouldn't think they would be of interest here."

"And you didn't meet anyone from steerage?" Jade asked. Inez's raised brows answered that foolish question.

"Tell me about these people, please. Start with the Kennicots."

"Jade, how can you suspect them? They are missionaries."

"So they say."

Inez released an exasperated sigh. "If you insist. I don't know what church they represent, if that's what you mean. But they are very devout in their own way."

"Meaning?"

"They held prayer services every evening in one of the ship's parlors."

"You went to one?"

Inez pulled back in shock. "You know perfectly well, Jade, that I am very devoted to our Catholic faith."

Making it all the more wonder that they associated with you, a known Papist. "But you never saw one of these prayer meetings or noticed who attended regularly?"

"I saw some passengers come and go to it when I took my evening stroll around the deck." She closed her eyes to conjure up a memory without the distraction of her present quarters. "I believe many of the second-class passengers and some of the staff attended regularly, but I never actually met any of them. I don't recall seeing Mr. Bennington attend."

"What about his aunt?"

"Oh, no. Miss Bennington suffered far too much from seasickness. I saw her only once at table with us, and once she took a turn around the deck. Otherwise her nephew sent for trays and dined with her in her room. He would stroll on the deck sometimes in the early morning and evening, poor young man. So pale. Never outside enough, and so used to whispering to his aunt that it became a habit with him, even with us."

"Who else attended?" asked Jade, unimpressed by Bennington's attention to his rich aunt. The prospect of an inheritance had a way of increasing devotion in people.

"I believe the Tremaines came on occasion. They are a pleasant enough young couple, but slightly common. So much slang. Mr. de Portillo seemed fond of them."

This news piqued Jade's interest. "Really," she mumbled to herself, remembering that the planted note in the room had seemed to be signed by Libby Tremaine. Before she could press her mother further on this association, Inez took another avenue of thought.

"I did meet one perfectly charming lady when the boat docked in London. She came on board looking for a Mr. Buttersmythe. So disappointed to find he wasn't on board, but she was charming, very elegant, very refined."

Everything I'm not. "You know perfectly well I don't enjoy meeting such people, Mother." Jade idly worked her pencil through her right-hand fingers.

"But you would have liked her. We chatted for a short while before she left. Now that I think on it, you have a com-

mon acquaintance. She knows Lord and Lady Dunbury. At
least she mentioned them."

"What was her name?"

"I believe she said she was a relation to your young pilot
David. Her name was Lilith Worthy."

CHAPTER 16

The Amazigh symbols are so important that the women mark them on their hands and feet with henna, a substance with its own baraka. Finally a symbol identifying a woman's clan or one that gives her special protection might be permanently tattooed in blue on a woman's chin, cheek, or forehead.

—The Traveler

"LILITH WORTHY!" The words exploded from Jade's mouth. "David's murderous mother was on the boat with you? Why didn't you tell me before?"

"Jade! Mind your tongue," scolded her mother. "She stepped on board in London, and you were only interested in the people that came to Tangier with me. Besides," she added, "you told me Mrs. Worthy's name was Olivia. I presumed this was his aunt."

Jade shook her head. "No. Her full name is Olivia Lilith Worthy, and she's evil to the bone. She had her own husband murdered."

Inez looked at her daughter with exasperation, her lips pursed, her brow furrowed. "That is preposterous. How can you speak of David's own mother that way? She might have been your mother-in-law."

"Praise the Lord for great favors she's not," said Jade. "And it isn't preposterous. I told you and Dad about this already." Then Jade remembered her mother had taken offense at Jade's portrayal of her dead beau's mother and left the room before Jade could go into detail. "You'll have to trust me on that, Mother."

Inez fidgeted with the sleeping rug. "From what you told me, David was a fine young man. I'm sorry for your loss, Jade. He would have been a good husband, I'm sure. But it's time you put him behind you and accepted someone else. You need to marry and settle down."

Jade tossed her pencil in the air and let it fall in a display of frustration. "Don't start on that again, Mother. I have a good job. I'm perfectly happy."

"Gallivanting around Africa, chasing wild animals? It's dangerous."

"It's exciting. It's adventurous. Remember adventure, Mother?"

"It's not appropriate for a young woman of your age. You should be married."

"Like Libby Tremaine?" Jade let out a derisive snort. "Now, there's a wonderful example for me. She flirts with anything in trousers." She shifted her overskirt and revealed her own pair underneath. "Would probably chase me if she saw me dressed like this."

Inez waved a hand in a dismissive gesture. "I grant you she is a silly girl and you're not, thank heavens. But why are you so obstinately against getting married?"

Jade stood up and started pacing the floor. "Because marriage changes people, at least the women." She turned and met her mother's gaze. "Consider what happened to you."

Inez shuddered. "I am aghast that you would say such a thing. How dare you speak to me that way."

Jade hurried over, knelt down, and sat back on her heels

beside her mother. "Mother, I love you dearly, but it's true. Remember when you and Dad first took me to Spain? I was only five. I saw you dance the flamenco one night. I was supposed to be in bed, but I crept over to the railing to look down at the party below and listen to the music." Jade's eyes glowed and a smile played across her lips as she recalled the scene. "You were wonderful, your skirts flaring, your heels clicking out the rhythm. You have no idea what an impression that made on me. For years I used to practice at night after you put me to bed. I'd swish my nightgown and tap my bare heels on the floor."

Jade placed one hand on her mother's arm. "I wanted to be like you, Mother. Maybe that's why I always got into trouble. I was trying to emulate the woman I saw that night. The woman you still are if you'd just look inside."

Her mother sat silent beside her, her eyes wide at Jade's revelation. Finally she spoke. "That's foolish. I'm a Spaniard. I danced a Spanish dance. What is so unusual about that?"

Jade shook her head. "It's *how* you danced, Mother. You had passion and a zest for life that night. You know, Dad told me once that you used to dance with the Gypsies. That's how he met you. What happened, Mother? Now you host boring dinner parties and sit on committees with tiresome, self-righteous busybodies. You deserve better than that."

"A wife has responsibilities, Jade."

"Yes, but that doesn't mean a wife must become tedious." Inez turned her head aside, and Jade instantly regretted her choice of words. "Mother, let's not fight. I am who I am partly because of you, partly because of Dad and the ranch hands, and partly because of that horrid war. Maybe I'm also the way I am because of my ancestry, *our* ancestry. If Zoulikha's story is true, it could explain your youth, as well as mine. Maybe it's why I love Africa so much. Anyway, I have an interesting job. I can travel. Traveling helps when the war intrudes in my mind."

Inez kept her head turned away. "But your father misses you at home." She sniffed once, as though she were fighting back tears.

Jade stroked her mother's back in a gentle caress. *And you do, too, but you're too proud to admit it.* "I get home. I'll get home again. Don't worry about that, Mother." Jade stood and extended her hands. "Come on. We're in Morocco in a *kasbah* having our own adventure, frightening as it's been. Let's go up to the roof and look out at the night."

Inez turned around and gave a weak smile. "You go on, dear. I'm tired. I think I'll just go to sleep."

"I'll stay with you until you do."

After her mother dozed off, Jade picked up her notebook and a pen, scooted closer to the coals, and poured out on paper everything she could remember seeing in Marrakech and in the village. If she hoped writing down her thoughts would help cleanse her mind and let her sleep, she was sadly mistaken.

She looked at her mother, lying on her side on the rug, her beautiful aristocratic face softened in sleep. *How can one woman be so wonderful and so exasperating at the same time?* Jade felt an ache in her chest and realized it was pity for her mother. She knew her father missed the Inez of yore, as well. She could read it in his eyes when he watched her take one of the horses through its exercises. *When this is over, I'm going to write to Dad and tell him to whisk Mother away somewhere. They could ride down into the Grand Canyon and camp with the Havasupai Indians.* The plan gave Jade some peace of mind, and she decided to try for sleep herself.

For more than half the night she tossed and turned on her mat, chasing sleep and Lilith Worthy. Ever since Jade first went to the Protectorate in search of David Worthy's half-brother, she'd found herself treading on his mother's shadow. But that's all Jade ever managed to uncover, a shadow. *A shadow eclipsing the sun.* The woman operated through others, people like Roger Forster, whom she hired to murder her husband, Gil, before he could find his bastard son. She kept her own lily-white fingers clean back in London, hiding her criminal existence under the veneer of an aristocratic widow in a high-end London neighborhood.

Inez hadn't recognize Lilith's name, but even if she had, Inez would not have been suspicious of Lilith's behavior. In her mother's mind, good breeding and manners made up for everything else. And now it seemed likely that Lilith had spied on her mother long enough to set up plans for her here in Morocco. Patrido Blanco de Portillo was involved, but who else had Lilith hired to do her dirty work? The Tremaines? The Kennicots? Someone in steerage?

Jade gave up trying to sleep. She tugged on her boots and crept up the winding stairs until she reached the corner rampart tower. From there she stepped out onto the flat roof and leaned on the rampart wall. The gibbous moon threw its pallid light over the *pisé* walls, transforming them to a warm golden red. She felt as if she'd stepped into a Maxfield Parrish painting and she was the girl on the wall.

The cold mountain air cleared her head and allowed her to sort out her questions. The bigger question in her mind was what in tarnation was Lilith up to now? That she still smuggled drugs seemed obvious based on the hashish hidden in the pouch. But what about those ancient Roman coins? Jade's pouch contained five of them. Judging by the number of bags she had seen, Lilith's people must have uncovered a hidden treasure trove of them, and Lilith wanted to get them out and back to her in London without anyone knowing. Or was the unknown man in charge of operations here doing that under her nose? That seemed dangerous and consequently unlikely. Did de Portillo know about them?

Yet Lilith could have done all this and more, and Jade would never have been the wiser. She and her mother would have gone over to Andalusia after a few days' tour. So there must be more to that other woman's plan.

The underlying answer came to Jade as she stared up at the thick belt of stars overhead, twinkling like the glowing coals in her room: revenge and a chance to remove Jade from any future interference.

And Mother was the bait. That tore it. As much as Jade objected to someone trying to kill her, she was almost accustomed to it by now. After all, several of the kaiser's air squadron had tried bombing most of the ambulance drivers at least once. But her mother? That went beyond good taste in her estimation.

"You want a fight, Lilith? Be careful what you wish for. It might come true," she whispered to the moon. She'd go back to Marrakech, find that missing amulet, round up de Portillo and whomever he worked for, and clear herself and her mother. Then, she'd head to England and, with Avery Dunbury's help, root out Lilith from wherever she was hiding and kick her drug-smuggling fanny from there to perdition.

Deciding on some course of action, however vague, seemed to settle Jade's mind. She returned to her room and drifted off to a dreamless sleep beside her mother.

If Jade thought making preparations meant getting together supplies for the return trip, she was mistaken. The *kahina* delegated that task to Bachir and Mohan. Instead, after shooting a roll of film around the village, Jade found herself sitting on a low wall near the well, learning the use of various herbs, the meaning of different symbols, and several words of power. As the afternoon wore on, Jade felt as if her head was spinning. Her mother sat nearby, her main interest being Jade's health.

"I don't understand why you are trying to learn all this nonsense," scolded Inez when they finally had a respite from lessons. "It's heathen nonsense."

"Now, Mother, you know as well as I do that you used to steep willow bark in hot water and take a spoonful for a headache. Using these herbs is no different. It's natural medicine. Zoulikha is a healer. And as far as these symbols and *jinni* go, I don't believe in them any more than you do, but they are obviously important to these people. I need Zoulikha to have confidence in me, and if learning this helps, then so be it. Besides," she added as she studied her mother's proud features, "didn't those Gypsies cast spells and read fortunes? I bet you had your fortune told once, right? Come on, Mother, admit it." Jade grinned. "Do they use crystal balls or tea leaves?"

Her mother blushed and looked away. "I may have visited them a time or two, though I'm certain your father has embellished the story beyond recognition. But this is a new age, Jade, and I want more for you than running amuck in the wilderness."

"Oh, I'm perfectly capable of running amuck in civilized situations, as well," said Jade with a playful laugh. "And I won't crack too many heads doing it. Of course, you can't make an amulet without breaking a few eggs." She laughed again at her own pun, stopping when she saw her mother's frown. "Oh, don't be so serious, Mother. We're here in this beautiful village, escaping death. Have some fun. You could learn this, too. Admit it, Mother. You're just dying to go to some of those artistic snobs taking over Taos and say 'Five in your eye' at them. By the time I get back with that amulet, you can have memorized a whole storehouse of curses. I heard one this morning. 'Damn you, oh son of ten men and a dog as the eleventh.' Isn't that wonderful?"

"Jade!"

"It gets better, Mother. You can also call someone a son of a woman who makes water in the street in front of others."

Inez put her hands to her face. "Where did you hear these horrid words?"

"I think Bachir made Mohan mad."

"Well, they are awful, and just what did you mean when you said 'by the time I get back with the amulet'? You're not leaving without me, young lady."

"You cannot come with me, Mother. I can't do what I need to do and also watch out for you."

Zoulikha returned to the well with Yamna and little Lallah before Inez could make a retort. All three wore ornate headdresses of finely woven green and gold fabric wrapped turban style and held in place by multiple silver chains draped across the forehead. Coins and small charms hung from the chains and jingled as they walked, to Lallah's delight.

"Come," Zoulikha said, "it is time to prepare for the feast. All the village joins us, happy that the amulet will be returned."

Jade was thinking that maybe they shouldn't count on their amulets before they were hatched, but kept the thought to herself, wondering what would happen if she didn't find it.

Yamna handed Lallah over to Inez, who petted and cooed over the pretty child, while Yamna drew water from the well and poured some over Zoulikha's and Jade's hands. Then she motioned for Jade to do the same for her as well as for Lallah and Inez.

Purified, they returned to the village where everyone had gathered in the *kasbah*'s courtyard. Many of the men wore their best *djellabas* and ornately embroidered slippers, but the women were the most impressive. They all sported their dowries in the form of chains of gold and silver across their foreheads and wore necklaces of fat amber beads that hung low over their chests. Every one of them had decorated their slippered feet and palms with intricate patterns in henna so that they appeared to wear ornate gloves and socks.

They'd also outdone themselves cooking. Even before Jade saw the food, the enticing aromas of cumin, lamb, chicken, onions, and bread greeted her. Platters of couscous topped with cucumbers and other savory vegetables sat amid a wide variety of *tajine*. Heaps of flatbread and platters of dates and sugared almonds rounded out the feast. Over all was the scent of mint, crushed and steeped with green tea and clumps of sugar for the ever-present beverage. Jade had just about resigned herself to enduring more tea when Yamna presented her with a cup of sweet white liquid.

"It is almond milk," said Yamna, "ground almonds mixed with goat's milk, sugar, and orange-flower water. It is a drink for special times."

"*Besmellāh,*" Jade said, taking the cup. She took a taste, steeling herself for some horrid concoction, but found it to be delicious. It reminded her of marzipan candy. "Thank you." They feasted together, and Jade was pleased to see that her mother actually seemed to enjoy the festivities. Twice Jade caught her laughing at something Yamna said, which made her wonder if her mother wasn't perhaps picking up parts of the language after all. She hoped so; it would make her stay here, however brief, more endurable.

Jade also watched Mohan and Bachir. That the two men did not get along was clear to her. She wondered what their story was and decided to ask Zoulikha at the first opportunity.

The meal completed, a few of the men went to the raised platform and picked up a type of drum called a *bendir*. It amounted to little more than a circular wooden frame with what appeared to be a goatskin stretched over it. They formed a small circle on the dais, sat down, and waited. The remaining men and women formed a ring shoulder to shoulder around the courtyard. Several small fires in the middle lit the circle. Jade was initially surprised to see men standing so close to women until she recalled that these people held their own traditions, often distinctly different from the Arabs in Marrakech.

Uncertain what she should do, Jade waited by her mother, Zoulikha, Yamna, and Lallah. No one moved, no one spoke. Suddenly Yamna raised her chin to the night sky and let out a piercing ululation, a cry that was both joyous and stirring. It ripped through the blackness in a long series of *lu lu lu*s that grew from the back of the throat and swelled into a battle charge. The cry made the hairs on Jade's arms tingle and she half expected to see an army swell out of the houses.

Immediately after the call, the men started to drum and chant. As they did, the other men and the women in the chain began to rock to and fro. After a time, as though on an unseen signal, the women, hennaed palms up, stepped in with tiny steps, then withdrew to the men. They repeated this several times before altering the step. Then the women quivered and sank to their knees before rising again. The men continued to rock to and fro, clapping time and chanting. The tempo didn't change, and the entire dance was very modest and dignified.

Standing beside her mother, little Lallah imitated the women's movements with all the serious deliberation a two-year-old could muster. Next to her stood Inez, rocking ever so slightly to the rhythm. Jade pretended not to notice. "What are they singing about?" she asked.

"They sing about the times of old when the Imazighen and the lion of our tribe roamed all over the *Maghreb,*" said Zoulikha. "Come, they will continue the dance to call *baraka* on you. We have other things to do."

Mohan, seeing them start to go, left the ring and took his daughter from them. "I will keep her beside me," he said, looking warily at Inez, "so that she may join the dance." Yamna nodded her agreement.

"What about you, Mother?" asked Jade. "Will you come or stay?"

Inez cast a long look at the dance. "Where are you going?"

"To a spring," said Zoulikha, "We will take bread to feed the water spirits there."

"I will stay here, then," said Inez and added quickly, "to help watch Lallah."

Yes, and perhaps dance, as well? The image made Jade smile. But she wasn't surprised at her mother's choice. The woman didn't court spirits. *Neither do I. The blasted things come to me.*

She followed the other two women by torchlight along a narrow path into the mountains. Jade stumbled and stubbed her booted feet several times in the dark and wondered how these two managed with just the thin leather slippers on their feet.

"Zoulikha," Jade began, "tell me about Bachir. Why did he make the long journey to find me? Why does Mohan dislike him?" She couldn't see their faces, but she saw Yamna's back stiffen.

"It is a difficult story," said Zoulikha after a moment's silence, "but I will tell you what I can. Bachir traveled to the south and fought in the Great War. Though the French are the newest invaders, he thought they would be strong allies later to help our people. While he was away, his mother arranged a marriage for him with a girl from a neighboring village, a granddaughter of the valley *kaid*."

Jade listened carefully, keeping an eye on Yamna's back as often as she could spare it from her own feet. The young woman walked on with a stiff, erect carriage as though this tale was difficult to endure.

"Her parents demanded a very high bride price for their daughter. Bachir's family is a fine one, but they do not have as many goats as some. Still, his mother felt this was a good alliance for her son, putting him close to a man of power and wealth." She stopped and caught her breath. Yamna turned and gave her mother her arm to assist her. Zoulikha shrugged her off and continued walking on her own.

"They were married when Bachir returned from fighting. If he did not go into the marriage with great joy, he did not oppose his mother's wishes," said Zoulikha. "But his wife died in childbirth with the baby."

"If you had been allowed by the girl's grandfather to tend to her, she would have lived," said Yamna.

"Perhaps. Perhaps not. But it is done. Bachir returned to

his parents, the grandfather blaming him for the girl's death. He is devoted to his village, so when I needed someone to bring you, he would not hear of anyone else going."

"Then why does Mohan dislike him? He argued with Bachir this morning and I don't remember him welcoming Bachir into the house yesterday. It was your husband who did that."

"My husband is a proud man," said Yamna before her mother could reply. "Lallah is very fond of Bachir, and Mohan does not like another man to take any of his daughter's affections."

Jade thought the answer came too quickly to be the complete truth. Perhaps that was all there was to it. Mohan obviously doted on his daughter, but she wondered if Mohan was protecting the child, as well. Bachir didn't seem to be a man who hurt children, but then she hadn't seen him around very many.

The opportunity to ask more questions disappeared with the soft sound of gurgling water. After about a twenty-minute walk, Jade saw the source, a bubbling spring. She noted brightly colored strips of fabric tied to the trees growing near the spring.

"We are here," said Zoulikha. "This water is sacred and the *jinni* here are at peace with our people. We will feed them to continue the peace and ask their help." She pointed to the fabric ribbons. "These are prayer offerings left by many women and men."

Zoulikha handed a round flatbread to Jade and motioned her to step forward to the little pool of water formed by a rock wall that looked too regular to be natural, and too hoary to be much newer than the mountain. There in the pool swam five little turtles. Jade obediently broke off bits of the loaf and tossed them into the pool. The turtles paddled over to the bread and nibbled.

"It is good. They accept your first gift. Now you must hold a piece for one to take from your hand."

As Jade stepped closer, torch in one hand and bread in the other, she noticed the spring emerged from a small cave. A design on the far wall caught her eye and she held the torch higher to see. Painted on the wall in red was a Barbary lion drawn in simple lines. Beside it was a handprint in white and the stick-woman figure of Astarte in red, represented as a triangle with a circular head on top and two crooked arms upraised in prayer. A crescent moon crowned her head like two horns.

"Painted by the first *kahina* to find refuge in this valley," said Zoulikha in response to Jade's unspoken question.

Jade remembered the turtles and squatted down next to the stone dam. She held out the bread just above water level and all five turtles swam over and began to feed. Several nibbled on her fingertips.

"That tickles," said Jade.

"They bless you. You have great *baraka*, Jade. Equal to our own. Sit here." She pointed to a flat stone near the pool.

Jade complied, handing her torch to Yamna, who stuck all of them in crevices along the cave's outside. Then Yamna opened up a woven pouch and took out several pots and small goat's-hair brushes. They pulled off Jade's boots and began the extensive process of decorating her feet with henna. When they finished with her feet, Zoulikha repeated the process with Jade's palms while Yamna applied some decorations to Jade's chin and forehead.

"Ouch," muttered Jade as the soft brush was replaced by a pointier stippling device for her upper forehead, just below the hairline.

The two women worked in absolute silence and the entire process took well over two hours. Zoulikha finished first and took out a strip of parchment from a hidden crevice. She mixed saffron in a bit of water, dipped a stylus into the mix and wrote some symbols on the paper. Next she put the paper into a bowl and poured a ladle of water from the spring over the paper. By now, Yamna had also finished. Jade felt relieved. Whatever the woman had done on Jade's forehead had hurt. She decidedly preferred feeding cute little pet turtles to being poked on the head.

"Drink the water," said Zoulikha as she handed the bowl to Jade.

"*Besmellāh,*" said Jade as she drank. The water had a slight tang to it from the saffron. She handed the bowl back to the old woman, who passed it on to Yamna.

Yamna took the wet parchment from the bowl's bottom and rolled it into a tiny scroll. Finally she placed the scroll in a little silver box that hung from a silver chain. A silver hand dangled below the box. Zoulikha slipped the chain around Jade's neck, leaving the box to lie atop her shirt. Jade felt for it and the comforting presence of David's ring, only to realize her mother still had the ring. An emptiness washed over her.

"You will be well protected now," the old women said. She pointed to Jade's hennaed feet. "Ash leaves and the snake guard your footsteps. The eye of the partridge is on your palms to watch for danger. Barley sheaths on your chin will keep you from eating poisonous foods. And the charm will increase the protection."

"What did you mark on my forehead?" asked Jade.

"You are the lioness. You will need the matched strength of the Barbary lion to join you. There are few left, but one keeps watch over this spring. We have put his paw print on your forehead. Three small spots below and two above. Because the print is made with five marks, it has more *baraka*."

And mother will have a conniption when she sees this. Thinking of her mother, Jade wondered if she'd actually be able to sneak off without her tomorrow.

"Have no fear," said Zoulikha when Jade asked. "Yamna will go back now and give her a cup of almond milk, but it will contain herbs. She will also spread the oil of the orange on her pillow to make her sleep. You will be gone with Mohan when she awakens." She nodded for her daughter to take a torch and return to the village.

"Mohan?" asked Jade. "Does not Bachir return with me?" She'd grown to trust the man in her own way. At least she knew his tricks.

"Mohan understands the importance of this amulet. It is his daughter's birthright. He insisted that he go. And he has been to Marrakech many times over the years to take his sister's pots and Yamna's rugs to sell in the market."

"You haven't told me yet what Elishat's amulet looks like. How will I know it?"

Zoulikha bent over and traced a two-by-three-inch rectangle in the dirt. "The talisman is a silver box, this big," she said. "On one side is the *kahina*'s hand." She raised her own hand with the fingers splayed. "On the front is the symbol of the first *kahina*." She indicated Astarte's symbol on the cave wall. "Inside is a written charm. The catch to open it is well hidden, so the box appears to be solid. Do not attempt to open it. To do so is to lose the *baraka*. Do not open the box you wear, either."

"I understand," said Jade. "I will do my best. Take good care of Mother for me. She will be worried and," she added after a moment's hesitation, "very angry."

Zoulikha grinned. "Such is the way of mothers. Their

children will always be their children no matter their age. Come, help my old bones to walk back."

"There is more to Mohan and Bachir's story than you told me, isn't there, Zoulikha?" asked Jade.

The old woman made a low hum, as though deliberating how much more to tell Jade. "Yes, there is, but it is not important to this trip."

Jade didn't press the issue any further and concentrated on keeping to the path in the torchlight. By the time Jade and Zoulikha returned to the village, the festivities had ended, and families had drifted to their own homes. Jade found her mother curled on her side in their room, sound asleep on her rug. Inez's lips twitched and her eyes darted back and forth under the closed lids.

She's dreaming. Jade wondered what her mother might dream about tonight. She hoped it was something happy *Something with Dad and the Gypsies.* Jade felt a rush of pride in her mother. She'd proven very brave throughout this affair, going so far as to attempt her own escape with a single nail. Jade draped part of the rug over her mother's back and shoulders for added warmth.

Sweet heavens, I've made a hash of this reunion with Mother. It pained Jade to always feel at odds with her. It wasn't the thought of returning to New Mexico that seemed odious, it was the role her mother wanted her to assume. *I definitely need to write to Dad, but in the meantime . . .* Jade took out her notebook and jotted a brief note to Inez, then left it by her mother's shoes where she'd be sure to find it.

Jade bent down and kissed Inez on the forehead, catching the scent of orange around her.

"Good night, Mother," she whispered. "I'll be back as soon as I can. Try to stay out of trouble while I'm gone."

CHAPTER 17

In Morocco it is the hallmark of politeness to serve any visitor hot mint tea.
A good rule of thumb: don't visit too many people in one day.

—The Traveler

YAMNA CAME FOR JADE several hours before dawn sent a glow of light over the mountains. While Jade hardly felt refreshed, she wasn't sorry to break this short night's rest. Her head throbbed behind her eyes and her temples, and her stomach churned. *Blasted dreams*. She cast an envious glance at her mother and watched her slow, deep breaths; the sleep of the innocent, or the heavily drugged.

Zoulikha waited for her outside in the village street. She handed a woman's tuniclike dress to Jade as well as an older *handira* and two brass *fibula* to hold it in place. "You will have need to dress as though you are one of us, I think." In the gloom, Jade thought she detected a faint smile on the old woman's face.

Reading the *kahina's* thoughts, Jade replied, "You said that I *am* one of you." The throbbing behind the eyes increased. *Blast it, but it hurts to talk*. Her hands shook as she took the garments from Zoulikha and a pair of low slippers from Yamna. Neither of them moved from in front of her.

"Tell me," said Zoulikha as she peered at Jade's troubled face.

Jade thought about asking what she meant, or telling her that she ate too much yesterday, but decided there was no use playing dumb with either of these two women, especially Zoulikha. The old *kahina* was too well versed in human nature.

She took a deep breath and steeled herself for the pain of talking and recollecting. "I dreamt I was in a garden of some kind, but all the flowers were arranged in rows and rows next to stones. It might have been a cemetery. I saw many . . ." She hesitated before speaking again and decided to use the euphemism preferred by the Amazigh people. "Many people who shun salt and iron. I saw a faceless woman in black. She might have been beautiful; I don't know. She seemed . . . diseased somehow."

Jade's voice dropped to a hush, filled with empathy for the pain she had witnessed in her dream, the same pain she now carried in her pounding head. "I think she cried. One tear fell, only one. But when it struck the ground, the flower there grew larger. But it was no longer a flower. It became a terrible tree, all twisted but dead. The rocks grew, as well, like walls. There was a man, at least I think he was a man. I think she seduced him because he clung to her like a lover before his body withered. Then the moon came over the sun and eclipsed it, but just before it did, I saw a silver box sticking out of the ground under the rocks. I went to reach for it, but my hand touched something else." She shuddered as she recalled the image. "I touched the shriveled corpse."

When Jade finished, she felt as though she'd been sleepwalking, just as she had in the Azilah tunnels. Only this time the urge to vomit, to purge herself of this memory, rose in her throat. Peering into the darkness, she saw that both Zoulikha and Yamna had their hands raised in front of their chests, exposing the partridge eyes painted in henna on their palms. She fought down the nausea.

"The water spirits have sent you a vision," Zoulikha said. "This dark woman is a *jenniya*, but while many of the people who shun salt and iron do not harm and some do good, there are those ruled by Shaitan, they are the *afrits*. This woman is one of his first disciples. Even her name, which we will not speak lest we summon her, means 'dark lady.' It was she who seduced Adam before Allah gave him Eve. Even now she brings death to any man she lies with."

"There is no need to speak her name to me," said Jade. "I know it already." Jade recognized the story from that first morning when Tremaine brought it up at breakfast. One of the more colorful characters who lived outside of Cimarron, New Mexico, had told it to her as a little girl. But Lilith Worthy had been a distant evil in Jade's mind that morning in Tangier when Mr. Kennicot named her as the serpent's daughter. Hearing it then hadn't affected her like last night's dream did. Now it came like a revelation from her subconscious, putting all of the evils she'd experienced since the war at this woman's feet.

Jade didn't need any mystical excuse for her dream. It made perfect sense that she'd dreamt of Lilith. The woman had been on her mind ever since Avery sent the warning in the telegram. As for the rest of the dream, she didn't very well understand it, but what dreams ever made sense? She knew the dream dealt with death which was Lilith's stock-in-trade. But while Jade didn't believe Zoulikha's claim that spirits sent it as a warning, she felt there was more to it than she knew. Whom did the shriveling corpse represent? Jade only hoped that if it *was* a warning, she'd understand it in time.

Zoulikha took some herbs from her pouch, crushed them, and dropped them into a cup of well water. "Drink this. It will help the pain."

Jade swallowed some of the concoction and recognized the bitter taste of willow bark. She downed the rest in a quick gulp and handed back the cup. *"Shukran."* Jade headed for their mounts, folded the garments, and added them into a large woven bag that hung like a pannier across her mule's rump. Next she threw in the leather pouch she'd taken from the *riad,* her compass, and a flashlight after putting in her spare dry cell. Mohan held the rope halter of his mule and hers, and Jade recognized two of the animals she'd purchased in Marrakech. Jade took one halter from Mohan and they started on foot from the village. In the dark, it was safer to lead the mules than to ride. From a distance, Jade thought she heard the coughing *harrumph* of a male lion.

Yes, well, good-bye to you, too, Izem. Watch over Mother for me.

Darkness promoted silence and neither of them spoke a word until many hours later when the sun broke over the eastern rim of the mountains. Mohan immediately stopped, pulled a prayer rug from one of his panniers, faced Mecca, and recited the morning prayers.

While he prayed, Jade said her own prayers silently, putting her mother's well-being in the Lord's hands. As an afterthought, she decided Zoulikha and Yamna could use some protection from her mother's ire once she discovered she'd been duped. How long could they keep her drugged? Probably not long enough. She opened a pannier and pulled out two loaves of flatbread and a chunk of goat's cheese. She broke the cheese in half and handed one to Mohan. They followed the simple breakfast with several pulls of water from their respective water skins.

"We can ride," said Mohan in Arabic. "We must go slow. The road is not easy."

Jade mounted up and moved in behind Mohan, who led the way through some of the remaining stands of tall cedars growing in the sheltered parts of the upper mountain, not yet cut down for firewood or ceiling beams. Spring flowers dotted the floor below, popping up through old needles in pink, yellow, white, and mauve. The scent of cedar washed over them each time their mules' hooves scraped across the forest litter.

"It is good of you to take me back to Marrakech, Mohan," said Jade. "I am sorry you had to leave Yamna and Lallah to do this."

"*Inshallah*, God willing, I must do what I can for my daughter. Lallah is a jewel dearest to my heart."

Jade smiled to think that this rough man of the mountain who worked so hard to eke out a living felt so much tenderness for a little girl. She thought of her own father, somewhere back on his mountain in New Mexico, and all the times he took her with him on the spring rides, checking on the flocks, teaching her how to track and hunt. There was something very special about the bond between a father and a daughter. An image flashed before her eyes, a distant memory aroused by the scent of cedars. It was her mother riding beside her. Jade remembered that last trip the three of them took. They camped out under the stars, laughing and seeing who could tell the tallest tale. Then later that summer, several wealthy Easterners and artists moved into Taos and Angel Fire, and Inez quit going with Jade and her father.

. . .

Why? Why would she care so much about these silly people that she would abandon her own daughter to play the role of a Spanish doña? Jade recalled the first time she noticed something seriously amiss. She was eleven and in high spirits over helping Dody, their foreman, brand the few calves from the small beef herd her dad kept along with the sheep and the horses. She came running into the ranch house, her eyes aglow with excitement, dirt smeared all over her face and britches, proudly holding her rope.

"I roped two calves from horseback, Mama," she said. "Dody said I did *real* good. He even made up one of his pis-sonnet poems about it." Without waiting, Jade had launched into the limerick. " 'Lil' Jade was as good with a lasso as any cowpoke from El Paso. When she got to ropin', the calf got to mopin', as Jade set to brandin' his a—' "

"Jade!" snapped her mother.

There had been a guest in the parlor at the time, a woman who'd recently arrived from Philadelphia. The lady had halted in midsip over her teacup and stared at Jade with horror, as if she'd seen a polecat loose in the parlor. Jade's mother sent Jade up to her room and ordered her to bathe and put on a dress. She ran up the stairs, tears streaming down her dirty face, making muddy rivulets in the grime. Didn't Mother love her anymore? Jade had expected a smile or perhaps a pat on the head for a reward, something to show that Inez was proud of her daughter's accomplishment. Jade had despised tea ever since.

She tried to focus now on her mother instead of her past sorrow. All she could see of that morning was the tired sadness on her mother's face. That's when it dawned on her. *Mother sacrificed her own freedom so that I'd have a chance to fit in.*

Inez saw that their world was changing, that the free Western spirit was giving way to city rules. Young Western ladies wanting to make their way had to do so by conforming to society and going to finishing school. It was an idea that Jade had balked at as much as a colt did a saddle. And while Jade had learned to play the role, she had bucked every chance she got, up to the day she enlisted in the ambulance unit.

The revelation shook Jade. Her tears were for Inez and the opportunities they'd lost together. All those years Jade had been trying to emulate the woman she'd watch dance in Spain, and all that time that woman was molding herself into a stranger. To give herself a moment to adjust, Jade tried to converse with Mohan. It wasn't an easy task riding behind him.

"It is good of Bachir to teach you and your family French."

Mohan shrugged. "I do not care to learn, but it is good for Lallah. It will help her to marry well. I stay with them during lessons because it is not right to leave Yamna alone with another man."

"Will Bachir tend your barley field for you while you are away?"

To Jade's surprise, Mohan shook his head so that the lock of hair hanging from behind his right ear shook violently. "My sister's husband will do it. I do not trust Bachir. He is the son of a one-eyed donkey and nine men. May his brain fly and his bladder be weakened." Mohan spat to the side to seal his curse. "He watches Yamna and has betrayed his people."

Inez bolted up from her sleeping mat, aware that something was amiss but not sure what. When she saw how bright the day was, she knew she'd overslept. *Someone slipped something into that almond milk on purpose.* Her glance fell on the note beside her shoes. Inez snatched it up and read.

"Do not worry about me, Mother. I didn't talk to any spirits last night, just some harmless turtles. I'll be back as soon as I can. I love you, and I'm proud of you. No other woman I know could have endured what you did and not caved in."

Jade is gone! Immediately, Inez ran from the *kasbah,* looking for Zoulikha. She spotted Yamna first, sitting outside of her house, turning a hand stone to grind grain into flour for the day's bread. Lallah played at her feet with her spinning shuttle.

Inez had no time for the charming scene. She stormed up to Yamna and demanded in English, "Where is Jade?"

Yamna might not have understood the first part of the question, but she definitely understood "Jade" and the imperious tone of Inez's voice. She rose gracefully, scooped up Lallah, and motioned for Inez to follow. She led her to Zoulikha, who was ministering to a woman suffering from morning sickness.

Inez paced in front of the doorway, waiting for the old woman to finish her task. The instant Zoulikha stepped over the threshold, Inez said one word. "Jade!" She punctuated it by stabbing her index finger to the ground next to her. She wanted her daughter here, now.

Zoulikha motioned for Yamna and Lallah to return home and shook her head. "Jade," she said as a softer echo of Inez's demand, and pointed to the north. "Marrakech." Then she followed it with "Inez," and gestured politely to the village. The meaning was clear. Jade had gone back to Marrakech and she was to remain here like so much excess baggage. Not while she had anything to say about it.

Inez stormed off through the village to one of the unoc-
cupied houses where she'd first seen her donkey stabled. The
little beast was still there, placidly chewing on some straw.
His soft ears went straight up, and he paused in midchew
when Inez grabbed a small saddle blanket and tossed it over
his back. She looked in vain for one of the little leather saddles and decided she didn't need it. *I rode bareback as a girl. I
can do it again.*

By now, Zoulikha had caught up with her, Bachir following fast in her wake. Inez barged past them, dragging behind her the sad little donkey, braying piteously at having his
breakfast rudely interrupted.

"*La la*, no, no," they called in Arabic.

Inez ignored them, hiked up her now sullied and ruined green dress to nearly indecent heights, and proceeded to
swing a leg over the beast. Once atop the donkey, she pointed
to herself, then north, making her meaning very clear. She
intended to follow Jade and she intended to go now.

Zoulikha's old shoulders sagged in defeat. She nodded
but came close enough to block the way. "You need food,"
she said in Arabic, pointing to her mouth, "and water." She
imitated drinking. "And Bachir." She pointed to the man
next to her.

Inez considered her chances on her own, decided they
weren't very good, and agreed. "Food and water," she said,
repeating their words. "And Bachir."

Mohan wouldn't elaborate on his statement, leaving Jade to
rethink all the past events. Bachir, a Berber from the Atlas,
just happened to know how to find the Azilah tunnels. He
entered those haunted tunnels, ostensibly to protect her with
salt, but that just happened to coincide with the dead man's

removal. Bachir also just happened to find out where her mother was hidden, and he brought her to his village rather than to the church. He also admitted that he needed more money to pay a bride price.

Zoulikha said that some of the women had reported their dowry bracelets were missing. Could Bachir have stolen those bracelets and the *kahina*'s amulet to sell? What was it he said when she'd asked him about remarrying? There was no *un-*married woman that he wanted. Was he trying to acquire Yamna?

Zoulikha had said something else, about initially seeing her missing amulet in the fortress of the valley's *kaid*. Bachir had married into that family. Could he have stolen the amulet? There were too many coincidences and twists to sustain credibility. Might he be playing both sides? He clearly had access to Zoulikha's house. If he stole the talisman, he may have offered to help the *kahina* just to cover his own tracks and to inhibit Jade's help. But Mohan must have seen through it all. Now he risked himself for his daughter's legacy.

They wended their way down the mountain trail, fording streams swelling with snow melt, and made it to a spring near the mountain base as night fell. Mohan started a fire and boiled water for the inevitable mint tea while Jade distributed bread and cheese. She took some comfort in knowing that her mother was safe with Zoulikha now. She trusted the old woman.

Late morning had stretched into late afternoon before Bachir could assemble the necessary supplies for their trip. Inez watched, wishing she could do something, feeling helpless in her inability to communicate. She settled for doing the one thing she knew how to do: care for their mounts. Besides two little donkeys for riding, there was the third mule Jade had purchased to use as a pack animal. Inez rubbed them down using an old woven bag in lieu of a cloth. Then she wheedled a knife from Bachir and set about cleaning their hooves. She noted with approval that Jade's mule had sound legs. The girl did know horseflesh.

Cleaning the animals helped a little. At least it made the time crawl less slowly. It didn't do much to lessen her anxiety, though. It was that horrid dream that did it. She saw Jade in shackles with other men and women, then dragged away to the ends of the earth. *Holy Mother. It's all this talk of symbols and charms. It's gotten to me, as well.* But something in the back of her mind told her that her daughter was walking into danger. Just as Jade had saved her, it was her turn to save Jade. She felt for the Roman coins they'd found in the leather pouch. Inez had kept them in a little leather bag she'd borrowed from Yamna. It was all the money Inez possessed right now and it might be needed. She tossed a blanket over the donkey's back, and called for Bachir.

CHAPTER 18

Handle your book bindings with respect.
Men toiled through hell to produce that coveted red leather.

—The Traveler

JADE WOKE UP STIFF, sore, and sleepy Wednesday morning. She attributed the stiffness to crossing the icy Oued Issil and the long walk those last twelve miles across the flat and rocky wasteland. *Stupid mule.* If Mohan's beast hadn't taken it into his stubborn head to investigate what looked like something edible at camp last night, he wouldn't have gotten that rock in his hoof. And if Mohan had checked his animal's feet to begin with rather than waiting until the poor beast started going lame, the rock wouldn't have cut in so far. Jade had taken it out and cleansed the wound as best she could with their limited water supply, but they'd ended up walking the last part of the journey and had lost valuable time, arriving in Marrakech after the gates had closed.

The soreness? Well, that was another issue. Apparently Mohan's mule didn't like having his hooves checked, which probably went a long way to explaining why the man had neglected doing it. At least the beast's teeth were good, if Jade's shoulder bite was any indication.

And the sleepiness? She chalked that up to camping out near the palm gardens. The area was filled with other people who'd either arrived too late to find a caravansary—a hostelry for both man and beast—inside the city or who preferred the outdoors to a crowded building. Jade and Mohan had ended up near a cluster of grunting, grumbling, ill-tempered, smelly camels and their equally noisy owners who snored all night long. She'd slept through quieter nights in a French farm cellar three miles from the front lines.

Jade might have done something about the situation herself, but by then she was supposed to be a Berber woman traveling in the company of her brother. She'd paused by a clump of ruined huts near the mountain's base and removed her boots and overskirt, rolled up her trouser legs, and donned a Berber headdress, the *handira*, and slippers. She'd put her boots in one of the panniers. With the aid of the henna tattoos, she'd transformed herself from an Anglo to one of the Imazighen. With the disguise came the required behavior to make it work, and that meant putting up with all the singing, chattering, and snoring around her.

After a necessary visit to the nearest private palm and a quick breakfast of bread, cheese, and dried apricots, Jade turned her attention to the business at hand. Chances were her adversaries were still holed up in the same house as before. But outside of de Portillo, Jade didn't have any idea who else was in Lilith's employ, if, in fact, she was the brains behind the operation.

In Tangier, de Portillo had claimed he was a leather merchant coming to Marrakech to buy goods. Marrakech and Fes were the two principal places where this coveted red leather was made, and since those leather bags bearing Lilith's seal were found in Marrakech, they were probably crafted there, as well. Jade estimated she had seen nearly one hundred bags in that room. Making so many would have taken longer than the time de Portillo had been here. After all, he couldn't have arrived in Marrakech much before she did. So if she could locate the leather worker who'd made the bags, she might be able to find out who the initial client was. That might tell her who else was working with the Spaniard. Then perhaps she could go to the French authorities. Surely they would listen, especially when she showed them the hashish.

Spit fire and save the matches. She'd left the bags of hashish and the gold coins in the village. Well, spilt milk and all that nonsense. No time to go back for them. She still had the leather bag and the charm the Little Owl had coughed up at the Azilah tunnels. She would use them to locate the bag maker and proceed from there. Jade debated having Mohan do the talking so she could continue her role as his sister, then decided against it. That amulet needed finding and he might be of more use inquiring at the silversmith's or anyone else likely to buy old silver. Her biggest concern was her imperfect Arabic; however, disguised as a Berber woman, she could claim it wasn't her first language. *Just so long as I don't run into a shopkeeper who speaks Tashelhit.*

"Mohan, if someone tried to sell the *kahina's* amulet, where would he go?"

Mohan rubbed his hand over his short beard. "Perhaps to a dealer of women's adornments? Someone who sells to the wealthy princes in the city?" He answered as though he were uncertain, like a student who looks to the teacher to see if he has given the correct reply.

"Do you know who they are? The dealers, not the princes."

Mohan shrugged. "In the souks."

She recalled she was originally supposed to meet someone to bargain for her mother's freedom in the Square of the Dead. "Would someone like that be in the *Jemaâ el-Fna*?"

Mohan shrugged again. "It is mostly storytellers, fortune tellers, and sellers of food there. Sometimes I sit there to sell my wife's rugs. But I do not think the rich princes buy from there."

Jade had another thought. The amulet might have more value as a talisman than as women's jewelry. "Is there anyone who sells charms in the souks who might have bought it?"

"Charms for one cannot be used by another. They are made special for a person."

Jade didn't press the issue, although she noted that Mohan didn't really answer her question. She'd locate the charm dealers herself. "You know better than I what Elishat's amulet looks like. Would you please ask about it in the souks?"

"I cannot buy it, if I find it," he protested.

"Just let it be known that there is a lady who is looking for something like that; someone who will pay a good price. Tell them it is a Nazarene woman if you have to. Just don't give my name. We will meet again at the eastern side of the Koutoubia mosque tower," she said. "Meet me just after the muezzin calls for evening prayer."

Mohan grunted what appeared to be an affirmative reply and headed into the old city. Jade waited a moment to see that her mules were secured, fed, and watered; then she skirted the *Medina* walls around the east side and entered at the *Bab Debbagh*, the tanner's gate, on the northeast edge. She assumed the leather workers would have shops close to their source of raw materials, but once she caught scent of the place, she realized she was wrong. No one would want to be close to this section of the city. Even the lepers chose the northwestern gate to haunt. This place reeked.

Wet sheepskins, some still holding their fleece, some denuded, lay in piles waiting for processing. They contributed the least to the stench. The processing took care of the rest, cultivating a bad smell into one that could curdle milk still in the cow. One section of mud-brick vats contained an assortment of nasty brews for tanning the hides, while another held rancid dyes for staining the leather. Piles of bird excrement, vats of urine and fish oils, one of lard, and yet another of brains waited to be mixed into the tanning vats.

Bad idea. Jade debated approaching the district from the other side, and decided it would take too much time. *God favors the bold,* she told herself. She covered her mouth and nose with her sleeve and plowed through, hoping to find someone who actually made bags at the other end of the district. *How in the name of St. Peter's bait bucket did they manage to actually work here?* She wasn't sure she could make it through without retching.

Several groups of men paused momentarily and looked at her, but no one harassed her or questioned what she was doing there. She caught a few comments regarding foolish women and ignorant mountain people, but paid them no mind. If they thought she was merely a lost Berber woman passing through, so much the better. Finally she pushed past the worst of the odors, through the vegetable dye vats and corresponding mounds of tamarisk fruits and tree bark, and found herself in a small set of *souks* where men stacked and bundled the leather. As far as she could see, no one actually sewed the leather here.

"*Shkara?*" she asked one man, using the word for a Berber

man's shoulder bag. When she received no reply, she held her own bag in front of him and tried the similar Arabic word. *"Chkairas?"*

The craftsman shook his head and pointed to the stack of his red-dyed leather. *"Ktab,* books." Apparently this leather all went to bind books. Jade went from leather worker to leather worker, always receiving the same reply or lack of one. Finally she came to the stall of a man who sat making *babouches,* leather slippers.

"Chkairas?" she asked.

The man, who looked to be in his sixties but might have been only thirty, squinted at Jade. She held up the leather bag around her neck. *"Chkairas?"* she repeated.

"Souk Serrajine," he said with a shrug, and pointed to the southwest.

The saddlemakers' district. *Wonderful. I went through Dante's third level of hell for nothing.* She started to leave when the man stopped her.

"Let me see," he said, and held out a hand for the bag. Jade handed it over, keeping one hand on the leather strap in case. The old man studied the shape and the seams with an intensity due in part, Jade suspected, to failing vision. Finally he nodded as though he'd come to some decision. "Go to the shop of Wahab Taboor."

"Wahab Taboor made this bag? Are you certain?"

"I know my own brother's work," he said.

Jade thanked him with "May your work prosper" and navigated the blind alleys, twists, turns, and general haphazard layout of the old city to find the correct *souk.* At times, even keeping a mosque tower in view became impossible as the street narrowed and grew dark from an intermittent roof of reeds and palm branches.

Periodically, the streets opened into more spacious avenues where Jade could get her bearings. Using her pocket watch, she lined up the hour hand with the sun, then picked the point halfway between noon and the hour hand. That was south. She set off again along a new maze where she jostled up against black-skinned slave women making purchases for their mistresses, Arab men, small boys, countless cats, and a few half-starved dogs that had the uncanny knack of lying down right in the middle of the road. Occasionally someone carrying a tray of food would trip over one of these poor brutes and then the dogs leaped into life, attacking whatever fell and bolting it down whole. Cries of *"Balek! Look out!"* rose so frequently from someone driving a donkey along that no one paid any heed to the donkey herder.

Finally as the muezzin called for noon prayers, effectively clearing the streets, Jade found a relatively straight and broad avenue heading south and took it. She emerged in the *Rhaba Kdima*, or old square, a former slave market, now completely occupied by vendors hawking promises of health to the few remaining customers, most of them men.

"I will make your potion," called one man as he held up what looked like the horn of a rhinoceros.

"My cure casts out demons," shouted another, only to be shouted down by a third who promised greater virility to any man, no matter how old. "The Sultan's stallions should want your prowess with my herbs."

Several women sat at some of the stalls, some as vendors, others as buyers while the shopkeeper diligently painted their hands with henna and traced their eyes with kohl. A movement near Jade's left eye made her start, and she turned and stared into the bulging eyes of a caged chameleon.

"I can cure your harm," said a man standing beside the

chameleon. "Do you lack children? Desire a son? Perhaps," he said as he eyed Jade's face and noticed her beauty, "you seek to charm some man?"

"No," said Jade. She started to press on, then stopped. If this was the district of the healers and charm sellers, then maybe someone here might know about Elishat's amulet. She turned back to the man. "I seek an amulet."

"I can make an amulet to protect you from harm from man and *jinni*," he said. "It will take three days. Or I can make one to help capture a man's heart. Also three days to make."

"No, I had a charm, a silver charm. It was taken."

"Ah," he said, his gaping mouth exposing many gaps in his teeth. Apparently, thought Jade, the man's charms had no protection against tooth decay. "You wish to curse the one who stole it?"

"No. I want to find it."

"Very difficult," said the man. "What did it look like?"

"I will draw it for you. Do you have paper?"

The man handed her a sheet of parchment, a quill pen, and a pot of ink. Jade sat on the low stool outside of his closetlike shop and sketched the amulet box. As if interested, the chameleon rotated one of his buglike eyes to watch. The other eyed an insect flying nearby. When Jade finished, she held up the paper.

The man pondered the sketch for a few moments, muttering to himself and shaking his turbaned head. "That charm bears very ancient symbols," he said finally. "I have never seen any like it."

"Someone stole it," said Jade. "Would they be able to sell it here?" She gestured to the entire *souk* to mean any of the healers, not this man in particular.

"No. To buy such a charm would be to risk everything if

the charm is indeed powerful. And the charm loses its holiness if it is worn by one who is unclean. Amulets are made for each person, not for all. You are Berber?" he asked, studying Jade's face and garb. She nodded. "Then someone of your tribe stole it?"

Jade pondered the question for a moment before answering. Zoulikha said she wore the talisman only when she performed healings or officiated at a birth, marriage, or at the women's gatherings. But she alone knew where she kept it hidden at the other times. So it seemed unlikely that it was taken by any outsider.

Jade had initially thought it had simply dropped off a chain sometime, but Zoulikha had been adamant that was not the case. And even if it had fallen, if anyone in the village found it they would not touch it, but call for Zoulikha immediately. Unless, of course, they intended to sell it. Poverty often made the unthinkable very tempting, and many of the villagers brought crops, rugs, and pots down the mountain to sell for tea and sugar. Once again her thoughts strayed to Bachir and his need for money to court another wife.

"Yes, but we do not know who," admitted Jade. It was clear this man had nothing more to offer, so she took her leave. "I thank you and wish Allah's blessings on you for your help." She plucked off one of the few coins left on the second of the three bangle bracelets to offer to him for his trouble.

The shopkeeper's eyes bugged almost as large as the chameleon's. "Ah," he said, reaching for the silver coin. "You wish for me to make a charm to help you find the lost charm?"

Jade shook her head. "*La, shukran*. Perhaps it will call to me," she added, using the phrase that Zoulikha had given. She rose to leave.

The man handled the money and seemed hesitant about

keeping it as he had sold nothing to Jade. Finally his conscience got the better of him and he handed it back.

Jade motioned with a flip of her hand that he should keep it. "For your trouble," she said.

"Charity is a virtue, lady, but to take charity when it is not needed . . ." He shrugged. "I can tell you this much in return. If the amulet is pleasing to look on, a foreign woman might buy it to wear. Ask the silversmiths who sell baubles to Nazarene women. They wear many shiny things and take pleasure in wearing old charms, too."

Jade pulled out the moon eclipsing the sun charm. "Would a Nazarene woman wear this?"

The man pointed at the charm. "Yes. I have seen such a woman with that symbol. A young woman with hair like the soft blushing red of dawn. But she did not wear this on a chain. She wore the symbol on a bag." He stooped and peered at Jade's bag. "Much like yours. Perhaps you can find her at the leather workers' *souk*."

"How can I find one Nazarene woman among so many in this city?" asked Jade, hoping for a more detailed description.

The charm maker shook his head. "Not so many Nazarene in Marrakech. This one is very bold. She makes eyes at all the young men."

Jade asked for directions to the leather workers' district, found she'd overshot the area, thanked the man again, and left. This time she headed due north, keeping her eyes peeled for a flirtatious young woman with reddish-blond hair—a woman who sounded a lot like Libby Tremaine.

CHAPTER 19

Jemaâ el-Fna translates to "the Square of the Dead," and gets its name from the Sultan's executions and displays of heads. Current residents must settle for more harmless entertainment. Come, listen to a storyteller weave a tale suitable for Arabian Nights, have your fortune told, or watch snake charmers mesmerize defanged, thick-bodied asps and undulating cobras. For a price, they might drape one around your neck. For even more, they might remove it.

—The Traveler

ROLLS AND WALLS OF GORGEOUS CARPETS woven in every conceivable color replaced the triangular herbal heaps, baskets of horn, and bug-eyed chameleons of the medicine dealers. They hung from makeshift scaffolding, rafters, and doors, some faded to gentler colors by the sun, others as vibrant as if straight from a dye vat. Since Jade appeared to the sellers as a Berber woman, one who made carpets herself, no one called to her to inspect the wares. In another time, she would have loved to. Everything from traditional Berber designs to exotic, kaleidoscopic patterns festooned the shops, hanging like flags. Red, the color of life, seemed most popular, if quantity was any guide, although autumn gold and deep indigo vied for second place.

As she moved through the carpet *souk,* she noted one open area with a few benches in front of an old *riad. A place to show and auction rugs?* She wished she could take out her camera and photograph everything, but it hardly fit with her disguise. She hurried along. Her path veered west again, and Jade looked for the first street going even remotely north and south. She found one and turned right. Within a few hundred yards, she became surrounded by the shops of metalsmiths, all making and selling delicate baubles and trinkets in brass, copper, and silver.

The metalsmiths. Jade looked around for Mohan, hoping to find him and see what he'd learned, but the crowds in this *souk* made it nearly impossible to identify any one person. Nearly a third of the men wore the shorter, calf-length *djellabas* and tight-fitting white skullcap that indicated traditional Berber garb. She toyed with inquiring herself, then decided against it. After all, it might seem suspicious with two people asking after the same amulet.

Finally, beyond the jewelry makers' district she found the *Souk Serrajine,* home to the saddle makers. The scent of leather here was much more pleasant than in the tannery district. Jade inhaled the aroma as she walked amid closet-sized stalls full of boots, saddles, and bridles. For a moment, it felt like the tack room in the barn at home. But her mission dictated action, not reminiscing. She wanted the people making bags. She found them just north of the saddles.

Once again she went from stall to stall, this time asking for Wahab Taboor.

"I am Wahab Taboor," said a small man with one good eye. The other was hidden under a white rag tied behind his head.

Jade held out the leather bag with the eclipse symbol stamped on it. She decided to take the offensive rather than simply ask if he had made it. "I have come about the bags."

Wahab took one look at the bag and threw his hands in the air. "First he sends a man of your peoples with his order.

Many 'if you please,' and 'Allah bless you.' Then he sends an Arab with a saber to bully me to hurry. And now the *Nazarene* sends his slave woman to annoy me? You tell your master that it will take three, maybe four more days to make these the way he wants. It would be faster if he did not want . . ." He hesitated and glanced about to see who was nearby. Then dropping his voice to a whisper he continued, "Certain objects sewn into the hidden side pouches."

So this man put the hashish inside. *Interesting*. It also distanced de Portillo from the drug. He could always claim that he did not know someone was using his pouches to smuggle hashish. Jade wondered if Wahab Taboor also slipped the gold into the bottom panel. Somehow she doubted it. All that gold would be a tremendous temptation.

"Does it take longer to put the items in the bottom or in the sides?" she asked in a roundabout way of finding out about the hidden gold.

Wahab cocked his head and peered at Jade with his one good eye. "This son of a jackal expects me to put something in the bottom, too? Is it not enough to make the bottom double thick with leather so it is stronger?"

That answered that, thought Jade. He didn't handle the gold. De Portillo or someone working for him made a slit in the seam and added the gold later. It wouldn't take a very large slit, either, as the coins were only slightly larger than an American nickel.

Jade wanted to ask who this Nazarene man was, but to do so would reveal that she wasn't the man's slave and had no business asking. Instead, she tried to find out how and where they'd be delivered. She needed to know if this man had relocated after her escape. "My master does not remember if he told you where to bring them this time."

"Bring them? Myself? Would he like for me to be the donkey that carries them, too?" Wahab spat on the ground. "Infidel, pig. Tell him that I do not leave my shop. I will send my worthless cousin with them to the same place as before, but it will cost him more. Fahd has a donkey's rear for brains, but passing the house with the white hand on the door scared even those wits out of him."

"I will tell him," said Jade. She started to go, hesitated, and turned back. "My master has heard that you have sold bags with that design to others, as well. It did not please him to hear this."

"I did not!" cried Wahab. He clutched the metal die with which he stamped the leather. "I have been told not to use the Nazarene's seal for anything else."

Jade believed him. So if Libby Tremaine had one of the bags, she must have gotten it from either de Portillo or whoever he was working for.

"I will tell my master. But if you wish to save your last remaining eye, do not displease him further."

Pondering what she'd learned, she left the shop just as the call came for afternoon prayer. This man, Wahab Taboor, made the leather bags, secreted the hashish in the two side panels, and stamped and embossed them for identification. He didn't receive orders directly from this man so there was no sense trying to find out if they came from Patrido de Portillo or from someone else. But since de Portillo didn't reside at the house where the bags were kept, she presumed he was only the courier and not the one ordering the merchandise. This other man wasn't an Arab, though. She'd heard him speak. Perhaps one of the French residents of Marrakech? But the voice hadn't sounded French.

Jade also knew that Wahab's cousin Fahd still delivered

the bags to the house and that this person had not relocated since her escape. This unknown man also had several native Moroccans working for him. *Wait a minute. What did Wahab say?* Jade closed her eyes to think. Something about the first man, the one who placed the order. *A man of your peoples.* Of course, the first man was Berber. But that wasn't much help. There were a lot of Berbers living in Marrakech. *Bachir?* The second messenger was an Arab, possibly the one who'd been left to guard her. He certainly would have looked intimidating to Wahab Taboor with his large size and dagger. *Probably hires a whole retinue of lackeys.*

As she mulled it over, it was a decent amount of information, but was it enough? Could she convince the French to watch for Fahd's delivery and catch these people red-handed? Somehow she doubted it, especially if they figured out that she was the same woman who'd fled Tangier under suspicion. Besides, the French preferred not to interfere with the Sultan's rule unless they had to. They'd probably consider an Arab stuffing hashish into bags as something for the Sultan's men, not them, to punish. Only when it came into their country would it matter. Having the Sultan mete out punishment would result only in Wahab being thrown into one of those horrid prison pits to rot and die while the mastermind went free. Or worse, the Sultan would assume she was behind the operation and toss her in, too.

If only she could find this woman that also had one of these bags. It certainly sounded like Libby Tremaine. If she could made her talk, make her tell the authorities where she'd gotten the bag, Jade might at least be able to clear herself and her mother of the murder and drug charges. Well, at least the drug charges.

This is a mess! She hoped Mohan was having better luck

locating that silver amulet. Since it was just midafternoon, she had a few hours before she was due to meet him at the Koutoubia tower. Her stomach growled and she realized she hadn't eaten anything since morning. She still had another bracelet full of silver coins, courtesy of the old woman. One of those coins ought to be worth something to eat. She broke one off by its link and went in search of some food vendors.

Her search, led by her nose, took her back south towards the *Jemaâ el-Fna*, and before she reached the square she ran across the dried-fruit market. She tried bargaining for a handful of anything—dates, raisins, almonds, or even sunflower seeds—but discovered that unless she wanted a full basket, she was out of luck. Her stomach growled again and informed her that only something substantial such as an entire cooked chicken would be acceptable. She headed for the main square.

Perhaps it was all the walking in the uncomfortable, heelless slippers, but her feet, calves, and knees ached. The first two problems didn't concern Jade too much; the last one did. Her left knee had an uncanny knack for hurting when she was in danger. Zoulikha claimed this gift, or curse, depending on your viewpoint, arose when death entered her body during the war. In particular, when she received her shrapnel wound, just before her sweetheart, David, was killed in a dogfight. Unfortunately her knee also ached just before rain, and right now, *both* of her knees hurt. How was she supposed to know if she was in danger?

Why can't I get a clear sign? Something that leaves no doubt, like maybe everything suddenly shifting to black and white, or a voice in my head that screams out, "Danger!"

Jade decided she'd rather be safe than sorry, so she paused a moment to take in the people around her. As far as she could tell everyone appeared to be intent on buying and selling produce, but as she turned she caught a movement in her peripheral vision. Someone darted back into the crowd. Was she being followed? She proceeded on her way, but every so often she suddenly looked behind her. Most of the time she saw nothing out of the ordinary, but once she had the feeling that someone didn't want to be seen.

Whoever it is, better not interrupt my meal.

The late-afternoon sun kept most people out of the square, but Jade noticed a few hardy vendors set up under makeshift shades. She passed a sleeping man, his head drooping on his chest, a clarinetlike instrument in his lap. Beside him was a circular basket, its lid weighted down with a stone. *Naptime for the snake charmer.* A few boys in ragged tunics ran across the square, playing something resembling a game of tag.

Jade found someone selling kabobs and purchased one with large chunks of chicken, squash, and onions, grilled over hot coals. She held the wooden skewer in her right hand, grabbed a chunk of chicken and squash with her teeth and had to remind herself not to bolt her food like a coyote on the run. She would be perfectly safe in this large, public square. After all, who would want to attack a harmless Berber woman in broad daylight?

The four boys raced by again, this time with a different aim than a game. They had sighted fresh prey in the guise of the rare non-Moroccans and raced ahead in pursuit of money. *"Baksheesh,"* they cried as they held out their hands and called for charity. They knew from experience that the few visitors, overwhelmed by the clamoring cries and outstretched hands, tossed coins just to make the youthful beggars go away.

Jade followed the urchins with her gaze as she ate and instantly recognized the boys' intended victims. Libby Tremaine strolled into the square with Woodard and Chloe Kennicot. Walter had lagged behind to watch a juggler toss and catch three lemons and a cucumber. At first, Jade stepped back to avoid being seen by them. That's when she noticed that the boys' pursuit of money held all the earmarks of a coordinated attack. Three of them managed to encircle Mrs. Tremaine, culling her from the herd, as it were. As they pressed forward, she held up her hands in front of her and stepped backward, distancing herself from the Kennicots. The fourth boy ran behind her and reached for her bag.

The bag. From a distance Jade recognized the leather pouch by its shape. The boys planned to steal her bag. In the meantime, the juggler had moved during his act so that Mr. Tremaine stood with his back to his wife, not noticing the assault.

Someone wanted that bag back. Jade couldn't let it happen. "Libby!" she shouted. She saw heads turn in her direction, searching for whoever had called. "Your bag. Hold on to your—"

Her next words were cut off when a man grabbed her from behind. Jade's reflexes took over, and her left elbow jabbed backward into his gut. Without waiting for him to react, she twisted to the right and stabbed the Arab in the cheek with the wooden skewer. The man howled in pain and released her, grabbing for the skewer, his fingers slipping on a greasy chunk of chicken and onion. While he struggled with the stick, Jade risked a glance to the others to see if Mrs. Tremaine still had the pouch. She did, and by now her husband and friends had rallied to her rescue. Jade darted away just as her assailant made another grab for her.

She took off running, but her slippers made it nearly impossible to gain any decent headway. None of the onlookers appeared interested in helping her, either. Instead they seemed to find the pursuit highly entertaining. Jade instinctively reached for her knife sheath on her boot, only there was no boot, much less a knife. *Spit fire and save matches!* The dagger was with her boots at the mule. She needed a good diversion, something that would stop her assailant in his tracks. She found it.

Jade ran towards the sleeping snake charmer and scooped up the basket next to him on the fly. Pivoting, she hurled the basket and its contents towards the Moroccan. The lid fell away, revealing one very perturbed cobra. The man screamed, flinging his arms in front of him. Jade didn't wait to see the outcome. She assumed that her attacker, the juggler, or someone else involved in the attacks would continue the pursuit. She needed to hide.

The easiest way to hide in plain sight was to break her profile, something many animals did. As she'd done in the past, Jade's mind raced through her experiences with wildlife and settled on a role model, several in fact. Many animals, when fleeing, flashed a bright spot of white. The predator focused on the white patch. Then when the prey dropped or folded its tail, it effectively disappeared from view.

Jade knew her predators had focused on a Berber woman wearing a striped cloak with the partridge eye in the center back. As soon as she found a dark passage between buildings and makeshift shops, she pulled off the cloak and headdress and tossed them aside, keeping the sharpened *fibula* pins for weapons. What emerged out the other end of the alley was a tourist in a plain brown blouse and brown trousers. Even the dark henna stains on her feet looked from a distance like nothing more than a pair of boots.

She didn't want to take too much of a chance. The plan

only worked for wildlife as long as they stayed still until the predator continued his search elsewhere. And since there weren't very many Europeans in the city, she'd stand out. Jade waited in the dark alley for another half hour before she decided it was safe to wait at the Koutoubia for Mohan.

Jade cursed her foolishness. Wahab Taboor must have sent someone such as his cousin Fahd to either de Portillo or the unknown man and asked why they were harassing him. They would have known someone, she to be more specific, was on to their smuggling plans. But the more Jade thought about it, the less sense that made. It would have taken Wahab a little time at least to locate his cousin and send him with the message. Then assuming cousin Fahd did make haste, he could not have made it to the smuggler's house that quickly. Jade had sensed someone following her shortly after she left his booth.

No, it seemed more likely that the smugglers were keeping an eye on Wahab for some reason. Perhaps they wanted to make sure no one else got one of the bags. Or maybe they hoped the person who owned one would come back for another. And she just happened to be carrying one. *St. Peter's goldfish, but I'm stupid. Might as well wear a sandwich sign identifying myself.*

She hoped they hadn't managed to get hold of Mrs. Tremaine's bag. Jade counted on it being stuffed with hashish and she wanted the officials to have a shot at seeing that one. In the meantime Jade wanted to find out how Libby actually got hold of the bag to begin with. Wahab claimed he hadn't sold one to anyone else. Maybe Fahd had decided to make some money on the side by selling one to Libby, or perhaps she knew the smuggler? Well, that was going to be a problem for the French to figure out. As soon as Jade met up with Mohan, she'd pay a visit to their offices and explain what she'd learned. It ought to be enough to at least clear her mother and herself of suspicion. She just wished she knew what to do about that blasted amulet.

Like a needle in a haystack around here. From what she could see, everyone and his camel had a protective amulet. Hopefully Mohan had experienced some luck making his inquiries. After all, he had a strong interest in retrieving his daughter's legacy. Jade pulled her pocket watch from her pocket. Five o'clock. About two hours until *Salat-ul-maghrib*, the evening prayer. She wasn't far from the mosque tower. She decided to lie low until the muezzin's call.

Finally there came the distinct wavering call and she heard, more than saw, the little cubbyholed shops being closed as most men left for the nearest mosque. She slipped out of hiding and walked to their appointed meeting spot. She spotted Mohan kneeling on an old mat, facing east, completing his evening prayers. Jade waited a respectable distance away until he was finished before approaching him.

"Mohan," she called in a soft voice. "What did you learn about the amulet?"

"You are fortunate," he said. "I have spoken to someone who says he can help us."

"Does he have the amulet?"

"No, but he may know where it can be found. Come. I told him I would bring you to him so you would hear this, too. I think he does not believe me. He wants to see you."

Jade's heart beat a little faster. If this man had reliable information, then perhaps her business here would be finished and she could take her mother to Spain and out of danger. It would be just as well. Right now she felt like she'd been bucked from a bronco. "Slow down, Mohan."

Mohan didn't slow down, and Jade was forced to again hasten her steps in the little heelless *babouches. How in tarnation does he trot in them?* By now both legs hurt, as well as her left elbow with which she'd jabbed her attacker in the gut.

He led her through the dried-fruit vendor's market and past a crumbling mosque. Turning right into a narrow alleyway after the mosque, he slowed and came to a small cube-shaped building with a stumpy minaret on top. Whatever tiles had once decorated the saint's shrine had fallen into disarray as the plasterwork crumbled from the walls. Behind it was an equally run-down building that probably housed whoever tended the local saint's grave.

"This man has information?" Jade asked, wondering what the keeper of an Islamic saint's tomb would know about an ancient Berber amulet. She bent down and rubbed her legs, easing the cramps and aches.

"Yes," said Mohan. "If you go inside, he will talk to you."

Jade started towards the low doorway, then paused. Why would this man welcome a Nazarene woman inside? Suddenly her general aches and pains dropped into the background as the pain in her left knee dominated. *It's a trap.* She wheeled about to run, but two burly Arabs already blocked the narrow alleyway. Jade pulled the *fibula* pins from her pockets and gripped them in each fist between her ring and middle fingers, letting the sharpened points stick out.

"Just try it," she said in English, backing away, scanning the periphery for an escape route. The low light made it difficult to tell if she stood in a dead-end passage or not, and the last thing she wanted was to get backed into a corner. She eyed the caretaker's hut, wondering if she could reach the roof. From there she might be able to run across the rooftops and flee.

One of the two men made a dash for her and received a gash across his face for his pains. Jade recognized his crooked nose. *My prison guard.* He attempted another lunge. This time Jade sliced across his forehead. She knew facial wounds bled freely and hoped the blood flow would temporarily blind him. His partner, more wary of her, edged forward cautiously. Jade feinted a move to her left, then darted right towards the hut. With one leap she managed to get her right foot onto the ledge of the narrow window slit, but the second man recovered quickly and reached for her legs.

Jade kicked out at his face, but without stout boots the force was not enough to do any damage. When he didn't let go of her right ankle, she hurled first one, then the second *fibula* pin at him. He dodged both, releasing her as the second one whizzed past his ear. In that moment Jade grabbed the low rooftop and scrambled up. Luck toyed with her. The ancient building's walls were in no condition to support her. A chunk of mud-brick and plaster broke loose in her hand.

For a fraction of a second Jade hung between capture and escape. The sudden lurch backward as the wall broke startled her, and had she given in to the confusion, capture would have been inevitable. But she hadn't spent the better part of a year dodging shell fire on the front lines in the Great War for nothing. Her finely honed reflexes kicked in, fueled by a combination of fear and anger. She grabbed for the wall with her left hand and hurled the dry mud-brick in her right at the man below her, aiming for his nose. Direct hit. Her attacker howled as blood poured out.

Jade didn't waste any more time pulling herself onto the roof. A quick survey of the surrounding buildings showed her the surest route of escape, one that would put several narrow streets between her and the pursuers by the time they doubled back out of the blind alley. The last thing she saw before she leaped from the rooftop was Mohan digging something up behind the abandoned caretaker's hut, muttering an incantation against the *jinn* guarding his prize.

She found a building whose upper rooms arched over the alley and connected to the building on the other side. Jade raced across the arch, putting one street between her and her pursuers. The next alley was little more than four feet across. Jade cleared it starting from a dead run across the rooftops, losing her slippers in the jump. Then the streets widened and she was forced to run along a row of buildings to put more distance between her and the men. She knew they would continue their pursuit, so she decided that doubling back behind them would be the safest course of action. Besides, her legs were starting to weaken.

She scooped up a handful of plaster and tossed it across the alley to the next roof, imitating the sound of her running and jumping along the roof. Then she dropped flat and lay still. She heard the two men race by, still shouting to each other. As soon as they had passed, she scuttled crablike in the other direction and dropped down into the side alley. The first thing she *wanted* to do was discover what Mohan had been up to. Common sense told her to find a hiding place first where she could safely spy on the area.

Jade limped back along the alley until she came to a cluster of shops two buildings away from the empty caretaker's hut. The merchants here had already closed down business for the day after evening prayers, and no one loitered nearby. Jade huddled in the buildings' shadow, listening for the sound of pursuit. *Silence.* Her ruse had worked. The pursuers were chasing her shadow now.

Slowly she crept closer, hugging the wall. The caretaker's

hut and the untended saint's tomb stood before her. Again she waited to see if anyone had stayed behind or returned. Her sore knee told her to be wary, but she knew part of the danger was tied to her not being in hiding rather than in the proximity of attackers. She darted over to the hut, again pressing her back to the wall; waiting, listening.

The only sound came from the singsong yowling of the territorial neighborhood cats. No humans loitered nearby. Jade ducked into the hut and strained to see through the gloom. Her hand reached out and felt at the dirt floor and found a small hole. Mohan had dug something up here. The amulet? Which meant that Mohan, not Bachir, was the traitor. She'd have to find Mohan. Maybe he went back to the caravansary to retrieve the mules. It was worth a try, and besides, she wanted her boots and the dagger she'd tucked into the sheath.

Jade slipped out of the hut and headed back into the more open street where she felt safer. She hadn't quite passed the old abandoned tomb when a hand shot out and grabbed her arm, pulling her inside.

CHAPTER 20

Tucked away in the cities and along the countryside are shrines to the Islamic saints.
They are usually tended by a holy man. Many people, especially women, come to these
shrines to beg favors of the saint. It is also an acceptable excuse to leave the harem.

—The Traveler

INEZ DID EVERYTHING SHE COULD to speed up their progress, short of carrying her donkey. The little animals set their own pace and no amount of cajoling, coaxing, pleading, or scolding would change it. She and Bachir had started late enough to begin with, and night seemed to fall early in the steeper valleys where their path led them. Patience was not Inez's strong point. Heaven knows it should have been after dealing with all of Jade's escapades throughout the years. She'd prayed for patience often enough. Somehow she seemed to end up instead with only a tremendously large share of stubborn determination: the same stubbornness of Jade's that drove Inez to distraction.

They made it halfway down the mountain the first day and now they were close to the foot of the mountains, trying to coax a balky little donkey to brave the Oued Issil. The river had risen from snowmelt, but had not reached anything resembling a dangerous flow. The donkey just didn't feel like going any farther. Inez didn't remember any of the animals going slowly on the way up the mountain. Apparently, this one liked going home, but didn't care to leave it. She'd just have to convince him that the trip was in his best interest.

Inez rummaged in the saddlebags for the tea-making supplies. Bachir, thinking she was thirsty, offered his water bag, but Inez declined with a smile and adding her thanks with a *shukran,* one of the Arabic words she'd picked up from Jade. "Sugar," she said.

Bachir shook his head, not understanding. "Sugar," she repeated, and made the motions of making tea.

"Ah," said Bachir. He nodded and grinned. *"Sūkkar,"* he said in Arabic, emphasizing the similarity between the two words. He reached into the supplies and handed over the sack of sugar loaf.

Inez thanked him and broke off several chunks, putting all but one in her dress pocket. She fed the other to her donkey. He took it greedily, licking the palm of her hand before nudging her for more. Inez handed the pouch of sugar back to Bachir, then gripped the animal's halter in her right hand, holding it close to his head. Then she took out another lump of sugar and held it with her left hand extended as far as she could. The donkey's nose quivered, and he strained against her grip to reach the treat.

"You want the sugar?" Inez asked in a soft, gentle voice. "Go get the sugar." She took a step towards the riverbed, and the donkey followed, his tongue extended as he tried to reach the treat. Step by step they went until they reached the bank. When her donkey balked, Inez fed him the sugar. Then she repeated the process, slowly but surely luring the animal across the stream. Bachir followed with his less recalcitrant beast and the pack mule.

When they made the other side, Inez's tattered dress was soaked from the hips down. The sun hadn't yet set, but already the air was chilling, and Inez began to shiver. Bachir hobbled the animals and started a fire. Reaching Marrakech and finding a mule-headed daughter would have to wait until tomorrow. In the meantime she needed some way to communicate with Bachir. She'd picked up some of the Moroccan Arabic already, matching repeated words with Jade's translations; words such as "amulet" and *"kahina,"* which played a role in this adventure they'd found themselves in. Others such as *"souk"* she'd learned from Jade earlier. Now, with these rudiments, she attempted to form a plan with Bachir. What words she didn't know she'd try to supplement with pictures scratched into the dirt. If that failed, maybe some of that Indian sign language she used to use with the old Navajo on their ranch would work.

Underneath her anxiety and fatigue she felt a new sensation: excitement, the thrill of being alive. Her pulse quickened as though she were a sapling coming to life in the spring, ready to burst forth into leaf. She hadn't felt this invigorated since she and Richard had ridden to what had become her new home in New Mexico. The thought of her husband brought a smile and a warmth to her face, quickly followed by a pang of regret as sorrow for lost opportunities rose to the forefront.

How many times had she passed up taking overnight trail rides with Richard because she had to entertain some new lawyer's wife or a territorial representative who might assist her husband's ranch? She'd taken pride in her role as a wife, doing what she could to further her husband's prospects. *I did all of it for you, Richard.* But did he know that? Or did he just see their worlds taking them in different directions?

I have to get home to him.

. . .

"Quiet. You're in danger." The voice came out in a husky whisper with a faint trace of an English accent. The grip on Jade's arm pinched like a vise.

Jade pulled back, but the grasp tightened. "Tell me something I don't know," she said. "Who are you?"

"Shh," admonished the hidden speaker. "They may still be near."

"Mr. Bennington?"

"The same." He moved out of the little bit of twilight that reached this alley. "We must stay out of the light so we won't be seen. Is your mother safe?"

"How do you know about my mother? What are you doing here?"

"Not so loud," Bennington cautioned. "We should go someplace else to talk."

"I'm not going anywhere until you let go of my arm," said Jade. The hand released her. She stepped back a pace and locked eyes with his. It was difficult to do with his dark glasses. The man matched Jade's height as she stood before him in her bare feet. His face was immaculately shaven except for his impeccably groomed blond mustache.

"Sorry," he whispered. "I needed to get your attention. It's rather a long story." Seeing Jade wait with her arms folded across her chest, he took a deep breath and continued. "As you already know, I was looking to engage a nurse in Tangier, someone to take my Aunt Viola back to London. I should never have let her talk me into bringing her out here on this trip, but I'd hoped the ocean voyage would be good for her. And selfishly, I wanted a chance to see the world."

"Go on."

"I was coming back to the hotel when I overheard Patrido de Portillo talking to the Tremaines. Common sort of people," he added as an aside. "Never did like them. Mrs. Tremaine especially. Always mocking my aunt, and de Portillo struck me as the sort who preys on older women. I felt he was looking for hints as to how well-off your dear mother was financially."

He shook his shoulders as if to pull himself back on track. "They were planning what I thought sounded like a rather childish joke on your mother," he said. "They were going to leave a note for her purporting to be from you. I believed they had seen that you and your mother tended to be, er, at odds with each other and simply wanted to play on that. I got the impression that you had angered them somehow at breakfast."

"And you did nothing about it?" Jade's voice was low, a menacing growl.

"I planned to. You must believe me, but just then the nurse I was looking for found me and I'm afraid I became rather caught up in my own domestic details. I wouldn't have thought any more about it, but later on, as I took my aunt to the boat, I heard the police were looking for you. Something about you claiming a kidnapping, and they accused you and your mother of committing murder. I tried to tell that Deschamp chap what I knew, but he wouldn't hear a bit of it."

"So you came all the way out here to warn me?" Jade didn't bother to hide her incredulousness. "How did you even know where to look?"

Mr. Bennington sniffed. "To answer your first question, what would you have me do? I felt partly responsible for not having warned you or your mother of what I deemed was a rude joke. But once I thought your mother was in danger, I couldn't abandon her. She was always so kind, inquiring after Aunt Viola on board and even offering to stay with her, a dear offer but one I never felt I should take advantage of. I should think you'd be a bit less critical of me, you know."

"Sorry," said Jade, her voice softening. "It's been a trying day."

"Apology accepted," said Bennington. "As to how I knew where to look, I wasn't certain, but I hazarded a guess. I knew Mr. de Portillo had engaged a motorcar to Marrakech. Imagine my surprise when I found that the Tremaines and the Kennicots had also decided to go to Marrakech together. I don't think the Kennicots planned to leave quite so soon, but it seems you took the second-to-last available car in Tangier, so they joined forces with the last car. It was too much of a coincidence to suit my mind."

"Impressive bit of detective work, Mr. Bennington," said Jade. "How in the world did you get here, then, if we took all the cars?"

"It was not easy," he whispered, pulling himself up very straight and tugging on his tweed shooting jacket. "Especially with the local French constabulary looking for you. If you must know, I hired a camel as far as Rabat and engaged a motorcar there. I only arrived yesterday. Then I heard this commotion in the square and saw those men attacking a native woman. Imagine my surprise when I saw your face and realized it was you."

"Thank you, Mr. Bennington. Perhaps with you telling the officials here what you know, they will apprehend these people." Jade recalled that she had no idea where de Portillo resided. "I don't suppose you know where any of them are staying, do you?"

"As a matter of fact, I do. Come with me."

Jade hesitated, partly because she wanted to know where

they were going first, and partly because, with her bare feet and aching joints, she really didn't want to go very far without getting her boots or at least another pair of those slippers.

Bennington noticed she wasn't right behind him and turned back. "What's wrong?" he whispered.

Jade pointed to her feet and legs. "War injury." As she voiced it, she realized the left knee still throbbed, which meant her attackers were probably on their way back. "We can't stay here. I should see the slipper merchant, too," she said, "to get something on my feet."

Bennington motioned for her to follow him as they passed silently down that alley, paralleling the dried-fruit market just south of them. After a quarter mile, Bennington pointed to a small garden area, hidden behind a house and screened off by latticework. "Why don't you hide in there," he suggested, "and I'll get some shoes for you."

Jade agreed, opened the old gate, and slipped inside. Through the latticework, she watched Bennington walk off to the open streets and turn north towards the *Souk Smata* where the *babouches* were made and sold. She hoped he could persuade someone to open shop at this hour. Jade found a low bench and sat down to wait, straightening her legs in front of her to ease the pain in her knee.

From the far side she heard the gate creak open. She tried to bolt, but the lattice fence was too high. Someone threw a chloroform-laced bag over her head.

"Very clever to double back," said an Arabic voice in English. Then his gloatings muted into a distant, throaty buzzing as everything went black.

CHAPTER 21

Above the great Bab Agnaou, the gate into the Kasbah, a greeting carved in elaborate script translates, "Enter with blessings, serene people." To emphasize that latter point, especially for anyone who couldn't read, heads of enemies were often hung from the gate. It was a practice the French decided was in bad taste, at least ornamentally, and banned it. Several nesting storks make up the deficit.

—The Traveler

INEZ SAT BY THE FIRESIDE, head bowed as she poked at the fire with one of the few branches they had left. They had made it down the mountain, but stopped after again crossing the snow-fed river. Bachir had insisted on halting among the cedars during the day to cut branches. At the time Inez had felt it was a waste of time. Surely, she thought, if they just pressed on they could make Marrakech after nightfall. But apparently Bachir had known the little donkeys' limits. Pausing to cut the branches had given the animals a chance to rest and forage. Without those respites, they might not have even reached the foot of the Atlas.

As soon as they had stopped for the night, Inez had learned the wisdom of Bachir's hesitation. A wind, formed by the descending mountain air hitting the hot air over the plains, blew the dried clay up into a thick red dust. It might have been passable during the daytime, but it obscured what little light was left. Inez remembered the open wells and brick pits from her passage in the other direction. She didn't relish falling into one of those in the dark. The dust storm didn't last long, but by then Inez was resigned to stopping for the night.

Funny how easily she'd slipped back into life on the trail. It had been years since she'd bedded down under the open sky, the Milky Way spread overhead like a casket of gems spilt out onto black velvet. She even remembered how to start a fire with flint and iron; a skill, along with her abilities to handle the animals, that went far in winning Bachir's approval. Those same two skills, along with her beauty and daring, had also won the heart of her husband.

She closed her eyes and recalled the day they'd met. He had come to Andalusia, looking for adventure and the remnants of his own Spanish past. He found her instead, dancing and singing with the Gypsies around their encampment. Richard rode up to the camp on a bay mare and dismounted. Inez took one look at his smiling, tanned face and wavy hair, the color of rich walnut, and felt her stomach flutter. She remembered the assured way that he walked, not cocky or swaggering like a few of the dons' sons she knew, but like a man in control of his life and with no need to prove it.

She'd danced up to him, swishing her full skirts and twirling in the uninhibited flamenco style of the Roma, as the Gypsies termed themselves. He responded by joining in, clapping the rhythm as he stepped lightly around her. She felt his warmth behind her back, and quivered when his arm brushed hers in passing.

Never had she felt so on fire, so alive, as she did then. They spent the rest of the afternoon together, riding across her family's estate. Few men could maintain her pace on a horse, and she led him in a wild chase. Eventually, after clearing a stream, he'd caught up to her and, in one sweeping motion, clasped her around the waist and lifted her off her saddle and onto his during a full gallop. Once she rested securely in his embrace, he drew to a halt and kissed her lips, eyes, and hair. She knew then that there would never be another man for her.

Afterward she took him home and introduced him to her parents. They were not impressed by an American cowboy, even if he did own land in New Mexico. They had other plans for their only child. Inez and Richard eloped the next night and were married by a sympathetic Benedictine priest in the village.

That memory fled in the face of another, this time in New Mexico. She and her husband had set up a camp in the mountains where his family had long ago been awarded land. Only they were not alone. A slender young girl in braided pigtails, jeans, and a denim shirt joined them. Together they dug a small pit in which to bury potatoes to bake under hot coals. Richard reclined on the grass with his guitar and played the song he'd learned from the Gypsies. This time it was little Jade who danced while Inez clapped out the rhythm. Inez had always wondered where Jade had learned the flamenco and why she hadn't joined in the dance herself that evening. Now she knew the answer to that first question.

She still wondered about the second.

The headache, the dank smell, the cold stone floor, and the curious squeaks seemed all too familiar. "I think I'm having what they call déjà vu," Jade mumbled. "I've been here before." She shifted her legs, found them unfettered, and sat up. That's when she heard something clank. A foot of stout iron chain bound her wrists to each other in front of her. Another six feet circled her waist and shackled her to the far wall, giving her just enough length to lie down or visit a slop bucket in the back corner.

"I know I've been here before."

The squeaking, which stopped when Jade moved, started up again. *Probably the same rats, too.* "Hi, fellows," she said to the rodents. "Remember me? I have it on good authority that you're actually *jinni* in disguise. So how about getting me out of here again. Can anyone pick a lock?" When the rats didn't come any closer, Jade slumped against the wall. "I forgot. You aren't supposed to like iron, are you."

She wondered how long she'd been unconscious. Was it still night? Did Bennington come back with those slippers, find her gone, and look for her? She should have known better than to go back to that caretaker's hut. Her assailants must have figured out her trick and doubled back themselves. Then it was just a matter of waiting for an opportunity, and she had handed it to them. *Or Bennington handed it to them.* Jade chased away the thought. After all, she had no evidence that he had betrayed her. But cynicism reared up in her mind and taunted her. No one could be that altruistic to travel alone over half the length of Morocco just to save her and her mother, could they?

She heard a key turn in the rusty lock and the door hinges creak. *Company.* A burly Arab stood in the doorway with a lantern in one hand and a chicken leg in the other. He bit off a chunk of meat and chewed, waiting as though wary of some trick. *Probably the same guard as last time.* Jade spotted his crooked nose and the relatively fresh red gashes striping his face. *Definitely the same guard.*

The guard tossed the bone to the floor and wiped his greasy lips with the back of his hand. He hung the lantern from a hook by the door and drew his dagger, a new one since Jade had taken his old one. Jade watched him approach her with the same slow steps that one would use to come close to a chained lion. *Time to test his nerve,* she thought. She waited without making any motion until he was inside her radius of movement. Then she leaped towards him, hands extended like claws, a snarl issuing from her throat. The man jumped up a foot and back two more in a lightning-fast move that would have made her old tomcat, Rupert, proud. Jade leaned back against the wall, chuckling.

"I'm glad to see you've retained your sense of humor, Miss del Cameron. You'll need it." The hushed voice came not from the guard, but from someone standing just outside the door in the shadows.

"It is safe," said the guard. "She has not gotten loose this time."

"Lucky for you she hasn't." Jade's captor stepped into the room and into the lamplight.

"The mules," exclaimed Inez, pointing to a pair of animals tied under a shelter of poles and palm fronds. She and Bachir had broken camp before dawn and arrived at the south palm gardens by late morning. Inez immediately recognized Jade and Mohan's animals by the distinctive design on the saddle blankets. After Bachir convinced the Arab overseeing the animal's care that Inez was the owner's mother, they were allowed to inspect the panniers, where they found Jade's boots. Inez stood on her tiptoes and pivoted around, searching for her daughter. "Jade!" she started to call.

Bachir put his hand out and shook his head to stop her. Using Inez's version of sign language, he touched his chest, then his lips, before pointing to a man who sold grain. Inez understood. He would talk to the man and find out when Jade had arrived.

Inez waited by their animals as Bachir dickered for both information and a reasonable price for caring for their donkeys and the mule. That's when she first noticed the crowd of men clustered at the far end of the field. They shouted and pressed forward, only to be driven back again. Something was definitely going on over there. Bachir came back with a frown. Inez didn't wait for him to try to tell her he had no news. She gathered he had little beyond knowing when Jade had arrived. Instead, she pointed to the commotion, grabbed Jade's boots, and led the way to the crowd.

"Bennington!" exclaimed Jade. "I should have guessed. I've got to quit being so trusting." She stared at his immaculately trimmed, creamy blond mustache and understood the Berber boy's description. It wasn't a red mustache, it was a blond one coated in the *bled*'s red dust. A third man peered around the doorframe. "And Mohan," she said, switching to Arabic laced with French when the first language failed her. "You son of a legless camel and three blind dogs. It was you, not Bachir, who betrayed your people, wasn't it?" The fact that he was not in chains told her as much, but she wanted to hear it from him.

Mohan straightened to his full five-foot, four-inch height. "I did not betray them. It is for the good of my people, for my daughter, to abandon the infidel ways of the *kahina*. I cannot let you find the amulet. I want her to marry a rich man in Marrakech and live in a fine house, not practice magic."

"Then you betray yourself, Mohan. What chance would I have to find one silver charm in all of the Atlas or even in Marrakech? None. Unless," she added, "you *really* believed it would call to me." Her emerald green eyes locked on him, staring as though to bore a hole in his own eyes.

Mohan threw his hand up in front of his face, palm out. "The evil eye!" he screamed in Arabic. "Five in your eye," he shouted to ward off the danger from her stare.

Jade laughed, her voice echoing in the chamber. "Your curse does no good, Mohan. I am the *kahina*'s right hand," she taunted him. "I have her vision. Shall I prove it? *You* stole the bracelets from the other women to sell for yourself. I can see it."

Mohan cowered against the outer wall, his hands outstretched in front of his face. Jade laughed and continued her tale. "You didn't care about your people, only about the money. Then you found a buyer. You told him about the amulet and promised to bring it next time. You stole it and buried it in the caretaker's hut on your last trip to sell rugs. You hoped the dead saint would protect you from the *jinni* when you came back for it. I saw you take it out. Did you rehide it? That won't help you now. The ones who shun light love treasure. They do not willingly give it up. They will chase the one who took it from them."

Mohan's face contorted in fear. He closed his eyes against her stare and covered his ears with his hands.

Jade raised her voice. "Your only hope is to return it to the *kahina*, Mohan."

"Stop." Bennington's soft librarian's whisper carried weight, enough to silence Mohan's whimpers. "Fool," he said to Mohan. "She cannot hurt you."

"The *jinni* can," moaned Mohan. "And she has the evil eye."

"Then give the amulet to *me*," suggested Bennington. He stood close to the doorframe, allowing the torch shadow to cover all but his clean-shaven chin. Now his soft, subdued voice carried a soothing quality such as one used with a frightened child.

Mohan shook his head. "No. I promised *her*."

Jade turned her head to hear better. *Her?* Libby Tremaine had one of the bags. Did he mean her? It seemed unlikely. Or had Lilith herself been here at one time? Until now Jade had had only her own inner gut feeling to indicate that Mrs. Worthy was behind this mess, but she decided to try to play her hunch at the first available opportunity.

"Fool," hissed Bennington. "Do you forget who I work for?" He waved his hand to dismiss the Berber. "I will pay you later, when you hand over the amulet. Wait in the court-yard."

Mohan raced up the stairs, leaving Jade alone with Bennington and the guard. Now was the time to voice her hunch. "So you and de Portillo work for Lilith Worthy," she said. She watched to gauge Bennington's initial response.

He shrugged. "I prefer to use the term 'partners.' Mr. de Portillo is merely a convenient courier."

"Does she think I'll interrupt this operation as I did the others? She forgets that I only found out about them by accident. I didn't know anything about this and would never have been the wiser if you hadn't pulled me into it by kidnapping my mother. I suppose Mother told you all about me on the boat and it made you nervous to think I was even going to be in the country. Or did you run into your boss when she visited the boat in London?"

"On the contrary," he said as he inspected his manicured nails and flicked away a speck of dirt, "that knowledge came to us through the contents of your mother's letter."

Jade remembered the opened envelope of the last letter

she'd received from her mother. She had always suspected that someone had been spying on her.

"Spies," Bennington hissed when Jade didn't make a comment. "You see, as easy as it is to smuggle *out* of Tangier, it is still hard to smuggle *into* anyplace else. And the French have gotten rather uppity about all the hashish that comes into France from Morocco. We needed a . . . what is that new term you Americans use? A fall guy. So your arrival provided an opportunity."

"And you kidnapped my mother as bait to get me."

Bennington leaned against the wall, thought better of it, and brushed the cobwebs and dirt from his sleeve. "Not just you. Don't you think a mother and daughter make a perfect criminal network? Mohan will tell the authorities where your charming mother is hiding and they will arrest her."

"And I presume you've been ordered to kill me? I've stepped on Lilith's smuggling operations one time too many."

Bennington shrugged. "You do tend to get in the way, but you overestimate your impact and underestimate the extent of our activities. Still, I think the reason is far more personal. *You* killed her son, David. He was everything to her."

David. Jade had always felt he risked himself too much as a pilot in order to win her acceptance to his marriage proposal. Apparently so did his mother. Perhaps he'd written to her about the American ambulancier that he was striving to impress. That could go a long way, Jade thought, to explaining why Mrs. Worthy hated her so much. Jade's unnerving dream of the dark lady popped unbidden into her mind. Part of it became clearer now. She understood the lone tear the dark lady had shed, and the subsequent terrible tree that grew from the gravestone, David's gravestone. In her unconscious mind, she'd understood Lilith's grief for a lost son, a grief that gave rise to a hideous vengeance centered on death.

"Then why drag me in here? Why didn't you and Lilith just kill me when you had a chance? It's a wonder you didn't do it when I hired the car. I presume that was one of your confederates there posing as Madame Laferriere?"

"Clever girl."

"I suppose you played on Libby Tremaine to write that note to Mother? And the man stabbed in the tunnels? Was he someone you couldn't trust anymore?"

"He was just a man we hired to capture your mother," Bennington replied. "But we could hardly leave him alive after that, could we?"

"Just like you can't afford to leave me alive now?" As she asked, forgetting that Bennington hadn't responded to the allegation against Libby, a new thought formed. Had Lilith returned on board ship, posing as the infirm Aunt Viola?

"On the contrary," said Bennington, "we need you alive to take the blame for this operation. If you turn up dead, then that takes the blame off of you. That little murder of the guide just sweetened the pot. So I'm not going to kill you. I'm sending you to hell instead. This evening, the slave market will have another addition to the usual fare. With any luck, you'll end up spending your life in a harem in Timbuktu."

"You'll pay for this, you bastard."

"Oh, no," said Bennington. "You're not my type, but I'm sure someone else will be glad to pay for you." The last Jade heard from him was his soft, husky laugh as it echoed down the stairs.

CHAPTER 22

*Slave markets used to occur on a weekly basis, generally in either
the old square or in the carpet district. Potential buyers eagerly bid on
black-skinned men from the south and blue-eyed Circassian women.
But the French also put a stop to this practice in 1912.*

—The Traveler

INEZ SECRETLY HOPED HER DAUGHTER was behind this commotion, just like when she'd put a box full of nesting mice in the church's piano bench, effectively proving that several of the choir members could hit high C. But the fact that she didn't hear Jade's voice above the general babble told her that her hopes were in vain. *Of all the times for her to not cause a ruckus, she'd have to pick this one.* As she came closer, she could tell that the men's voices weren't angry, just excited.

"Stand back, please. No, I do not want your rug. Hey, there! Get that camel away before he chews on my spars."

An American. Inez pushed through the crowd with Bachir's help and came face-to-face with a yellow biplane and one frazzled pilot doing his best to protect it. He held his leather flight helmet by the straps and swatted at the Dromedary intent on taking a nibble out of the plane. Inez turned to Bachir and made a sweeping gesture to the crowd, followed by shooing motions. Bachir nodded and set to work.

"*Imshi,* go away!" Bachir said, and waved away the men closest to the plane. Inez couldn't tell what else he said, but judging from the wide-eyed expressions, it probably involved curses and an army of evil spirits haunting this machine. Whatever he said, it proved effective.

"Thank you," said the American. He patted the biplane. "I've been stuck here for the past two hours, afraid to leave her alone. It's a good thing you happened along. . . ." The man stopped in midthought, his gaze taking in Inez's features. Then after a few seconds' study, he held out his right hand. "Pardon me for staring, ma'am, but you must be Mrs. del Cameron."

"Yes, I am," said Inez as she shook his hand. "But how did you know?"

"My name is Sam Featherstone. Avery Dunbury received a message from Jade. Said you'd been kidnapped. I came to rescue you." He ran a hand through his mop of straight brown hair, which had flopped over one eyebrow. "It appears you don't need my help anymore."

With what appeared to be a very casual and proper glance, Inez sized up Sam as she might a new horse. What she saw agreed with her. "Your gallantry is greatly appreciated, Mr. Featherstone. But don't be too certain that I no longer need your assistance."

Sam made a quick survey of the area. "Where *is* Jade?"

"That, Mr. Featherstone, is the question of the hour and why I am very glad you have arrived."

Jade pulled every trick she could think of to free herself but, unfortunately, her repertoire was limited. The rats, which had proven themselves useful with the leather bindings, were useless against iron, and there was nothing handy that would serve as a hammer and anvil to break the chains. The guard seemed mildly amused by her pretenses at fainting and needing water, and was far too wary of her after the last time to risk another ruse. That left trying to pull the chain out of the wall. If she'd hoped to have some help from rotting brick work, she was sadly mistaken. The bolt was driven into a stout stone pillar and secured with well-made mortar.

Exhausted, she sat on the floor, toying with the padlock that secured the iron band around her waist. Could she pick it? Lock picking was never a skill Jade had bothered to learn. She had watched her father do it once when they'd lost the key to a document box. He'd used two tools, but told her that one could work if you raked it hard across the tumblers. *Well, what do I have to lose?*

She searched for something to use as a tool. A *fibula* might have worked, if she hadn't already used them to elude capture. She had no knife except for one tucked into her boots, which were back with the mules. The smooth little amulet around her neck wouldn't do either. *Mother would probably say if I hadn't bobbed my hair, I'd still have hairpins.* Her gaze strayed to one of the resident rats chewing on something in the nearest corner.

"You wouldn't have any ideas, would you?" she asked. The rat bared his yellow teeth at a second rodent who'd come to inspect the first one's intended meal. At first Jade didn't recognize the contested prize, then as she let her eyes adjust to the dim light seeping through the door, she identified it. *The chicken bone.*

The bone was out of hand's reach, but not out of reach of her foot. Jade worked the iron waist binding up as high as it would go and extended her right foot towards the corner.

She could barely see the bone in this position, but she was more concerned about how the rat would feel about a succulent bare toe poking him. She pulled back, found a broken piece of ceiling plaster, and tossed it at the rat. The surly rodent waddled to safety, giving Jade a chance to snare the bone with her toes. Success! To her delight, it was a well-gnawed leg bone, partially sharpened at one end.

"Thanks, buddy. I owe you. If I get out of here, I promise never to call a rotten person a rat again."

Jade shimmied around in the snug band and inserted the sharpened bone tip into the lock. Too wide. She held the bone against the stone wall and studied it before beginning the process of reshaping it. It should look like a key, she thought, with a slightly wider tip to turn the pins inside the lock. Jade rubbed the bone against the stone, slowly abrading it. Gradually she wore away the back half of the hollow bone. Next she gently filed away the sides, careful not to snap the increasingly fragile tool or lose the enlarged tip. Every few minutes, she tested it in the lock. As soon as it slipped in freely, she went to work trying to jimmy the pins inside.

She tried to imagine a key and how it turned. She concentrated on feeling any resistance to her bone pick as it swiveled and pushed the inner workings. She turned an ear to the lock, bowing low over her waist, straining to hear any clicks. *Nothing.*

Finally in her frustration, she smacked the makeshift key against the wall, driving it deeper into the tumbler. *Now I've done it,* she thought. *Probably wedged it in there for good or broken it.* She grabbed the bone's end, gave it a gentle twist, and raked it out of the keyhole at the same time. The lock clicked open. Recovering from her astonishment, Jade quickly removed the padlock and opened the waist iron. She let the chain and the heavy iron band slip silently down to the floor. *Now for the door*. She'd worry about the wrist irons later, when she was clear of the house.

As if on cue, the door opened and the guard entered. This time he carried an old flintlock pistol and it was pointed directly at her. The slash marks on his face blazed like a brand in the ruddy glow of the lantern resting at his feet. With his free hand, he hung the key outside the cell, picked up the lantern, and hung it on a hook inside by the door.

"Good," he said in heavily accented English. "You have saved me the trouble of unchaining you." He grinned, revealing rows of stained teeth. "Now we will go to the marketplace."

Inez finished summarizing the events from her kidnapping to the present as she, Bachir, and Sam walked into the *Medina,* to the caravan hostelries where most travelers lodged themselves and their animals. When Inez saw the assorted camels, mules, donkey, and rare horse stabled in the lower quarters, she wondered why Jade hadn't come here with her animals. Perhaps her daughter had hoped to avoid detection by staying outside the gates, just as she and Bachir had done.

Bachir excused himself in French, first pointing to his eyes and ears and then to the caravansary in an effort to communicate that he was going to try to gather information on Jade's whereabouts. Sam, who had learned a smattering of French during the Great War, managed to understand his intent.

Sam rubbed a hand across his stubbled chin and frowned. "Maybe she's not in any trouble, Mrs. del Cameron. If she didn't know you were following her, it's not surprising that you haven't run across her yet."

"Please, Mr. Featherstone. This is my daughter we are talking about. If you have known her for any amount of time, then you know she has a penchant for finding trouble and entering into the thick of it."

Sam grinned. "That she does." The grin faded and his brows furrowed as worry washed over his face. "Did she give any hint as to what she planned to do? Where she intended to go?"

"She didn't confide in me." The statement held a note of hurt rather than of blame. "Once Mr. Bachir returns, I hope he can lead us back to that house in which I was held. If he can, then I intend to bring along a herd of French soldiers."

Sam smiled at the use of the word "herd." It reminded him of the tale Jade told about her mutt dog and his own penchant for herding and picking up skunks. She'd named the animal Kaloff the Dog as a joke in itself. He erased the smile as soon as Inez turned back to him. "Something amusing you, Mr. Featherstone?" Inez asked.

"No, ma'am. Um, well, I was just imagining that dog of Jade's running herd on the French."

"Ah, you know about Kaloff, then?" She sighed. "I'm coming to believe that Jade and that dog are two of a kind, both completely untrainable."

"If I may say so, ma'am, sometimes you just have to let a creature be what God made it to be. My father once told me there are two kinds of animals: critters and varmints. The first are happy inside the fences. The varmints are happiest outside." He looked up as Bachir returned in a hurry, his arms swinging wide arcs as he waved them forward. "Looks like our friend here has some news. After you, ma'am."

"Come quickly," said Bachir in French. "*Allala* Jade." He turned and pushed his way past a crowd of people busy inspecting a live chicken hanging by its feet. The crowd resisted and, after finally parting ranks for Bachir, closed up and glared at Inez and Sam, who had to elbow their way past. The chicken was the only one that didn't mutter curses and imprecations at them.

"Do you have any idea where we're going?" Sam called over the din to Inez.

"No, but wherever it is, we aren't making much headway. And we're losing Bachir. We must press on harder, Mr. Featherstone."

Sam took the lead and shoved with renewed force through that group, but more clusters loomed ahead in the narrow streets as people came out for the late-afternoon business. Start shouting *"Balek,"* Inez suggested. "It's what the donkey men yell. To clear the way, that is."

"Balek. Balek!" yelled Sam. Immediately, the crowds moved to the side to avoid an oncoming donkey. Sam grabbed Inez's hand and towed her along after him before the people closed back and separated them. "Works like Moses parting the sea," he said. *"Balek!"* They caught up with Bachir.

"Where are we going?" asked Sam in his rudimentary French as they hurried after the Berber.

Bachir yelled over his shoulder, *"Souk Joutia Zrabi."*

The guard took no chances with Jade this time. There were too many places for her to hide between the old palatial *riad* and the carpet auction district. He knew firsthand how feisty she could be and his face now bore the new marks to prove it. He hauled Jade at pistol point up the stairs to the central courtyard and shoved her down hard onto a threadbare rug.

Jade didn't go down without a fight. She lashed out with both feet, but the guard neatly sidestepped her kicks and added one of his own in her ribs.

The blow, while not hard enough to break bone, knocked the air out of Jade's lungs. Tears flooded her eyes as she gasped for breath, her chained hands reflexively grasping her side. Her pulse pounded in her ears, and for a moment she lost her vision as exhaustion, pain, and thirst joined forces to overwhelm her. By the time her head cleared, the guard had rolled her up in the rug. She gagged on the carpet's stale scent.

"Do not fear, little one," said the guard in a mocking voice. "The rug is thin so you can breathe. My master said to drug you, but who would buy a limp rag? This will take enough fight out of you so that you will fetch a very good price. Perhaps I should buy you myself, huh? I could teach you obedience."

An explosive sneeze cut short Jade's muffled curses.

The guard lifted her up and slung her over his right shoulder. Jade tried kicking, then rolling, but each attempt required oxygen, and the carpet kept that in limited supply. She concentrated on tilting her head so she faced the open end and took a deep breath. It was enough to give her fresh courage and strength. This time instead of trying to kick her legs, she swung her entire body like a bar, using the point where the guard gripped her around the waist as a fulcrum.

Contact! She caught the guard in the throat with her legs. In retaliation, he slammed her down across her stomach on a donkey and tied her in place. She felt the pressure of the rope grip her across the shoulders and pull her head down. He passed the rope under the animal's stomach and attached the other end to her ankles.

Her head swam, her ears buzzed, and for a moment Jade

lost consciousness. Her next recollections were vague impressions of sounds: people haggling over prices, a water seller ringing his bell, the tremulous notes from a snake charmer's reed, all mingled with the donkey's rhythmic clopping step. She tried to sort out the voices for some clue as to her route. To the best of her knowledge, she'd passed the Square of the Dead, and gone through the fruit vendors' market, followed by that of the herbalists'. The donkey stopped soon after and her bonds were loosened. Jade waited, biding her time and energy. *What was north of the herbalists? The carpet dealers?* She remembered the little plaza with benches set for auctions. Through her rug, she caught the guard's words and managed to understand enough of his Arabic.

"I have a woman to sell."

"Where?"

"Here." The guard patted the rug over Jade's back.

"What? You bring her like this?"

"We did not want anyone to see her before she went on the market. Do you understand?" Jade heard the clink of coins and knew that news of her kidnapping had been stifled by a bribe. "Do not ask any questions. She wears the tattoos of a Berber. Sell her as such. Sell her to someone from far away. She must not stay here."

"I cannot guarantee who will bid and who will not bid."

"You can do a lot with your tongue to sway the right bidder. Do you want the French to get word of your sales again?"

"Take her in there with the others and write your name on the books so I know who receives the money."

"I have been told you may keep the money. It is your payment to sell her far. And my dagger," he added, "is your payment if you fail." Jade heard a jingling of metal. "There is the key. But do not release her yourself. Give the key to the one who buys her."

The conversation did not go unnoticed by the surrounding people. Jade heard the hum of murmuring voices, like bees. The buzz became louder as news of this unusual woman went from person to person. By the time the guard hauled Jade off the donkey and toted her into a nearby building, the voices had reached a clamoring din. The guard slid her off his shoulder and plopped her onto the floor.

"Careful," said the auctioneer. "Do not bruise my goods."

"The bruise won't show right away," said the guard with a growl, but Jade suspected he unrolled the rug more gently than he probably wanted.

"Achoo," Jade sneezed, then struggled to her feet before she could be manhandled further.

The guard took one last look at Jade and shoved a finger in front of the auctioneer's nose. "Remember. Sell her far away." He picked up the old rug and stomped out the door into a large, covered courtyard.

Immediately, the five women hiding in the shadows against the far wall ventured forward. It was as though the multi-hued tile work came to life. Their brilliantly colored caftans glittered as bits of gold embroidery caught the lamplight. The auctioneer clapped his hands twice and an old crone rose from a tattered cushion, a ragged crow in black among a flock of songbirds.

"Clean her," the auctioneer commanded. Jade recognized the old woman as the one Patrido de Portillo had pointed out to her during the breakfast in Tangier. Jade studied the young women edging timidly forward to view her and recognized them by their general height and numbers as the young women she'd seen in tow. They clustered around her, eager now to inspect this unusual woman who'd come rolled up like a packet of fish in an old newspaper. One of them reached out a tentative finger to touch Jade's short black hair, and the old woman barked at them. Immediately, like birds startled from their crumbs, they fluttered back a few paces. Then they settled, unwilling to completely vacate the area in the hopes that they could edge forward again.

The old woman dipped one end of her black robe in a dribbling wall fountain and swiped at Jade's face. Jade pulled back and swatted at the crone with her chained hands. "Get away from me," she said in French before adding an *imshi* in Arabic. Whether the woman understood or not, she didn't appear to want to risk getting struck by the chains and returned to her cushion.

Jade took the opportunity to quickly examine her newest prison, but found little to encourage her hopes of escape. The building might have been a home at one time, based on the mosaic of turquoise, blue, and red wall tiles. Now this room at least seemed to be a storage room for rugs waiting to be auctioned off in the airy courtyard. Half of the room held rolled-up carpets. The rest was devoted to some low cushions, a teapot, and a brazier for heating the water. Goods other than rugs were destined to go on sale today.

True to most homes in Morocco, there were no windows looking out on the ground floor. All light came in from the open skylight in the central courtyard on the other side of the door. A skylight she couldn't reach even when she was put up for auction. Jade surmised she was in the carpet sellers' *souk* and that the area had been selected for the secretive slave auction. She tried the door. Locked. *Can't let the merchandise slip out.*

The auctioneer's voice sounded from outside the door.

The slave mart had begun with the male slaves. From the auctioneer's description, most of his goods were boys with an occasional beggarly man thrown in for heavy work. The girls edged forward to listen at the door. They conversed among themselves in nervous voices in a language Jade didn't know. Normally her heart would have gone out to them in their plight, but hers wasn't any better. She decided her best chance lay in being as disagreeable as possible to forestall any bidding. Then, when she'd created maximum confusion, she'd make a break for it and run like she had a hive of angry hornets on her tail.

The auctioneer announced the sale of some rare beauties, and the girls whispered again and held each other. The youngest stifled a sob. *Okay. Before I bolt, I'll knock out the auctioneer*. If Jade could put a halt to the auction for the day, she might be able to get the French military in to save these girls before they were sold. She turned and gently shooed them from the door, then pointed to herself in an effort to tell them that she would go first.

She heard the exterior bolt slide back and stepped back and to the side, waiting for the door to open inward. It did and she blinked against the late-afternoon sunshine filtering down through the skylight. The auctioneer tried to push her back to get one of the other girls. Jade refused and stood her ground. With a tired sigh, the man took hold of her arm and pulled her outside, shutting the door behind him.

"What am I bid for this . . ." Immediately Jade slammed her elbow up and into the man's ribs.

He doubled over and the crowd roared their delight at the unexpected entertainment. Jade never gave him a chance to regain his breath. She immediately jumped behind him, threw her wrist chains over his head, and pulled back, his throat caught in her irons.

The little man was no match for Jade, even in her exhausted condition. She had youth, well-honed muscles, and a great deal of rage on her side. As she watched, his face turned red, then purple. Jade had no intention of killing him; just rendering him unconscious would do.

"Ahmad," the auctioneer squeaked to a large Arab who had just returned from handing off a male slave, "help me."

Ahmad grabbed Jade's waist from behind in a hard grip while his second hand forced her to relax her vicelike hold on the auctioneer's throat. The auctioneer slid down in front of her, his hands clawing at his neck while he gasped for air. Jade raised both her legs and kicked back. She felt contact, but not in a vulnerable spot, and without boots she didn't manage to inflict any damage. *The hell with that*. She leaned forward and sank her teeth into her assailant's hand.

By this time, the auctioneer had regained his breath and at least part of his voice. "A very strong woman. A hard worker." As his brawny assistant howled from Jade's savage bite, the auctioneer added, "Good teeth."

The crowd laughed, clapped, and hooted, but no one placed any bids. If anything, some of the men seemed to be placing wagers as to the outcome. "She is a lion from the Atlas," suggested one spectator, and the other laughed.

"A man of the desert would know how to tame this creature," suggested the auctioneer, apparently remembering his orders to sell her to someone from far away. "Who will give me five hundred dinar?"

Jade twisted in Ahmad's grip and punched him in the face, her chains striking him on the chin.

"A hundred dinar? Fifty?"

Just as Jade thought she had a chance to strike another blow and completely destroy all chances of being sold, someone from the crowd tossed a leather bag at the auctioneer's feet. A gold coin spilled partly out of the open mouth and glittered on the stone floor.

"Sold," croaked the auctioneer.

CHAPTER 23

Someone forgot to tell the slave traders that they are out of business.
I have it on good authority that the auctions still take place in secret.

—The Traveler

No sooner had the auctioneer gasped the word "Sold!"
than the burly assistant released Jade as readily as he would
a nearly grown and very scrappy Barbary lion cub. Jade
dropped to the stone floor with a thud, her face just inches
from the little leather sack.

"Do not let her escape, Ahmad," shouted the auctioneer.
Before Jade could recover her breath and get up, the big Arab
planted a foot on her back and pressed down. The auctioneer squatted and reached a tentative hand towards his money.
Jade snarled at him, and he scrambled back.

A pair of booted feet stepped in front of her. There was
something familiar about them. "You may release her," said a
man in very poor French. *Something very familiar*.

"Sam!" exclaimed Jade to the boots' occupant. "Am I
ever glad to see you." Sam extended a hand, which she took,
and helped her to her feet. The auctioneer made good use

of Jade's preoccupation and snatched his money before she could revert back to a wild beast.

"Sam, my mother—"

"Is safe outside with Bachir," he finished for her. "Let's get out of here." He took the key from the auctioneer and unlocked the wrist irons.

He started to lead her away but she dug in with both feet planted firmly. "No," she said, shaking her short black curls. "Those other girls. I can't let them be sold." She pointed to the adjoining room, where even as they spoke Ahmad was leading out the younger and more timid of the women. She pulled back from the man's grip with all the force of a mewling kitten, a striking contrast to Jade's behavior.

"By all means," said Sam. He stepped quickly around to the auctioneer. "The sale is over."

"What do you mean?" demanded the auctioneer. "If you want this girl, buy her as you did the wild cat."

Sam inched closer, maneuvering behind the man's left side. "I said, the sale is over."

"Your French is very bad," retorted the auctioneer with a sneer.

"But my aim is not." Sam pulled a Colt revolver from his holster and shoved it into the man's flesh just below the ribs. Ahmad took a step towards Sam, but the auctioneer waved him back.

"The sale is over," called the auctioneer, waving his arms to disperse the crowd. "Please go home."

The crowd disbanded without too much grumbling. After all, it had been a far more entertaining sale than usual. A few coins exchanged hands as the previously made bets on Jade versus Ahmad were won or lost.

Ahmad didn't back away with the crowd until Sam pointed the gun at him. The size of the huge pistol clearly intimidated the guard, who was more used to bullying chained men and helpless women.

"And I will take the other girls with me," added Sam.

As the crowd left the building's courtyard, Inez and Bachir pushed their way inside while Sam kept his Colt trained on the two slavers. Inez ran over to her daughter, opened her mouth to say something, decided against it, and settled for stroking Jade's hair.

Jade saw her mother's lower lip tremble and knew that her mother had undergone a tremendous amount of emotional and physical pain to get to her. She longed to hug her mother as she could her dad, but settled for something that would not likely be rejected. She took her mother's hand and gave a gentle squeeze. Her mother returned it and held on tightly while her other hand caressed her daughter's wrists where the irons had bruised them. Even that gentle touch hurt, but Jade wasn't about to wince and end the first maternal touch she'd experienced in several years. She fought back the tears welling up behind her eyes and swallowed down the tightness in her throat.

"Mother," said Jade with a tender smile. "Why am I not surprised to see you here?" She gently pulled her hand free of Inez's tight grip and kissed her mother's hand. "It's a wonderful surprise at that. Will you let the other young ladies out, please? And Sam, I think our two friends here should see what it is like to be locked up inside for a while."

Inez coaxed the girls outside while Jade kept an eye on Ahmad, swinging the wrist irons in a way that suggested she'd like to strike him with them. "Jade, there's an old woman in here," said Inez. "What do we do about her?"

"Leave the hag in there with these two. They deserve each other."

While Inez shushed the young women, who huddled about her like chicks around a protective hen, Jade and Sam prodded the two slave dealers into the little storage room and drew the bolt across the door.

"That won't hold them for long," said Sam. "They'll be pounding on the doors as soon as we leave."

"Let them. By the way, Sam, thanks again for your timely rescue." She touched his arm, then his chin as though she needed tangible proof that he really stood before her. "My stars! I can't believe you're here. How did you know where to look? How did you find Mother? What—?"

Sam hushed the last question with one finger on her lips. Jade felt giddy and light-headed, a sensation she might have attributed in large part to fatigue and hunger, except it increased when he drew nearer. Her pulse quickened.

He took her hands in his and came closer still, his dark eyes gazing into hers. Sam leaned in to kiss her, saw Inez standing off to his left still occupied with the girls, and quickly pulled Jade off to the opposite room. "Best make sure there are no more slaves in this room, as well," he called over his shoulder.

No sooner had he drawn her around the corner than he enveloped Jade in his arms and pulled her close. His lips found hers, his pencil-thin mustache brushing her upper lip, cheek, and neck as his mouth explored and caressed every available exposed inch.

Jade, still relatively breathless from her rough handling by Ahmad, found his gentle but urgent kisses equally disarming. Only this time, still caught up in the surprise of seeing him, her reaction was to surrender. She responded to his caresses by clinging to him and letting her senses take over. His scent of soap, sweat, and leather smelled like an intoxicating perfume to her, one that made her breath come in short, panting gasps. Her skin noted the tickle of his mustache, the scrape of his chin and cheek stubble. She felt his body heat and the warmth of his breath. Her ears concentrated on the gravelly bass murmurs, and all this rushed in to fill the void left behind when release replaced fear.

Her heart pounded faster just as it did during her fight and her skin grew flushed and warm. Her pores opened to release the heat and carry away her own musky scent. Every hair stood alert to receive a caress, each nerve alive, and, for a moment, everything dissolved from around her except for his scent, touch, and her own heartbeat.

Then a stray sound intruded, her mother's querulous voice calling for her to help with the girls.

"Um, Sam," she managed in between his kisses.

He nibbled at her neck. "What?"

"Sam, my mother is out there."

"Very nice lady." His lips strayed to her earlobe.

"She's calling. She'll be in here any moment."

Sam released her and stepped back, his face tight with passion, his movements conveying self-restraint. "Sorry," he said, a bit sheepish. "I'm just so damned happy to see you alive."

With her mother nearby, Jade's usual reserve took over and she widened the space between them. "That makes two of us. I hate to think what would have happened if you hadn't shown up in time." She patted down her errant hair, more out of nervousness than from concern for her appearance.

Sam grinned. "Yes, that guard might have ended up in a very bad way if I hadn't stopped you."

Jade chuckled and discovered that it hurt to laugh. "Presumably you are the aid Dunbury mentioned in my telegram." She took his arm and walked with him back into the courtyard. Her mother arched one brow and inspected them both from across the room. Jade's free hand instinctively went to her uppermost shirt button to see if it was still fastened. It wasn't. Her fingers fumbled with the button. "I must admit you were the last person I expected to see, Sam. The last I heard, you were back on Marsabit, filming the elephants."

"That's right," he said, slowing his pace to extend his time alone with Jade. "Stayed about two weeks and made a dandy film. Then I headed for Mombasa and caught the first boat that eventually took me back to the States."

Jade stopped and turned to him. "You went back through Nairobi and didn't say good-bye?" Hurt and disappointment seeped into her voice.

"Well, to be honest, after our last meeting, I wasn't sure you wanted to see me again. I sort of made a promise to myself that when I came back, and I had *every* intention of coming back," he added, "it was going to be as a whole man and not some pinioned bird." He patted his right leg, the one that was wooden from the knee down.

Jade knew about his prosthetic leg, a fact she had discovered when they were chained together in the desert last January. But she didn't know what he meant by this promise to himself. She looked up into his eyes, as dark as ebony shadows and filled with their own secrets. "I don't understand."

Sam grinned, his white teeth flashing in what could only be described as an ornery, cat-and-canary grin. "Wait till you see her. My Jenny is the prettiest thing you ever laid eyes on."

Jade knew that his "Jenny" referred to the pilots' beloved

Curtis JN4-D2 plane in which many American pilots had trained. "Your plane?" she gasped in an excited breath.

Sam nodded, as happy as a kid with his first bicycle. "You bet. My friends in Indiana, the Bert Boys, fixed me up." Seeing Jade's confused look he explained, "That's what I call them. One is Ro*bert* and his twin brother is Gil*bert*. They got the rudder pedals rigged up for hand controls, and I sold the elephant movie to an outfit in California for enough money to make the payment. I own her free and clear." He paused and his dark eyes twinkled. "I own you, too, now. Bought and paid for."

Jade made a soft scoffing snort and folded her arms across her chest. "And just where did you happen to get the money, Mister?"

"Um, your mother had this bag of coins and . . ."

"So if anyone owns me, it's Mother. Come on, Sam, she's waiting, and it's never a good idea to keep Mother waiting."

Jade and Sam joined Inez, Bachir, and the covey of animated young ladies. Jade made the formal introduction of Sam to her mother, and Sam explained how he had managed to come to the rescue.

"After I got my plane, I wanted to head back to Africa and show it off to, er, the Thompsons," he said, referring to the coffee-farming couple that he and Jade knew. He cast a sheepish glance at Inez, who studied him with the intensity of someone who wasn't the least bit fooled by his pretenses.

"Madeline Thompson is the one who wrote that adventure book, *Stalking Death*, based on me, Mother," explained Jade.

Inez nodded. "Ah yes, the one I had to read to find out what you've really been doing in Africa." She smiled at Sam. "Please continue your story, Mr. Featherstone."

"Yes, ma'am. I put my plane on a freighter and headed

to London first to show the Dunburys. By the way, Beverly is doing fine with her impending motherhood. Anyway, I was on the point of leaving for Mombasa when Avery got your telegram, Jade. We took the plane off, and I flew to France and on to Spain."

"You flew? How did you manage fuel?"

"Avery took care of all that. He's got a lot of pull. He arranged for a shipment of gas to go out of France to Casablanca. It was all in place by the time I took off from Spain."

"What about your return trip?"

"Some soldiers are supposed to bring gas down here to Marrakech in their next convoy of supplies." He reached into his trouser pocket and pulled out a sheet of fine paper, now slightly crumpled. He unfolded it and tried to smooth out the creases. "Before I forget, I have another message from Avery. Seems he's been busy investigating Mrs. Worthy and found some information you might find interesting." He offered the paper to Jade.

She snatched it from his hand, her entire focus on Avery's letter. She read silently, poring over each word. When she stopped, her eyes held a distant look, as though trying to see beyond time and place.

"What does it say, Jade?" prompted her mother.

"Oh, sorry, Mother, Sam. Not much really. I'll read it to you."

Dear Jade,

Beverly and I have been hoping and praying that you have already found your mother alive and well. I know Sam will do everything in his power to help you. I won't stop there, either. I have few connections with the consulate in Tangier, but I'm using what I have to expedite a thorough search and investigation. I've uncovered a bit of Lilith's past. Her maiden name, which was no secret, was Clowes. Her father held an estate in the north country, most of it going to her older brother, Hampton, who by all appearances is a regular sort of chap, albeit a bit of a recluse. Her father prompted her into marrying Gil Worthy, so Bev and I have our doubts that it was ever a love match. No surprise there, either, considering the outcome. But what I did uncover by way of enduring a tediously boring weekend hosting some couples from Lilith's home turf is that Lilith had a lover before her wedding.

My sources aren't sure. I had them a bit tipsy by then, but they think his name was Mathers Pellyn. It's a Cornish surname but I don't know that he came from there directly. By all accounts he was a roguish sort involved in several shady enterprises that no one can seem to recall specifically. A bit of a rake, too, so I don't wonder that Lilith's father disapproved. With a little more prompting, and a lot more of my best scotch, we learned that Lilith continued the affair long into her engagement and marriage. It ended only when Pellyn found it in his best interest to leave the country before a few gentlemen claimed his hide. What I find most interesting is that he left England about a year before Gil went looking for David's half brother. My sources weren't 100 percent certain, but they understood that the man had gone to Africa and settled in Mombasa.

Beverly sends her love, and says she cannot wait for the baby to come so she can take the little tyke home to Africa. She expects both you and Sam here for the christening sometime in September.

Avery

Inez spoke first. "I don't understand the significance of this news, Jade." She looked to Sam to see if he did.

"It appears Avery found the woman's initial connection in Africa," said Sam.

Jade nodded. "We always wondered how an upper-class lady in London would have been able to hire anyone to kill her husband a continent away. Chances are Lilith didn't stop corresponding with this Pellyn once he left England, and Avery says the man was involved in questionable activities."

"Cornwall has seen a lot of smuggling in the past," said Sam. "And if he was Cornish—"

"Right," continued Jade. "Chances are he started new operations in Mombasa. That's probably how Lilith became involved in smuggling."

"That is an amazing story," said Inez. "I am gratified to know that my daughter has such devoted friends as the Dunburys and Mr. Featherstone to help you." She cast a quick glance at Jade and added, "You certainly need them." She turned her attention to her daughter. "However did you manage to end up in a slave auction?"

"Mother," exclaimed Jade, "I might ask how you managed to get kidnapped to begin with, so please do not cast stones."

Sam laughed. "Like mother, like daughter. I guess apples don't fall too far from the tree." Both women glared at him. Sam shoved his hands in his pockets and looked away.

"But how did all of you meet up and then find me at the slave sale?" asked Jade.

"We met Mr. Featherstone near the southern palm gardens. He was protecting his plane from the crowds."

"And after Bachir told everyone the plane was cursed, I took one look at your mother and figured out who she was. We weren't sure where to look for you, but Bachir heard the locals jabbering about an unusual woman going up for sale," said Sam. "One who had to be carried in wrapped in a carpet. We figured it could only be you and ran over as fast as we could. I was prepared to shoot the auctioneer, but your mother had another idea."

Inez, who now had two women clinging to her hands and three others busily examining her dirty dress, took the cue and explained further. "I had the Roman coins you'd found in that pouch. Mr. Featherstone's plan, while certainly effective, seemed more likely to bring one of you to bodily harm."

"Please tell me you didn't give all the coins to that horrid man," said Jade. "We need some for evidence."

Inez patted her pocket, and Jade heard several coins clink together. "Only two. The rest are here."

Jade breathed a deep sigh of relief.

"We would have gone higher," said Sam, "but it was beginning to look like the man might pay just to get you off his hands." No one laughed, and Sam looked from one woman to the other, his brows upturned in confusion. "But it's all over now, right? Everyone is safe?"

Jade shook her head. "It's *not* over, Sam. Mother and I are being framed for a murder we didn't commit. I know who's behind it now and I intend to get proof before they escape." She gently swatted away one of the girls, who was now examining Jade's trousers. "We need to do something with these girls first. I feel like I'm back in the dormitory in London. Mother, would you be so kind as to escort your chickens to the French authorities? Bachir can show you the way."

"And leave you to get in trouble again? No." She tried to fold her arms across her chest, only to be stopped in midgesture by one of the girls, who'd begun a serious study of her left sleeve. "Bachir can escort these ladies on his own."

Bachir, who had stayed in the background because he

didn't understand the English conversation, did get the gist of this recent topic. He spoke up for the first time, demanding to be let in on the plans. "I remind you, *Allala* Jade, that you have promised your help to my village. We do not have the amulet yet."

Jade's shoulders drooped as she felt his mild chastisement. She took her promises seriously. This one just had a hard time competing with the need to clear her own and her mother's name. "You are right, Bachir. I'm sorry. Forgive me. But I hadn't forgotten. In fact, I have uncovered some news. Mohan stole the amulet to keep his daughter from becoming the *kahina*. He wants her to be a proper Muslim girl and marry into a rich household. I think he plans to sell the charm to the man who took me prisoner."

"Mohan would also like to be sheik," Bachir said. "May the son of a dung raker be given fever without perspiration to cool him. He is not worthy of Yamna or the little girl."

"You haven't told us who took you prisoner, Jade," said Inez, ignoring Bachir's colorful curse.

"Your proper Mr. Bennington, Mother. And he's in partnership with your charming boat companion, Lilith Worthy."

Inez's left hand flew to her mouth as she gasped. Since one of the girls still had hold of her sleeve at the time, the frayed fabric ripped. The girls let go of Inez and clustered around the fabric instead, examining their new prize. "You cannot be serious, Jade. Mr. Bennington is a perfect gentleman. It's true we never saw him often, he was so devoted to his aunt. He's . . ."

"A low-down, cheating, drug-dealing, murderous, son of a one-eyed rattlesnake," said Jade.

"You forgot 'no-good' and 'lying,' " added Sam. "Maybe he's really that Mathers Pellyn."

"But his aunt . . ." protested Inez.

"I wouldn't be surprised if the aunt isn't Lilith herself, along to oversee operations, then clear out of Morocco to some safe harbor," said Jade. "Avery said she'd left London."

Bachir held up his hand for them to stop and waited for Jade to repeat the conversation in French. So that Sam could also follow, she explained how they knew both Bennington and de Portillo, the other part of the smuggling ring. Jade also described what she'd learned from the leather worker, Wahab Taboor.

"Surely you have enough evidence now to go to the French officials, Jade," said Sam. "You have names, the location of that house where you were prisoner. I'm a witness to their attempts to sell you off."

"But outside of the coins, I have nothing tangible. Just my word, and right now that doesn't count for much. I'm not even sure owning those Roman coins would be a crime. It would help a lot if we had another one of those pouches with the hashish." Jade stopped as she remembered the attempt to steal Mrs. Tremaine's pouch. "Libby Tremaine has one of those pouches."

"Are you saying Libby Tremaine is one of the smugglers, too?" asked Inez.

Jade shook her head. "At first I thought so, but not anymore. I think the delivery man, Fahd, must have kept one back to sell for his troubles, not knowing what was hidden inside. But Bennington must have found out Libby purchased it. It would explain why someone tried very hard to steal it from her. For all I know, they succeeded. I didn't wait around to find out."

Bachir, arms folded in frustration because the conversation had again switched to English, demanded information.

"These new foreigners," he said after Jade finished, "they would probably not stay in the *Medina* if they are visitors. They would have rooms in Gueliz."

"Of course," said Jade. "So we take the girls to Gueliz, and Mother can hand them over to the authorities while I look for the Tremaines." As she finished, she noticed that the assorted young ladies had now discovered Jade's boots, which her mother had brought from the saddlebag. One of them put the left one on and a second was talking excitedly about the other.

"My boots! Mother, thank you."

Jade claimed the boots, much to the chagrin of the little creatures. But when she looked for the dagger, she found the sheath empty. She turned abruptly to the girls, her right hand outstretched. "My knife," she said in Arabic. They only looked at her with huge eyes, puzzled. Thinking they didn't understand, she made stabbing motions with her hand. The girls' eyes widened even farther and one began to cower.

"Jade, you are frightening them," scolded Inez. The coterie of damsels huddled behind Inez like ducklings under a mother hen when a hawk looms overhead.

Jade immediately stopped her pantomime and shushed the girl. "I'm sorry, I . . . oh, you deal with them, Mother. Mohan must have taken my dagger, the one I took from the guard." She sat down to pull on her boots and two girls insisted on helping her. Jade shooed them back to Inez.

"We're not going to accomplish anything until we get rid of this clutch of chicks," Jade said. "And the sun will set soon. I don't want to try to run herd on them in these narrow alleys once it gets dark."

They followed Bachir south through the rug market and west through the medicine healers' *souk,* urging the girls forward when one of them stopped to examine a caged gecko or another succumbed to the scent of rose oil. The girls, while still shy of Sam and Bachir, seemed to have lost all fear of them and looked on the outing as tremendous fun. It grew more difficult to keep them together once Bachir took them south to the *Jemaâ el-Fna*. The snake charmers and jugglers were in full force, as were assorted sellers of sweets and oranges. Jade found herself more than once wishing she had their border collie with them to nip at their heels now and then.

To keep them halfway content, she used one of her silver bangles and let them each pick out a silken scarf. With such prizes in their hands, they grew less distracted by the other assorted temptations. Jade breathed a sigh of relief. From the square, she could see the tower of Koutoubia mosque, a sure guideline directing them west to the edge of the city and on to the French village of Gueliz, less than a mile beyond.

They exited the *Medina* from the *Bab el Jedid* as the sun set and the call to prayer wafted on quivering notes from the red mosque tower. The glow of lamps shining ahead from Gueliz acted as their new beacon until they finally stumbled into the French district. Jade stopped them in front of a café to organize their plan.

"I would prefer that Mother and I do not show our faces just yet in the headquarters in case they feel like arresting us first and asking questions later. I don't think we should entrust these girls to some rough officers. They need someone motherly to take care of them. So, Sam, would you kindly take these poor creatures and see if you can find some married officer whose wife can figure out what to do with them?"

"Anything else you want me to tell them while I'm there?"

"Tell them everything. Tell them how you just happened to save me and who kidnapped me and Mother. Tell them about Wahab Taboor in the leather workers' *souk* and the hashish in the bags and about Bennington and Patrido de Portillo. Just don't tell them where to find Mother and me."

"I don't know where this house is you were kidnapped in. How can I tell them where to go?"

"Bachir knows how to get there. He can draw them a map or something. It's one of those old *riads* north of the Bahia Palace." She repeated the latter in French for Bachir's benefit, and he agreed.

"And what do you have planned for me?" asked Inez. Despite her tattered and dirty costume and her uncombed hair, she still managed to convey an aura of courtliness with her head held high and carriage erect.

"Well, Mother, you can sit and have dinner at this café, or you can come with me to find out where the Tremaines are staying."

"I shall go with you, Jade. I don't think it's safe to leave you out of my sight. The next thing I'd know, you'd be heading back up the mountain without me."

"Fine. Shall we all meet back here in an hour?"

The girls were reluctant to go anywhere without Jade or her mother, but after some persuasive smiles and nods from Inez and a gift of the remains of her bracelets from Jade, they went off in company of Sam and Bachir to find a married French officer.

Jade and her mother patrolled the cafés, restaurants, and various inns, asking for the Tremaines or the Kennicots. They finally located a woman at a private house who let rooms for lodging.

"Yes," she said, "I have an American couple staying here

and an English pair. But I have not seen either of them today. I think they went into the *Medina* earlier. I saw the American girl yesterday following a different man."

Jade assumed the other couple was the Kennicots. But the man? "Was this lone man a Spaniard?"

The woman shook her head. "No, a small man, very slender. Maybe as tall as you. Very soft-spoken. He did not seem as interested in her as she was in him."

"Bennington," said Jade after she thanked the woman for her trouble. "The question is, Is Libby in trouble or in cahoots?"

"Well, either way, Jade, we cannot do anything since we don't know where they are."

Jade grinned. "Yes, we can, Mother. We can search their rooms. Maybe we'll find something incriminating."

But the landlady had no intention of letting two such disreputable-looking women sit and wait for her tenants in their rooms, no matter how much Jade pleaded friendship and devotion to the Tremaines. Finally, exasperated by her lack of success, she suggested they go to the café to wait for Sam and Bachir.

No sooner had they arrived than Sam came running out of the café to greet them. His tense posture and down-turned mouth carried the hint of potential bad news. "Jade. Which of those couples had that leather bag you were looking for?"

"The Tremaines."

"That's what I was afraid of. You don't need to look for the missus anymore."

"Why?"

"Because she's dead."

CHAPTER 24

A popular gathering spot within the Medina *is the* hammam.
This is a public bath and steam room, separate for men and women.
It is a place to socialize, to gossip, as well as to bathe.

—The Traveler

"DEAD? ARE YOU POSITIVE?" Jade heard her mother gasp beside her.

"What happened?" asked Inez.

Sam shrugged. "Not entirely sure. We took those girls to the home of Lieutenant Joubert. Then after his wife took charge of them, I told him about all this other nonsense. He seemed only mildly curious. To be honest, I'm not sure he believed me. Then when I mentioned the Tremaines' name to him, he sat up straighter than starched socks. He told me Mrs. Tremaine died earlier this afternoon at something called a *hammam*."

"What is that?" asked Inez.

"It's a public bath," answered Jade. She turned back to Sam. "Did she drown?"

"No. But when I asked him how she did die, he wouldn't tell me."

"Where is her body now?"

Sam jerked a thumb back over his shoulder. "In what passes for a morgue at the French hospital. I presume you want to go there. I think her husband is there, along with the Kennicots."

"Then I most certainly think we should go." She took a few steps and stopped. "Wait a minute. What did Lieutenant Joubert say about us?" She pointed to her mother and herself.

Sam ran his hand through his brown hair, shoving the longer strands on top back from his forehead. "He's gotten a report about you all right, but I don't think he's going to arrest you. I got the impression that he doesn't believe a proper American lady and her daughter could be behind any sort of drug-smuggling-and-murder scheme."

Inez raised her head higher and tilted her chin up. "I resent that. How dare he belittle my daughter's ability to wreak havoc. And," she added after a very short hesitation, "mine, as well."

Jade laughed. "He shouldn't underestimate Western women, right, Mother?"

Sam led the way to the hospital where a Sister of Charity met them and escorted all of them to a small room that served as a resting area for families. There they saw Mr. Tremaine seated in a plain wooden chair, his face in his hands. Mrs. Kennicot sat to his left side. Her right hand rested on Mr. Tremaine's shoulder while her husband did his best to utter consoling words on the other side. Both of them glanced up then stared openly at Inez and Jade's bedraggled appearances. They paid scant attention to Sam and none to Bachir.

Inez spoke first. "Mr. Tremaine. We just heard about Libby. We're very sorry. Is there anything we can do?"

Walter Tremaine peered at her through reddened eyes.

His nose resembled a ripe strawberry, only his glistened with mucus rather than dew. Sam pulled out a pocket handkerchief and handed it over to him. He blew once and handed the handkerchief back to Sam. Sam refused it with a wave of his hand.

"Keep it," he said. "Can you tell us what happened?"

Walter blinked at Sam, not recognizing him and not comprehending Sam's role in his own personal tragedy. Then he looked back at Inez and a shuddering sigh emerged, his upper body shivering. "Oh, Mrs. del Cameron. Thank heaven you're all right. I can't tell you how I've regretted that nasty trick my Libby played on you. I don't know where she got the idea, but I'm sure she didn't think you would be kidnapped."

"I forgive you both," said Inez. Her voice, while absolutely sincere, came out with the gravity of a queen forgiving an underling for some misstep. "Enough about that. Tell us what happened to your wife."

Walter looked at Mr. Kennicot for advice. Kennicot nodded. "Tell her, Walter. Cleanse your soul."

Walter sighed again, his shoulders sagging in defeat. "Libby and I were married rather hurriedly back in the States. She thought"—he hesitated, and Mrs. Kennicot patted his shoulder for comfort and encouragement—"she thought she was in a family way, you know." He swiped his nose again with Sam's kerchief. "But she found out on board ship that she wasn't. Didn't matter to me. I was happy to have her for my wife. She . . . she *was* a swell girl."

His head drooped. "But I think she only married me to save her reputation. I got the distinct impression her eye was roving for a sugar daddy, if you know the term. She spent far too much time with that de Portillo fellow for my taste. And now it looks like she also fancied that Bennington." He sniffed, fighting back tears. "I don't know what she saw in him. Seemed rather sissified to me."

"You've seen Bennington recently?" asked Jade.

Walter shook his head. "I haven't, but she did, I think. Saw him somewhere in the city two days ago. Took it into her head to wander around trying to find him after that. Then this afternoon she suddenly got all gaga about going into one of those public bathing places. Said she wanted to experience what it was like to be in a harem with someone scrubbing her and sitting around in a steam room in her alltogether drinking mint tea." He blushed, his cheeks matching his eyes and nose for color.

"Had she talked about that before?" asked Jade.

"No. We were walking around the *Medina,* and she suddenly just up and decided to go into that bath place. Told us to come back for her in two hours." He sat up straighter and waggled a finger in the air. "This blasted city is dangerous enough. Someone tried to rob us yesterday. I told her not to go there, but she had to have her way."

Mrs. Kennicot spoke up for the first time. "I had the distinct impression that she saw Mr. Bennington go inside."

Jade arched one eyebrow in an expression of inquiry and nodded for Mrs. Kennicot to continue.

"You see, we were a little apart from the men at the time, and suddenly Libby pointed towards the *hammam* and said, 'Oh, there goes Mr. B.' That's when she went back to Walter and insisted she try the *hammam* herself."

Mr. Tremaine jerked his shoulder out from under Mrs. Kennicot's hand and snarled at her. "And you let her go in there? You didn't tell me?"

"But, Walter, I knew that the men and women don't go into the same area. There was no chance of her meeting him inside. If I'd stopped her, she would have just waited outside for him to exit. This seems much more harmless." She tried to pat him on the arm again.

Walter swatted her away like he would an odious insect. "Well, it wasn't harmless. Someone killed her."

Jade leaned in closer now, her face inches from Mr. Tremaine's. "You don't think this was an accident? Why do you think someone killed her?"

Mrs. Kennicot answered for him. "Because of what the other women inside reported. Libby was in the hot room waiting for a massage and scrubbing. Of course the other women noticed her, being a foreigner and all. Apparently the locals shave . . ." She remembered the men and blushed. "Anyway, they reported that she sat alone, looking around. Then she suddenly acted as though she saw something that shocked or surprised her. They just put it down to bad manners, staring and all that." She blushed again. "Shortly after, they said a woman who works at the *hammam* brought her mint tea to drink. She drank some and immediately fell over."

"She was poisoned, don't you see?" said Walter.

"But what works that fast?" asked Sam.

"She didn't die right away," said Mr. Kennicot. "The women went to her aid and said her eyes were staring, and she was struggling to breathe. She was sweating more than they thought natural despite the steamy room. They tried to get her to stand but she couldn't seem to move. She died within a half hour."

"We just now got her here," said Mr. Kennicot. "You can imagine how they weren't about to let any men into the women's bathing room until everyone was dressed. Even then, some of the women refused to turn over Libby's body until they felt she was decent."

"Someone put something in her tea," shouted Walter. He pounded his right fist on the chair arm repeatedly. Inez wedged herself between Mr. Kennicot and Mr. Tremaine and whispered something soothing in the latter's ear.

Sam took Jade aside. "What can kill that fast with paralysis?" he whispered.

"Offhand, if I was back home, I'd guess dogbane. Out here?" She shrugged, then raised an index finger to wait, and thought for a minute. "I saw a flowering shrub on my way through the mountains. It grew all over. Bachir called it something in French that basically translated to 'laurel rose.' I think it's actually oleander. That has similar effects to dogbane. Very fast."

"I don't suppose it matters *how* she was killed as much as why or by whom," added Sam.

"She saw something or someone," said Jade in a near whisper, as though thinking aloud. "And they didn't want to be recognized." She balled her right hand into a fist and smacked it into her left. "But her death may mean Bennington and de Portillo will move out before anyone else discovers them. I need to get back inside that *riad* before they take away the bags. Tonight."

"Whoa there, Simba Jike. How are you going to do that?" asked Sam. "It's after sundown. The city gates are closed till sunrise tomorrow."

"So? I'll go over the wall." She hesitated a moment then added, "Just don't tell Mother."

Sam took hold of her arm. "Wait a minute. I know I can't stop you, and you know I'm not letting you go in there alone. But just how are *we* going to keep this from your mother?"

"Tell her we're going to ask around for more information."

"You're going to lie to your mother?"

"No. I don't lie to my mother. I just don't plan on telling her *where* we're going to ask around. In fact, I don't even plan on telling her anything. That's *your* job." She poked him in the chest with a finger. "Tell her we'll meet her back at the boarding house where the Tremaines have rooms. But do it fast and meet me over by the *Bab Agnaou*. Bachir can direct you. Tell him I'm going to get his amulet."

"Where are you going now?"

"To find my mule. Unless Mohan stole everything, my flashlight and some other supplies are in that saddlebag."

The great horseshoe-shaped gate into Marrakech's Kasbah loomed overhead. Build from slate-blue stone, its massive height grew out of layer upon layer of arches, each one nesting atop the other in concentric horseshoes. Elegantly simple rather than opulent, the architecture said "I am not frivolous. I am powerful."

Like the other gates, it stood closed, admitting no one. Jade never planned to get into the city there, but it made a conveniently recognizable rallying point, and just around the corner stood scalable, unguarded ramparts. She found her mule still hobbled among the palms, happily dozing. She extracted her light, tested it, then rummaged around some more and pulled out an old compass before she slipped back to the gate. On seeing it again, she recalled Zoulikha's reported vision of the amulet. She'd seen a great gate made of many arches—perhaps this one.

"Just how do you plan to get over the wall, Jade?" whispered Sam when they joined forces.

"See those indentations in the clay?" she asked, pointing with her flashlight to the regularly spaced, squared-off holes high above her. A pigeon roosting inside one squinted against the glare. "Those are left over from the framework used to build this wall. We use them for hand- and footholds." She turned off the light and shoved it into her side pocket.

"Those are a good twelve feet off the ground, and I don't see a ladder around."

"Come with me." Jade crooked her index finger and wiggled it. Then she led the way to the west along the ramparts until they turned a corner and headed north. At this point the indentations went down to about a foot above ground level. "We scale here."

Sam eyed the spacing and nodded. "You're right. This spot provides the easiest access." He locked the fingers of both hands together and held them low in front of him. "Step up."

Jade stepped into his hands and pushed herself up, until her right foot found a secure toehold about four feet off the ground. Then she grabbed for some handholds, tested them to see that the clay held, and slipped her left foot out of Sam's hands.

"Be careful, Jade," Sam cautioned. "I'll try to catch you if you fall, but I don't think it will do either of us any good."

Jade didn't reply. For one, the wall stood a fraction of an inch from her face. For another, she had no intention of falling, and Sam knew it. But climbing in the dark required all her concentration. The indentations looked deceptively deep and wide from below, but many of them still held chunks of timber inside and barely accommodated her boot tips. Several times the brittle and broken clay crumbled under pressure, causing her to scoot sideways along the wall until she found a better hold above her. Finally she scrambled up onto a shelf that ran along the outer edges just below the top. The summit was only a few feet above her, close enough to swing a leg over.

"I made it, Sam," she whispered. "Your turn. Can you do it with your leg?"

Jade had seen him climb trees well enough with his false leg, but wasn't certain how well he'd do scaling a wall when he couldn't feel half the toeholds. "I can look for some rope if you need it." Her only answer came in the form of some mutterings and the sound of a boot scraping hard clay.

Inez had too much experience of human nature in general, and her daughter in particular, to be fooled by Sam's story. She knew full well that Jade had no intention of letting go so easily, and with the gates to the old city closed for the night, that meant only one thing: Jade planned to climb over the wall. Inez adjusted her torn sleeves and smoothed the front of her ruined dress. *Let her go, then.* For once she knew someone would be with Jade. The question was, Did her daughter have Mr. Featherstone wrapped around her little finger?

She thought about the meeting between Jade and Sam at the slave market. Not for one moment did she believe his statement about looking for other slaves in the opposite room. She'd seen how he gazed at her daughter. It was the same look her Richard had when they'd first met. Inez smiled. This Sam had other traits in common with her husband: bravery, determination, and a clear head.

Maybe my Jade has finally met her match. If anyone looked like he could handle her, that young man stood the best chance. Still, Inez had every intention of keeping her own eye on her daughter. She waited only a few seconds after Sam left her. Then she motioned to Bachir and followed the young American pilot.

Bachir held out his hands and made a slight shrug as if to ask what in the world were they doing now.

Inez pointed and whispered one word: "Jade."

Bachir nodded and fell in step with Inez as they tailed Sam to the *Bab Agnaou* and then to the rampart wall beyond. The pair hunkered low behind a palm and watched as first Jade, then Sam, climbed the rampart. The two stayed at the top for a while, and Inez presumed Jade was taking her bearings. She saw her daughter point to the northeast before disappearing over the wall. Once Sam joined Jade, Inez pointed to herself and Bachir, then to the wall. At first Bachir shook his head vigorously. He pointed to Inez and back to Gueliz, then to himself and the wall, indicating that he would go, but she should wait behind. Inez's answer was to hurry to the same spot where she'd seen Sam begin, and shove her right foot into one of the framing holes.

Bachir held out both hands and patted the air, signifying that she should wait a moment. He pantomimed first his ascent, then reaching down from the top to give her assistance. Inez nodded. She didn't really think she needed the help, but it occurred to her that it might not be dignified to climb with a strange Moroccan man peering up her torn dress at her underthings. Once Bachir made the ledge, he lay flat on his stomach, his left side pressed against the remaining rampart wall. He extended his right hand and waited for Inez to join him.

She climbed with the agility of a goat, ignoring the minor scrapes on her knees and her knuckles. Her pulse increased and she felt a flush of heat bathe her neck and face. She hadn't felt so exhilarated in years, and it was the memory of first meeting Richard that reawakened it in her. She couldn't wait to tell her husband. Better yet, she thought, maybe she'd show him. *First I'll get on a horse and lead him in a chase up into the high country. And later? I wonder if that old hunting shack is still standing?* A fresh warmth blossomed up from her neck and she knew she was blushing. *Better focus on the hand grips, or there won't be a "later."*

"*Alalla* Inez," whispered Bachir above her. She tilted her head back enough to see his hand without throwing herself off balance, took a better grasp of the wall, and reached for him with her left hand. He gripped her wrist and pulled her up as she found new footholds. Once she made the narrow ledge, she hitched up her tattered dress and threw a leg over the top. Bachir wasted no time climbing up and was sitting on the wall as she scrambled onto her stomach. In the dark she could barely make out the ground below, but at least this spot had a garden on the other side rather than another wall.

"Lower me down," she said in English, knowing Bachir wouldn't understand the words as much as her actions. As she spoke she scooted her legs over the other side while she clung to the top. Bachir lay down on the wall and grabbed both her wrists. When she'd inched down as far as she could, she nodded for him to release her. Inez dropped the last few feet and landed on her backside.

Before Inez could regain her breath and her remaining shreds of dignity, Bachir stood beside her and was helping her to her feet. He grinned, his brown teeth barely visible.

"Jade," he said, and pointed through the garden.

Inez swiped her hand across her rear end to brush off the dust. "Jade," she repeated.

"Do you have any idea where we're going?" asked Sam in a hushed voice.

Rather than head out in any sort of straight line, they'd

followed the wall south, a garden of sorts to their left. Then they turned east with the wall until they reached what passed for a major street in this city. That meant it was not only straight for more than fifteen yards, it would also admit a donkey *and* a pedestrian at the same time.

Jade nodded once, then bobbed her head from side to side. "More or less," she finally admitted. "But I needed to start out where I started the first time I came into the city." She positioned herself with her right side to the wall and jerked her thumb to the right. "That big gate, the *Bab Agnaou*, is just around the corner. That way," she continued as she pointed ahead of her, "is a mosque and some ruins of an old palace. Not far past those are some streets that run nearly north. Lots of palatial homes tucked away there. The one we want is off on one of the side streets."

"Does this street have a name?"

"Probably, but," she added with a grin, "I don't know it. I imagine the French call it Rue something-or-other."

"And I suppose you have some sort of plan in mind once you find it?"

"You bet your sweet ascot I do. Climb up to the roof of the house next door, go across to the intended roof, and go down the stairs into the courtyard." She hesitated as she remembered the state of those stairs. "By the way, the steps are broken at the bottom so we will have to jump down the last couple feet or five."

Sam sighed. "Great, more climbing and dropping. And once we're inside?"

"We find Bennington."

The streets ahead of them were empty now, with only a hint of music drifting down from the *Jemaâ el-Fna*. Everyone else was indoors, sitting down to their late suppers.

They crept past the silent mosque and hesitated as the ruins of El Badi Palace loomed to their right. The *kee-uk* of a Little Owl echoed from the ruins, making it seem eerier. By day the vast site of broken walls and empty pools looked interesting. By night it appeared treacherous and haunted by every *jinn* known to man. As if to emphasize that last point, something rustled in the debris. A pair of eyes glowed from another corner and gave chase to the sound.

Several streets, ranging from narrow covered alleys to open thoroughfares at least six feet wide, opened up to their left. Jade studied two in particular before deciding on one. A placard placed by the French proclaimed it as the Rue Riad Zitoun el Kdim. Jade pointed to it and whispered, "See? I was right."

Sam pushed her ahead of him. "Move along, my little slave. By the way, your flashlight is on."

Jade pulled the light from her pocket and slid back the metal switch. "Blast it. It must have come on when I jammed it in the pocket."

They met very few people on their way north up the street. Only a few men passed them, hurrying home to dinner after having completed business or prayers. As one opened a door into a lamplit entryway, the scents of lamb and cumin drifted out into the night air along with the fragrant, clean smell of mint.

Suddenly Jade stopped, causing Sam to bump into her. She studied the doors of several houses on one side of the street, then crossed and examined those on the other, paying particular attention to the knockers. Three were large metal rings, one was shaped like a flat hand, fingers together, and another looked like a large insect cast from metal.

"This way," she whispered, and turned down a narrow

side street. As they wended deeper into the passages, Jade hugged the walls and skulked more than walked. Sam followed her lead and placed his right hand on his Colt revolver, ready to draw it if danger threatened.

Finally she stopped in front of a boarded door with hands painted across it. She pointed first to Bennington's house. Next she pointed to the abandoned one, then up to the roof and over to Bennington's roof. Sam nodded, but when Jade started for the door, he stopped her. "Me first," he mouthed. He pushed in the door and crawled between the old barricades into the dark entryway. Jade followed, her flashlight on to light the way.

They moved left, then a sharp right again in the once beautifully enameled *chicane*. Dead silence met them, daring them to intrude into the shunned interior. Unsure how long her light would last, Jade wanted to get up to the rooftop as quickly as possible. "Hurry," she coaxed as she led Sam through the dead courtyard to the back rooms.

They found the narrow flight of steps up to the second floor and again up to the rooftop, emerging in the cool, evening air. Overhead the first stars appeared in the sky. Sam gently took hold of Jade's arm and stopped her from crossing to Bennington's roof.

"Before we go in there," he whispered, "I want to know your plan. Give me some idea of the layout of the rooms and where to go."

"It's designed just like this house," said Jade. "We go down the stairs to the back rooms, a kitchen of sorts. There's the central courtyard, but the fountain trickles there and some of the trees are still alive." She traced out a sketch in the dusty stucco of the rooftop. "The room where I saw the bags was here." She made an *X*. "It must have been some sort of bathing room at some time, a private *hammam,* but it's dry now. This door over here"—she marked a circle—"is where I found Mother. The steps down into their dungeon are over here in this room." Jade tapped the sketch and looked into Sam's eyes, now as black as the night sky. "I have no idea where anything else is. None of the rooms upstairs looked inhabited."

"So Bennington may not even be here," said Sam. "The house may be empty except for the guard."

"That's right. I don't expect to see de Portillo again until the shipment is ready to go. Since you've got the gun, I'll leave the guard to you. Do whatever you have to do, Sam. I'll hunt for Bennington and Mohan." She gripped her knife. "That little Atlas weasel knows where the amulet is."

Sam edged closer to Jade until only an inch separated their faces. "And what do you plan to do if Bennington isn't here?"

Jade's answer emerged from deep within, her low voice a predatory growl. "We wait!"

CHAPTER 25

*The most sumptuous palace today is the Bahia Palace, now the home of Resident
General Lyautey. But even his home holds no candle to the legendary opulence
and wealth that was the El Badi Palace. Alas, its beauty is now no more than
a shadowy ghost, like an aged crone left to remember her glorious youth.*

—The Traveler

SAM AND JADE CREPT DOWN THE STEPS from the rooftop to the
second floor. There they paused to reconnoiter and listen for
voices, footsteps, anything that spoke of the occupants. All
they heard was the soft, irregular padding of booted feet below them. Whoever paced, walked alone. Judging by the listless steps, frequent pauses, and random directional changes,
the lone guard suffered from boredom.

Jade crept to the latticework railing and peered through
the decorative curves and loops. She saw the guard from his
chest down, his upper torso out of view. The man was inspecting a ripened orange on the gnarled tree. He turned and
continued his listless patrol towards the front. She sniffed,
searching for the scent of a meal under preparation. The
air was dry and musty. Not even the cleansing scent of mint
reached her.

Sam joined her and they watched for a few moments
more to determine the guard's movement pattern. In that

time the guard strayed from the front entry to the middle of the courtyard, but no farther back than that. Jade pointed to the steps leading down to the ground floor and led the way. She sensed more than heard Sam pad behind her, his clean scent of leather and natural musk a soothing reminder of a strong ally.

Sam. A part of her still couldn't believe he was here, that he had come all this way to save her. It was a very flattering thought, one that brought a pleasant tingle to her back and arms and made her pulse quicken. Another part of her wondered what her mother thought of him and his rescue. The sound of the approaching guard shoved such matters back. She held up her hand for Sam to stop. Below her the steps gave way to emptiness. They couldn't drop down until the guard went back to the front.

The guard didn't go back. For several minutes he stood by the tree. Jade had spent many hours waiting in a cramped blind before, silently watching for wildlife and hardly daring to shift position lest she scare off a potential meal or photograph. But this was different. Now she was hunting a human and there was no blind to hide her. If he should choose to wander farther back, they would be found.

Beads of sweat formed on Jade's forehead and upper lip. She became painfully aware of her heartbeat, which now sounded like a kettle drum hammering away in her chest. Still she remained frozen in place on the last step before the drop. Like the lioness whose nickname she bore, her muscles tensed to pounce if the guard should discover them. Had he heard them? Was he waiting for them to slip up and make a sound?

Something small plopped onto the hard floor of the courtyard, followed by the sound of slurping. *Sweet Millard Fillmore on a pogo stick. He's eating the blasted orange.*

It occurred to her that this was actually the ideal time to get him, while his hands were full and his attention elsewhere. She pointed to herself and the opposite corner of the courtyard, then to Sam and the nearer corner. She'd jump down and distract the guard's attention while Sam did his best to slip behind him.

She squatted down and sat on the bottom step. Then she grabbed hold of the step and slid off. Sam shoved his pistol in his holster before she made the drop, and he knelt down to take hold of her wrists. When she hung suspended a foot off the ground, he bent over as far as he could and lowered her softly to the floor. She waited for Sam to get ready, then ran to the opposite corner of the courtyard.

The guard was her old friend from the dungeon, the one she'd bested and later scarred by the shrine. He recognized her immediately, a fact plainly registered by the glowering brows and sudden intake of breath. But the element of surprise played into Jade's hands. With that inhalation came a segment of orange. The man's futile grab for his lone flintlock pistol was aborted by a fit of choking. Jade ducked behind a corner pillar in case he managed to squeeze off a lucky shot. The guard, red in the face and still coughing, pulled his weapon, but the click of the hammer he heard came from next to his ear.

"I wouldn't do that if I were you," said Sam, his Colt revolver pressed against the man's temple. "Hand it over." The guard dutifully placed his weapon in Sam's palm while Jade pulled the man's new dagger from his sash.

"Miss me?" she asked. The guard glared at her. "Glad to see you got a new knife. I sort of lost the old one." She slipped it into her boot sheath.

"You will pay for this, infidel woman," he said, spitting the words out along with an orange seed.

"Easy there, pal," said Sam. "I'd rather not shoot you, but I will if you insist on this kind of rowdy behavior. Now put your hands behind your back for the nice lady." He pushed the Colt against the man's head for emphasis. The guard complied.

Jade relieved him of his long, colorful silken sash and sliced it in half along the width. She used one strip to lash his wrists together, palms up, making certain to keep the knot below his hands where his fingers couldn't work them. Enough remained of the lengthy sash to bind his hands to his ankles once they had him in the cell. She used the other half for a gag. When she finished, she took the guard's flintlock pistol from Sam and stuck it into her waistband.

"Where do you want him?" asked Sam. "That nasty cellar sounds like a good spot to me."

Jade grinned. "I'm sure he'd agree. I'd hate to keep him from his furry little friends down there." She stopped just as Sam started to drag the man away. "Wait. Not the cellar. I don't want him using the rats to get loose, like I did." She looked around the courtyard until her gaze lit on a familiar door. "We'll put him in the same room they kept Mother in."

Inez couldn't figure out how she could have lost sight of her daughter so quickly after Jade and Mr. Featherstone had gone over the rampart wall. Surely it hadn't taken her and Bachir that long to climb up, but when they got to the top there was no sign of them. Still she hadn't worried. Bachir seemed to know just where she'd gone. Odd, how she trusted this little man whom she couldn't even speak to. But she knew he had a stake in this expedition, as well.

She had seen how he watched Yamna during the French-language lesson. His look, though always discreet and respectful, had a note of longing to it, and his praise when she recited her lesson correctly had far more warmth than when the same praise was given to Mohan. No, Inez had seen that look before. It was the look of a man hopelessly in love. She saw it in Sam's eyes, too. *Is it still in Richard's eyes when he looks at me?* She didn't dwell on that thought. There would be time when she returned home.

Mohan also wanted this amulet back and wanted it badly enough to have traveled all the way to Tangier to find Jade. Inez didn't like to dwell on that last part. It went against all rational thought, and Inez had always been a rational being, even in her wilder youth when she spent days at a time camping with the Gypsies. Oh, she'd had her palm read and played the game of letting one of the old women make a love spell for her, but she never believed any of it. So just how did this man know where to look for Jade? Her head reminded her of the answer. The old woman, that *kahina* person, told him where to look, but that only pushed the question back a step. How did the old woman know *who* Jade was, much less *where* she was?

In her mind she pictured that odd lion's-claw tattoo that Jade tried to hide. She'd written home about it, glossing over the details. Some sort of native tribute for killing a troublesome hyena, but Inez knew there was more to the story than that. What bothered her most was the fact that she had to read about it in an overdramatized, romantic novel by the wife of a coffee farmer who had been on the expedition with Jade. No, there was definitely more to her daughter than what Jade cared to tell, and that hurt. The fact that it hurt surprised Inez. She missed her daughter. She wanted to be close to her. Instead, Jade had a secret life. *Just like I did at the Gypsy camps.*

A man coming from the opposite direction passed them, a flaming torch in his hand to light the way. The scent of smoke, grease, and burning wood hung heavy in his wake. In an instant a vivid memory flashed into Inez's brain like a living scene, overwhelming the present as it imposed faces, sounds, and scents from the past.

All around her, men sang and played fierce flamenco-style songs on old guitars while women beat tambourines and danced in a whirl of vibrant colors. Inez had danced with them, flipping her skirts, flashing her legs, and pounding her booted feet. When it was over, she collapsed by the fire, laughing. She saw the old Gypsy woman's wrinkled face and gap-toothed smile inches from her own face as the woman conjured up her predictions from the campfire. *Freedom is a wild horse. Once you catch it and corral it, it is no longer free. You will lose yourself, my child, and find yourself again in a far land where houses rise from the living clay.*

Inez staggered under the memory's weight, and Bachir hurried back to her, respectfully supporting her around the shoulders to keep her from sinking. She gratefully gave in to his help as she took a deep breath and rallied herself.

He pointed behind them to the darkened ruin of the old palace. "El Badi," he said. *"Jinni."* He pointed from the ruins to Inez as if to suggest the *jinni* were responsible for her present weakness.

"I'm all right," she said, waving a hand to indicate nothing was physically wrong. She stood up straight and stared at the red buildings around her, seeing them as if for the first time. Inez always thought her home in New Mexico close to the Taos pueblos fulfilled that Gypsy's prediction, especially when she "found" herself there as a mother with responsibilities. Now she knew the truth. She'd corralled herself in a self-imposed prison of propriety for all those years. *These* houses, manufactured in the same manner, were what the old Gypsy meant. *This,* not the United States, was the far land where she'd "find herself," not physically but emotionally.

Bachir waited a moment while she composed herself, glancing nervously back into the dark at the ruins. Inez watched him put out his open palm, the sign against the evil eye, for protection. Once she felt in control of her legs, she smiled and nodded for him to proceed.

Jade almost felt sorry for the guard as they shoved him into the empty little room. This was the third time she'd humiliated him; the first when she escaped from the cellar, the second when she'd scratched him with the *fibula* by the old tomb, and now. Maybe this last time hurt less, knowing she'd needed the help of a man and a gun to get him. *Probably not.* It certainly wouldn't bode well for him if Bennington found him like this, but she planned to solve that dilemma by taking care of Bennington herself.

After they bound his ankles behind him to his wrists, Jade checked the floor for broken tiles. She pushed into a far corner anything that might be usable to cut his bonds loose. They had no sooner shut the door and drawn the bolt when they heard the front door open.

"The last killing went too far, I tell you."

Jade recognized de Portillo's voice even as she and Sam scurried to the safety of the back room.

"You worry too much, Patrido," said another voice, barely audible in its half-hushed tone. Jade knew it for Bennington's. "The girl needed to die. She knew too much. Besides, it will be blamed on the two del Cameron women, as will the death of the man I had left in the Azilah tunnels. Not that it matters. By now the young bitch should be on her way to Timbuktu or some Arab sheik's harem."

"I'm surprised you didn't kill her when you had the chance," said de Portillo.

"Fool. If the French found her body, they would start to look elsewhere for a killer, which means us. As long as she is alive and presumed on the run, she's the main suspect and no one will watch you. Besides," Bennington added, "she needs to suffer for a very long time."

"Just so you know what you are doing. But I still do not like it. I did not buy into murder."

"Are you thinking of running out on me now, Patrido?" The voice took on a new note of menace, emphasized by the soft, threatening tone. "I would not suggest that at all. Not if *you* wish to live."

The voices came closer as the two speakers passed through the courtyard.

"Damn," said Bennington in a stronger voice, one that made the soft whisper seem more like a facade. "Where is that fool guard?"

"Probably sleeping," said de Portillo. "Maybe downstairs guarding our new prisoner."

Jade's attention went to full alert at that last statement. *Who did they have in the cellar now? It sure as hell better not be Mother again.* She stopped herself when she realized that was impossible. She'd left her mother with Bachir, the Kennicots, and Mr. Tremaine back at the hospital.

"How much longer until the shipment is ready?" asked de Portillo. "It is getting dangerous to remain here."

"Tomorrow," said Bennington. "After that fool Wahab talked to del Cameron, I encouraged him to speed up his work." Bennington laughed. "He didn't need those two toes to stitch leather, anyway. Come on, let's visit our friend Mohan and convince him to show me where he hid that amulet."

"I fail to see your interest in that silver trinket. You can buy them everywhere," said de Portillo.

"This one is ancient, dating from the founding of Carthage. It will be worth a small fortune to the right collector. Besides, I am very intrigued by the legends surrounding it. It is said to be a thing of power."

"Then *you* go," said de Portillo. "I'm staying here to watch over my bags since that fool guard isn't doing his job."

Jade heard de Portillo cross the courtyard to the old bathing room where the bags were stored, while Bennington headed to the front to gain access to the cellar. As soon as they were both out of earshot, she turned to Sam. "You take care of de Portillo. Don't let him get away. Lock him in there, shoot him, whatever."

"Let me guess, Jade. You're planning on taking on Bennington yourself. Why? Once he's in the cellar, we can lock him in there with that Mohan fellow. We'd have them all in one tidy package."

"I need to follow Bennington and get that amulet back, Sam. Mohan's the only one who knows where it is."

"So we get Mohan out when we lock up Bennington," Sam argued. "He'll probably be so grateful to be free he'd take you right to it."

Jade shook her head. "I doubt I'd be able to convince him to reveal his new hiding place as well as Bennington can. I intend to follow them."

If Sam wanted to argue the foolishness of her scheme some more, he lost his chance as Bennington and Mohan came back up the steps.

"Remember," Bennington said, "give me this rare amulet

and you'll live. Lead me on a wild goose chase and you'll die slowly and very painfully." Their footsteps died out as they wended around the entryway's turns towards the door.

Jade faced Sam and claimed his mouth in one brief but smoldering kiss. "Wait for me," she said as she released him and raced down the courtyard to the door.

"Jade," Sam hissed after her, trying his best not to alert de Portillo, but he was too late. The Spaniard had heard the extra pair of feet in the courtyard and hurried out of the storeroom.

"Is that you, Hassan? Where the devil have you been?" yelled de Portillo.

"Hiding," said Sam as he raced up behind de Portillo and landed a solid punch to his temple.

Bachir pulled Inez back into a darkened side street as Mohan's pleas alerted them to the approaching danger. Mohan spoke French, so she couldn't make out the words but thought he said something about a body. Behind her, she heard Bachir's sudden intake of breath, followed by a whispered repetition of Mohan's words.

"El Badi," Bachir hissed.

Oh, thought Inez. *So that's what he said.* Inez waited for Mohan and whoever was with him to pass, eyes alert and muscles tensed for flight or fight. As soon as the whimpering Berber stumbled by, Bennington right behind him, Inez felt her ire rise and her fists clench. That man had used her and imprisoned her daughter, and no one did that to a del Cameron. For a moment, she toyed with the idea of following Bennington and capturing him herself. That idea vanished with the sight of her daughter skulking past her in the shadows, tailing the others.

And just where is Mr. Featherstone? Inez reverted to the role of protective mother. Then she remembered that de Portillo was part of this smuggling group, as well. If Jade and Sam had arrived at the house together, and Sam now stayed behind, it must be because he was either dealing with de Portillo or lying in wait for him. Either way, he probably needed assistance. She turned to Bachir and pointed to him. "Sam Featherstone," she said, and then motioned up the street where they had been heading. She next pointed to herself, then back down the street where Jade had gone. "Jade. El Badi."

Bachir stubbornly refused with a firm shake of his head and his arms folded across his chest. He pointed to himself, then to Inez to show he intended to stay with her. He hadn't counted on the imperial nature of Doña Inez Maria Isabella de Vincente del Cameron.

Inez straightened to her full height, chin raised. Despite her tattered clothes and sooty face, she looked every inch a queen, or in this case, a descendent of the first *kahina*. She shooshed him with both hands and, without another word of argument, turned and followed her daughter, leaving Bachir to find Sam.

Jade tailed Bennington and Mohan, at times relying more on sound than on sight. After the first turns out of their immediate alleyways, Mohan stuck to the lamplit street. Jade knew she'd be more easily spotted if Bennington turned around to look behind him. That meant staying farther back and hugging the walls. Twice she flattened herself into an entryway, her back pressed so tightly against the door that if anyone had opened the portal from inside, she'd have fallen backward.

Once she felt she was being followed, but couldn't see anyone. Since her left knee didn't ache, she brushed it off as an overactive imagination or more likely Sam and continued on. Wherever Mohan was going, it was not back to the old tomb. It was only when she saw the El Badi Palace ruins that she knew where he'd rehidden the amulet.

El Badi's broken shell loomed ahead, the wall around it visible only as a black emptiness in the distant light from the torches scattered along the street intersections. From this distance the walls were apparent by the absence of anything else. To the east, north, or west, the eye sought out and found dim streets; here the impression of a doorway, there a rooftop with stars overhead. To the south loomed nothing but unbroken wall, an empty black space, and where there were gaps, more black wall beyond. Only the stars flickering above let the eye know when the wall ended and the sky began.

By day, the old palace was more a corpse than a building; the few shreds of majesty it wore were more mocking than grand, like a tarnished imperial ring on a desiccated mummy. By night the flickering torchlights transformed this sleeping corpse of a ruin into the waking dead, as sandy red walls became black like old, smeared blood that flowed with every shimmy of the torch's fire. Every shadow jiggled as though alive, rendering the ancient palace truly frightening.

The mass of rubble and rock proved itself alive to the ear, as well. Scurrying and scratching came from above, the more fearful noises rolled up from below as it settled into itself. Hollow echoes like that of decomposition erupted from the bowels of underground passages. Something fluttered from an upper corner nook. A restless stork? An owl? A *jinn?*

Jade watched from the nearest corner as Bennington prodded Mohan with a gun and muttered threats around the old rampart and forward into the ruins. Still Mohan held back, clutching his own protective talisman. He seemed to be weighing the danger of torture from Bennington against that of a *jinn* angered at losing its treasure. You could dig up treasure during the day if you had salt and iron to protect yourself, but not at night when the *jinni* were awake. She heard a painful outcry, quickly stifled. Then the pair, like the cry, were swallowed up inside El Badi. Jade followed.

Once they were inside, not even the city's torches assisted them, and the last sliver of moon wouldn't rise until after two a.m. Only a myriad of stars lent illumination. Anyone without the reflective eyes of nocturnal animals was out of luck. Jade fingered her flashlight, tempted to switch it on and muffle the light under a shirttail, but in this blackness even that would be a dead giveaway to Bennington. Luckily Bennington also carried a flashlight in his left hand and turned it on. Something small rustled in the weeds as the beam swept across it. Higher up in the walls, two large round eyes glowed back at them. They blinked independently, then disappeared as the disturbed owl took off.

"Where is it?" hissed Bennington. "I'm losing patience with you."

"We should wait until daylight," Mohan said, his voice tremulous with fear. "It is too dangerous at night. I have no salt or iron with me."

Bennington's right hand waved a tiny revolver, a Derringer. "I have plenty of iron here as well as lead. And there's more iron hanging from my belt. But it's not the *jinni* that will taste it if you don't give me that amulet."

"It is not for you," protested Mohan. "I promised the dark lady. She will be angry."

"You have no idea how angry," agreed Bennington with a chuckle. "Which is why you should give it to me now. I promise she'll get it."

Still Mohan stalled. "It's too hard to see. I might miss the spot."

Bennington shoved the flashlight in Mohan's hands. "Move!" he commanded. "You're too much of a coward here to have gone very far even during the daytime. So I know it's close." Jade heard a click as Bennington pulled back the hammer on the Derringer. "Find it."

Mohan moved up against the wall by the old entrance and followed it, counting paces aloud. Then, having identified which corridor to take, he turned left and walked through a pavilion and entered what was once an opulent courtyard of sunken gardens and pools. Jade crept up to the side of them, waiting for Mohan's next move. Rather than proceed farther into the courtyard, he stopped and strained his eyes in the blackness, looking for a landmark.

Bennington obliged by sweeping the area with the flashlight. Jade dropped and lay flat on the ground behind a long untended shrub and waited until the beam passed overhead. Then she peeked through the weeds.

The Berber apparently recognized a spot, for he went to a chunk of fallen *pisé* near one of the smaller pools. He stopped only fifteen yards from Jade's hiding place. Bennington followed and stood close behind him. Mohan dropped to his knees and rolled the chunk aside, then dug with one hand, the other still clutching his own amulet. Jade caught snatches of words, but whether they were incantations or pleas, she couldn't tell. Soon the glint of silver winked back from Bennington's light. Mohan had unearthed the talisman, the silver box carried by his tribe's *kahina* since the days when Carthage was founded. From one of the near walls, a Little Owl sounded its questioning *kee-uk* from the opposite wall.

"The *jinni* are angry," wailed Mohan.

In a flash, Jade's dream returned to her: the stone walls, the talisman in the earth—it pointed to this ruin. It was the remainder of the dream that terrified her now. She'd seen the talisman replaced by the withered body of a man. *My stars! He'll kill Mohan!* With this thought came another, more fleeting recollection. In the dream, it was a female form that made the man wither. The idea tickled at Jade's subconscious.

There was no time to spend on the second thought. Mohan's life was at stake. Time to end this once and for all. Jade drew the Arab guard's flintlock pistol and took a bead on Bennington's right hand, the one holding the pistol. Jade's other hand held her flashlight, her finger poised to switch it on. She counted on Bennington's attention being focused on the amulet. She hadn't reckoned on what came next.

As soon as Mohan picked up the amulet and stood, Bennington pulled the knife from its sheath and rammed it into Mohan's chest. The Berber dropped to his knees, the light falling from his left hand. His right hand still gripped the amulet as he clutched his chest in disbelief.

That's when Jade turned on her light. Bennington wheeled around and squinted against the beam just as Jade fired.

CHAPTER 26

Sultan Ahmed al Mansour ed-Dahbi built the El Badi palace in the late 1500s,
using gold and onyx in unheard-of quantities and trading the country's sugar
for marble. He asked a visionary at one of his banquets what the man thought
of his magnificent home. The visionary replied that it would make a
big pile of earth when it was demolished. It did.

—The Traveler

As soon as Sam landed the punch, he knew it wasn't enough.
De Portillo reeled under the blow, but didn't fall. Sam stepped
up and aimed a left for the jaw, but de Portillo twisted away
and escaped with only a glancing blow across his left cheek.
Sam's immediate jab with his right, however, landed squarely
on de Portillo's nose.

Like a Spanish bull, de Portillo didn't go down easily.
Sam's element of surprise gone, de Portillo fought back with
ferocity and the advantage of having little conscience. He
lashed out with his right foot and kicked Sam on his right
shin with the intention of cracking a bone.

"You'll have to do better than that, man," said Sam as he
took the blow without so much as a wince of pain. "It's hard
to break an oak leg."

De Portillo, now thoroughly enraged, roared with anger and
charged Sam. Sam met the rush and braced both hands against
de Portillo's shoulders. Whatever advantage de Portillo had in

size and anger, Sam had more than gained with Jade's good-bye kiss. When the Spaniard pushed Sam over backwards, Sam took the fall with his left foot firmly planted in de Portillo's gut. The lighter American used his enemy's momentum and pushed up and over, before rolling off his shoulder to one side.

He heard de Portillo land with a heavy thud, the side of his head hitting the fountain's marble rim. Sam sprang to his feet, ready to launch himself on top of the fallen man, but the Spaniard didn't stir. Sam's tanned, angular face paled as he worried that the man was dead. He hadn't intended to kill him, just knock him senseless. Then to his relief he saw de Portillo's chest rise and fall. *Good. He's still alive.*

He was in the process of deciding what to do with him when Bachir ran in. Sam swiped his unruly forelock out of his eyes and to the side. "Help me here, Bachir," he said in his muddied French.

Bachir took one arm and Sam the other and, together, they dragged de Portillo to an empty room similar to the one the guard was in, and bolted the door on him.

"Where is Jade's mother?" Sam asked after they had de Portillo safely squared away.

Bachir rolled his eyes like he'd never met anyone quite as exasperating as Inez. "Jade," he answered.

Sam laughed. "Two peas in a pod." But his laugh was cut short as he remembered he didn't know where Bennington was, and so consequently where Jade had gone. He grabbed Bachir by the shoulders and faced him. "Do you know where they went?"

Bachir nodded. "El Badi. Come."

The old flintlock went off with a loud, pulsing *whoomp* that nearly muffled the pop from Bennington's little Derringer.

Jade didn't need to hear the return fire, though, to know to duck. She had seen the hatred that quickly replaced Bennington's initial shock at seeing her free. But even then the flintlock's recoil took away the necessity of ducking by knocking Jade on her backside. She hit the ground, rolling. The return shot passed over her head.

Bennington's face writhed in pain and as the lead ball clipped his hand a high scream erupted, a scream that Jade could barely hear after the flintlock's low percussive jolt in her ears. Bennington's little pistol flew from his grip and clattered into an empty pool on the other side of the aisle. Jade heard it plunk into water. Pool's not quite empty, she thought as she turned onto her knees.

When Jade got to her feet she realized she'd dropped her own flashlight. It must have landed on the switch, because it went out. Bennington's light was still on, its glow hazy in the powdery smoke that belched from her pistol's muzzle. Jade scrambled to her feet as Bennington retrieved the light from the ground. He pulled the amulet from Mohan's dead fingers and ran deeper into the ruins, leaving Jade engulfed in darkness.

Most ears would have lumped the nearly simultaneous gunshots as one shot with an echo. Inez had more familiarity with firearms. She heard two distinct reports; the deep, booming pulse of a black-powder weapon and the shorter pop of a small-caliber pistol. *Who fired first?* Inez didn't think Jade had carried a pistol, especially not one of those little pocket-sized models, but she might have taken the guard's flintlock. That meant Jade had fired first. It also meant she was out of shots unless she had a brace of pistols.

Inez hesitated by the gates into the ruins and listened

for the sound of a groan or anything that indicated someone wounded. Nothing. But that was no relief. It might mean her daughter was dead. *Impossible. Isn't it?* Somehow Jade always seemed indestructible, surviving throws by unbroken horses and bulls, falls off roofs and out of trees, and one fistfight with an older boy who made the mistake of saying that girls couldn't shoot straight.

Inez's fear for her daughter rose to a panic. She ran into the ruin in the direction she'd heard the shots and tripped over Mohan's corpse.

It took several minutes of blinking before Jade's eyes lost the afterburn from the flintlock's flash. She hoped it was worse for her enemy, but didn't count on it. In the meantime she tracked by sound, listening for any footfalls. Bennington would first put distance between them, but Jade knew that once the noises stopped she needed to be more cautious. Bennington's gun might be down in a watery pit, but that might not be his only weapon.

As she crept along, that vision from her dream tickled her brain again. It made a little more sense now. After all, Mohan kept saying he had promised the amulet to "her" and not to Bennington. Jade surmised that it was Lilith who originally bought Mohan's supply of stolen bracelets. He probably told her of this wonderful silver amulet and took it, intending to sell it to her. So if Lilith was behind the initial theft, she'd essentially sealed Mohan's doom even if she were hiding safely away on a ship disguised as Bennington's aunt. But as logical as it sounded to Jade's head, her gut reaction was that it was all wrong.

Jade's left knee ached fiercely and she threw a glance to the star-studded sky. *Okay, rain's not imminent. That means someone's trying to kill me.* She almost laughed. *Tell me something I don't know.* She started to take another step and hesitated. Maybe the knee could be useful after all. Maybe it would hurt less if she were farther away from Bennington. In other words, she could gauge the pain and play a game of "hot and cold" like children did.

Right, and get killed for making a wrong choice. She decided to find out if Bennington had another gun. Jade groped around on the ground until she found a handful of broken stones and brickwork. She tossed one somewhere in the direction she'd last heard any noise. No one fired. She tossed another a few yards in front of her first throw. This time her efforts were rewarded by the scuffing of leather soles over stone pavement. Bennington was headed towards an open arch on the other side, exiting the courtyard. Jade followed, careful to avoid the sunken pools around her.

The pain increased at the arch entrance. *I'm getting warmer.* What if Bennington was waiting on the other side? Jade pulled the guard's curved blade and gripped it in her right hand, hilt facing forward, the blade paralleling her forearm with the unsharpened edge against her skin. She took a step towards the arch. A stabbing pain in her left knee held her back. *Can't wait here forever.* Taking a deep breath, Jade mentally readied herself for an attack on the other side, and darted through the arch, shrieking like a banshee to unnerve her opponent.

A suggestion of movement to her right caught her eye, a shadow within a shadow. She wheeled, keeping her knees bent and ready to dance off to either side. Bennington's flashlight flared on, its beam hitting Jade's eyes. The light burned painfully in her fully dilated pupils, and Jade fought the urge to shut her eyes. Instead, she kept her fists up in a boxer's stance and focused at the ground in front of her. The decision saved her life.

The new afterburn image on her retina reduced everything directly in her line of vision to a black hole. That meant she never saw Bennington's feet. But as long as she used her peripheral vision, she could see the blade driving down towards her left. Her left arm swung up, blocking the blow by pushing up against Bennington's right arm. His left hand still aimed that blinding beam at Jade's face. Her right hand shot out and twisted clockwise as she dug the tip of the curved blade into Bennington's right elbow.

Bennington screamed and the flashlight flew out of his grasp, spinning like a top. With each spin its light cast an eerie bit of illumination on the scene. The effect played tricks on the mind. First Jade's opponent stood in front of her, then two feet to the left in a herky-jerky motion from one spot to the other like a poorly crafted nickelodeon movie. Her mind wanted to predict the next move, but Jade knew she needed to rely on sound again for those brief flashes of information. Finally the light came to rest in a stand of overgrown weeds.

As Jade's vision returned to normal, she could see Bennington's stance more clearly. She took in the long knife, its four-inch blade dark with Mohan's blood. Something about the knife as it came at her before had looked very familiar. *That's my knife!* Bennington must have taken it from her when she was first captured. *Be danged if I'm letting him stab me with my own blade.* Bennington shook his injured left arm, trying to regain its use. His face contorted in pain and rage. Then his hand made a jerking movement towards a low jacket pocket. Jade felt her pulse quicken. *It will call to you. So that's where the amulet is.* It didn't stay there. Bennington pulled it out and slipped it into a more secure side trouser pocket.

"Hand it over and I'll let you go," Jade said.

"You're a terrible liar," hissed Bennington. "And I don't intend to let *you* go."

Bennington lunged forward, slicing at her side. Jade parried the move, pushing his blade away. Then with a flick of the wrist she exposed her dagger's sharpened inner curve. She jerked her hand back, slicing at Bennington's forearm. Unlike her own knife, which she kept well honed, the dagger had a poor edge. She succeeded only in ripping the coat sleeve.

It was time to get serious. So far she'd only defended herself, but Bennington clearly intended to kill her as he had Mohan. Jade didn't plan to kill Bennington, but she needed to come to grips with killing in self-defense. Still a dead prisoner couldn't be questioned, couldn't help her prove her innocence. She ran through her options, her mind flipping through all the fighting advice her father's chief wrangler, Dody Higgins, ever gave her.

"Hamstringing 'em'll keep 'em from runnin' but not from fightin'. If you can't get their knife, you best take care they can't see straight. Head wounds bleed something fierce." Well, she thought, it had worked with the guard. Why not here?

A stray sound came from the courtyard on the other side of the archway, as a dislodged stone clattered into one of the empty pools.

"Your cavalry arriving, perhaps?" hissed Bennington.

"Only the *jinni*," Jade replied. "They want their amulet back."

One of the resident cats, startled by the noise, dashed between them. "There's one now," said Jade. She took advantage of the momentary distraction to slice at Bennington's face.

He screamed again as the blade slashed up from his nose

and over his left eye. It was in the high-pitched outcry that Jade found the answer to her dream's confusing images.

"Give it up, Lilith. You're not going to get away this time."

Inez fumbled around Mohan's corpse, looking for some sort of weapon before she went to Jade's defense. *Blast it. Didn't this man at least carry a knife?* Then she remembered. He was a prisoner. They don't let prisoners carry knives. *A rock. That would be something.* She abandoned her search of Mohan and inched around on her hands and knees, feeling for a decent-sized chunk of stone or wall.

She moved slowly, aware that she could easily tumble into a pit if she wasn't careful. Her right hand brushed against something cold. *Metal. A gun? A knife?* Her fingers gingerly followed the shape in case it was a knife. No point in slicing her own fingers grabbing for a sharp blade. But this object had no sharp edges. It felt tubular.

A flashlight! Jade wouldn't have left it behind on purpose. Maybe Bennington dropped one. Either way, it was something to keep. She could at least find her way around in this desolate place, and it felt heavy enough to serve as a cudgel. Her fingers found the switch and slid it forward. For one brief fraction of a second, the empty courtyard lay exposed before her. Then the light died just as Inez heard a shrieking battle cry.

"So you figured it out, did you? Clever bitch." Lilith Worthy spat as a trickle of blood ran over her false mustache and lips. Blood flowed freely down over the left eye, but she could still see with her right.

Jade watched Lilith's shadowy form circle her, looking

for an opening. She kept one eye on the woman's blade, the other on the rest of her. So far, Lilith had shown some skill with a knife, not at all what one would expect from a proper, upper-class English widow. At least it might have surprised someone else, but Jade had long known that Lilith's sedate role as Olivia L. Worthy was a facade.

"You won't live to tell anyone, though," the woman said in a husky growl. "You've harried me too long. You don't deserve to live." She lunged again towards Jade, but with her vision rendered two-dimensional, she misgauged the distance.

"That's right, Lilith," said Jade as she dodged the attack, letting her opponent wear herself down. "Your little empire is in ruins. So is all this because I've broken up your drug trade? Or is it because I foiled your plans to be Empress of Abyssinia?"

"You witch!" Lilith spat, another spray of blood arcing out. "You think you hurt me then? My *empire,* as you call it, is hardly destroyed." Her voice rose in pitch and quivered with more than rage. An edge of despair crept in. "You took my son from me. My *son!* First you killed him, then you destroyed his good name by finding that bastard half brother." She punctuated the last word with another stabbing charge.

Jade sidestepped again, but this time she took a slice at Lilith's leg, cutting the edge of the pocket along with some skin. A bit of silver chain dangled out. "I didn't kill David, and you did more to destroy the family honor by having your husband murdered." As she spoke, she tested Lilith's skill by feinting with her dagger. Lilith responded by swiping at Jade's quickly retracted hand rather than moving towards her more exposed side.

Jade's move wasn't perfect, unfortunately. With only starlight and the faint glow of Lilith's fallen light to see by, she also misjudged her distance. She sliced into air rather than flesh, but it confirmed her growing suspicions about Lilith's training. The woman knew a little about how to fight with a knife. But she *only* fought with the knife. She didn't see beyond it. Jade, on the other hand, had learned from the ranch hands back home and knew a few more tricks involving elbows, knees, and a fist. *Time to take care of that other eye.*

"Think you have me now, do you? Think again." Lilith continued circling Jade, looking for an opening. "Still trying for that amulet?"

Jade took a few steps back till she heard something grittier than weeds under her boots. She kicked out at Lilith with her left leg, then quickly dropped low as Lilith jumped to Jade's right, avoiding the kick. Jade was ready for the move. She sliced at Lilith's left thigh, this time penetrating the bottom of the pocket and deeper into the leg. In the meantime she grabbed a handful of pebbles and dirt with her left hand.

Lilith didn't even cry out as Jade's dagger made this fresh gash. Her rage seemed to make her inured to pain. "You'll have to do better than that, lovey," she hissed. She caught the amulet with her left hand as it spilled out of the pocket.

"Give me the amulet, Lilith. It can't mean anything to you."

"It's mine. It has power. I can feel it." She gripped the knife more tightly and waved it around, making pretenses at another strike. "Does it give protection? You want it to protect yourself from me? Is that it?" She stabbed at the air in front of her, making certain Jade couldn't get in too close.

"I already know the magic phrase for protection against vermin like you, Lilith." She tossed the handful of gravel at the woman's face with an open hand. "Here's five in your eye."

. . .

Inez waited for a moment after the light went out, committing everything she'd seen to memory. If she followed the inner wall, she would avoid most of the sunken spots. *Most* of them. There seemed to be another, smaller pit at each corner. But she needed to hurry. She could hear Jade and Bennington fighting on the other side of the archway. With any luck, they would be so intent on each other that they wouldn't hear her approaching. If she could get in close, she could hit Bennington from behind with the flashlight. She shook the flashlight in irritation and was rewarded when the beam reappeared. Fearing it wouldn't last much longer, she turned off the switch and proceeded in the dark as before.

She stumbled on a pile of debris, sending a stone clattering to the ground. It scared one of the feral cats, which tore off through the archway with a parting hiss. "Aya, sons of biscuits," Inez muttered under her breath as she grabbed for her stubbed toe. Just then she heard a scream of pain from the other side of the archway. *Jade?* Inez forgot about her foot and made double time for the arch and her daughter.

Lilith threw her hands up to block the sand and grit, but in doing so she left herself wide open to attack. Jade switched her dagger to her left hand and charged in, swinging the blade to distract Lilith's attention. Then she drove a hard right fist at Lilith's diaphragm. The blow should have disabled her opponent, doubling the woman over in a gripping pain as she gasped for breath. But Lilith had also retreated several steps from the flying debris. Jade's punch merely grazed the woman's midsection.

Still blinking madly in an effort to clear her right eye of grit, Lilith swung her blade down towards Jade's neck. Jade anticipated the attack, having discovered that Mrs. Worthy still saw her knife as her only weapon. She grabbed Lilith's wrist and pushed her arm back, twisting as she held on. Slowly she drove the arm up, then Jade suddenly reversed herself and pulled, using Lilith's forward push to bring the arm all the way down and around to Lilith's back.

"Drop the knife," Jade ordered. She jabbed Lilith's right elbow with her dagger. "Drop it now." The knife fell at Jade's feet. She heard someone else coming from the arch and hoped it was Sam. "Now give me the amulet."

With her right arm pinned behind her and Jade's blade pressed to her back, there was little Lilith could do.

She did it, anyway. Jade had to give the woman credit. She was a fast learner. Perhaps she felt Jade's grip relax slightly. Perhaps she heard the approaching footsteps and, knowing it wasn't de Portillo, decided this was her last chance to escape. Whatever gave her the impetus, Lilith took the chance. She rammed her head back against Jade's, spun around, and pulled her wrist free when Jade stumbled. For a fleeting moment, Lilith hesitated, as if trying to decide whether to grapple for Jade's dagger and stab her or flee. Someone to the side shone a flashlight on her face. The appearance of reinforcements made the decision for her.

Jade made one desperate grab for Lilith, but it was too late. The woman ran from her and the light towards a distant enclosure. Jade gripped the dagger in her right hand, pulled back, and threw with all the force she could muster. Lilith had too much of a head start, and the blade clattered to the pavement behind her.

CHAPTER 27

El Badi Palace stood for 114 years, after which it was gutted, sending its beauty
to other palaces, like a captive woman sold into a distant harem,
and leaving its empty husk behind in a big pile of earth.

—The Traveler

"Come on, Sam," yelled Jade as she started running after Lilith.

"I'm not . . . Sam." Short panting breaths broke the words, as though the speaker were unused to sprinting.

Jade spun around. "Mother! What in blue blazes are you doing here?"

"There is no time for that," Inez said. She tugged on Jade's sleeve, trying to slow her down. "Are you all right? We should get out of here before he comes back."

Jade shook her head. "Bennington isn't a he. That's Olivia Lilith Worthy, David's mother. Give me the flashlight. I have to find her."

Inez stumbled and Jade slowed for a moment. "Forget the . . . amulet."

"It's not *just* the amulet, Mother. Lilith cannot get away. You have no idea what that woman has done. Now, either wait here or find Sam." Jade stooped and picked up her own knife, the one Lilith had dropped, and took off running, not waiting for an answer or the light.

• • •

Sam followed Bachir through the short maze of side alleys to the main street, then south as quickly as Sam could manage with a false leg. His right hand kept straying to his Colt as though he couldn't wait to shoot someone. In the back of his mind he wondered if it would ever be possible to spend time with Jade without her running headlong into danger. Possible, but highly unlikely given her temperament, he supposed. If that was the case, would he ever get used to it? Probably not. Could he accept it? Maybe. After all, that spirit was what had attracted him in the first place.

You go and buy a woman, and what does she do? Runs off after another man.

They met no one on the streets, and very few lights burned through the upper screened windows. The faint cry of a restless child was shushed by a woman's voice cooing an Arabic lullaby. The most active life as the time neared midnight was a dozing, swaybacked mule, swishing its tail and stamping a hoof as the flies irritated him. Even the cats seemed to have vacated the area, or else Sam and Bachir's hurried steps chased them away.

"El Badi," said Bachir, pointing to a distant shadowy ruin ahead of them.

"I see someone," said Sam. "It's not Jade."

"It is her mother."

Where was Jade? Had Bennington gone someplace else? Had he taken Jade? The thought that he'd lost her again made Sam's guts twist.

"Mrs. del Cameron," Sam called out. "Are you all right? Where's Jade?"

"Oh, Mr. Featherstone. And Bachir," she added with a nod of genuine appreciation for her Berber ally. "I'm so glad you're here. Jade has run off into the ruin, chasing that terrible woman."

"Woman?" exclaimed Sam. "I thought she was following Bennington."

"She was, but Bennington is really a woman. Apparently the mother of Jade's former beau."

"Mrs. Worthy?" Sam smacked his forehead with his open palm. "That would explain why Mrs. Tremaine was poisoned. She must have seen Lilith in that steam bath and figured out that Bennington was really a woman in disguise."

Inez nodded. "When I found Jade and this Lilith person, they were fighting with knives, but Jade had the upper hand." Pride tinged her voice. "And to think," she mumbled to herself, "that I used to scold Jade for letting the men teach her that." She sighed. "Jade had her, too, but I must have startled them and the woman got away."

Sam reached for Inez and held her firmly but gently by the shoulders. "Where did they go?"

Inez pointed in the general direction with her left hand. "There's a big courtyard, then an arch on the other side with some large rooms. Before I came out to find you, I followed for a while. I ended up in some room that looked as if it once held columns, judging by all the circular depressions in the floor. That is when I quit. I had my light off and slipped in one and twisted my ankle.

"Are you hurt badly?" Sam asked.

Inez shook her head. "I'm fine. But we have to go find Jade. I think she ran underground. At least I thought I heard sounds below me." She wiggled her fingers to show walking and pointed to the ground.

Bachir could not follow the conversation, but he recognized the hand gestures. *"Cachot,"* he said.

"Dungeon," Sam translated. He started to run into the ruin, but stopped at the broken entryway. "We're going to need more light than that little fading flashlight you're holding." Inez shut it off to preserve the cell. "We need a lantern or a torch. *Incendiez. Lumière,*" he added to Bachir.

Bachir nodded and ran back to one of the nearest streets, his hairlock bobbing. He returned with one of the street lanterns, a piece of bamboo taken from the street's canopy, and a dirty rag. Inez tore the bottom foot of fabric from her ripped dress and added it to the cause. After Sam wrapped the materials around the bamboo and secured it with a knot, he lit a makeshift torch from the lantern and handed it to Bachir.

"Let's go," he said, and led the way into the ruin.

Jade followed Lilith deeper into the ruins. For a while it was easy, as Mrs. Worthy used the flashlight to guide her way. By now Jade's eyes had readjusted to the dim starlight and every once in a while she saw something glisten on a bit of mosaic floor or a stone: blood. As long as the light moved, Jade moved, too. She tracked her prey back into what had once been stables and stopped. The light went out.

Knowing Lilith might be lying in wait or possibly backtracking, Jade froze, every sense on alert. She tried to get into the woman's mind, to think as she would. *She has no real weapon.* That meant her best bet was to lie low and escape later, or lie in ambush. *How badly does she hate me?* The answer came back in Lilith's own words, echoing Jade's own doubts. *You killed my son!* No cobra had ever spat as much venom as Lilith had in that one short phrase. No, Lilith wouldn't just hide like a frightened mouse. She'd feed on her pain and rage like a wounded Cape buffalo, waiting and planning her next move. *She won't stop until she's killed me.*

A slight noise reached her, a leather sole slapping on stone. Then another. Both had a hollowness to them. *An echo?* Then it registered in her brain. Lilith had found steps leading underground.

Jade moved cautiously in the direction of the first sound and found the steps leading down. She took her time, planting each foot carefully. In the meantime she listened. She also focused on her left knee. Once more she needed it to play the game of hot and cold. Presently it only ached a little, a pain she would have ignored previously. At the bottom of the stairs she found herself in what seemed to be a tunnel. She felt the walls, noting the low arched ceiling above her and the narrowness of the passage. She heard a noise ahead and followed it.

Spit fire. It's darker than a bat's innards down here.

The blackness of the tunnels became absolute until she couldn't see her hand when she moved it across her face. It was as though this was no mere *absence* of light; it was an entity itself. It closed in on her, making her feel smothered.

Think, she commanded herself. *Animals live in this darkness and survive. I can, too. Touch. That's the sense. Touch and sound.*

She felt along the left-hand wall, using it as a guide. Every so often her fingers touched cold metal and cracked wood rather than stone and mud brick. *Doors.* She didn't try any of them. If Lilith had gone inside one of the rooms, she'd have heard the noise already. Those hinges wouldn't open without a serious protest.

Another sound came from ahead. Again Jade followed. This time her fingers felt a gap in the wall. As they wrapped around the old doorjamb, Jade knew this room had lost its door. Was Lilith inside? She waited and listened for breathing but heard only silence. Was it a trap? Should she go in?

She edged her body against the inner frame and snaked her hand along the inner wall. Her fingertips brushed against metals chains. Jade groped down the chain and found the wrist iron at the other end. It was occupied, at least partially. The rest of the skeleton had long since fallen away and probably been consumed by rats. Only the lower arm bones and hand remained, held together tenuously against the ages by mummified sinew.

The thumb broke loose and Jade felt the bones slip. She grabbed for the radius and ulna before they hit the floor and alerted Lilith. She mentally apologized to the long-forgotten prisoner left to rot in this ancient dungeon. *Sorry.* Then just as she knelt to lay the bone on the ground, she hesitated. She couldn't just keep following Lilith through these passages. For all she knew the woman had already backtracked. *No. I need to lure Lilith to where I want her. Time for some light.*

She pulled her kerchief from her back pocket and tied it around the arm bones. Then she fumbled deep into her trouser pockets. The tin of matches had been taken from her back when she was first captured, but she remembered that they'd spilled out in her pocket. Sure enough, down in the recesses of the seam lay one lone match, the one they hadn't bothered to fish out.

She wouldn't light her grisly torch yet. Once the dry handkerchief caught and burned, she'd only have a few minutes of light to work with.

"We can't just all wander in there," whispered Sam. The three of them stood at the entrance to the dungeons. "We need to flush this woman out, and one of us needs to stay up here in case she comes out." He repeated his statement to Bachir in his own particular brand of garbled French.

"I will wait here," said Bachir. He hoisted the curved dagger that Jade had thrown. He'd found it on the ground near the back of the courtyard.

"Good," said Sam. "Mrs. del Cameron, you should stay here, too. Hide back in the stables, maybe."

Inez stood her ground, hands at her hips. "You do not order me about, Mr. Featherstone. This horrid person is not going to run out just because you are chasing her. If you truly want to bring her into the open, you'll need to offer her what she wants."

"I'm afraid to ask what that might be, ma'am."

"Vengeance on Jade, Mr. Featherstone. I think it is obvious. I will be the bait."

Jade slipped back out into the narrow tunnel, feeling her way. She soon discovered that the blasted place was laid out like the streets of the *Medina,* with no rhyme or reason. They branched off, sometimes into dead ends, sometimes looping back on themselves, seemingly at the whim of the builder. By now she had lost her sense of direction—perhaps what the builder had intended. *It will call to you.* Well, why not? Jade listened and was rewarded with a faint sound like an ethereal humming coming from the left-hand tunnel. *As good a choice as any.*

Time to light the torch. She struck the lone match against the rough walls and set the flame to the handkerchief. The flame burned blue, not providing much light, but perhaps that was better. Then when it went out her eyes would take less time to adjust. In the short time available she covered as much ground as possible and made a small amount of noise. She needed to let Lilith know where she was, to draw her out, but at the same time not make it appear too obvious.

Most of the kerchief had burned and the gristle sputtered and smoked. It seemed her plan had failed. Then, at the far end of one corridor, Jade saw a glint of light. The humming sounded louder now. She let her macabre torch burn itself out as she waited for Lilith to make her move.

Perhaps it was simply the result of stress and fatigue coupled with holding a smoldering, dismembered skeleton arm in a maze of black tunnels, but Jade would have sworn she heard voices. *Not again.* This was no time to hallucinate. She gave her head a quick shake to clear it, but a faint murmur persisted, a voice disturbed and growing in anger. This time another recognizable voice overrode the others: a faint whisper calling her name.

"Jade. Jade."

That's Mother. The tunnels' echo distorted the sound, making it difficult to pinpoint the source. Jade moved, hoping to hear from another location and triangulate her mother's position. She hadn't gone far when she saw the glow of lantern light washing over the walls.

"Jade? Where are you?"

Jade watched as her mother crept past along the distant corridor. To her horror, a shadow slipped out from where she'd originally seen a faint light. *Lilith. And now she's stalking Mother.*

Sam didn't know why he was so surprised. Did he expect someone like Jade to have an ordinary, sit-at-home mother? He could have said no to her plan, *should* have said no. But what the hell good would it have done? Even Bachir didn't try to dissuade her and agreed to wait at the top with the torch in case Bennington slipped back out.

There's a man with a sense of self-preservation. But Bachir,

Sam noted, seemed more confident. The man had positively come to new life once he'd seen Mohan's corpse.

And Sam had to admit it. The plan was the best one yet. His own unspoken idea of going into the tunnel and shooting it out with anyone not Jade might have worked. Then again he might have shot Jade instead. So he grudgingly went along with Inez's plan.

Can't stop a damn tornado, anyway. Just get out of its way and let her run.

Besides, he thought, he wasn't trying to catch de Portillo or some burly Arab guard. He was after a lone widow. How hard could that be? *She nearly bested Jade in a knife fight. That's how hard. And she's not a widow. She had her husband murdered.* He gripped his Colt and readied the flashlight that Inez had given him in exchange for the lantern. He counted on the light coming back on dimly enough so he could follow Inez without being seen. *This better work.*

Jade's torch gave a few feeble sizzles. The kerchief was long gone to ash, but its heat had ignited the residual pockets of dried flesh and sinew around the hand and wrist joints. As a torch it was useless, making more smoke than light. As a weapon it still held value, and so Jade kept it in her left hand. One by one, the small wrist bones loosened and dropped to the floor as the connective tissue burned or melted away.

"Jade, where are you?" whispered her mother.

The other voice and the hum increased in intensity, buzzing in Jade's head.

Inez's lantern threw jerking pulses of light like flaming shadows behind her. One of those shadows took human form, creeping with hunched back and bent knees as it stalked Jade's mother. The shadow passed the end of Jade's intersecting corridor. To Jade's horror, she saw what looked like a long, sharp digit extend from the shadow's fist. Lilith must have found another weapon.

Jade hurried down her corridor and came up a few feet behind Lilith, close enough to see the iron spike in her hand. "Mother, run!"

As she shouted, she gripped her own knife. This time, she would kill without hesitation to save her mother. Jade charged after her enemy, clearing the distance in two leaps. But both her warning and her attack came too late.

Lilith grabbed Inez from behind, one arm around her throat, the other knocking the torch to the ground. She pivoted herself and her prisoner around, placing Inez between Jade and herself. "Stop right there, bitch!" screamed Lilith. She held a rusty but still sharp iron spike to Inez's throat. "Stop or I'll stab her."

Jade dug in her bootheels and plowed to a halt less than a foot away from her mother. She held both the knife and the skeletal arm ready to attack. "Let her go, Lilith. If you hurt her, so help me, I'll kill you."

Lilith sneered, her once delicate lips twisted in a snarling grimace, blood coating her false mustache. Her blond wig hung awry, exposing bits of her natural taffy-brown hair. But what made her a truly hideous apparition were the streaks of clotted blood draping down over one side of her face, like fringes of a scarf.

"You'd like to do that, wouldn't you?" Lilith said, the words coming out in a hiss. "And you probably would, so I'm going to use your dear mother as a hostage to see myself safely away." She tightened her vicelike grip around Inez's throat. "Hello there, Inez. Want to come with me and stay with my dear auntie?" A shrill, hysterical laugh burst from her lips.

"Ever wonder why you never saw the two of us together? Oh, Mrs. del Cameron," she said in a high, quivering falsetto, "how kind of you to ask after me and my dear nephew."

Around them, the hum rose in pitch like a disapproving murmur. Jade tried to meet her mother's eyes for some sign, some clue. All she noted was that Inez appeared unduly calm. She didn't even seem to notice the sounds. But Lilith did. Jade saw her shake her head quickly and blink, as though trying to drive off a persistent insect. Then Jade noted something else. Her mother was taking very tiny steps backward, driving Lilith inch by painfully slow inch back down the corridor. Jade kept pace. She had no idea what her mother had in mind, but she needed to maintain the same distance so that Lilith wouldn't notice they were moving.

Lilith laughed, the edge of hysteria in her voice. "I can do many voices. I can even be a French woman. Isn't that right, Jade?" She switched to a well-schooled French accent. "Yes, you may rent my automobile." Then Lilith's voice grew cold as she addressed Jade again in English. "Now listen to me, bitch. You are going to drop your knife and that ridiculous thing in your other hand. Otherwise, Mummy here takes a spike to the throat. Oh, and yes, I get to keep the amulet. There must be something very powerful hidden inside of such a pretty little box. Either way, it's ancient and that means it's worth a fortune."

Jade hesitated for two seconds, enough to meet her mother's eyes and gauge her resolve. She lowered her right hand and let the knife slip from her grip. It clattered onto the stone floor, and Jade watched as Lilith's stiff posture relaxed now that she didn't perceive Jade as a viable threat. Lilith's kept the spike to Inez's throat, but raised her elbow and tried to brush her ear.

"The amulet won't do you any good, Lilith," said Jade. "It wasn't made for you. Aren't you afraid of the *jinni*? Don't you hear them? They're angry."

"Drop those bones, too," said Lilith.

Jade let her left arm droop, just as she had the right. The arm bones dangled loosely in her hand. "There are lots of *jinni* in these old tunnels. You know, the people that shun light and salt. Mohan already paid the price. Will you?" She let the bones clatter to the floor and took a tiny step forward.

Lilith, unconsciously caught up in the reverse motion, pulled back, dragging Inez with her. "You must be mad if you think I believe in such rubbish." She continued to back away, keeping her eye on Jade. Her head twitched in jerky motions. But now Jade let her go. She understood. Three steps later Lilith backed straight into Sam's Colt revolver, its muzzle pressed against the back of her head.

"I actually like a bit of salt myself," said Sam. Then he flipped the gun and whacked her upside the head with the grip.

Lilith released her hold on Inez, who immediately turned and slammed her fist into Lilith's face. "What was that phrase again, Jade?" Inez asked as she massaged her knuckles. "Five in your eye?" The humming and the buzzing voice stopped.

Jade ran to her mother as Lilith slumped unconscious into Sam's arms. "Yes, Mother," she said with a laugh. "That's exactly right." The two women embraced without another word, but Jade glanced up over her mother's head and smiled into Sam's eyes. Her lips moved in a silent "Thanks."

CHAPTER 28

*Scholars will continue to speculate about the origins of the Berber people and
argue language, blue eyes, and skin tones in defense of their favorite thesis. No one seems
to pay much consideration to the legendary warrior queen in these debates. For myself,
I can't help but notice the uncanny resemblance of the words Amazigh and Amazon,
the legendary warrior women from Libya, itself part of the mysterious* Maghreb.

—The Traveler

JADE WATCHED AS A PAIR OF PIGEONS fluttered down from the
cedar beams to the alabaster fountain. One stayed on the
fountain's slippery rim to drink. The other dropped down to
the hexagonal pool on the floor, inlaid in turquoise and white
mosaic stars. Swallows swooped in and out of the courtyard,
now drinking, now clinging to the ornately carved stucco
work along the courtyard walls. The pigeons, having satisfied their thirst, took up residence in a citrus tree and cooed
their devotion to each other. The scent of jasmine permeated
the air, tantalizing the nostrils with promises of romance and
love. No outside noises disturbed the tranquillity of this interior garden.

"I'm going to die of boredom in here. I want to go out
into the *Medina* so I can finish my photographs," said Jade. "I
can't imagine how the vizier's favorite wife endured living in
this prison." She turned to her companions. "That's what it is,
you know. A beautiful, exotic prison."

"I admit that this isolation could grow tedious," admitted Inez, "but I still think it was very gracious of the Resident General to house us here in Bahia Palace. He's been very kind to us, trying to make up for Deschamp not believing you in Tangier." She brushed her hands across the folds of her navy blue dress. "I am happy you had the foresight to pack an additional set of clothes for me in the carpetbag. I just wish we had proper chairs and beds rather than these low divans."

"Better than sleeping on the floor, Mother," Jade replied. "At least if we had to be temporarily incarcerated, we're in a much nicer jail than Lilith is in. I wonder how much longer until they believe they have all the details sorted out?" She leaned against the courtyard doorway and nudged Sam with her elbow.

"What about you, Sam? Are they cutting you loose anytime soon?"

"I'm free to go whenever I want," he said. "I've twice told them everything I know. I think they just like hearing the part about you fighting the slave handler."

Inez rose from her seat on the divan and joined Sam and her daughter. Together they walked into the courtyard and strolled in the garden.

"I want to thank you again, Mr. Featherstone," said Inez and she took Sam's arm. "I do hope you won't fly off too soon. I believe that General Lyautey is letting you keep your room for as long as you like. Isn't that true?"

"It's true, ma'am, but I still think it was a rotten joke to give me the room belonging to the favorite wife's eunuch, no matter how nice a room it is." Jade turned her laugh into a cough and looked away. "I heard that," said Sam. "But to answer your question, Mrs. del Cameron, I'm staying another two days. The general offered to set up refueling stations

starting in Casablanca and on into Algeria and French Soma-
lia. Avery's taken over providing me with fuel once I'm back
in British East Africa, starting with Archer's post. And," he
added, "you don't need me anymore, not even to get back to
Tangier. Jade still has that automobile."

"Are you going to stay in East Africa long?" asked Jade.

"Do you want me to?"

She nodded, finding it surprisingly hard to meet his dark,
cocoa-brown eyes. "I think I'd like that." She felt her mother's
gaze studying her and quickly moved the discussion along.
"What are your plans for your next film? Lions? Rhinos?"

"I'd like to get the Thompsons to help out with a full
documentary on the struggles of coffee farming. It could be
very dramatic. What about yourselves? How long before the
Frenchies turn you two ladies loose?"

"We actually shouldn't be here too much longer. Patrido
de Portillo is talking, and the evidence against Lilith as Bennington is very deep. The authorities have collected the drugs
and the Roman gold from the house. I think they're more
excited about the gold than blocking the export of hashish.
You can see the avarice in their eyes." Jade shook her head in
disgust.

"At least Mr. de Portillo didn't know about the kidnapping plot or that poor Arab man's murder," said Inez. "I'd
hate to think a Spaniard could be so evil."

"No, Mother. He's just a nice, well-mannered drug smuggler. But he did know who Bennington was all along."

"I'm confused," said Sam. "Didn't you say, Mrs. del Cameron, that Lilith Worthy visited you when the boat docked in
London?"

"Yes, she did. I suppose she wanted to make certain I was
really on board."

"And then," continued Jade, "she got off, but came back on as Bennington."

"Then who came on with her as Bennington's aunt?" asked Inez.

"No one. There were so many people embarking and disembarking, no one on board noticed. Later, everyone just assumed there was an aunt, something Lilith took care of when she posed that one time as Aunt Viola."

"I never did see them together," said Inez as though to herself. "No one ever saw much of them at all, really."

"The better to maintain her disguise. Women have successfully posed as men in tighter situations, like in the Civil War, and it's not easy. But it does explain the perpetually impeccably groomed mustache and clean-shaven chin. She always stayed in the shadow or wore a hat and glasses."

"I just assumed he, er, she wasn't used to the light," said Inez.

"So what's going to happen to Lilith?" asked Sam. "Seems she should be held on more than just this murder, kidnapping, and smuggling."

"That's the question of the day, really," admitted Jade. "The Brits want her in connection with the problems in the Northern Territory, running guns into Abyssinia last January and smuggling drugs in East Africa the year before that. The French want her over this hashish smuggling and Libby Tremaine's murder. Seems the only crime no one cares about is that poor devil she had killed in the tunnels. At least not unless the Sultan wants a crack at her for it. All I know is, whoever has custody of her better watch her closely. That woman has connections everywhere, probably more than we'll ever know. I can't imagine that she doesn't have some sort of escape plan."

As if to emphasize Jade's last point, two pigeons flapped their wings and took flight up towards the open skylight above the gardens.

Inez kept her eyes on Jade's face as she watched the birds escape from the palace. She placed a gentle hand on her arm. "You did well, Jade. You rescued me. You captured that horrid woman. With your help, Mr. Featherstone," she added. "And you found Zoulikha's precious ancestral amulet."

Jade fingered her own amulet, hanging around her neck next to David's ring, which her mother had returned to her. "Bachir took it back to the village yesterday. I wrapped it up very carefully so no one else would handle it again except the rightful *kahina*. It should be safe in Zoulikha's hand by tomorrow morning." Jade watched the colored light from the glass windows turn the water from the fountain into pink, gold, and pale blue drops of liquid light. "I wonder what Bachir will do now?"

"I imagine he'll get married," said Inez. Jade looked up suddenly, her eyes questioning. Inez smiled a cat-and-canary grin as though pleased to have noted something that her daughter had missed. "I believe he's in love with Yamna, and I suspect the feeling is mutual. That alliance should also put him in good standing to become the next village sheik."

"Mohan would have been," added Jade, "but old Izemrasen must have figured him out. Mohan not only stole silver bracelets to sell, he was also likely one of the many mountain people bringing in hashish to sell."

"Was he actually growing plants and harvesting the resin for hashish?" asked Sam.

Jade shook her head. "Not that I saw, unless he had a hidden garden far away from the village. But I remember Zoulikha saying she once thought she saw the charm in the district *kaid*'s big *kasbah*. I gathered the *kaid* and Zoulikha's

husband did not see eye to eye. Mohan might have been helping the *kaid* deliver hashish down the mountain in return for
the backing to succeed Izemrasen as sheik. But that's only a
hypothesis. It's probably how he met Lilith to begin with, but
we'll never know for certain. He's dead and Lilith is acting as
silent as the proverbial grave."

She shivered for a moment as she recalled part of her
dream before leaving the mountain. "I dreamed about his
death, you know. I saw Lilith as the dark lady mourning in
a cemetery. I saw her shed a tear of grief but it sprouted into
something twisted and vile. Like the Lilith of the Adam stories, she drew Mohan into her web, sucking the life from him
and eventually killing him."

"Still it's sad, what happened to Mohan," said Inez. "In
his heart he was only trying to do what he felt was best for
his daughter." She stroked Jade's short wavy hair, shimmer-
ing blue-black in the light. "Sometimes even parents with the
best intentions make mistakes."

Jade heard the yearning in her mother's voice and pivoted
to see her more clearly. "Mother? Are you trying to tell me
something?"

"Should I leave?" asked Sam.

"No, Mr. Featherstone," said Inez. She put a hand on his
arm to ensure him of his welcome. "I just think maybe I tried
too hard to force Jade to become more like those Taos people,
those boring, tedious, silly—"

Jade laughed and caught her mother up in a bear hug.
"Oh, Mother, I love you. And I'm sorry if I've given you fits. I
just hate to see you try to emulate those women. I think we're
more alike than either of us might want to admit."

"Mr. Featherstone explained that to me, Jade. Something
about critters and . . ."

"Um, ladies," interjected Sam, ignoring Jade's raised eyebrows. "So you trust this Bachir to get the amulet back safely?" Jade nodded.

"Are you sorry you couldn't go back with him?" Inez asked.

Jade shrugged. "Maybe. But it's probably better this way." She turned and grinned. "I don't think I could have handled any more mint tea. So, Sam. You plan to film life in Happy Valley, right? That should be interesting. As soon as we have the Resident General's blessing to leave this marble sepulcher, I want to photograph Marrakech. I already have pictures of the Amazigh village. I could manage two articles out of this trip for the magazine, and maybe another on Tangier once I drive Mother back in my trusty Panhard."

"And after that, it's on to Andalusia," said Inez. "This time, I will not take no for an answer from my cousin. I will get my stallion."

"I believe you will at that, Mother. How can he possibly say no to a descendent of the great *kahina*. I just wish I could be with you to see the look on Dad's face when you bring it back and tell him all about your adventure." She tilted her head and peered at her mother. "How much do you plan to tell him, anyway?"

"Oh, probably all of it. But not all at once," said Inez with a teasing grin. "I think it will be more fun that way."

"Poor Mr. del Cameron," murmured Sam. "He doesn't stand a chance." Inez and Jade both laughed.

Jade broke loose of the others and paced out into the courtyard. "I just wish they'd tell us we can go."

"It's just as well that we stay here, Jade," said Inez. "You still aren't fit to be seen with all that henna staining your hands and chin."

"They're fading, Mother, and please do not start in on my appearance again."

"I'm not. I suppose you could hide your hands with gloves. And enough powder might cover the chin." She studied Jade's forehead and frowned. "But that mark just below your hairline doesn't seem to be fading. And it's blue, not black or brown."

"Really?" Jade knelt down on the floor by the pool and stared at her reflection. "Oh, dear. I hate to tell you this, Mother, but that one's not going away. It seems our mountain friends made me a permanent member of the tribe." She fidgeted with the curls over her face. "I can always wear my hair in bangs, I guess. It's small." She stood and brushed the damp off her trouser knees. "But after all, we are Amazigh people, Mother."

Inez's lips formed a coy grin. "Maybe, but I will always be a Spaniard first." She stepped onto the hard mosaic floor, raised her arms above her head to her right, and clapped out a staccato rhythm. As she did, she struck her heel down hard and followed it with three rapid steps in place. The clatter of her heels on the enamel sounded like a retort, sharp and defiant.

"Olé!" shouted Sam as his hands took up the rhythm. Jade laughed, her teeth flashing like pearls in the sunlight as she joined her mother in a wild flamenco.

Jade felt a twinge of sadness when she and her mother rode the last mile up the mountain trail to the Berber village, but it had been a wonderful trip. And it was all her mother's idea. She'd read the disappointment in Jade's eyes when she handed the amulet over to Bachir to take back. So once the authorities were satisfied and released them, they used one of the ten Roman coins given to them as a reward to buy mules and supplies. They camped along the way, singing songs and getting to know each other all over again. They shared tales of past adventures; many of Inez's were eye-openers to Jade.

If they'd entertained any notion of surprising Zoulikha with their visit, they were mistaken. No sooner had their mounts stepped into the valley than the pair was met by the entire village. Leading the group was Zoulikha, decked in full regalia with silver chains and bangles across her headdress and chest. Lying on top of them all was the precious amulet. Behind her was Bachir, proudly standing next to Yamna and holding Lallah's hand.

Inez and Jade looked at each other and grinned. Then, as one, the village women raised their chins to the sky and burst forth in a joyous ululation.

AUTHOR'S NOTES

IT IS ALWAYS DIFFICULT TO TRANSCRIBE languages that use different characters from those found in the English alphabet. Such is the case with the Berber and Moroccan Arabic words found in this book. For example, *jinn* is frequently written as *djin* or *jnun*. I chose *jinn* for two reasons: it was easier for me to type and it's easier for the reader to read. For other spellings, I referred to the *Lonely Planet Moroccan Arabic Phrasebook*. In some instances, I took words from books of that time. For example, Marrakesh is rendered Marrakech in many writings of the period.

Many excellent resources exist on historical Morocco, most from the American or European perspective, and since that was Jade's viewpoint, they served my purpose. Budgett Meakin provides us with three accounts: *The Land of the Moors* (1901), *The Moors* (1902), and *Life in Morocco* (1905). George Edmund Holt published a 1914 account of Tangier in *Morocco the Bizarre, or, Life in the Sunset Land*. Novelist Edith Wharton describes the drive from Casablanca to Marrakech and the red city itself during her 1917 trip in her memoir *In Morocco*. Her book has been reprinted, but without the valuable photographs found in old copies.

Old Morocco and the Forbidden Atlas by C. E. Andrews gives a good account of Marrakech and the Atlas Mountains in 1921. Highly recommended is *Ritual and Belief in Morocco* (1926) by Edward Westermarck, especially if you wish to learn more excellent curses. This is a continuation of Mr. Westermarck's studies on Moroccan culture begun in *The Belief in Spirits in Morocco* (1920) and continued in *Wit and Wisdom in Morocco: A Study of Native Proverbs* (1931).

Several *National Geographic* articles are well worth looking up: "Morocco, the Land of the Extreme West" (March 1906), "Scenes From North Africa" (September 1907), "A Journey in Morocco: The Land of the Moors" (August 1911), "The Two Great Moorish Religious Dances" (August 1911), "Across French and Spanish Morocco" (March 1925), and "Beyond the Grand Atlas" (March 1932). A description of Tangier can also be found in Jade's rival publication, *Travel* (November 1910), with "Across the Doorstep of Morocco."

I cannot do credit in this novel to the incredible richness of Amazigh (Berber) culture, so to any Imazighen who read this book I do apologize for any mistakes I have made. There are some very good modern treatises on Berber culture and their art. These begin with *Berber Art: An Introduction* by Jeanne D'Ucel (1932) and continue with *Saints and Sorcerers: A Moroccan Journey* by Nina Epton (1958), and *The Berbers* by Michael Brett and Elizabeth Fentress (1996). *Amazigh Arts in Morocco: Women Shaping Berber Identity* by Cynthia J. Becker (2006) focuses more on the Ait Khabbash who live south of the Atlas. My personal favorite was *Imazighen: The Vanishing Traditions of Berber Women* by Margaret Courtney-Clarke and Geraldine Brooks (1996). There are some books that one simply has to possess. This is one of them. One of the most poignant accounts of the hardship of life in the Atlas Mountains comes from *Mountains Forgotten by God* by Brick Oussaid (1989).

This is a personal memoir from a young Berber man who grew up in incredible poverty.

And what about the *kahina*? One can read about her in *Colonial Histories, Post-Colonial Memories: The Legend of the Kahina, a North African Heroine* by Abdelmajid Hannoum (2001), but I'm partial to an article found in *The Amazigh Voice* (June 1996): "The Daring Daughters of Kahena" by Ann Marie Maxwell.

In the end, I invite you to visit Morocco and experience the *Maghreb* for yourself. It's a beautiful, friendly country.

The Berber clan in this book is of my own devising.

Photo by Joe Arruda

Suzanne Arruda, a zookeeper turned science teacher and freelance writer, is the author of several biographies for young adults as well as science and nature articles for adults and children. An avid hiker, outdoorswoman, and a member of Women in the Outdoors, she lives in Kansas with her husband. You can reach her at www.suzannearruda.com.

JADE DEL CAMERON
BECOMES AN INTREPID AVIATOR

in the next mystery adventure from

SUZANNE ARRUDA

THE
LEOPARD'S
PREY

Available in hardcover from Obsidian in January 2009
Read on for an excerpt. . . .

I'LL BE FINE.

Jade del Cameron wondered if those famous last words would soon end up gracing her headstone. The plan had seemed like a good one at the time, but it had been daylight then, the sun warm and benevolent. She'd watched the two Americans, Wayne Anderson and Franklin Cutter, enter the blind twenty yards away, and heard the three Kikuyu assistants settle into the tree that grew beside her. Soon after, darkness had swooped down upon the African landscape, a mythical black bird—immense, terrible, and predatory, devouring Jade's previous cockiness. Her quivering limbs told her this had been one of her less intelligent ideas.

I'm safer in here than in that Model T ambulance during the Great War, with shells pounding around me. But her heart didn't believe her. It raced until the dull roaring filled her inner ears with a sound akin to a raging river. She took a deep breath and tried to relax by shifting her legs. The right calf immediately cramped, and she flexed her foot to relieve it. The cramp quit, but the left leg started twitching, the muscles fatigued from maintaining one position for over six hours in a two-foot-wide-by-three-foot-long-and-four-foot-high enclosure, built for something much smaller than a five-foot, seven-inch woman.

Get a grip on yourself. You've sat in blinds for longer than this before. That was from her head. Her stomach responded with, *Yeah, but never as leopard bait.* She shivered, her sweat-soaked shirt sucking heat from her body. When she had first entered the cage of lashed limbs, its stifling warmth had stolen every breath. Then, as Africa released its captured heat like a nightly sacrifice to Ngai, the Maker, she longed for some of that warmth. And all just to save a bit of Africa from itself.

The leopard in question was one of a pair that had menaced the pastoral tribes for several months. Both were slated for death for their crimes, the male first. It wasn't his fault. Easy game had diminished as the colonists expanded their farms. The pair of young cats, hungry and desperate, had first taken to the goats, conveniently clustered into low pens. On his last raid, the male was driven off by a brave villager, but not before the cat had slashed the man's leg and bitten him in the thigh. Worse yet, at least as far as the residents of Parklands north of Nairobi were concerned, the cat had been seen stalking someone's dog. The terrified boxer had raced onto the veranda and into his master's house through a partially open window, his tail between his legs, leaving a puddle of urine on the new rug imported all the way from Turkey.

The arrival of the Perkins and Daley Zoological Company soon after this incident had seemed like a godsend to all. They wanted specimens for American zoos, the villagers and settlers wanted the leopards gone, and the goats and dogs wanted not to be eaten. It looked as if everyone, except the goats that would still be consumed eventually, would get his wish. The company suited Jade's purposes, as well. She wanted to save these cats from extermination, and she needed the money.

Writing articles for the *Traveler* paid well enough, but traveling anywhere to write about a new location had grown more expensive, especially with the current petrol shortage. Even her photographic film seemed to cost more every time she picked up an order. It also gnawed at Jade's conscience to take advantage of her friends, the Dunburys, by staying at their home. She longed for more independence. So after asking about the company and finding that they had a reputation for honesty, she hired on as a wrangler and photographer. Somehow, she hadn't counted on ending up as leopard bait.

From lashed-together tree limbs, the company had built a double cage, one half for a goat, the other half for the cat. The leopard would try to get the goat from outside, but wouldn't be able to drive its claws through the tight network of vegetation. It would finally notice that it could more easily see the prey if it looked through the open doorway into the empty half.

The illusion of accessibility was maintained by a double layer of bars, each constructed of branches lashed at right angles to one another, and each layer separated by a foot of space. In theory, the cat would enter, tripping the mechanism that would drop the door behind it. The men in the nearby tree would jump down and secure the door before the cat could get out. In theory.

This male had proved wary, and after two nights of sniffing and snarling around the outside of the cage, he'd slipped away and stalked the village instead. The Kikuyu said they'd heard his asthmatic "chuff" outside of the injured man's hut.

Jade hadn't been with the men those first two nights. So when they and two of the closest settlers, Alwyn Chalmers and Charles Harding, said the cat would now turn man killer and needed to be shot, Jade intervened with this solution, which now had her questioning her sanity. If the cat wanted a human, she argued, let it smell and see a human in the cage. For obvious reasons, no one else had volunteered to be the literal "scapegoat."

Perhaps Jade had never really believed that the leopard would turn man eater just because it had tasted human blood. It sounded like an old wives' tale. In fact, she doubted the cat would even approach a cage with a human in it. But the settlers wanted the animal eradicated, and the expedition didn't want to waste any more time trying to capture this pair. She was their last chance. Wild Africa, Jade noted, was disappearing, one animal at a time. She intended to save these two leopards even if it meant shipping them to a new home in Cincinnati or New York.

So why are my palms sweating? Jade knew why. She felt vulnerable. What if the leopard threw itself on top of the cage? Would the lashings hold against one hundred to one hundred forty pounds of snarling muscle? Did she trust the men to immediately release her once the animal was caged next to her? *Why the hell didn't I bring my rifle?*

Of course, there wasn't room to aim and fire, and anyway, the purpose was to save the cat, not kill it. With her right hand she reached down to the sheath on her boot, her fingers grazing the smooth antler-bone knife hilt. If she had to, she could cut the lashings and escape.

Just relax. Cutter and Anderson are out there. The two Americans seemed competent enough. Or maybe it was just their thick Chicago accents that gave the illusion of toughness. Both of them were solidly built, but could they handle a furious leopard?

Take a nap. It's going to be dawn soon. Hard to nap when her heart was pounding one hundred times a minute. She felt her lungs constrict, as though the walls were closing in on her. She tugged at her shirt collar and gasped. *It's the cage!* That was it. Suddenly she needed to get out, to feel air on her face and space around her body. Unfortunately, the release pin was on the outside.

She shoved her slender fingers up through the narrow gap and felt for the toggle. Nothing! *Where's the blasted pin?* Jade forced her hand up farther, her knuckles scraping the rough wood, drawing blood. Her fingertips grazed the toggle, and for the first time, she wished she'd grown long fingernails. *Just a little farther.* There! Her index finger had the pin. She started to push it when she heard a tubercular cough.

Leopard! Jade jerked her fingers back inside the cage as something powerful brushed up against it. The soft glow from the gibbous moon, which had previously penetrated her compartment, disappeared as the leopard's body blocked it. The animal sniffed, short whuffing snorts, as he analyzed her scent. When he exhaled, the hot scent of stale carrion flooded the enclosure. Jade instinctively pressed her back against the opposite side as the leopard snarled, the sound deep and rasping like a heavy saw through hard timber.

The cat pushed his shoulder against the cage, testing it. The lashings creaked under the pressure, and Jade felt subtle movement in the wood along her spine. Her sanctuary shifted a fraction but held. She slid her knife from its sheath and waited for the next jolt.

It came from on top when the leopard jumped up to try to gain entry from above. The limbs groaned, but the green wood didn't crack. Jade heard the cat's claws scrape against the cage as he tried to find a point of entry. In the moonlight, she could see his form more clearly than before. She thought she detected a thinness about his middle. The animal was more than hungry. He was ravenous. His raspy snarls grew in volume. So did his repeated scratching and probing.

A thin piece of leather snapped, two limbs separated and a paw appeared above her. His claws swiped at empty air as he tried to reach her. Time to get him off the roof. She reached up with her knife and pricked the soft padding. The leopard withdrew the paw with an angry scream and jumped off the cage and away from her.

He landed near the open door, and for the first time, the two stared at each other. The leopard's eyes glowed with the night shine of a nocturnal animal, reflecting every fragment of moonlight back at her. Jade knew the men were getting worried out there, and if it was anything like what she felt, they would soon finish off this cat. No doubt the only reason they hadn't tried to shoot it yet was fear of accidentally shooting her. She needed to draw the animal in. Jade pricked her finger on her knife-edge, and let the scent of her own blood fill the cage.

The cat stalked her with an unnerving slowness, his broad head low between his shoulders, pausing after each step. His pale amber eyes never left hers, hypnotizing his prey into immobility. Beads of cold sweat formed on Jade's brow. She could literally feel them ooze out of her pores, a creeping sensation. She didn't move. There was no place to run.

Another step and the cat hit the release catch. The door dropped, but the animal had hesitated again and it only hit him across the top of his rump and tail. The capture crew didn't know that. They only heard the door swing downward followed by a high-pitched snarl.

Jade heard the men jump from the trees. *He's going to back out of the cage and kill them!* She needed to bring him in all the way. She forced her hand, the one she'd pricked, through the narrow openings and swiped at the cat, taunting him. A splinter made a fresh gash and a few drops of blood landed on his nose.

"Come on, *chui*," she yelled, goading the leopard with his Swahili name. "Dinner's waiting." The scent of blood drove the starving and infuriated animal to a fever pitch. He charged forward, slamming into the partition just as Jade jerked her hand back into her compartment.

She knew the men were now sliding the wooden beams across the door to secure it, but she couldn't hear them. Her senses only noted the hideous, enraged screams and those eyes—those furious, smoldering yellow eyes, glowing with hatred.

Jade didn't wait for the men to pull the pin and let her out. She sliced the lashings from her side of the prison and tumbled out into the African night, gasping for air.

One cat, one bit of Africa was saved from a death sentence, but somehow, Jade doubted that he'd ever be grateful to her. She heard a truck door slam and looked up to see one of her bosses approach. Brooklyn-born Hank Daley was built like a wrestler whose muscles had gone to flab over the years. His five foot, six inches were capped by a sun-reddened face and receding hairline. A seven-inch scar on his right arm and a missing pinky finger on his right hand testified to his having survived some difficult captures in the past.

"That was one hell of a job, Jade," he said, hitching up his pants. "I thought for a moment we were going to lose one of my men. You're quite a daredevil." The forty-three-year-old second-in-command pulled a cigarette from his shirt pocket, struck a match on a boot nail, and puffed away. Together they watched as the other men loaded the cage and the furious cat into the truck.

Jade hugged herself to keep from shivering, not from cold, but as an aftereffect of the rush of danger. She tried to divert herself by asking, "What's next?"

"Well, there's that other leopard a little farther north, the one by Harding's spread," Daley said, his cigarette bobbing as he spoke. "And I still need a young rhino, some zebra, a baboon or two. Got a line on some ostrich. I also want a cheetah. I understand you have a male. Care to sell him?"

Jade shook her head. "Biscuit's not for sale, Mr. Daley. He saved my life and the life of a good friend this past January."

"Biscuit, hunh." He rubbed his chin stubble. "Well, if you should change your mind . . ."

"All loaded up, boss." The speaker, Wayne Anderson, was a bulky, five-foot, ten-inch man with a shock of carrot red hair. He flashed a big smile at Jade. Next to him stood Franklin Cutter, a well-muscled, wiry man with straw blond hair.

"Thanks, Wayne," said Daley. "You and Frank go in the truck with the cat." He nodded toward the Dodge truck, now surrounded by the Kikuyu men who stood guard over the leopard, singing a song about a brave warrior. "I'll take the Africans back with me."

Jade and her boss walked toward a hill where they'd left the other vehicles, another Dodge truck and Jade's 1915 Indian Big Twin motorcycle, which she'd purchased after she sold the French Panhard she'd acquired in Morocco that spring. After unloading the leopard at the Nairobi warehouse, the men would drive on to Alwyn Chalmers' farm and catch what little sleep they could before the next night's work began.

A soft noise in front of them attracted Jade's attention. "Someone's coming." She made out two figures. One was slender and walked with the erect carriage and sure step of youth. The other clung to him, a hunched form tottering with age.

"Jambo," Jade called in greeting.

"Jambo, Simba Jike," said the man, calling Jade by her Swahili name of "lioness." He was a Wakamba, judging by his filed teeth. Probably from the nearby village. "This woman is my mother. She says she must speak to you."

Jade turned her attention to the old woman clutching her son's arm. She wore a leather apron stained red with soil and clutched a monkey fur cloak around her back and shoulders. Her shaved head and gnarled hands showed the liver spots of great age, but what most startled Jade were her dead eyes. Milky white, they still managed to lock onto Jade's own green eyes as though the crone could still see.

"Mother, what did you want?" asked Jade in Swahili. Her son translated.

Immediately the woman spoke two short sentences with a strength and volume that belied her great age and bent figure. Jade's Wakamba was rudimentary at best, since she'd spent more time recently studying Kikuyu and a smattering of Maasai, but she did catch the word for danger, which she made a point of learning in any language.

"My mother says that you will face danger and must beware. She says you must always watch for the madness in the eyes of a killer."

Jade felt a cold chill ripple down her spine. She looked into the old woman's blind eyes, but in her mind, all she saw was the leopard's hateful stare.